SANDBURN

Courtney Hargrove

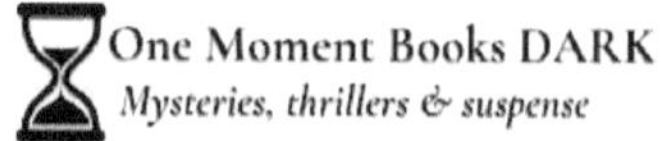
One Moment Books DARK
Mysteries, thrillers & suspense

"We love a missing person suspense saga and *The Expat Wife* delivers. It's like a Switzerland vacation on the page. This riveting journey took us to Lucerne and had us glued to the page."

—Addison McKnight, author of *An Imperfect Plan*

"The story is filled with intrigue and nail-biting thrills. The twists and turns provided more than enough suspense to keep me on the edge of my seat…The characters were authentic and relatable. The story was superbly written and had me guessing until the end."

—Readers' Favorite

"An unputdownable psychological thriller that'll have you reading long into the night. I loved this book—the dynamics between the characters makes this an addictive read."

—BookGirlBrown_Reviews

Also by the Author

Memoir:

Hargrove tells all: From JFK Jr. to Leonardo DiCaprio, from Taylor Swift to 2Pac to Tom Cruise to Harry and Meghan, she's had a front-row seat to key moments in pop-culture history. Be the first to devour her exclusive encounters with the biggest stars!

Psychological suspense:

Welcome to Switzerland in winter: Snow upon snow, everywhere to disappear, nowhere to hide...
Try this atmospheric, twisty and suspenseful mystery set in one of the most beautiful places in the world (Book 1 in the Expatriate Mysteries series).

Available wherever books are sold online

For my Mom, the best person I ever knew.

Author's Note

I'm thrilled to bring Book 2 of the Expatriate Mysteries into the world. *Sandburn* is its own story, so you needn't have read Book 1, *The Expat Wife*, to immerse yourself in this moody mystery.

Then again, readers of *The Expat Wife* might notice some intriguing parallels in *Sandburn,* almost as if there's an alternate universe at play between the two stories and timelines. If you notice these easter eggs, I'd love to hear your takes and reactions. Let me know on social media; all my handles and links can be found on Linktree.

I hope to hear from you, and I truly hope you enjoy *Sandburn.* xoCourtney

The North Cape, Massachusetts
Canada
Maine
Plum Island
Atlantic Ocean
Castle Neck
Magenta Shores
The Sable found drifting
Marlin Bay
The Bay
The Cap
Rogue's Rock
Rusty Lantern
Lighthouse
Langsford St
Washington St
127
Goodstone
Lost Island
The River
Wailing Beach
The Saltbox
Millers' House
135
Sandburn Marina
Oyster's Home
The Schooner
The Pearl
Sandburn
127
Clam Shanty
Western Ave
Eastern Ave

1

I plunge my rake into the ground and sift through wet earth with razor-sharp tines, finding only small rocks and undersized clams. I go again, careful not to break any soft shells, then kneel and use my hands to feel for mollusks. I grip onto a good-sized clam and ease it out. It nearly covers my palm, so it goes in the basket. By law, anything under two inches must be tucked back into its subterranean home.

I hear a boat cutting through the choppy water in the distance. These days I'm hypersensitive to the sound of a motor where you don't expect it, especially a powerful one before seven a.m. at low tide near the saltmarsh, where anything grander than a skiff risks beaching itself.

I straighten up, squinting as the sun's rays obliterate the dawn and usher in morning on the river, but all I see is Oyster raising his tool like the Grim Reaper, stretching his aching body. The shape of a clamming fork is part rake, part scythe. My old friend cuts a lonesome silhouette, and the sight of his labor brings a lump to my throat. Next to him is a hole in the horizon where my father, sovereign of the sand, one of a long line of North Shore clammers, once stood. But after fifty years on the mudflats,

Nicholas Banks disappeared on a dark, calm night, and a piece of Sandburn history was erased.

It's been four months since my father and my husband, Dutch expatriate Clive Hooghiemster, vanished on what should've been a quick boat trip to the pub. We never found a trace of the men apart from my father's drifting sixteen-footer. I'm the only one still searching for them, the last one holding out hope they can be found. People around these parts are quick to accept that when the sea swallows you up, it doesn't always spit you back out.

Not me. I put my life in New York on hold and went on hiatus from my job as a television news producer to find out what happened to my family. I'm not leaving Sandburn, the place where I grew up and learned about tides and shellfish and making out in the dunes without getting sand in inconvenient crevices, until I do.

It's almost time to pack up and move to another beach, like ditching a slot machine that doesn't pay out. There are four others on this mudflat today, including Old Caleb, the grouchiest clammer in three states. I head over to Oyster, who's working the sand with more skill than I'll ever possess.

"You short today?" I ask him.

He is, by a lot. His basket has about ten gritty clams in it.

"Don't you worry about me," Oyster, who's seventy-something but has the skeleton of an eighty-five-year-old, grunts as he attacks the ground with his rake. Clamming's funny like that; it's literally backbreaking work that people do into their nineties. Oyster's already had his first back surgery, which is one less than Old Caleb. That tends to happen after decades bent over holes and sand piles.

"Almost ready to move on?"

"A-yep. Green crabs been around here. Bad sign."

The motor grows louder. It doesn't sound like a lobster boat or a fishing charter. It's something more urgent, and I tell myself it's not about me. I shiver anyway.

"What's *he* doing here?" Oyster sees him before I do.

I brush scraggly strands of hair, dry and sun-bleached thanks to my unplanned new outdoor lifestyle, out of my eyes, and catch sight of a marine patrol cruiser.

My friend and long-ago ex-boyfriend Ben Cassidy is at the helm, and he's idling perilously close to shore.

"Our permits are up-to-date, Ben," I yell. "You know they are."

"They found something," Ben shouts back to me.

"*What?*"

"Isla," he says. "Something orange."

I drop my basket and rake and wade out to meet him.

"Over by the house?" As the water gets deeper, I'm forced to take big, high steps

like a one-woman marching band with no instruments.

Ben shakes his head. "By Rogue's Rock."

"*The lighthouse?*" My heart sinks, and the nausea I've learned to live with blossoms and spreads in my stomach. "That makes no sense."

Oyster calls out over the idling motor. "I've got your gear! Go!"

Ben, who's wearing his usual royal-blue windbreaker and Sandburn Marine Patrol baseball cap, reaches down and grabs my hand. I clamber over the side in my heavy waders, and as I take my place next to him, he flips the blue lights on and speeds toward the bay.

"Any chance it's an old buoy?" I ask.

I already know it's not a buoy. If it was, Ben wouldn't be here picking me up, triggering me, setting the stress spigot inside me to full blast.

"No," he confirms.

I look back as the boat revs up. Oyster is watching us go, hand over his brow to block the glare of the morning sun, a sad, sunken expression on his face.

I stand with Ben at the helm, not caring that I reek of sulfur and sweat and dirt.

"I can't see a scenario where it could've gotten to the lighthouse by itself," I yell over the sound of the motor, the wind, the boat cutting through the chop. We both know what "it" is, but the cops are going to make me confirm it for them.

Ben looks at me, says nothing, then brings his focus back to the water.

As we approach the glass house on the point, a monstrosity built by summer people with too much money, Ben speeds up as if he thinks I'm going to dive off the boat and break into it. He needn't worry. I'm craftier about my spying nowadays, only visiting the house under cover of night when I have the bay to myself. It has everything to do with my family's disappearance, and I'll do what I must to uncover its secrets. I can't see the woman who lives in it now, but she's there, I'm sure of it. She's always home.

We're approaching Rogue's Rock, a cursed underwater

boulder where the ghosts of pirates and crew whose vessels foundered there are said to haunt it to this day.

"It can't be my father's," I yell to Ben as he downshifts. "The tide was going the other direction that night, toward Goodstone. We'll have to check the charts. Get an expert to figure out where he could be—"

"Isla."

"What?"

"It's been four months. No tide expert can trace a...a piece of clothing over that period. Ebbs, flows, winter storms. It could've been hitched on a branch or did a circuit or two around Lost Island."

He squints, and I notice crows' feet deepening around his brown eyes. He's thirty-five, a year older than me, and he's spent his days outdoors since we played in the surf as toddlers. Annoyingly, I suspect he'll continue to grow more attractive as he ages.

"How do you know?" I challenge him. "Are you suddenly a geologist? An oceanographer?"

The gaping maw of the Atlantic comes into view. Captain Cassandra Broussard's boat, the *Courage*, is steaming toward the Lorenson Bank. She'll be looking for cod, I expect. She's back from her winter fishing port in North Carolina, killing time and preparing for bluefin season in June.

Ben downshifts and we float toward the old lighthouse, a white cylinder built in 1801 that guided many a ship over the centuries. The place is usually deadsville until high season, but this morning it's crawling with people. A Coast Guard cutter is anchored on the other side of the point, a white van is parked by the former lightkeeper's house, and Sandburn's police chief is talking to a uniformed coastie.

Ben stops the boat and drops anchor. I'm already clambering onto the rocky shoreline.

"Careful!" Ben shouts. The rocks are uneven, slippery, jagged and range in size from soccer balls to large buoys. I make it to the paved parking area and march up to the Sandburn Police Chief, ignoring the coastie who regards me with some suspicion but says nothing. He's got stripes, which means he's a big enough deal, which in turn makes me less inclined to show unearned respect.

"I'm surprised you let me anywhere near this place," I say to the chief.

"This is Lieutenant Flack," Chief Lilith Wen replies, nodding to the Coast Guard bigwig. "I have something to show you, and I'm going to need you to stay calm."

2

have a million replies to that, none of them fit for current company. I would argue that ordering a person to stay calm has never once caused a person to stay calm in the history of humankind.

"A coastie found it on a routine patrol this morning," Lilith says. "We lucked out. He's followed your family's case and knew about the orange fleece."

"Show me," I say, swallowing bile. I take a breath and steel myself; for me, with this case, it is always either total collapse or brutal focus. Today, right now, I need the latter.

Lilith walks toward the van with me squishing in my boots alongside her. She was four years ahead of me in school. My mother hired her to babysit me during the summer I turned nine and Lilith was thirteen. Her parents were summer people who fell in love with Sandburn, so her father moved his law practice to nearby Beverly and the Wen family became year-rounders when Lilith was fourteen.

I see the sopping wet orange jacket in the arms of a cop I know from the initial search months ago.

"I'm sorry about your father," Sergeant Carter Waring says. He's got black hair cropped close to his scalp. He's about my height and gives good eye contact. "My father was there when he saved that fisherman who went overboard out by the Grand Banks. Still talks about it."

"Thank you," I reply, resisting the urge to point out my husband is missing, too.

The locals never could bring themselves to mourn my husband with any gusto. Clive was an oversized foreigner who recently started hanging out with the clammer's daughter. My father was a legend. A lot of people around here miss him for his cinematically manly ways, how he could tie any knot, fill in as a tuna boat captain, dig up clams, put out a fire, and volunteer at the soup kitchen when times are tough and the fishing community can't make ends meet, even with three part-time jobs. Others, mostly women, miss Nick Banks for his rugged good looks. That second part nauseated me from the day I understood I had a Hot Dad. This is a curse, trust me.

I hold the fleece, let it weigh on me. It's soggy and heavy with grit, shell shards, sugar kelp. I notice something odd: As much detritus is clinging to it, the fleece has retained its fluorescence. It's a brand of outdoor wear made for people who work in the grey hours.

I check the tag. *Size L.* Maine Man brand. Lilith surely knows it was his, but she needs me to triple-confirm it.

"It's Nick's. That's his blood," I tell the cops as I run it between my hands like pizza dough, checking every inch, seeing the stain in the shape of Texas my father could never get out. "He was always cutting his hands on shucking knives or fishhooks."

I hold up the soaking fleece. "Does anything strike you as odd?"

Lilith pauses, thinks about her answer, knowing that with me, questions are usually loaded. "Everything about this is odd," she replies. "I'm as surprised as you that it turned up here."

"It's too clean," I tell her.

"What are you talking about?" Lilith reaches out, rolls a bit of material between two slim fingers, makes a face like I'm an idiot. "It's covered in seaweed and shells."

"It's not *dirty*." I hold the fleece closer to her face. "If it's been in the water for months, why isn't it browned, blackened, muddy? Parts of it are as clean as it was the day he went missing."

I wondered if I'd feel a connection to the garment, like a medium at a séance. But the hit is stronger than that; it's like I'm holding his soul.

"Still think two healthy men got drunk at some mystery pub no one saw them at, fell overboard and rode the tide toward Greenland?" I ask Lilith with the calm demeanor I was ordered to maintain. "Because no one saw them at the Rusty Lantern or any other bar that night."

"You know that's not our primary theory," the chief retorts, her expression professional and flat, like she doesn't know me. "It had to be a consideration. It still is."

"Oh? What about his coat? Every witness said he was last seen with his brown jacket on, which he would have been wearing *over* the fleece when he left the house. How's a tide going to undress him piece by piece?"

A tide won't. But a human will. A killer. A person who saw my husband and my father out on the water and mistook them for the wrong people in the wrong place at the wrong time. I don't know why the guys never made it to the Rusty Lantern, but I'd bet everything they didn't disappear from natural causes. Lilith doesn't answer my rhetorical question, so I keep going.

"Nothing else was found? Nothing from…"

She shakes her head. "Nothing of Clive's. I'm sorry."

The Coast Guard lieutenant has been glaring at me from the side for a while now. He's got a pale face, narrow shoulders, narrow hips. He reminds me of a paperclip. Apparently, he thinks I've spent enough time with my father's last-known fashion item.

"Ma'am, we're going to need you to move away from the scene."

He reaches out to touch my shoulder. I jerk away.

"I'm going to need you to keep your hands off me."

He doesn't know me. He doesn't know how many of his kind I've had to face down since it happened. He's six two, easy, and I'm five nine. He tries to use his size and deep voice to intimidate, but I have access to sensitive parts of him that will feel pain if he tries to touch me again.

"*Isla*." Lilith rebukes me. To him, she says, "I'm sorry. It's an emotional time."

"Don't apologize for me. Show me where it was found."

"Tide's coming in," a younger coastie, a fellow with a crew cut and thin red lips, says from behind the lieutenant.

I point to the shore. "There's time. Over there?"

Both coasties nod.

I navigate down the rocks on the other side, away from Ben's boat where he remains with an eye on me, and as the coastie said, the last bit of sand and the lower rocks are about to be swallowed by seawater. I can see where the fleece had lain half in the sand, half on a rock. The sand around the spot is the hard, packed, unblemished kind that's only revealed at low tide.

Unblemished, that is, except for one indentation. One mistake.

"Whose footprint is that?" I turn and ask the paperclip and the police chief, who remain on flat land above me. "We know it's not the petty officer's. Coasties don't work barefoot, last time I checked."

"Calling that a footprint is a stretch," the lieutenant says.

"It's the footprint of an adult male."

Lilith says to him quietly, "Isla has a…sense of sand. She's usually right."

Always, actually, but since I can't prove what I know every time, I'll take her weak praise.

"Isn't it obvious?" I crouch and trace the mark lightly with one finger. "The outline is clear. Narrow side of the foot, then space for the arch here. Five toes. Heel."

"I don't see any clear shape…" The young coastie steps forward and slips on the slimy rock, catching himself before he goes down.

"Look closer," I say, nodding to the rock he almost broke his neck on. "Someone was trying to plant the fleece without leaving evidence he was here, but he slipped and left a footprint in the sand. They recovered quickly and assumed the mark would disappear. Or they didn't notice it."

I pull out my phone and snap a picture of the indentations.

The coastie nods like an excited child. "Yes! Like I just did…"

"But you had boots on," I continue as he nods. At least someone around here gets me. "So we can rule out your people."

I head back up the rocks, ignoring the coastie's outstretched hand.

"The fleece didn't wash up on its own," I tell Lilith when I'm on even ground. "It was placed here as the tide was going out, just in time for your shift change and the new patrol to conveniently find it. I look for Nick and Clive every day. Whatever I'm doing, I search for them. Out digging. At the marina. The mall. Picking up takeout. If this fleece had been floating around the North Cape all these months, I would've found it."

I use my hand to make an awning over my eyes and stare out at the sea as if I'll see the little red boat motoring back to me, Dad at the rudder and Clive keeping watch on the bow.

Lilith's hands are in her pockets. She's looking at Lieutenant Paperclip.

"We've got to get back to work," he says, as if investigating my family's disappearance is an optional side trip.

A feeding frenzy or a coordinated attack—you never know with gulls—erupts over the water in front of us. Shrieking birds swarm, flying in from all corners, hovering over our heads, flapping, circling and diving. Their flash mobs are triggered by things we can't see: a smell, a crumb, a view of another bird dropping a scrap. As if from heaven, a giant splotch of bird crap plops onto the ground in front of the lieutenant. *Damn.* This isn't my day. He doesn't flinch.

"Thank you, Lieutenant," Lilith says. "We can take it from here."

He nods to both of us and stalks off, followed by the young one, who no one bothered introducing.

I say to Lilith, "Call me when you're done with the fleece. I'll come pick it up."

I turn and head down the rocks, now covered from a fast-rising tide. That's what my waders are for.

"Isla!" The Chief yells after me. I don't look back. "Stay away from that house. Don't go stirring things up again. It'll only make things worse…"

I've no doubt Lilith would have me arrested if I tried to search the glass house and its grounds again. I'd assumed I had an open invitation to Harold and Millicent Miller's summer home in the days after my family disappeared. I frequented their property and searched their woods, knocked gently on their door for permission to search the shed and my father's workspace on the bottom floor, paced the beach looking for anything I'd missed.

Within weeks, Harold Miller told me in no uncertain terms to stay away from the house on the point. And by "told," I mean he put my name on a restraining order that

remains in effect for another year unless a merciful person directs the judge to quash it.

There is, so far, no mercy in this town.

I slap one booted foot on the stern of the Harbormaster's boat, grab Ben's outstretched hand, and pull myself up, water pouring off my waders.

3

"**H**ome?" Ben asks me as he swings the boat away from the shrinking jetty.

I nod, then remember my manners. "Thank you."

The others at the mudflat will have taken care of my equipment, and Oyster will sort and sell the few clams I dug up.

Ben's got his wayfarers on, but I don't need to look into his eyes to know he's dying to hear what happened. I fill him in, yelling over the motor and the pounding spray.

"This changes everything," I conclude. "Now we know there was nothing natural about their disappearance. It wasn't an angry sea that took Nick and Clive. It was one or more angry human beings."

"Isla…"

Again, Ben gives the house on the point a wide berth. I grip the metal railing and try to catch a glimpse of the woman who lives there, but the place is lifeless.

"Ben." I clear my throat. "Please don't be another person who writes me off. I *know* you believe I'm onto something. This sudden find stinks to high heaven."

The sea spray hits my face like cold needles.

"I have to keep pushing to find out what happened. I know I've ruffled some feathers, but—"

"*Some* feathers?" Ben looks at me before turning back to the water. "You've dumped a pack of foxes into a flock of chickens. The town is covered in feathers you've ruffled."

"Can you blame me?"

His Adam's apple bobs as he swallows. I know that neck well. I've been there many times.

Ben is the last one standing. Even Oyster is trying to be Switzerland between me and the locals, who think I'm obsessed, stirring things up, and in denial. Your basic small-town bullshit. This town, this cape, takes care of its own. But months into my family's disappearance, the inhabitants are weary.

Ben's cutting back through the bay, heading around Dolphin Spit. We pass Old Caleb speeding down the river in search of a fresh digging ground, and we all wave as is the custom in Sandburn, though Caleb's greeting is a begrudging half-salute. We're almost at my father's house. I can see the gangway and the private dock leading to the home that should be a sanctuary bursting with life, but the windows are eyes that don't see, the front door is a soulless, wordless mouth, the porch is an empty void where people once rocked and visited and watched the sun set. It is a still life.

Ben downshifts and slides the 46-footer into a smooth landing against the dock. I hop onto the newly refinished wooden slats, my sneaker crushing an old crab shell dropped by a satiated gull. The dock refurbishment was one of the odd jobs the other clammers did to try to make up for my father being gone. Hard labor is their love language.

As I tie him off, Ben looks at me oddly, because he thinks he's not staying. How wrong he is.

"I need to show you something," I say, standing over him, hands on my hips.

He checks his phone, frowns, and then steps onto my dock.

I lead him up to the house. The Banks family's four-bedroom saltbox, the one my grandfather inherited and then passed down to my father, is worth a fortune thanks to rich summer people putting in obscene offers every year. This skyrocketing value makes no nevermind to my father, who's less likely to sell his family home than his own kidney.

Everyone who sells to the summer people regrets it. They got nowhere to live that's as heavenly as this place, and the extra money goes away fast.

We don't talk about how most of the people who sell have no choice. There's no living in commercial fishing anymore. People have three jobs, medical bills they can't pay, mortgages they can't keep up with, drug addictions they can't shake.

I peel off my waders, flicking the straps off my shoulders and hopping as I pull off the attached boots, and leave the jumpsuit-style gear on the porch like a deflated human. I pad inside in my socks, scanning the sunroom for signs anyone's been here, or *is* here. Maybe Clive and Nick have been stumbling around the Eastern Seaboard with bad cases of amnesia and finally found their way home. Maybe they're reclining in the living room as we speak, waiting for someone to bring them hot chocolate and remind them who they are.

I blink and the preposterous thoughts dissolve. Detailed

fantasies swarm your mind when nothing is known. With a vanishing, all that's left are the stories you tell yourself.

As I move through the kitchen, I feel Ben's presence behind me in a way I didn't on the boat where the open air was a buffer. Inside, it's quiet, small, private, and his six-foot-two lacrosse-player's frame guards me. I feel a charge when his arm brushes mine. He smells of work and salt and soap. Maybe I should feel guilty about these pangs in the midst of a desperate search for my husband, but I don't. Ben will always be a chapter in my story, the marrow in my bones, an audience to my childhood memories. I'm OK with that, though I doubt Clive would be, which is why he'll never know.

"I haven't been in here in years," Ben says, giving the place a once-over as we move to the kitchen.

I daresay his tone is almost wistful. Neither of us points out that the last time he was here we were caught on the sofa by my father, who screamed *Arghhhh…my eyes! Get a room!* I was eighteen, Ben nineteen.

I lead him to the den, my father's cave, a sunken living room fit for an eighteenth century seaman. My father's reading glasses remain on the end table where he left them, untouched. I've been dusting around them. Nothing is amiss, and I'm acutely aware the brown sofa Ben and I used to fool around on is still here.

Ben adjusts his baseball cap and takes in the scene. My father's cave is dotted with collectibles, including vintage maps and seafaring journals. A picture of him with a mullet holding the biggest striped bass he ever caught, a forty incher, shares a wall with a black-and-white image of his great-great-great-grandfather knee deep in mud, glaring like they did in the olden days, brimmed hat sitting cockeyed on his head, surrounded by sand piles and tide pools. Back then they used the kind of old-fashioned wicker baskets a tradwife influencer would pack with blueberry muffins.

Nick, whose life's work depends on being sandbound, nonetheless attracts ships in bottles from well-meaning gifters. He's kept a few, including a delicate antique passed down from my great-great grandfather; a collector's item given as a Christmas present; and a tacky, bulbous bottle given to him by a favorite aunt, wherein a pirate is flamboyantly pointing his sword at a cowering deckhand.

I move to the back of the room, where my father's nautical map of the North Cape takes up half the wall. I reach up, pull the tab, and unroll my own map so it covers my father's. I turn to look Ben in the eye.

"It's time to answer the questions law enforcement clearly aren't going to. How did two grown men vanish into thin air on a smooth river on a calm night and leave no trace behind?" I clear my throat. "And how are we going to get access to the house on the point to find out?"

I don't mention the mystery woman. No one wants to hear about her anymore, so I'll deal with her on my own.

Ben steps forward to get a good look at my wall of mess. I found this map rolled up in my great-great-grandfather's cedar trunk. It's now dotted with sticky notes of varying colors, slashes of red question marks, angry exclamation points. I've drawn a route in red marker illustrating where I know Nick and Clive were, and where I think they went.

Ben's studying it, his face unreadable.

I stand to the side like a teacher, tapping the map as I go.

"We're here," I say, pointing to a yellow thumbtack. My finger traces the dotted line I drew to the Rusty Lantern pub, which is about two miles away if you take a right off our dock and set off due northeast. It's about halfway between the saltbox and the lighthouse by boat. "This is where they were heading, but no one saw them docking there, walking through the door, or drinking at the bar. No credit card or bank records show they bought anything that night, let alone beer."

I point to the squiggly lines I drew along the coastline with a blue Sharpie. "The tide was coming in, so the current in the river was strong against them."

Ben is nodding.

"Now. Where did they *actually* go? Two witnesses have come forward, so we only have a vague idea of where they were before eleven p.m."

I trace the next red line I drew from our house to the Sandburn Marina, which is in the opposite direction of the Rusty Lantern. I slap my palm on the red dot at the marina.

"It's a mile away in the opposite direction," I tell Ben, who knows this better than I. "The first witness is Theodore Rainwater." I tap a stick figure I drew, which is bigger than the marina's main building. I never said I was an artist. "Theodore saw Nick and Clive passing by the marina in the *Sable* about ten-thirty, but he said there was something in the boat with them."

Normal people don't name their skiffs. But my father, who was driving a boat at age seven and had his own at twelve, wasn't about to buy me one, so he made his seem larger than life when I was a child. We named it the *Sable*, the French word for sand.

"The famous red buoy," Ben says.

"Right. Theodore said it looked like a buoy, but we don't know how it got in the boat or what the guys were doing with it, or if it even was a buoy. Was it something they found in the water on the way to the pub, and they were heading back to find its owner or dispose of it? The marina lights stay on overnight, but not so bright you'd be able to make out everything inside a small boat floating twenty yards off the docks."

"And the security footage from that night was lost, so we might never know."

"Conveniently lost," I clarify. "Then we've got Big Kev, who says he saw the guys speeding up toward Plum Island, my father with his brown coat on, no sign of a bright orange fleece and nothing resembling a buoy between the men in the boat. That was around eleven."

"Big Kev isn't the best eyewitness." Ben makes a cringe face.

"We can't be sure *what* he saw," I agree. "By all accounts he was three sheets to the wind that night. Par for the course. This is the guy who once told everyone he saw Godzilla on Magenta Shores."

"Who do you think left the fleece on the rocks?" Ben asks me.

"That's the million-dollar question."

He shakes his head. "The million-dollar question is *if* a person put it there."

This is the petty arguing we do. It's one of many reasons why we didn't work as a couple.

"There is no way the orange fleece made its way to Rogue's Rock by itself unless it sprouted flippers," I hit back. "You didn't see what I saw. It was a setup."

What I always think about, what never leaves my mind, is that the person or people who took my husband and my father away from me could have been someone in Sandburn. Someone I know. Someone my father knew.

"How could the person be sure it wouldn't be pulled back out by high tide? They risked having that piece of evidence lost forever if it was taken out to sea."

"Asked and answered," I remind him. "They placed the fleece there just before the Coast Guard shift changed at low tide. They knew a neon-colored item at their precious lighthouse, which the coasties won't let anyone near anymore, would draw attention in time."

"Let's say I can get on board with that theory," Ben says. "Why did they do it?"

"Good question. I don't think we're supposed to know yet," I tell him. "I think this is the beginning of…something. Part of a plan, or covering up a plan that went wrong. I've always said people around here know more than they're saying."

Ben agrees. I can see it in his eyes.

"Now." I jab my finger at the photo I took surreptitiously the day Lil let me examine my father's boat. It shows sand sprinkled under the tiller. "None of this testimony makes any sense, because you and I know my father was at three separate beaches that night—and all of them are miles in the opposite direction from the marina and Plum Island. So when were they at those beaches, and *why*?"

I throw my hands up. I feel as lost as the men are sometimes.

"That's the picture you're working from?" He asks, stepping forward to get a better look. "When was that taken?"

Ben doesn't doubt me about sand, not ever. Not even when we were little.

"The day after they went missing," I reply.

"Oh…" He removes the tack and takes down the photo to examine it. "Huh."

"*Huh*, what?"

"I think I might be able to help you with the order of events," he says.

"*What?* How? What do you see?"

"It's not what I see," he says, turning to me. "It's what you *don't* see."

4

The lobster boat Ice Maiden found my father's skiff at the mouth of Marlin Bay on a frigid October morning. The *Maiden* almost hit the *Sable* in the low light of the blue hour as it drifted aimlessly at the edge of the Atlantic like a drunk ghost was at the wheel, its lights and motor off.

The lobsterman swerved just in time, catching the *Sable* in his light beams when it floated close.

An empty boat adrift around here is an automatic emergency. The captain called it in, marked the coordinates, and tied a line to tow it. Marine patrol arrived first followed by the Coast Guard, and after that the North Cape community descended and did what it does best, what it's been doing for centuries.

I was dead asleep when the police chief tapped on my bedroom window. I wear earplugs and use a white noise app, and it was dark in my room, so I thought Nick and Clive, my father and husband, were still tossing back a few cold ones.

No, the chief said when I stumbled to the front door to meet her. *It's morning now.*

With five more words, she dismantled my life: *We found your father's boat.*

Law enforcement, with military and local fishers' help, launched a massive air, land and sea search. They dispatched Coast Guard helicopters, the Harbor Master's fleet of two boats, fishing vessels that weren't already on the open ocean. Everyone came out. The clammers, the lobstermen. Then came the sword boats out of Marlin Bay Harbor and the tuna fleet out of Goodstone.

I hopped from vessel to vessel helping with the search for the first twenty-four hours. And then, when it seemed like everyone was still out on the water except me and the police chief, I went to see her at the station.

"I need to see it," I told her. "I have to see the boat for myself."

"Forensics isn't done with it," Lilith said, her voice cracking from exhaustion and concern. "There's nothing you can do with the boat now, Isla. It will keep until the right people go over it."

"It'll be too late," I argued. "Please, Lilith. Chief Wen. I need to see it *now*." Before the sand dried and fell off, before the evidence the cops didn't care about disappeared forever.

"I can't—"

"Supervise me. I won't touch anything. Two minutes. That's all I'm asking." I choked it out. I wasn't holding back tears—I was holding back a storm, a tsunami, a catastrophic collapse of my emotional building blocks.

She paused. I pushed. "There's no point trying to search the entire east coast," I pointed out. "They're flailing out there. No one can explain how the guys got from my father's house to the bay without being seen anywhere near the Rusty Lantern. Maybe I can narrow things down if I can check the boat before the evidence is compromised."

If every person on the Eastern Seaboard came out to help, we still couldn't cover all the inlets, spits, nooks, estuaries, harbors, marshes, tide pools, islands, boats, ships, private docks, or marinas. And then there's the Atlantic Ocean, where some believed my father's boat could've miraculously ended up, dumped Nick and Clive out in the great wide ocean for some inexplicable reason, then floated back to Marlin Bay against the tide.

Lilith sighed to let me know I was putting her in a real position, then led me to the garage next to the police station.

She stopped at the closed door. "I need you to answer few questions first."

In the daylight I noticed how tired her eyes were. She and everyone else in town were giving everything. I needed more.

"I've told you what I know." I eyed the garage door.

As soon as Lilith set foot in my father's house the day the men disappeared, even before I put on clothes or brushed my teeth, I surrendered every scrap of memory I possessed. The night before, Nick and Clive were bonding in the den, and I'd taken the chance to slip out to read a good book in my childhood room. About nine, Clive popped his head in, told me they were going for beers at the Rusty Lantern, and put his crossed fingers in the air. He gave me a peck, then left. This was a breakthrough. My father and Clive had what I'd call a chemistry issue. Clive was having to work hard to get Nick to latch on to his big-city executive ways. Clive though my father was cool as Indiana Jones, but with a clamming fork instead of a whip.

"Nick planned to hit the flats before six the next morning, and the Lantern closes at ten sharp on weekdays in low season," Lilith said. "Was it normal for him to go out on the river that late for a beer they could've had at home on their private deck?"

"Well…no," I replied. "But Clive and I were flying back to New York the next day. I figured it was my father's way of bonding with Clive. I guess I…well, my father and I had spent a lot of time talking about the old days and people Clive didn't know. I realized at the last minute that Clive was feeling excluded, so I left them alone. It made sense that would lead to a last drink at the Lantern."

Lilith nodded as if she understood, but I was pretty sure I hadn't convinced her of whatever she needed convincing about.

"So the plan was for Nick to go out clamming early the next day, then dash back home after processing his haul and drive you both to catch an afternoon flight out of Boston?" She asked.

"Yes. I had to work the following day."

"You're still at World Cable News?"

"You know I am, Lil. I'm a producer on the evening show. Can I go in now?"

"One more thing," Lilith said. "Was there tension between your father and your husband? They'd only met once before, right? You had a…whirlwind romance."

"What does that have to do with anything?"

She didn't answer. My turn to sigh.

"No," I replied. "There was no tension. In fact, as you know, we made this extended trip because Clive was trying to convince me to move back here. He was sick of the city. He wanted to work remotely in an idyllic Massachusetts town."

Lilith raised her eyebrows.

"I know, I know." I had to acknowledge her silent point. Sandburn—the whole North Cape, really—is idyllic on a one-dimensional post card, but in real life it's a three-dimensional mess.

The chief tapped the keypad. The garage door grated and squeaked open. I ducked under it before she could change her mind. The aluminum boat was perched on a trailer, so the bow was up to my neck. Without my father in it, it was like a wraith. It mocked me. The boat knew everything, but it couldn't tell me.

I examined the scratched-up underside with its green and brown discoloration from years in the water, then the rim and the cleats. I went over every inch of the boat my father had owned since the early 2000s.

"There's no obvious blood, and even if there was, we'd be safe assuming it could be a from his work," Lilith said, unprompted. "We have to treat it like misadventure until we know more. We know Nick was drinking—"

"They each had two fingers of bourbon after a full meal," I said. "They're both over six feet tall. I wouldn't call that 'drinking.'" I used air quotes.

"You've got one more minute," Lilith said.

I moved faster, examined the hull, and saw what I needed on the pointed nose of the red boat. I swabbed the bow with my finger. I worked the grit between my thumb and forefinger. I shone my phone's light on it.

I held my finger out. "The boat was at the Millers' house."

"I'm sure it was," Lilith replied. "Your father was their part-time handyman."

"I'm saying he—and this boat—were there *last night*. Sometime after ten."

My father did odd jobs for Millicent and Harold Miller at their house on the point for years, putting in so many hours that they gave him a workspace.

"How could you possibly know that?" Lilith asked through a yawn, making a point of checking her watch.

"The sand at that site is different," I explained. "Always has been. Construction of the Millers' house took two years. There are still cigarette buts from the workers, flakes and glass shards no other sand around here has, flecks of concrete. You don't have to be an expert to know the sand from that beach. It's got more mica than almost any other part of the North Shore."

Lilith shook her head. "There's no way to tell *when* the sand got there."

"Oh?" I leveled a gaze at her. "Remember the rain we got that day? What if I told you I helped my father bail out the boat? That we wiped down every inch of the inside? This sand is new, and it's from the Millers' beach."

"Time to go." The chief waved me in as if I was a toddler on the jungle gym.

"Can you at least cordon off the scene?"

"*What* scene?" I could see how exasperated the chief was, but I didn't have the bandwidth to worry about her. My father might've been clinging to an ice floe halfway to Newfoundland. "There's no evidence anything happened on the point. Go home, Isla. Or go help search some more. Whatever you need to do. Let me do my job."

She led the way toward the door. I raced around the other side of the boat and took a close look at the motor and the tiller. With my trusty phone light, I saw it immediately.

"Isla!"

"I didn't touch anything," I assured her as I step off the crate. "Oh, and by the way, I'm right."

She paused. I pounced. "There's sand from the Millers' place on the underside of the tiller. Where Nick would've been steering. His boat was at the house that night, and so was he. And probably Clive, too. I'm telling you that the answers are at the house on the point. We need to interview the Millers."

I didn't tell her I found sand from at least two other beaches the *Sable* visited that night. It was becoming clear that the cops weren't going to take my findings seriously.

"You can't prove when the particles got there," the chief said, right on cue.

"I just did."

"We're going in circles," Lilith said.

"Then stop swerving, and we'll both be standing in the same spot."

They say you're born with your first memory. I was born in the sand. I remember the feeling of it in my diapers, in the folds at the back of my knees, between my toes, in my ears. My mother would spend afternoons trying to clean me up before I got an ear infection as I wriggled like a sandworm. Everyone comes to Sandburn and gushes about the water and the waves.

It's not the ocean for me. It's the sand, powdery or packed or brown or white, the ecosystem, the shells, the dancing seagrass and waving eelgrass, even mermaid grass in some patches in these parts, moving slowly through thick air when it's 97 degrees and 110 percent humidity.

When I was young, the shore was my playroom, the rocks my toys, the shells my treasure. I was told never to go in the water without an adult, and so rarely was an adult there that I learned to play above the waterline, never treading beyond where the waves lapped on the shore. My mother would be home or at work at the television station she worked at in Boston, and my father would take me clamming with him. I don't think my mother ever knew about the times he forgot about me, and why the sand became my security blanket.

Most people I run into find the sand the most annoying part of the beach.

But when you look close, what at first appears as beige grit becomes crystals in a spectrum of colors and textures, and the whole of it becomes the thing you're phobic about and can't touch, or it becomes the thing you can't live without. You crave the feel of it on your feet, between your toes, even your teeth. Without it you're not at home.

I know when sand is too hot to step on and how to keep it off my towel when I lay it out. I know when a hole is too deep; I was ten the first time I stopped a child from being buried alive. I screamed, and his parents saw him and pulled him out before the sand walls collapsed, hundreds of pounds of earth, and you never would've gotten that child out. He would've died inhaling microscopic pebbles shaved from prehistoric stone.

I know sand like I know my own mind, like a fish knows the water, like a mother knows the cry of her baby.

5

Ben moves closer, his shoulder brushing mine as he holds the photo between us. "*Your* picture shows sand sprinkled on the bottom of the boat, and only you would be able to eyeball it and know it was a blend of sand from different places."

"Right," I agree. "But I can't say which order the men were at those three beaches."

"What if you could?" He asks. I feel his warm breath on my cheek. "I was at the police station when they were compiling the file, and I saw photos the cops took *before* his boat was offloaded onto the ramp that night. The images are different from yours in one key way: The sand is lined up under the tiller in three distinct piles, like anthills."

"*What?* You mean, as if someone—"

"As if someone deliberately left those piles to send a message. But when the boat was tipped and towed, the piles collapsed and mixed together."

I smack Ben in the shoulder as if this is his fault. "*Ow.*"

"Why didn't I know this?" I'm pacing now. Things are unraveling—for whoever did this. I'm done being passive, restraining order or no restraining order.

"Because no one was looking for it, and anyway, it would've just been…more sand. Based on what you've told me about the different beaches, I think I can tell you what order the piles were in."

"Oh?" I give him a sly smile.

Nothing about this is funny, but if Ben can identify types of sand with any level of success, he's been listening to me more than I thought. I once showed him samples I collected from various beaches under a high-school microscope, and he watched it become a collection of jewels, pink and purple and white, cream and smooth and pointy, oblong and snowflake-shaped. Like snowflakes, every grain is unique, and like a snowbank, every beach is different.

I pop the cap on my marker and circle the house on the point. It's already the biggest red mark on the map. The mystery woman in the house is the key to everything, I'm sure of it. And I can't get to her.

Ben says, "First pile was sand from Magenta Shores. The middle pile was uniform sand from Wailing Beach. Third was from the point."

"My father was leaving me breadcrumbs," I say, bouncing on my heels. "We need to do a grid search of those beaches."

"You did that early on," he points out. "And found nothing."

"I was looking for big things. Signs of a struggle, stained sand, body parts. I wasn't looking for the little things. The deliberate things."

I'm picking out more tacks and string from the basket on the side table. "I'm going to put together a new plan. No more tiptoeing and waiting."

"I'll leave you to it," Ben says, yawning.

"Wait—you're going?"

He nods mid-yawn, then tips the bill of his cap to me. "Turning the boat in for next shift. I gotta get Lola to school."

Lola. She'd be…six-ish now.

"Meet us at the Lantern tonight," I say. "I'll have a plan ready so we can talk about next steps."

I follow him out to the dock and watch him hop into the boat.

"I'll see," he says.

With that, he guns the engine and pulls out in a wide circle, leaving a frothy wake behind him.

I'm stuck for a moment, emotionally exhausted, once again on my back foot with him. I didn't know he'd worked the night shift before taking me to the lighthouse.

If I'd known Ben Cassidy was going to be a problem my whole life, I never would've kissed him that first time in the dunes so long ago.

Later, after a hurried lunch of cold leftover noodles, I drag my father's metal detector out of the shed. I make the fifteen-minute trip down the river and around the peninsula to Magenta Shores, landing swiftly and hopping out with bare feet.

A storm is coming. A heavy layer of cloud blocks the sun. The breeze has kicked up so the yellowed winter beachgrass by the dunes shimmies and flattens.

Today's events have changed everything. I swooned through an endless winter, hibernating and capitulating to those saying to me, *Stop. Rest. They're gone. In spring, we'll plan a proper fishermen's goodbye.*

There was no rest, but there was defeat. There was nowhere left to look, no more leads to follow, no more witnesses to interrogate. There were ice sheets on the river and gale-force winds I couldn't battle with a craft so light as the *Sable*.

Now my father is doing the talking, guiding me, showing me where he and Clive are with a million miniscule grains forming three solid clues.

It's a clear sight to Goodstone from here, and I imagine what would've brought the men here that October night. I pull the detector out and walk barefoot over cold sand that's alive and menacingly colorful, like bruised skin spidered with broken blood vessels. Magenta Shores is named for the layers of pink quartz and garnet, its deep colors only revealed when the storms come and the winds blow away the white powder everyone sees in summer, leaving the heavier minerals behind, like art.

I run the detector over the ground in a grid search from waterline to the dunes. At the top of the dunes the land turns to dirt and grass, with trails going up and around Devil's Hill. If I let myself, I'd be felled by hopelessness from the breadth of this place. But I know my father, and whatever he left for me, he'd have left it in sand. That's our language.

I wave the coil over a suspicious lump and am rewarded with a *beeeeeep*.

I crouch and force the packed sand away. Nothing. I dig deeper, feeling for pockets or loose sand from disturbances. My fingers find it. An old can with some red branding still visible, possibly a 1980s soda. I tuck it in my pocket—I never leave litter behind—and keep going.

There's a downside to metal detectors: They're finicky, they love false positives, and since I don't know what I'm looking for, I can't apply certain filters. Salt water, minerals, aluminum foil from a beach picnic or tabs on a beer can could set it off. It's not that I think Nick was in the middle of a crisis burying things for me to find, but…well, unless he was, I'm lost.

Where would Nicholas Banks hide something for me, where would he leave a mark? This isn't the woods, so there will be no trees etched with shards of glass, no pebble formations, branches broken to say, *I was here. Follow my tracks.*

I considered he could've torn up beachgrass along the dunes to leave a pattern, a clue, a word with foliage, but no; he wouldn't expect me to examine grass. Plus, whatever happened, it's safe to assume he didn't have time for fancy landscaping. This is about sand. I trudge up a steep dune, my feet digging deep and sending sand sliding down the already eroding mounds. I make it to the top, to the edge of the beachgrass before sand becomes dirt, then turn back. *Nothing, nothing, nothing.*

I shuffle back down, buried up to my ankles, the sand cold but comforting. I stare out at the sea, letting the wind blow my hair until it tangles and scratches my eyes. The skies are greenish-grey and night is coming. I have a few minutes left to pick a spot and commit to it.

Think. Imagine what it was like that night. My father is on this beach for some reason. It's pitch dark. The *Sable* is beached. Is Clive still with him? Is my husband incapacitated, or already lost?

Where would you go to leave something, anything, for your daughter, without getting caught by whatever it is you're afraid of or running from? What could you manage while a kidnapper had a gun to your head?

He would've brought his assailants here on purpose.

But no—wait. He *wouldn't*.

Don't be myopic and panicky.

Magenta Shores. Purple sand. They're not necessarily the same thing.

A hundred meters away is the tip to this peninsula, a triangular patch of beach accessible only to those with a boat. Nick and I would go when I was young to avoid crowds, and because it wasn't far from our house. We stopped going when I hit high school, partly because I was too cool to hang out with Dad when I didn't have to and partly because there's no good clamming there.

That place meant something to my father and me. I searched it early on, but again, I was running on supposition and guesswork. Now I *know*.

I push off and speed down the peninsula to the cap. The light is fading fast.

I ground the boat again and hop out. I stand silent, still, wind like my father's breath in my ears.

Where would you go, Dad?

Above the high-water mark, Isla girl. Straight up the middle.

I stand on the narrowest part of the point, then walk forward, bisecting the beach and running the coil slowly in front of me. The beach grass starts after twenty paces, poking out of the purple. I keep going through it, letting it brush my legs.

The sky darkens another notch. I hear the *beeeep*.

I drop down on all fours and paw at the ground like a dog. I use my fingers to let the cool layers, the red, then magenta, then pale grey and beige and pink, run through my fingers. Still careful, like digging for soft shells. It could be small, whatever it is. Or a piece of clothing, or his hair.

I feel something. Four inches down, buried deep in the packed stuff, is a metal piece. Not a can. I pull it out, then shine my flashlight.

I gasp, alone, and I wonder if I made a sound.

6

It's a key. Not an old rusty one. A shiny new one. It's small, so not a door key. A safe? A lockbox, a trunk, a storage shed. This is my father's gift.

I'm sick to think I didn't find this sooner, but I try to forgive myself. Without Ben, I'd never have known the sand deposits on the *Sable*'s floor were deliberate.

Before I go, I stay on the ground and feel around for anything else, any sign of my father, of his blood, a message, a piece of him. There is nothing.

I make it home before dark and get straight to work coming through every crack and cranny to find the hole that fits the key. My great-great-grandfather's chest. The attic. The shed. I kick baseboards and bounce on floorboards, but nothing loosens. My father kept important things in three places: His den, his grandfather's cedar chest, and his workspace at the Millers' place.

As night falls, I've found nothing the key would theoretically fit into.

I'll search again tomorrow. There are places to hide things that are not in plain sight in the fading light.

I rifle through my old jewelry box and find a silver chain. I never wear jewelry, but my mother gave me shiny trinkets in my teen years to counterbalance her absence, and the box was a junior-high-school graduation present. I string the chain through the key's hole and fasten the clasp, wearing it like a charm.

I freshen up and jump in the boat. Ben is the only one I can share this find with, the only one who can help me find the hole that goes with the key, and my best hope of finding him is at the Rusty Lantern.

As I speed by the house on the point, I see a figure moving through the open-plan living room, but I can't tell if it's the mystery woman. I visit the glass house most nights and it's always ablaze, lights pouring out of every room even when only one person is home. It's like a boat-in cinema, but instead of a movie screen, I have a window into a life unfolding in real time.

All I want to do is burst in and ask the woman where the Millers are. Look into her eyes and see her reaction, decide whether she could've killed them or knows who did, or if she's a kindly long-lost niece watching the summer house while her elder relatives winter elsewhere. But it's not just the Millers I can't approach; it's the house itself. The property. Even the water directly outside it.

I speed up as I hit a straight shot past Dolphin Spit toward the pub glowing in the distance. It's cold tonight, and I haven't wrapped up properly. The wind and the tide are against me.

What happened that night between here and the Lantern? The thought haunts me like a demon. Some days, I imagine Poseidon, god of the seas and rivers, creator of storms and floods, rose up with his trident and sucked my family down into a watery tomb.

The pub is a lone beacon on a darkened shoreline, its

signature swinging lantern acting as a lodestar to all who venture near. I slow the boat as I make it safely to the Lantern, as you would 99.9999999 percent of the time, and tie up next to Oyster's skiff at the pub's small dock. I stride around to the entrance that faces the ocean. A blast of warmth hits me as I step inside the bar and restaurant. It's packed tonight, and I make a beeline for my father's honorary booth. Oyster and Joe are keeping it warm for him, but there's no sign of Ben.

"How'd you do today?" I ask as I slide in next to Joe.

"Hit my quota." Joe Manion, a second-generation clammer in his forties, raises his drink, which I'm pretty sure is his beloved alcohol-free Tom Collins, otherwise known as club soda with a lemon wedge. "Lost Island at low tide'll do it."

Cassandra Broussard, a tuna-boat captain from Goodstone, casts a shadow over our table, her fish-shaped brass cigarette lighter in hand and a cascade of braids falling over her shoulders. She fixes on me.

"I heard what they found today. Sorry. He is missed."

"Thank you," I reply.

She turns to Oyster. "Heard y'all raided the flats today after the red tide kept you away. You fit to go out again tomorrow with that back a yours?" Her scratchy ribbing has a flavor of fondness to it.

"Never a time we're not ready," Oyster replies. "It's the ocean that's not ready for us."

Cassandra, a lifelong fisher not much older than I am whose catches outperform most boats most seasons, says to me, "Call me if you ever decide to get out of the sand and do a real job with a real captain."

Her dig is extra hilarious because she, like everyone around here, knows I'm a temporary clammer, a placeholder for my father so the town doesn't yank his coveted commercial license.

"What about you?" I ask her pointedly. "You catch enough cod today to pay the mortgage?"

Cassandra's eyes harden. "Who told you I was fishing today?"

I'd meant to poke her, not anger her. I don't know which nerve I hit, but I say calmly, "I saw the *Courage* coming out of Goodstone this morning. I never heard of you letting anyone else at the helm."

"You've been gone a long time. You don't know much."

She flicks her lighter irritably and heads out for a smoke.

I sweep the room now that everyone's attention has moved on from me. It's a mudraker's ball; this morning's success on the flats explains the festive atmosphere on a random weeknight. Many of my father's friends are here, along with a bunch of my frenemies. The air is thick with spare cash and eighties music.

Oyster tosses back the dregs of his beer, then slams the glass on the table like an aging frat boy. Salt-hardened spikes of white hair stick out from under the grey baseball cap he never takes off. He's absorbed a sustained attack from the sun, and he's craggy now, a few years from wizened, his pale skin permanently tanned. His stubble is never fully shorn and his eyebrows run unapologetically wild.

"I need a drink," I say. "Oyster? Another one?"

"A nightcap."

"I'll go." I direct a raised eyebrow Joe's way.

Joe is nursing his "cocktail" and shakes his head.

I slip out of the booth and wind my way past men stinking of

BO and fish guts, the creaky wooden floor under my sneakers slippery with layers of grit no broom can eradicate.

I look out for Ben with a sinking feeling. I suspect he has no intention of meeting me tonight. I've come up with an order to things, a way to attack this mystery while working around obstacles, the biggest of which is the state-of-the-art security system at the house on the point, and I was hoping he'd work alongside me. He's the only person I can show the key to.

In my peripheral vision, I see movement out the window on the left side of the pub. There's a man in the parking lot chatting on his cellphone. It's not Ben, but something about him makes me look twice. His back is to the window, but I can see he's tall and slight with jet-black hair. He's wearing jeans and a tech-bro vest. My instincts clang like a night buoy. A stranger skulking around this bar full of locals in the off-season won't go unnoticed.

I belly up to the bar and wait for Rusty to finish pouring a row of whiskeys. I watch the man. *Turn around. Let me see your face.*

"Isla? *Isla*—what are you having?"

"Oh. Sorry, Rusty." I snap out of it and pay attention to the Lantern's red-faced proprietor, who was a football star at Sandburn High when I was in elementary school. "Another cider for me and a nightcap for Oyster."

Rusty reaches for the crème de cassis, a sickly cordial Oyster's sipped last thing every night since mammoths roamed the earth.

I look to the window again. The stranger is gesturing at nobody and vibrating with impatience. If he'd just do a quarter-turn toward the pub, I could see a profile, catch a glimpse of a nose, a chin, a jawline.

Someone taps me on the shoulder from the side, then moves in front of me. It's another man with jet-black hair, but this one I know. His hair has thick waves, and the look is completed with a trendy beard and a fitted, striped button-down shirt more suited to a Boston night club than an old fishers' dive.

"Luke Kastic," I say. "Shouldn't you be out scaring kittens or selling drugs to kindergarteners?"

"Isla Banks," he drawls. "I'll forgive your foul mood. I heard about the jacket. Shame. Real shame."

I point to the striped bass clock on the wall behind the bar.

"Fuck off back to Mommy," I say coolly, even though I want to gouge his eyes out with my shucking knife. "Isn't it time for your bottle?"

He steps to me so our thighs touch. His skin emanates twin odors of liquor and cologne. "Is that your knife or are you just happy to see me?" He says, standing over me, reaching out to brush away a strand of hair out of my eye.

"Get off me. You gonna touch Oyster or Ben like that?" I slap his hand away and step around him.

"Ah, beautiful Isla," Luke says, his heavy, dark eyes smoldering in that practiced way they have since he first met a girl who liked bad boys and suddenly realized he was one. "Let me know when you're ready to consummate this spark of ours. We've done the will-they-or-won't they for long enough, dontcha think?"

His mouth curls into a lopsided grin. This is the face, the demeanor, the personality disorder, of a man who could've killed my family. Problem is, both he and his even scummier older brother have alibis. I haven't been able to break them yet, but I'll keep trying even though I never thought it was them. The evidence keeps bringing me back to the Millers' house on the point. But the Kastics, a family with two brothers that would rip your skin off so much as look at you, have to be in the mix. I'd just need to figure out what their motive would be beyond then fact they're garden-variety psychopaths.

"Spoiler alert," I reply. "It's won't they."

I push past Luke, who moves on to terrorize someone else, and I look out the window. The man is still there. I still can't see his face, but I don't need to. I swear I know him.

Rusty slides the pint of cider to me over the slick wooden bar, and I catch it in my palm. I bring the drinks back to our booth, setting Oyster's cordial in front of him and taking a swig of my cider.

At first glance, the man doesn't much resemble my husband, who's strong, is always trying to lose that last ten pounds, and has thinning light-brown hair.

Yet this stranger's very being is familiar to me. I see the things that can't be concealed by clothes and hair and fashion choices. A smell. A gait. A resting face. How a person leans, how he stands.

It's Clive. As ridiculous as the thought is, I know it's my husband. My heart is pounding and I can't catch my breath.

Oyster meets my gaze. I look out the window. The man has ended his call and is walking away, leaving me again.

"I have to go."

I set down my drink and run after the man, bumping into angry fishers as I do, knocking a drink and getting a few *What the fucks*, but I don't have time to care.

I'm fast, but not fast enough. The cold night wallops me as I burst out into the lot. I weave through beat-up pickup trucks and battered Hondas. The gulls are quiet, the streets equally so in low season. The man has disappeared into the night.

I didn't see or hear a car pull out, nor did I see him approach one. He's just gone. Again.

Why didn't I run outside immediately? Why didn't I drop everything to confront him, even if I might be wrong about his identity?

My indecisive mind had its reasons, including that a husband who disappeared on a routine nighttime boat trip doesn't show up out of the blue four months later casually chit-chatting where everyone can see him. Obviously, that thin man wasn't my husband.

But…what if he had amnesia and lost weight and dyed his hair and forgot who he was and doesn't know why he came back here?

What if he was held hostage and is under strict instructions not to contact anyone from his past?

The guy's probably in town looking at real estate. The summer people are infesting our town and driving prices up like wealthy vermin.

I swing around the back of the pub and find Oyster has followed me out, his arms in the air. Cassandra is leaning against the building, coolly puffing on her cigarette.

"I'll be at your place by six-thirty," I tell Oyster as I run by.

"She's going to that house, isn't she? Don't do it!" He calls after me. "Damn it, Isla!"

Cassandra's raspy voice adds, "That girl's gonna get herself arrested."

I jump in my father's boat and start it up.

Let my friends report back to everyone in the bar that poor Isla Banks is chasing ghosts.

I can't argue.

My boat slices through saltwater at max speed. If I'm fast enough, I can hop in the truck and try to catch up with Clive. Up ahead, the house on the point guides me. It's lit up like a fire tonight, standing alone on the point, an overpriced architectural fail with black railings guarding two white-painted cement decks, like a cellblock for rich people. The builders promised the town it would blend, swore that its inhabitants wanted to be one with nature, but the structure is an insult to the sand that anchors it.

As I'm passing the property, the lights in the house shut down at once. The sky is suddenly dark. I blink and lose my bearings. The picture windows are as black as the midnight sea, and so is the air around me.

7

I slow the boat while I adjust to the darkness.

Then, suddenly, I'm blinded. I blink then cover my eyes as floodlights illuminate the beach. I'm on show. I panic and shift into neutral. I rub my eyes and open them halfway to slowly allow the light back in.

"Hey! You!" It's an urgent call I can barely hear over my own anxious confusion. I squint into the white light.

A slim figure is on the beach in front of the glass house, jumping up and down waving their arms above their head, as if signaling for help.

"I can't see you," I shout. "Can you turn the light off?"

The spotlight stays on. I float closer to shore. The sound of the sea, the lullaby of my childhood, rises in a symphony of waves licking the hull, stripers nipping at the water's surface, and a thin March wind singing through the seagrass.

The woman steps forward, entering the water, the surf lapping over her bare feet. Her frantic calls make me think she's in trouble, and now I have a choice: Help this stranger I've been spying on for months, or chase the man I believe is my husband wearing a bizarre disguise.

I rub my eyes until I can see again, then turn the boat and back in until the stern is just touching sand. I hop out, grab the stern line, stab my PVC stake in the sand, tie off. The process is speedy, automatic.

My new friend, the mystery woman I've only seen from afar, is watching every move. "I wish I had that kind of skill," she says.

The first time I hear her voice, it matches my imagination—whispery, low, honey-smooth—in all ways but one. She has an English accent, if I'm not mistaken. I'll need to hear more to be sure. Could be Australian. Could be a rich-person's affect. *Luvvy, daahhling, fetch me some tea, won't you?*

"I don't have long," I say. "If the tide goes out too far my boat'll be stuck here until morning. So—you need help? What's wrong?"

"Help?" She lets out a soft, tinkling laugh. Close up, she's as put-together as she appeared through my binocular lens, that slick mahogany hair tied back without a flyaway in sight and dressed in a spotless wide-leg beige linen pants and an oversized black cardigan. "No, no. I want to invite you in for a drink. It's time we met properly." She offers her hand. "I'm Charlotte James."

We engage in a solid shake. She has red lips painted with a subtle gloss and big brown eyes framed with long lashes.

"Nice to meet you," I say. "I'm—"

"I know who you are, Isla," she says, meeting my gaze with the confidence of a championship boxer who's been thrown in the ring with a child. "Come. Have a drink with me."

I follow her toward the house. This is the first time I've set foot on this beach in months. Charlotte quickly gains ten paces on me. I'm hanging back to look for the cameras the Millers supposedly installed after my family disappeared. It was on the restraining order application: *Victims are so frightened of defendant that they installed a state-of-the-art security system at great cost to them.* I see several cameras on the house, and I'm told there are some in the woods.

As I catch up to Charlotte, I hear, "Oh, darn." She pats her pants pockets.

She calls out to me, "I think I dropped my bloody housekeys! Ugh."

"I'll use my flashlight. Hang on." I fish my phone out of my pocket and turn on the light. "Where do you think you lost them?"

"About where you're standing," she calls back. The wind carries her voice away, but I manage to discern the words. I scan the sand. Thankfully, it's not just a key; it's a ring of keys with a neon-yellow rubber duckie.

"Got 'em!" I yell back.

The spotlight shuts off.

I pause, blink, then find my way in the dark.

Turn around. Run away. You're committing a felony by walking on this sand.

"Sorry!" Charlotte trills. "I hit the wrong button. I'm still not used to this house…"

She waits for me at the side door. I've been here many times. Summers during high school, when the house was so new you could eat off the floors, I'd sometimes drop off my father's forgotten lunch or power tool when he was working a shift for the Millers.

As I enter the home for the first time in years, I'm struck by

Charlotte's housekeeping ethos. There's sand on the black soapstone flooring the Millers always kept squeaky clean, and as I venture into the foyer, I see scratch marks on the delicate material. A collection of raincoats, hoodies, a blue windbreaker, an olive-green fleece hang on hooks on the wall. There are flip-flops a pair of new aqua water shoes on a mat beneath.

To say I'm hearing alarm bells would be an understatement; the noise is more like the bellowing horns of a fleet of cargo ships navigating through fog in the Drake Passage. *Don't go any further.*

"Is your husband in?" I ask.

"Husband?" my host repeats absently, as if I've confused her. "It's a beautiful place, isn't it? Wait until you see the view. Ah, but you've been here before, haven't you…"

That confirms it—she's English, and from a posh pocket of the country. I've dealt with plenty of British guests on our show at WCN. Plus, Clive's grandmother is from Cornwall. My husband pops into my head, his thinning sandy hair, his shy smile—

Don't get emotional. Keep your head clear.

This invitation is a gift, and I don't intend to squander it. I see nothing of my father's in the foyer.

As Charlotte mounts the stairs, I stop to examine the darkened ground floor. At the far end there's the door to a second primary suite with glass walls facing the water. Tucked under the staircase on this end is a room the Millers use like a basement, which is where my father's workstation is. It has a shiny new padlock on it. I instinctively feel for the key resting at the base of my neck.

"I love the peaceful beauty of this place. I can see why you spend so much time here at night," Charlotte says as she hits the top of the steps. I take the stairs two at a time and make it halfway before she turns to watch me ascend.

She's telling me she's seen me when I thought I was hidden in the dark, bobbing in the seagrass and watching the house. So this is how we're doing it. Games. Passive aggression. Fine, I'll play.

I make it to the open-plan living room, and I immediately understand why she knew all along that I was surveilling her property. I can see the spot behind the seagrass where I "hide." I can see how the moonlight on a clear night bounces off the water. How the lights inside the house don't prevent its occupants from catching a glimpse of a small boat floating just offshore.

Then again, maybe I *did* know. Part of me wanted to be seen. I wanted to taunt her, bait her, unnerve her, without breaching the order. But I didn't grasp how crisply obvious I must've been.

The space is open, airy, and decorated in a beach-minimalist aesthetic. The off-white marble shelves above the bar I watched so often from far away are backlit, bathing the premium liquors in an amber glow.

"Drink?" Charlotte slips behind the bar and smiles. She's removed her cardigan to reveal a loose white top, a hint of cleavage, and a necklace with a teardrop pink quartz pendant. "I've just mixed some martinis."

She reaches under the bar and brings up a glass pitcher half-filled with clear liquid. This suggests to me she's either a raging alcoholic or she planned our "impromptu" meeting, which means I'd be unwise to consume anything she offers me.

I slide onto the same stool I've watched her sit on. We face each other. She sets a martini glass in front of me, drops a green olive into it, and pours me a drink. I pick up my glass, put the edge to my mouth. She waits.

Don't drink it.

I sip, expecting the delicious buzz of an ice-cold premium vodka martini. I almost retch, but I think I hide it well enough. It's *gin*; I despise gin.

"I know what happened to you," Charlotte says, gesturing to me with her glass. "I feel awful about it. I can't imagine losing two of the most important people in my life in one night."

She cocks her head and attempts an empathetic pout.

I swirl my drink with its bobbing green olive that reminds me of an eyeball.

"They are lost," I reply. "Not gone. We're still looking." *We,* meaning *I.*

She raises her eyebrows and sets down her martini. "Oh? You think your husband and father are still alive?" She gazes out the windows at the black ocean. "Yes, yes, of course…one must never lose hope. I admire your positivity."

Who said anything about positivity? I'm driven by rage and grief. I take a fake sip of my drink, then set the glass down too hard so it splashes.

"Oh, dear!" I cry. "I'm so clumsy. Do you have a napkin handy?"

She's already checking under the bar. She comes up with a clean washcloth and sops up the alcohol as I move my glass, spilling even more.

"Never mind," she says with a half-smile. "I can pour you another one."

"Thank you, but I probably shouldn't, as delicious as these are," I smile back. "Drinking and boating and all that…"

She gives the glass bar one last flourish with the cloth and sets it down.

I change the subject. I want to see how she reacts.

"If you know about me," I say carefully, "you must know I'm not legally allowed to be here. Could you tell the couple who own this place that it was all a misunderstanding and I never meant to bother them? I was in a panic about my family. One day, I hope I can apologize to them myself."

The sympathetic cock of the head again.

She is better at this than I am.

"Tell you what," she says. "No hard feelings on my end. I'm not scared of you. You're welcome to have a look around, and in fact, there's something I want to show you."

"I'd love the tour," I smile, then want to kick myself. Why would I need "the tour" when I've been here before?

"Of course," she says.

She slips off her stool and moves toward the windows. Charlotte doesn't walk, she glides. She's a figure skater and I'm a rhino on roller skates, and every road is covered in speedbumps. I take what's left of my drink and follow.

"I want you to know you have carte blanche to come here," she says, staring out at the water. "They didn't like being accused of being involved. I mean, you can understand that."

I assume "they" are the Millers, but their connection to her is still a mystery.

She turns to me, her voice sharpening. "They gave your father a second job as a lifeline. They knew clammers are always scrabbling to make a living. Their hearts broke for you. I think they would've forgiven you, and that's why you're welcome to stop by whenever you want. Just let me know when you're coming by so I don't press the panic button."

Careful what you wish for, Charlotte old girl. I ask, "Are you renting from the Millers? Are they coming back for summer?"

"We're not sure," she says, back to studying the sea now.

"Are they OK? I mean, are they sick or…?" *Are they dead? Are you a stranger who killed them and stole their home?*

She laughs, and once again I can't tell if her tinkling giggle is genuine or not. "Those two are fit as fiddles. They're almost eighty now, but you'd never know it."

One point in favor of her actually knowing them. She turns and I realize her glass is empty. I take another fake sip of mine, leaving some in there, most of the rest sopped up by the dishtowel. I follow her back to the bar and set my glass down next to hers.

"Look," she says. "I know what you've been through. Everyone in town gets it. That's why I invited you here. This is my contribution to helping you move on."

Everyone in town? I've been told no one knows her. Has seen her. Would recognize her. Monkey Borg down at the Gas 'n' Gulp swore he'd never seen the petite brunette who I "claimed" was squatting in the glass house. The few Clam Shanty servers I convinced to talk to me swore they never heard of her. My father's clammer friends insist they never met the mystery woman I spoke of. *Have they all been lying to me?*

Charlotte meets my gaze, and I can see her light brown eyes are flecked with yellow.

"What are you looking for, Isla?"

I stare back at her. It is the broadest of inquiries, one whose answer can range from *My lost contact lens* to *Inner peace*.

"I'll know when I find it," I reply.

Among other things, I'm looking for signs a man lives here. She's hiding something, and I want to know what it is. I'm hoping it's not the mummified corpses of the Millers. Or, god forbid, of my father and my husband.

"I have something to show you," she says. "Downstairs."

"I'm intrigued," I reply, because that seems to be what she's hoping for. "Can I use the bathroom real quick?"

"Of course." She points. "It's around the corner over there."

I remember. I lock myself in, loudly lift the toilet seat, then open her cabinets, rifle around, look for medications, blood stains, anything resembling a clue. The guest bathroom is sterile. I can't think of a way to talk myself upstairs right now to check the rest of the house.

I flush, run my hands under the water, and emerge to find Charlotte waiting near to the door, like she'd been listening. She's holding the rubber duckie keychain.

"I was going through the house, and I found a storeroom downstairs," she says, flipping through her jangling keys. "Naturally I had to get in there. My—" she clears her throat. "*I*, um, I got the padlock off with some wire cutters the landscapers loaned me."

She smiles conspiratorially. "To me, it's a whole lot of junk. But to a local fisherman—oh, I'm sorry, what is the term these days?"

"Clammer."

"No, sorry, I meant—"

Why do British people say sorry so much? "Fishers," I say, though the term hasn't caught on in the fishing community. Most people around here, including women, say "fishermen" to cover everyone who works the sea or the sand.

"*Fishers*," she repeats. "Anyway, this room is full of things they found while this place was being built. They kept everything. Old ropes and buoys and paraphernalia. I imagine some of it might even be from colonial times. Would you like to have a look?"

Do I want to go down to your locked room without knowing who you really are or who else is in the house in the middle of nowhere?

"Sure!"

"Come, then," Charlotte purrs. "Wait 'til you see."

I follow her downstairs to my father's workroom. I've been waiting months for this, but the moment is anticlimactic. I fail to believe that Charlotte, my close escort, would let me in if there was anything incriminating, any obvious clues, any blood or evidence in the room.

She's holding a small key. It's flimsier than the one around my neck. She slides it into the padlock and turns it with a click. I have my hand on the knife in my pocket. The door swings open, and I'm hit by a sickening smell, like a mixture of bleach and fish guts and…garbage? A dead animal? No way to know where exactly it's coming from, or if it's a general odor. The space is packed to the rafters.

I feel pain like a punch to the gut when I look to the back corner.

My father's neat, orderly workstation is boxed in by junk.

Someone has piled more stuff atop his pristine worktop. I can see his pencils. A ruler. Sawdust that would've been shaved by his hand. The knickknacks that tell you the little things about a person, every clam-related gift he received for every holiday: Clam shirts, a mug with *Don't be Shellfish—Get Me My Coffee!*, clam calendars.

Charlotte is opening an old cardboard box stacked on top of other cardboard boxes, the dry, squeaky sound grating on my nerves.

"This is what I wanted to show you."

She reaches into the box, then pulls an item out gingerly as if it's a museum artifact.

I have to stop myself from lunging at her and wrestling it from her hands.

8

I never thought I'd see it again. The tool they never found, the one I told Lilith and the other cops about, the one my father literally could not live contentedly without.

My father's clamming fork. A fourteen incher.

It's got rust on the tines and gunk on the stainless steel ferrule bolstering the wooden handle. Four letters burned into it, engraved, shellacked.

Nick.

"Where did you get that?" I snap, then remind myself to remain calm and nice and easy, like tapioca pudding. Any misstep, any provocation, and she can call the cops, who are guaranteed to side with her.

Charlotte holds out the rake. "I told you—it was here," she blinks. "I thought you should see it."

I take it, feel the weight of it, run my thumb over the engraving of his name. Embossing your rake isn't normal clammer protocol. It's pretty uncool, actually, but when I was young, I wanted to come up with something really special, an offering that wasn't a lump of pottery I cobbled together at school or a book or a gift certificate to a fancy dinner in Boston my father would never cash in. He used this rake until it got wobbly, then kept it in the *Sable* for luck and a backup. That the Millers and this strange woman have it is both validating and terrifying.

"The police might want to look at it. And some other things down here, too, I reckon," Charlotte says, reaching out for me to give her the rake. I don't want to. My grip is firmly on the wooden handle. She takes it from the wrong end, from the sharpened tines, before I can warn her. She doesn't get pricked, though, and sets it back into the box without injury.

"I agree," I say. "Let's call them now. There could be evidence—"

"Now? Would Millie and Harold want that? I don't know," she says with an exaggerated thinking face. "You're welcome to call them if you feel it's appropriate."

I can't get a handle on whether she's fucking with me or if she really likes me or if she's just rich and bored, if she's trying to make friends or if she's trying to show off. I want to take the fork. I have every right to it. But if she's not giving it up voluntarily, I'm not going to rile her up. I'm an emotional hostage, and I suspect she knows it. I can't call law enforcement until I have more to give them. I don't have time for jail and from what I'm told, violating the restraining order again is an automatic arrest.

Charlotte watches my expression carefully, which is irritating because I'm certain I'm showing a slideshow of emotions.

She says, "Next time you come, let's figure out a plan, shall we? I hate to see you out of the loop, left out in the cold, when your family's still missing. It's so...*tragic*."

"Have you checked his workspace?"

I don't wait for permission. I clamber over boxes, an old window screen, and a folding chair to get to my father's workbench. I run my hands over the unfinished surface, over the toolmarks and grooves, but find no hastily scrawled notes or clues. I don't see any recently scrubbed areas, disturbed cobwebs, rolled up carpet, suspicious stains, or anything that would lead me to believe that anything happened to Nick or Clive here. I'm not ruling out that this woman has the Millers buried under the floor.

Charlotte emits a delicate cough, and I take my cue. We exit the room and she secures the padlock, slipping the key into her pocket. It's just me and her in the darkened hallway.

"You know," she says. "We hear so much about your father. But no one seems to talk much about your husband. That must be hard."

I clear my throat, and it echoes in the emptiness as if I'd shouted. No one has ever said this out loud to me. Sandburn locals didn't know Clive before he vanished, and they learned of his Dutch nationality and his job at a non-profit in Manhattan from news sites and online sleuths, all of whom slunk away when they were told the search was off and there was no conspiracy or whodunnit. It's been a relief not having to talk about Clive and my marriage.

"I hadn't noticed," I say, suddenly wanting to get the hell out of here.

"I read in the news that you met in the park in spring. How romantic."

We met when Clive spilled a drink on me at an outdoor bar. He was somewhat apologetic, but also laughing. I didn't know whether the man with the sharp-edged accent was preternaturally good-humored or an asshole, but the way things happened after that, I ended up learning the answer in due time.

"Well," Charlotte breathes when I don't take the bait, "I suppose you have an early morning, with your clamming and all." Her face is in shadow so I can't read her expression.

"What are you doing tomorrow night?" She asks as she moves around me to get to the front door. She throws it open and I step out onto the sand, trying to think of a classy answer.

"It'll be a full moon," she goes on. "Apparently that does something to the tides? I'm having a few people over for dinner and I'd love it if you came. I'll get some nice vodka." She tilts her head and offers a knowing glance.

"Oh, no, I—I mean, it's, I—"

"Gin isn't for everyone," she winks. "It is for the queen and me. God rest her soul. I make a splendid dirty vodka martini. See you tomorrow? Say, eight?"

She leans in for two cheek kisses and I feel compelled to allow it. It's weird, warm and soft. She pulls away and closes the door. The floodlights come on outside.

The inside lights go out one by one as I make my way down the beach, slowly, always searching, as if somehow there's a clue that survived through two blizzards and a flood since October.

But I know there's not, and it kills me.

I was so, so close.

I raced here after Lilith let me inspect the *Sable* the day after my family vanished. The Millers were oddly detached, telling me how concerned they were, but hesitating when I told them I needed to search their beach. I didn't have time to analyze their odd reactions, and I walked every inch of their property.

The only footprints I could identify were mine and the Millers', but I could see other people had been there the night before. I noticed a trail of disturbed sand leading from the edge of their woods down to the shoreline, where someone or something had clearly been dragged, and whomever had done it had wiped their own footprints as they went. I knew a boat had been there hours before, too, because the indent of the bow was still there.

I stood in the sand, called Lilith and begged her to send a forensics team and some dogs. She'd snapped, *Everyone's searching for your family. Let us do our jobs.* I returned the next day to find someone had raked the beach from end to end, from woods to shore.

A month later, the elderly couple supposedly packed up and left town before their annual Thanksgiving party, which I viewed as suspicious. I don't believe in coincidences. The townspeople of Sandburn viewed the Millers abruptly kicking rocks as shrug-worthy.

You should have left them alone. That's what happens when you accuse people of murder and trespass on their property.

No one will help me anymore. Something about how I'm oozing trouble nowadays and they don't want it rubbing off on them.

I speed home, shivering as I feel eyes on me for no good reason. The boat's headlights illuminate only the stretch of black water directly ahead of me. A great white shark could be shadowing me and I wouldn't know it.

I park hurriedly, clumsily, slamming portside into the dock, using my phone's flashlight to cut through the horror-movie darkness. The neighbors on either side are summer people, so their homes are empty and battened down, their water shut off and the electricity cut. I've never owned a home; it rarely occurs to me to leave a light on for myself. You don't have to do that in Manhattan.

I flip on lights in the sunroom, then the kitchen, then the living room. I lean in and turn on the lamp on the side table where my father's reading glasses have remained untouched. The weak yellow glow bathes the wooden tabletop, highlighting the thin outline of dust around the spectacles where my cleaning cloth doesn't reach. My heartbeat goes into overdrive as I realize the ring of dust has been breached; the glasses are askew. Only by half a centimeter, but it's enough.

I whirl, the sound of my breathing taking up the room.

"*Hello?*" It's as reflexive as it is pointless. I whip my knife out of my pocket and wish my father's shotgun was handy.

Did I notice the glasses were in place last night? I'm sure I did…but I've been alone here for months, and the days blend into one another. I'm certain I sat here last night reading, and that's when I noted the glasses were exactly in their place. I check them every time I walk into this room.

They're my security blanket. I have to believe my father will come home, put them back on, look down at his nose at me, and speak his calming words. *Breathe, Isla girl. You've got this.*

For a moment, he's with me again.

I'm OK, I'll be OK.

I can't call Lilith and freak out about half a centimeter. I think about trying Angélica, but she doesn't need more stress. I can't lay my agony on top of her own. She and my father were married in all but name, and she was a later-life stepsomething I never knew I needed. We didn't necessarily need a label, but at a get-to-know you girls' night out, one of us blurted out *stepsomething* over sangria as we came to the giddy realization we adored each other, which was lucky because she and my father were smitten.

My urge to call Ben, to implore him to come over and help me figure out how this can all be over, is overwhelming. But if he's with Michele, texting or calling could be bad for him.

I stay quiet and listen for any creak, heavy breathing, scratching, or thumping. Holding my knife out and ready to strike, I spin in slow motion like I've seen cops do on television, and search the house top to bottom, checking doors and windows. I usually make sure to batten down the hatches, but one of the windows doesn't have a lock, and the saltbox isn't Fort Knox. I grab my father's shotgun, check there are rounds in it, and head up to the attic.

I grab a selection of handblown glass Christmas ornaments and head back downstairs, laying them on the floor under windows, figuring they'll crunch loudly under a burglar's foot. *Home Alone*-level burglar protection is as advanced as I'm going to get tonight. I shove furniture against the front and back doors, lay ornaments outside my bedroom door, lock it, and push the chest of drawers up against it.

I take the gun to bed along with a glass of water and my laptop. Propped up on pillows, I do a deep dive into Charlotte James. I have a name and a face now. Before tonight, she was a ghost, a nameless figure in a window, and according to some, a figment of my imagination.

9

After four hours' sleep, I toss my gear into the truck and spend an hour cruising around town, checking the only inn that's open this time of year, spying on driveways and the town's public lot, looking for anything out of the ordinary, a car that doesn't belong, maybe the dark-haired thin man from the pub out for a morning jog.

Nothing jumps out at me. The man was not my husband. I fell asleep last night scrolling through every photo of Clive I have, and I still can't picture the thick, tall Dutchman I married as a thin, spindly, dark-haired dude in a vest. No matter what my gut says.

It's my turn to drive today. I arrive at Oyster's house in the woods at six-fifteen, before sunrise. The two-story colonial is surrounded by maple trees and towering oaks. It's an acre away from the Millers' house on the point, which means Oyster's place is about as close as I can get to it legally.

Snout, a blocky-headed, pit-bull-ish mutt with a spotty coat, bounds out and slaps his paws on my open window, greeting me like he's taking my order at a fast-food drive thru.

"Hey, boy," I coo as his tail threatens to detach with the force

65

of his wagging. "You coming out with us this morning? We can sure use that nose of yours."

Oyster rescued him from a sandbar that was about to be washed out by a moon tide seven years ago, and the vet says Snout's pushing eighty in human years.

I lean over and manage to push open the passenger door. "This way, Snouty!" He knows what to do. He rounds the truck, hops in and sits next to me. Oyster's pulling his sled along the driveway.

I step out of the truck and try to help him, but he shoos me away. He's a man, I'm a girl.

I see a figure in the window, and I smile and wave. "Hi, Agnes!"

I tilt my head toward Snout sitting tall in the driver's seat, his pointy ears sticking up like Batman. He doesn't come out to the flats unless Agnes isn't well.

"How is she?" I ask Oyster as I lower the truck-bed gate.

"Fine," he says, tossing his bucket in.

"But Snout—"

"She's not been sleeping well. Some'em's keeping her up nights." He slams the door shut.

"Oh?"

"Noises. She's convinced someone's in the woods at night."

"Can I go in and say a quick hello?"

He hasn't invited me in for years. I knew Agnes when I was young, and I never forgot her kindness. She used to sing to me when she babysat while my mother was pursuing her dream of being a newscaster. I was six when Tanya Banks said, *Isla, a woman needs to be her own person. A mother and a wife is no good when that's her only identity. Never give up yourself.*

Agnes was diagnosed with multiple sclerosis five years ago, and Oyster won't talk about it, not unless you're a certain person in a certain situation, like an old-man clammer who bought him a drink. I don't know if Agnes doesn't like me, or if Oyster doesn't want anyone seeing her decline, or what. It's guesswork. The only thing *not* in question is how much he loves her.

He moves to the passenger seat as I shut the truck-bed gate with a slam. I turn and stifle a scream. Agnes is standing in front of me. She's wearing a flowing floral maxi-dress and a white cardigan, her loose, silver-white locks blowing in the breeze.

"Isla. Don't go to that house. You understand?"

Her voice is gravelly, like she hasn't used it for a while. I have no idea what to say, or what she means.

"I..I mean, I—" I'm not going to tell her she's too late.

"Stay away from there. Swear to it."

"Gotta hit the tide!" Oyster bellows cluelessly out the passenger-side window. Agnes slips away, out of her husband's sight.

I slide into the truck and drive away, wondering what Agnes's cryptic warning was about.

After speed-clamming at Flanagan's Nub, a rich mudflat behind Lost Island, I drop Oyster at home and head to Ben's.

I park around the bend from his house and walk the quiet one-way road along the river toward Bass Beach. He lives across from the thriving flat, a handy location for a clammer who doesn't relish a long commute.

He's checking the cover his pleasure cruiser parked in the side yard, his strong arms yanking at the ropes to tighten everything up this morning's wind. He's in jeans and his usual windbreaker, his hair a caramel shade of brown you don't see much. He never changes in my eyes. Ben will always be the boy in the sand, the one I explored the seaside with while our fathers dug together, raced the surf, learned how to run on sand like it was solid as tarmac.

When our fathers fell out over the possibility of bringing clam farming to Sandburn, Ben and I separated, too. We met again in junior high school and it was like meeting the missing piece of myself.

I'm about to sneak up on him when I hear female voices.

Shit. I could run and make it back around the bend before she sees me. But I don't, and I'm not sure why.

Michele is leaving the house in full medical garb, blue scrubs and comfortable sneakers, clutching Lola's hand as they traverse the walkway.

"Hey," I say. "Hi." This cozy domestic scene takes the wind out of me.

I figured Michele and Ben were probably together again, but there was a reason I never asked, never confirmed, never wanted details. In the months between the searches in October and finding the fleece yesterday, Ben and I kept a distance. Winter tore roofs off homes and eroded our coastline further, blocked roads, paths, crossings, kept us indoors much of the time. Clamming was less an invigorating way of life and more a hurried chore where you freeze in your heavy waders, hands chapped and covered in thick gloves so you can't feel the sand through the rake. There was no reason to see Ben, whose days are packed. He's a father with three jobs.

"Isla!" Lola calls. She lets go of her mother's hand, runs to me and wraps her little arms around my waist.

"Hi, sweetheart." I hug her back. "I haven't seen you in too long."

When we pull apart, Michele sends a glare toward Ben, who's pretending to focus on tightening the same rope he's been yanking for several minutes.

"Don't mind us," Michele says fake-brightly in a way Lola wouldn't notice, but comes through to me loud and clear. "Lola's off to her playgroup. Say bye to Aunt Isla."

"Isla?" Lola stays put.

"Yes, sweetie?" Right now, in my black hole of a life, she's an angel reminding me that not everything in the world is utter shit.

"Can we build sandcastles again, and then can we go wading for quahogs?"

"Sandcastles and quahogs?" My mind races. Oh, right. Two years ago. She couldn't have been older than four. I came home for a week that summer, and Ben brought Lola to a beach barbecue and I spent most of my time with her, legs splayed out, covered in sand, hands digging down and through, building, crafting, creating, dreaming. She begged me to teach her about clamming. Since it was high tide, I showed her how to look among the pebbles and rocks in the shallows for quahogs, otherwise known as hard-shells or chowder clams.

"How did you remember that?" I ask her.

"She still talks about it," Michele says flatly. "What we do has ripple effects. Like when you bond with someone and then forget about them."

I crouch to Lola's level, brush some hair out of her eyes. "I'd love to build sandcastles with you again."

"But no digging holes to play in," she says solemnly.

"That's right," I say. "Holes are dangerous. But building up, we can do that as tall and grand as the sand will hold up."

"When?"

I look up at Michele.

"Yes, when?" Lola's mother asks.

"Anytime. Seems like you're busy with school and fun activities," I say. "I'm free this weekend if you are."

"Supposed to be a storm," Michele says.

I look Lola in her eyes. "As soon as it's warm again, you ask your mommy and daddy when you can meet me in the sand, and I'll be there."

Lola throws her arms around me again, and when we pull apart, Michele takes the girl's hand heads to her Toyota.

"You two enjoy your day," Michele throws back to Ben and me.

I don't know why Agnes is cold to me, but I know why Michele is. She was homecoming queen at Sandburn High, the prettiest, petite-est, whitest-toothed thing you ever saw, and she had her eye on Ben, the hot varsity lacrosse player with the semi-mullet and a Jeep, from day one of her freshman year. She's a year younger than I am, Ben's a year ahead of me. She got him in the end, but she still blames me for everything that ever went wrong between them.

Ben stops pretending to strengthen the bonds of the cover on his pleasure cruiser—he has three boats—and waves to his daughter. "Bye, sweetie. Be good. I'll be there to pick you up when you're done."

With Lola and Michele motoring away and safely out of earshot, I walk up to Ben. "I'm sorry."

"For what?"

"I didn't mean to cause trouble."

"There's no trouble." He won't look at me.

I stand in front of him and find his eyes.

"Do you have an hour to help me walk Wailing Beach?"

He pauses, his attention on the grey water frosted with whitecaps. "I found something, Ben…I found something huge at Magenta Shores."

"What?" His eyes go wide. He can't help himself.

"Grab your metal detector," I smile. "I'll tell you on the way."

10

en walks ahead, barefoot like me despite the chill, and I
race to catch up. An hour into combing the beach, we've
gotten nowhere. We ditched our metal detectors early
on, and we've been pacing in bare feet as if we could possibly feel
what lies deep in the sand.

"Nick wasn't running around burying things in the midst of
whatever was happening that night," Ben says.

"No." I fall in next to him.

The sand squeaks and sings beneath our feet. There are all
sorts of scientific explanations for the sounds Wailing Beach
makes when you tread on it. Some experts say it's the shear of
the round, silica-heavy sand grains grinding against themselves,
but the truth is no one knows for sure why the beach cries and
sings. It's usually more of a squeak, anyway, like a bed with
broken springs. Sometimes it doesn't make any sound at all. The
tiniest variable, a grain of pollen among the grains, can silence it.

"So what the hell was your father's Wailing Beach clue
about?" Ben shakes his head harder as if he can loosen the answer
to his own question. "This is getting us nowhere."

A tennis ball rolls past him, and in one long stride he

effortlessly scoops it up and throws it halfway to Maine. A porky, smiling, drooling pit bull terrier sprints after it, a laughing dog dad lagging far behind.

Ben stops, turns to me. "This doesn't feel right."

"I know what you mean. It feels like we're searching for a grain of sand on—"

"On a beach of a trillion grains," Ben agrees.

This is a central, widely used beach, even in winter, because it's close to the richest clam flats and is easily accessible to the public by car, foot, or boat.

I stand at the edge of the waterline. The Millers' place looms in the distance, shining on the point, quiet, ugly, full of secrets. Everything comes back to that cursed house. I know it like I know my own father.

I plop down and hug my knees. Ben sits next to me.

"It would help if we had a clue what we were looking for," he says. "Something that goes with the key you found, maybe? Can I see the key?"

I nod, and he reaches over and touches my chest, fingering the key, moving his face so close to mine his hair almost brushes my nose. If I didn't know better, I'd say he knows exactly what he's doing.

"What do you think it goes to?" I lean back slightly and he lets the key drop against my chest bone.

"Hard to say. Could be a safety deposit box, padlock, gate…"

"I couldn't find anything at home it would possibly fit into."

I decide not to tell him I poked around Nick's workspace at the Millers' house, not yet, not until I know what Charlotte's motives are. I cyberstalked her last night and found very little about her, which isn't surprising. I had the same problem before my first official date with Clive, because European citizens' private information and data are better protected than ours. When I'm researching American sources for a news story, I can find out everything from a person's childhood address to their favorite candy bar to the names and favorite candy bars of all their distant cousins.

Job connections platform LinkedIn is Charlotte's top search result, but her page is set to private, which means only her photo, title, and a "500+" connections" tag are visible. She calls herself an "Independent international marketing consultant." In her profile photo, which looks recent enough, she went with a head tilt and a friendly but not flirty smile and a collared shirt. It screams *I'm trying hard to seem approachable yet professional.*

Nothing came up with a reverse image search. I was half-hoping for a mugshot or a friend's social media page revealing a messy, drunken night out with Charlotte, but nada. Same with Charlotte's Facebook page. That has a different headshot showing her laughing and looking off in the distance, as if we caught her frozen in a moment of joy. But that was all there is.

"Maybe there's nothing to find," I say. "Maybe my father's clue is about the name of the beach, some sort of cipher. Or…maybe the sand in the boat was just *there*, and not a clue at all."

"I don't think so," Ben replies. "Those piles were very distinct."

"Could you have gotten the beach wrong? Could the sand have been from somewhere else?"

Ben sighs. "It's possible."

"Crap."

We sit together in a way we haven't in years, wrapped in quiet, entertained by the lapping waves and the crying gulls.

"How's Oyster?" He asks after a few moments. "I don't see him much anymore."

"Yeah…we like to go to the flats no one else bothers with."

"Isla's famous sense of sand," he half smiles.

"Isla's illustrious insistence on getting away from other people," I retort. He laughs, and I think of how much I miss that sound when I'm not here.

"How's Agnes doing?"

"I couldn't tell you for sure," I reply. "You know how private Oyster is. He barely lets me near her, and when I run into her, she's clearly uncomfortable. I've known her my whole life, but she'll barely speak to me."

"I guess you can kind of understand it," he observes.

"What are you talking about?" I ask sharply. "Our families have been friends for generations."

He turns to me with an odd expression on his face.

I squeak, "Not because of Jack?"

Ben is unmoved and makes no reply, so I go on. "Because it was my father who found Jack in his bunk? Because he carried Jack up the dock? Because of that, somehow Agnes blames our family? What are you saying?"

Oyster and Agnes Farnsworth's son died of a heroin overdose before Fentanyl was the scourge. He died at sea, and the sword-boat captain had to cut his trip short to bring him home. It's an ugly part of Sandburn history, and it changed Oyster and Agnes forever. Agnes used to be a local socialite, as much as Sandburn does socialites. She was the pristinely put-together head of the North Cape Tourism Board and proud mom of a sixteen-year-old boy who insisted on going to sea to learn the trade when he could've been in school, who fell in with a bad crowd, who was offered drugs like they were lollipops.

Ben uses the silence to switch to a new topic. "What next?" He asks. "What's this plan you talked about?"

Find the Millers. Squeeze some answers out of Charlotte. Search the property for something that fits the key.

"I need to get a look at those photos of the sand piles in the boat," I reply. "If I can check them myself, I'll know if we're looking on the right beach. Can you…?"

I give him my special begging face, the one that's only for him, and he melts like maple candy in hot water.

"I can try," he says. "And I'll put my ear to the ground and see if I hear any chatter about the fleece down at the station."

I check the time. I need to get ready for tonight's dinner party, where I'll have to make small talk with strangers while committing a felony. I throw a parting test at my old friend.

"You seen the woman in the glass house yet?" I ask, watching his face like a forensic psychologist.

"Nah," he says. "I don't know if anyone has. I still think you saw a house sitter or a cleaner. I'm sure things will be back to normal when the Millers come back for the summer. You?"

"Nah." I stand and offer my hand to him, but he's already springing up. "Just seen her from a distance when I spy on the house at night."

"Ha, ha," he says, though he has to know I'm not joking.

We're both lying, and in his case, I have to wonder why. His tells are as loud as a foghorn. He has more than one. First, he sniffs. Then, after the lie, he wipes his mouth with the back of his hand as if to erase what he's done.

11

The glass house takes shape as it comes at me in the darkness. It's black on the outside and yellow-white in the middle, like a rectangular creme egg. Whether it will be my savior or my demise, whether it holds answers or doom, I will enter. Even though it's illegal, because I haven't been invited by the right people. Only the Millers can override the restraining order. I imagine such a risky outing would be a high if I was someone who fed off adrenaline.

But no; adrenaline feeds off me. It weakens me, clouds my mind.

I know more about what I'm walking into than I did last night, but also less. Does Charlotte have a plan for me? Does she need a friend, maybe a drinking buddy? Is she a serial killer or a bored marketing executive, or something in between?

I carry a bottle of Massachusetts's finest chardonnay up the beach, then ring the bell at the side door.

The porch light isn't on, but the full moon is enough to light my way. I knock, then ring again. A gust of wind kicks up loose sand around me and I have to spit it out. It occurs to me Charlotte might expect me to enter from the front door, so I trudge through the sand around the house, and find the grand entrance lit up. I ring the bell. I'm positive she said eight o'clock.

The lights go out. I stand in place. They come back on.

The door flies open. "Hello?"

What the hell is going on?

"Uh…hi, Charlotte. I brought you this." I hold the wine out, but she doesn't take it. "I'm here for the dinner party you mentioned last night?"

She stares at me like a zombie. Before I can decide whether to argue or run, she says, "That's Thursday."

The hell it is.

Everything I want to say will piss her off, so I take a moment to think of something polite.

"Oh, no worries, *dahling.*" She snaps out of it and puts on the charm. "Come in. I was just about to mix a drink."

We sit at the bar like two old friends having a catchup, sipping cocktails and picking at a charcuterie board she threw together.

As promised, Charlotte used vodka this time. The dirty martinis are cloudy with olive juice, and they remind me of the saltwater I use to wash off the clams, tinged with green-grey and with bits of debris floating in it.

"What brought you to Sandburn all the way from England?" I ask.

She smiles, but doesn't correct me, doesn't deign to tell me about her origin story.

"What's not to love?" She raises her drink toward the glass wall and the full moon behind it. "Look…I needed a place to recharge. This opportunity came up and I pounced on it. You know our stiff upper lip, right? It's a cultural relic. I needed some space to focus on a project that I wasn't able to do properly in the city," she says. "Coming here has been absolutely life changing."

She's managed to talk more than at any point since I've known her but has told me nothing. All I want to do is put down my glass and search the place.

I shadowed her in the kitchen while she constructed the charcuterie, but saw nothing that would fit my key. I padded downstairs to "hang my jacket" while she sliced up the brie, and I tried my key in the padlock to my father's workroom. No dice.

Now I'm having to make nice, mimic a relaxed person, and make small talk with a woman who might be a murderer.

"This house is certainly peaceful," I lie. I think it's abhorrent.

My father hated this place. The Millers destroyed the point when they built the house as a second home when I was young, stealing a carpet of sand that was once a thriving clam flat. Now you can only legally approach this stretch of beach by boat, which means the veteran clammers couldn't drag their sleds from the road anymore, and you can only harvest below the waterline at low tide before you're officially trespassing.

Nick stayed away for a while. But then, out of nowhere, he was drawn back here by something, maybe nostalgia, and got close enough to the Millers to get hired as their handyman.

"My turn," Charlotte drawls. "Why were you in such a hurry to leave this grand place and live in a box in the big city?"

I sip my drink, hoping the infusion of vodka will dull my urge to strap her to a chair and force her to tell me where the Millers, and maybe my family, are.

"There was nothing for me here," I say. "I didn't want to

spend my life in the dirt looking for something that's dwindling every year and is barely enough to support the people who used to make a good living from it. By the time I hit college, I'd seen everything this place had to offer, I guess."

"That's it?" She asks, eyes narrowing. "A simple, small town girl heads to the big city to make something of herself? The cliché? Something tells me you're no cliché. Surely there's a story about why you left this place. You're a part of it. I know all about you and your sand, Isla Banks. What made you run from it?"

Actually, there's every chance I'm a walking cliché, because there's nothing new under the sun, and I only had two choices when I came of age: stay or go. I'm not sure what kind of in between there is.

As I'm thinking of how to respond, she refreshes both our drinks and hops off the stool. "Let's go outside!"

I take my drink and follow her. The full moon is spectacular, the light pollution almost nil where we are on the point. The stars pack the sky like flaming polka dots.

Charlotte disappears, and I step around the corner of the house and watch her walk down the steps to the sunken barbecue area where the Millers installed a pizza oven and a firepit. She's pressing buttons. I notice the hot tub is uncovered, and is now lit up in flashing, changing rainbow lights, bubbling like a boiling cauldron.

She places her glass on the flagstones of the hot tub and then, out of nowhere, strips down to her bra and underwear. Half naked and grinning, she says, "Now you'll come in the hot tub with me."

It's a command, not an invitation, and right then I know I'm going to do it. We both know I don't have a choice. She doesn't have a bathing suit that would fit me, and I say as much.

She giggles. "We call it a swimming costume, and there's no call for such things. That's what underwear is for."

I do as I'm told, turning away to remove my key necklace and wrap it up in my shirt, then slide into the water before she can get a good look at my non-matching underwear and fraying bra straps.

We sink in on opposite sides of the steaming tub, which could fit six people at a squeeze. She puts her arms on the stonework deck and picks up her martini. The top halves of her breasts are bobbing up like tennis balls. Water beads off her skin like she'd moisturized with oil out of the shower, and the steam creates tendrils falling to the side of her face.

"You never answered my question," she says.

I did, but she wants more; she wants my damage, my baggage, my trauma, served up to a stranger bearing liquid truth serum. I swig some of my martini, the salty liquor suddenly tasting off, like lukewarm pickle juice.

I can see the spot where I used to play high on the beach at the edge of the wood when I grew tired of "helping" the clammers. I'd burrow in the beachgrass and the sand looking for treasure, and every piece of sea glass or intact shell brought pure delight. I was five, six, seven when my father brought me here. The clammers would show me how to dig fast enough to beat the tide, and my father and I would race alongside the veteran diggers who were picking the fruit of the sea that kept their mortgages paid and their children fed. Oyster was always alongside us, helping, guiding, showing us how to make a living at it.

"There's only nature and the sound of the water here for a kid," I say. "We were raised half feral when raising your kids half feral was out of style. My father would lose himself digging, and in the stories he and the old clammers told. I was alone so much that sometimes, it felt like he'd never come back. My friends were gulls, marsh rabbits. One time I made friends with a stray dog. I named him Scruffy."

She says, "Idyllic. And yet you couldn't wait to get out."

"Doesn't everyone leave the nest at some point?" I sip my drink out of pure necessity. This woman makes me tense. "You of all people know about wanting to see the world, being an expat and all."

She closes her eyes for a moment.

"Give it all the fancy names you want, but sand is just a shit-ton of grit," she says, shocking me with her sudden use of crass language and her abrupt change of topic. She opens her eyes halfway. "Don't you hate it when it gets everywhere, all over your shoes and your car and between your toes? There's nothing glamorous about sand."

"I never saw *glamour* in it," I clarify. "And you're right about tracking it. It gets everywhere, and it's different on every beach, and even on different parts of the same beach. Did you know you can trace specific sand grains back to whoever carried them, from where, and sometimes, even when?"

Her mask drops for a millisecond. Her eyes stab like icicles, her lip curls in anger. *Ah, there it is.* And then she snaps back to Ms. Cool Brittania. Did the real Charlotte join us for that blip in time? I'm leaning toward yes. I'll play her game. She's clever and charismatic, but I'm relentless.

"Where are the Millers?" I blurt.

She doesn't miss a beat. "Living their best lives, I expect," she smiles. "You know, Harold and Millie are very kind good people. I wouldn't want anyone to hurt them or take advantage of them."

"Then we agree on something," I say. "And yet you let me into their home when you knew they didn't want me here. Why?"

"I think you know why."

"No," I say. "I really don't."

The enigmatic smile again. "I needed to see for myself what kind of threat you are," she says, sending a chill down my spine.

"And?" I ask.

"Unclear," she replies.

After we dry off and re-dress, I say, "Next time, I'll have you over to my place. I'll make you *my* version of a killer cocktail."

She puts a finger to her lips as if to shush herself. "Lemme guess…old fashioneds?"

"Cosmopolitans." I want her to know I see what she's doing; I'm certain her mentioning of my preferred tipple was a message.

"I'd love to come to yours," she says. "But I meant it when I said the dinner party is Thursday. It's actually more of a happy hour. Please come."

Three nights in the same week with this stranger? I don't even see my best friends that often.

"I'll be here," I say.

She waves goodbye and I feel her watching me walk down the sand.

I shiver as a cold wind kicks up, and halfway down the beach I realize I left my coat inside.

I run back, because Charlotte's turning lights out like she's heading straight to bed. I ring the bell, shivering. Nothing. I bounce on my heels, hug myself. The weather took a turn, and I need to get home before the swells grow too high.

I ring, ring, ring. I bang and yell. "Charlotte! Charlottttttte! Open up!"

I run back to the sand and try to catch her attention inside from the beach, waving my arms. "Charlotte! Hey! It's Isla! Open up!"

Finally, I hear shuffling inside, and the sound of the door unlocking. "Isla? Is that you?"

She throws open the door, this time with an irritated expression. "What's the shouting about?"

"I forgot my jacket. My housekeys are in the pocket."

"I see. I'll go get them." She slams the door shut, and I hear her lock it.

The door opens a minute later. She hands me my jacket. "I trust you have everything now?"

Before I can say yes, she closes the door in my face and triple-locks it. *Click. Click. Clack.*

I feel exposed on the river alone. The dark sea, the aggressive moon, the aloneness is no longer serene, but unnerving. A sense of unease consumes me until I shiver. That alone is an upsetting prospect, because this land and the stretch of water that borders it has been my safe space for a lifetime.

The boat slams the dock. I'm exhausted and distracted. I left lights on for myself this time, but the darkened, empty homes on either side make my house less of a sanctuary and more of a target. I'm suddenly not a magnet and a safety net for my husband and father to come home to, but a sitting duck.

I let myself in, lock the door behind me, and pad toward the kitchen.

I gasp when I see the beam of a flashlight bobbing in the living room. I *knew* something was going on when that fleece turned up. I knew someone had moved my father's glasses on the living-room table. Something is terribly wrong, and I fight not to let my panic turn into heavy breathing.

I've lost the beam. The light is gone.

I'm frozen in place. Maybe they don't know I'm here. I wait two long seconds, and then I take one quiet step forward, and someone grabs me and covers my mouth with a gloved hand before I can grab my phone or yell for help.

12

"I'll let you go if you promise not to scream."

The man's hiss makes my limbs go limp. It's my husband's voice, but with a violent intruder's arm attached to it. It's too much to reconcile, so I don't.

"Promise me."

I nod best I can while constrained by his bear hug, then turn around and yell at him, because *fuck him*. For everything.

"*Clive?* What the hell is going on? Wha- *why* do you look like that?"

This is such a far cry from the reunion I'd dreamt about I have no idea how to react.

"*Shh*…Isla, please." His voice is a scratchy whisper-scream. "It's not safe. I'm so sorry—"

"You're *sorry?*"

He is, as I knew in my gut, the man from the Rusty Lantern, also known as my husband of nearly a year. He's lost at least twenty pounds, dyed his hair black, and grown a short beard. His garb is cartoonishly burglaresque, one fedora away from looking like a pantomime prowler.

"You left me…" I choke the words out. "I thought you were dead!"

"I know. I *know*," he appears only about fifty percent as sorry as I think he should be. "It's not how I thought any of this would turn out."

He's two inches from my face. "I've only got a minute. I'll explain everything as soon as I can, but right now I have to go."

I step back and regard the man who promised to love and cherish me as long as we both shall live. I'm thinking how I can call the cops if I want to. My phone is in my pocket.

"Where did we meet?" I ask him.

"What? This isn't the time—"

"Answer the question…if you can."

"Bryant Park. Isla, it's *me*. Listen—"

"Where in Bryant Park?"

Irritated sigh. Yep, this is my husband alright.

"At the bar." His voice softens slightly. "After I spilled your drink, you said if I didn't replace it immediately, you'd report me to the wine police."

Sue me. It was happy hour and I'd skipped lunch that day.

"Oh, and honey…Christmas ornaments under the windows?" He takes me gently by the shoulders. "Doesn't work in real life. You should get fix the lock on that window if you want to feel more secure."

My bravado is seeping away, my adrenaline running out, and sadness is taking over. "What happened to you? Where's my father?"

Clive winces. "I can't tell you what you want to know right now," he says, then leans in for a hard kiss. He pulls away and I lick my lips. His are dry, hard, different than I remember. "I'm so, so sorry, darling. I need you to trust me, and know that as soon as it's safe, I'll tell you everything."

"I do trust you," I say, my voice cracking. "And you can trust *me*! Tell me, Clive! Stay, and we'll go to the police and launch a new search for my father and—"

I'm saying all the normal things a person would, but my husband is acting like I shouldn't be asking questions, like he's an international spy and a bunch of assassins are about to descend on Sandburn and I need to be casual about this ludicrous situation. *Ok, bye again, babe! I trust you!*

"Later. I promise." Another dry, closed-mouthed slam of a kiss comes down on me. "Don't call anyone. Not yet. Give me two days. Forty-eight hours. Then I'll tell you everything, and we can bring in Lilith and whomever else needs to know."

I barely recognize this person. I feel numb, like I'm talking to a stranger.

"Where's my father, Clive? What happened to him?" My Dad wouldn't be pulling this kind of secret-squirrel bullshit on me after disappearing for four months. He'd gather me up and deal me in, and we'd be handling whatever this is together. Something's terribly wrong.

"Two days, Isla. Everything will become clear," Clive says, backing away slowly. "It's too dangerous right now. Go about your life as normal. Go out to the flats with Oyster tomorrow. Hang at the Lantern, do your grocery shopping, whatever. If you ever trusted me, I'm asking you to have faith that everything happening right now is to keep you safe."

He searches my face in the most obnoxious way possible: By shining his flashlight in my eyes.

I squint and bring my hand up to shield my corneas from being lasered off my eyeballs.

I blink, gather myself, and say as calmly as I can, "Tell me what happened to my father before you leave this house. If you want me to keep quiet for forty-eight hours, that's the deal."

He pauses. "I guess it is unreasonable to leave you hanging. But you're not going to like it."

"Try me." I fight back panic. *Please let him be alive. Please, please, please.*

"I don't know," Clive says, wincing as if bracing for me to hit him. "I swear on my mother's life, I don't know what happened to him, or if he's alive or not. I know this doesn't give you what you need. But it's the truth."

I open my mouth to push for more information, but before I can form words, Clive Hooghiemster, Dutch citizen, American resident, the man I love, the second-longest relationship I ever had, blasts out the front of the house.

I leave the ornaments under the windows and curl up in bed, hugging my pillow like a child with a security blanket. My husband left before I could ask a million questions, including the most important one of all:

Where the hell have you been?

Not to mention, *Why were you hanging outside the Rusty Lantern where anyone could see you? Why did you break into your wife's house? What about your job?*

Clive works for a nonprofit in Manhattan called Finance for All. He took a position there after years working as the Chief Financial Officer for a startup in Amsterdam. When he first told me what he did for a living, I thought, *Yay, Finance for All! They're giving money to the poor! What an interesting guy!*

No, he'd chuckled when I'd suggested something so outlandish. *We encourage children from every walk of life to get into a finance career. We offer scholarships, increase diversity, put on events at lower-income schools.*

Clive's boss still hasn't called me to offer support or condolences. After a few weeks, when the Coast Guard bowed out and the police decided they'd talked to enough witnesses, I realized I'd have to deal with our apartment and both our jobs, that it was up to me to look after three full-grown adults' personal lives, finances, and bills.

Finance For All's human resources department doesn't answer their phone. When HR finally replied to one of my emails, all they'd say was, *His checks should keep coming until the agreed date.* I wrote back instantly: *But how long is that?* I never received a response. Surely the day will come when they'll tell me somberly, regretfully, that Clive is no longer employed because he hasn't been showing up for work. He should have life insurance through them, too, and possibly a 401k and a pension, but no one will talk to me. With Clive alive and well, everything changes.

As for my job, most days I wake up expecting to be let go, but I don't care. Life in suspended animation will numb you as well as any drug. Layoffs in the media industry roll on, and the faster the corporate overlords teach AI to do our jobs the faster they decimate their newsrooms. I called my executive producer the day Nick and Clive went missing, and she arranged for WCN to pay out my accrued vacation, plus six weeks paid leave. My paychecks stopped two months ago.

I pick up my phone, desperate for support, another perspective, a sane person to tell me how any of this is possible.

Clive assumed I'd call Lilith first. But my hand scrolls to Ben's name.

Don't tell anyone. It's too dangerous. Trust me, Isla.

I lock my screen.

I'll give my husband, the man who once saved a kitten from a sewer on the streets of New York City, the benefit of the doubt. My husband is a kind man. A nice guy, a good guy. If he were here, he'd tell you himself.

With all of that racing through my mind, I still can't shake something he said: *How does he know I've been clamming with Oyster in the mornings?*

13

I drag myself out of bed at seven a.m. after spending half the night jumping at every noise and shadow. I grab a protein bar, throw on my knee-high boots—no need for full waders today—and throw my bucket and tools in the back of my father's truck. Oyster and I are driving separately, so I have no built-in reason to visit Agnes and attempt to ask her why she warned me. Agnes Farnsworth is no alarmist; she's got the constitution of a pioneer.

Oyster pulls up behind me at Bass Beach. We're not looking for the unicorn today, that unsullied flat where no one goes, where we can have the place to ourselves as we dig for treasure. We're going for the easy bet. Problem is, so is everyone else.

I hop out of the truck and grab my tools, racing ahead, Snout beating me by a mile. I'm looking at some speed clamming today, because I have other work to do. Diggers are already bent over, legs straddling holes and mud piles.

A few of them stop, watch me, wait. Not Old Caleb, though. He pretends not to notice, swinging his rake like he's angry at the sand. Linda offers me a kind smile and a friendly wave. Shep is here today, watching me and Oyster, throwing us a nod. He's an ex-Navy pilot who retired early from his job selling mutual funds ten years ago and became one of the most prolific mudrakers on the cape.

If Oyster is the captain of Sandburn's shellfishers, Shep Clancy is the mayor, but only until my father returns to reclaim his rightful place. He's six-foot-five of sinew and bone, hair shorn to military standards, and he's the last person you'd expect to take to clamming as he has, given how far he has to travel to reach the ground.

I survey the expanse of rippled ground that will become the ocean floor again in a few hours. *Ah, there it is.* A patch too dry and too close to seagrass to be considered ideal. But clams are there. I don't know why I know; I just do. Snout finds it, too, and paws at the sand.

"Good boy," I tell him, scruffling his neck before jabbing at it with my rake.

Oyster walks with me, and a few others move away from their own piles.

"Like lemmings," Oyster mutters under his breath. "Why can't they stay in their own space?"

He knows why. Because I always find the clams. My father was good; oh, he was fast, he was strong, he had instincts. But he never had the eye I do. Snout is sniffing the spot I pointed out. There's room for everyone.

Oyster and I get to work racing the tide.

As we load up the truck with full baskets, Oyster remarks, "Brokers'er only over Marlin Bay today. Not enough staff at Sandburn Marina, or somesuch."

This is bad news for me. Angélica works over in Marlin Bay most mornings. Of all days to have to look her in the eyes, to absorb one of her soft, warm hugs and say nothing of what I know.

The Marlin Bay Marina is alive with boats coming in and casting off, crew fixing nylon nets, and the loading and unloading of fishing vessels. The whitecaps are up and the ocean is licking the docks' old wooden slats like a hungry monster. The air is so thick with brine you can taste it.

The warehouse is buzzing with processors in the cold morning, all of them in warm clothes and waterproof gear. Oyster and I drag our sleds toward the brokers in the back, heads down, bodies pulling the weight across the cement floor. I see her before she sees me. Five-foot-two of curves and thick, dark waves gathered up in a hairnet, Angélica Vega is cutting and sorting and cleaning fish alongside a dozen other workers.

"Hi, Angie," I say, hoping she doesn't hear.

She turns, drops a dead fish with a *splat*, opens her arms to hug me, then seems to remember her bloody gloves. She makes a motion as if trying to wrap her arms around the world.

"Guapa," she smiles. "It's been too long. How are you?"

"I'm good, Angel," I say, my eyes getting misty because it's been a while. Angélica and my father have been together for fifteen years. Her eyes lost their sparkle when he disappeared. "You in processing today?"

"Aye…some days it's fish guts and garbage, and some days it's blue ocean and sunsets," she smiles. She's what we call a Jane of all Trades in the fishing community. She can mend nets, fish, serve as a deckhand, drive a boat, gut and filet a striped bass.

"I would ask how you are *really*, but…" She smiles, wriggles her bloody gloved fingers, and tilts her head to my dirty, smelly shellfish haul. "Another time."

"Another time," I reply, beyond relieved.

I should be asking how *she* is, but I find it difficult to look her in the eye given what I know. The day after the men vanished, Angélica had to be sectioned, and she was whisked into a mental health facility thanks to her son Jorge, my de facto stepbrother, who saw his mother go catatonic when he landed in Boston from San Francisco. It was almost as if she waited for him to arrive before she gave herself permission to shut down. She was in the hospital for weeks, and then again for another week two months ago.

I can't be real with her right now, can't watch her eyes cloud over, risk her crying when I'm on the edge myself. I'm a horrible person. It's easier dealing with clams, so I wave her goodbye. But she doesn't let me go. She steps to me and whispers, "I need to talk to you, guapa. It's important."

"Let's have lunch soon," I say. "I'll text you."

No, I won't. I can't handle Angélica's grief on top of my own right now. I'm in the thick of it and I have no bandwidth for more mess. I adore her, but I can't help her. I tried, before. It did nothing. She's so far from getting over my father's loss it's like she hasn't even made the start line.

Oyster's at the front of the line now, and I hurry over to calculate my catch for the broker. Everything we sell must go through official dealers, who are the only ones legally allowed to sell to restaurants and stores. A good clammer won't try to sell broken soft shells, nor will she try to skirt size rules.

There's no nudge-nudge-wink-wink on the mudflats. You take

care of the sea or you don't eat. Any softshell under two inches goes back. If you have a recreational permit, you take no more than your allotted poundage and you don't try to sell them under the table. If you have no permit, you'll be chased off faster than a dog at a cattery.

I fill out my form and take my receipt. Oyster's waiting for me, Snout sitting next to him like a good boy. He knows everyone here, and even non-dog-lovers grudgingly allow him inside because he doesn't bother anyone, as long as he recognizes you. He's even nice to the Kastic brothers, because they're not strangers. And they say dogs can sense evil.

After Oyster and I part ways in the parking lot, I head to the Sandburn Town Hall to resume my search for the Millers. My initial investigation after they left town was hindered by a restraining order, by exhaustion, and by law enforcement claiming there was nothing amiss.

There was, though, and I'm convinced the Millers themselves became victims of foul play. It's no coincidence they left Sandburn before their beloved beachside family holidays and haven't been heard from by since. I'm not going to be gaslit into believing something so ridiculous.

As my father's old truck rattles and clangs down Main Street, I relish the last days of thin traffic and unintrusive locals. Soon, the roads will be clogged with summer people and even worse, weekenders who come for the world's best chowder and fried clams. We are, for better or worse, famous for what we do with mollusks.

I stand in the hallway on the third floor of the Town Hall and peek through the glass into the town clerk's office. There are two men standing around looking bored while Wanda fiddles with paperwork behind the reception desk. I press my back against the wall a foot from the door and, ten minutes of doomscrolling and playing with my cuticles later, the men exit.

I slip in. Wanda looks up from shuffling papers.

"Awwww, no. Not today." She shakes her head as if I'm her bookie come to break her legs. "I'm sorry about everything, you know I am, but I don't have time."

"*Wanda*." I make a sad face. "I'm not here to bother you. I'm looking for an update. It's been three months since I was last here. I figure as a taxpaying citizen, that's a reasonable gap."

"You haven't paid taxes in this town your entire life."

"But my house does. My father does. Did." The familiar lump rises in my throat. I'm well aware I use sarcasm and humor to deflect the persistent agony of emptiness and uncertainty that eats me alive, but sometimes the dose isn't nearly potent enough.

"OK." She sighs. "What are you looking for?"

Wanda, who I've known since her granddaughter and I got caught shooting spitballs at the substitute teacher in fourth grade, sets down her papers.

"Has there been any movement on the Millers' place? Anyone sniffing around to buy or sell, anyone or asking about it or—"

"This isn't a real estate office." She goes back to shuffling papers. I don't know why anyone needs paper in the workplace anymore. But local government loves their hard copies. "I've told you a million times I don't know who lives there, and you know I'm not going to give out private information."

Who lives there.

Private information.

If the townspeople don't know Charlotte exists, if Wanda doesn't know there's a slick interloper living in the Millers' house, she wouldn't be talking about a *who*. Just like the rest of the locals, Wanda swore to me she never saw my mystery woman around, yet Charlotte seemed to give them away: *I know what you've been through. Everyone in town gets it.*

"You're right. I don't want to put you in a bad position," I say to Wanda, knowing better than to pull the widow card because she hasn't been moved by that since the new year. The goodwill this town had toward me seeped out slowly, like air from a balloon with a tiny pinprick in it, and then the balloon popped and the sentiment flipped from *Poor Isla* to *It's Time to Move on, Isla*. "But you have to admit it's strange how the Millers just…vanished." I wave my arms in a swooshing motion. "No forwarding address. No ads looking for renters, no goodbyes."

"Grown-ass American citizens are not required to tell the government about their comings and goings," Wanda says, though I suspect she's softening judging by the abrupt weakening of her voice.

She knows something's off. Anyone with two brain cells to rub together does. Wanda gazes at the ceiling as if praying to god for guidance to deal with Isla Banks. She moves to the counter. I hear voices in the hallway.

"I can tell you one thing," she says in a stage whisper. "They haven't paid their property taxes. They're in arrears."

"And that's a big deal?" I've never owned property, so I don't have a clue about how much it costs or what the penalties and deadlines are.

"It is," Wanda says, straightening up. The voices draw near. "Massachusetts has the most arcane and brutal foreclosure laws you ever heard of. You don't pay, they start legal proceedings. It happens fast. You can lose your house before you know it."

"You can?" I need clarification. *Shit.* Is someone paying property tax on my father's house, my current home? Should I be? "So, if a hypothetical homeowner neglects to pay their property tax bill in a certain amount of time, the government can swoop in and take their house?"

She nods. Her eyes dart toward the door.

"How long do the Millers have before they're in trouble?"

She clears her throat, holds up three fingers.

"Months?"

Wanda shakes her head, then pastes on a smile to greet the couple seeking her town clerk skills who have just burst in. How dare they.

"Weeks?" I cough it out. She cocks her chin in my direction; I read it as *Yes.*

"I owe you one," I say, and head for the door.

I don't bother asking why the status of the Millers' taxes is at the tip of her tongue in a town with a population of eight thousand people. Nothing right now is as it seems, because everyone around here is lying to me.

As I push the door open, a bright-blue flyer with neon yellow lettering on the community bulletin board catches my eye: *Join us at the 24th Annual Bowling for Clammers event. Marlin Bay Lanes & Brewery, 6 p.m.*

I'd forgotten about tonight's fundraiser for struggling mudrakers. Who can blame me, considering no one bothered to invite the daughter of the most prolific clammer on the North Cape?

I peel out of the parking lot and chug along Main Street, past the old meeting house from the seventeen hundreds. I pass the fanciest restaurant in town, The Pearl, which has a boat-up-dock and will be unbearably crowded starting next month when the summer people come to clean out their homes before Memorial Day.

Just past the Sandburn Marina is the world-famous Clam Shanty. They have the best chowder and fried clams on planet earth, which no one can deny because it's etched on their sign: *The Best Fried Clams on Planet Earth.* They opted for a period instead of an exclamation point, so it's all rather serious. People cross state lines and oceans to sample their clam-forward cuisine.

I park in the gravel lot and walk into the restaurant that used to be someone's house. It'd call the architectural style "sprawling ranch with Colonial undertones." It's got weathered white wooden slats and black trim on the windows.

I push open the squeaky screen door, and as I'd hoped, the long, narrow space with its infamous slanted floors is nearly empty before the lunch rush. When breakfast for so many workers around here is five a.m., lunch is any time after ten.

I head to the counter as Matty emerges from the cramped kitchen, wiping hands on his apron.

"What can I getcha?" He says, then realizes who's in front of him. "Oh. Isla. How ya doing?"

"I'm hanging in there," I say, trying for pain in the eyes without getting too emotional. I can't afford for this to get awkward. "I'm still looking, you know, like everyone. I…well, Matty, you know how I'm also looking for the Millers, that nice couple over on the point?"

The concern drains from his face, replaced by tension. *Tough.* If I have to lose two of my favorite people in one night, the townspeople can face a few hard questions.

The Millers were as addicted to this restaurant as anyone. They used to get their housekeeper to bring in Clam Shanty twice a week. In winter, they pay an exorbitant amount of money to get gallons of it shipped to them in the Boston suburb they live in half the year. Matty would pack the containers in ice and charge them quadruple for the trouble, *plus* shipping. His legendary New England hole-in-the-wall isn't on any delivery apps. You wait in his line or you don't eat—unless you're willing to outbid his ego.

"I was curious to know if they've been ordering their usual deliveries this year," I say. "I know you ship it to them in the offseason. My dad was their caretaker, and he'd always tell me how they loved your food so much they couldn't live without it over the winter." Throw in some folksy memories and compliments, stoke the guilt.

"Isla, I don't want to get involved. I'm sorry for what happened, but I don't talk about my customers."

If I had a dollar for every time an unhelpful person said how sorry they are, I could officially quit my job.

"Come on, Matty," I push. "There's no such thing as chowder-client privilege. How will you feel if something terrible happened to them and no one bothered searching?"

He crosses his arms over his chest and glances at the door, as if hoping an entire football team will storm in looking for soup and save his ass.

"I suppose I can tell you what *didn't* happen," he says. "They didn't order their usuals this season."

"Not once?"

"Not once."

"That's not good." They left Sandburn in early November. Their usual departure time is just after Thanksgiving.

I *knew* there was something wrong. If I can prove the Millers met a tragic end, the greater chance I have of exposing Charlotte, if that's her real name.

I can smell the vats of creamy chowder simmering in industrial iron pots.

"I'll take a cold quart to go, please." He nods. "And some frites."

"That'll be a minute."

"And extra aioli."

14

Back at home, I heat up my clam chowder and eat my frites lukewarm, drenching them in Matty's homemade garlic aioli. Since the fleece was found I keep forgetting to eat, so when I'm faced with food I turn ravenous.

I conduct a security check of the house, remove the useless ornaments under the windows, and hide my father's gun under my bed behind some guest pillows he'd stuffed down there. I lay several strips of duct tape on the window with the broken lock. Tape won't keep anyone out, but it'll alert me if someone tries.

I make a mental note to go to the hardware store to get a new lock so I at least feel safer.

Once I'm freshly showered and changed into relatively clean jeans and a black button-down top that hides the key around my neck, I head out.

I drive to Marlin Bay and struggle to find a spot in the packed lot. When it's time for the fishing community to step up, they do it big.

The tournament is well underway. The oblong space vibrates with a cacophony of hurtling balls and slamming pins across twenty lanes, of screaming victory and growling failure.

I stroll the threadbare carpet between the bar area and the bowlers, looking for Ben, hoping Michele isn't here. I don't want to be in a battle with her. She can have him all to herself—once my father is found. It's low-lit in here, with funky lavender lights and flashing neon signs giving glamour to a gritty place. They can dazzle us with lights, but they can't eliminate the smell of feet.

It takes time for my eyes to adjust and find his lane. He's standing, arms crossed, watching a teammate bowl. When the guy throws a gutter ball, Ben folds over and slaps his knees in sympathy.

I stay out of the eyeline of his group best I can, hissing his name to get his attention.

"Bennn. *Pssst*. Ben!"

He turns, along with a few others, because one of my hisses happens during a lull between turns. When he sees me, he hurdles the railing out of the pit and meets me on the carpet.

"What'er you doing here?" He's acting like I crashed his proctologist appointment and am most unwelcome.

"Nice to see you, too." I pull a strand of dry, sun-bleached hair out of my eyes. I'm overdue for a haircut.

"Now's not a good time." His eyes are darting around the room.

"Michele is going to have to get used to the fact I live in Sandburn, too," I say. "I'm no threat to her, so can we dial back the cloak and dagger?"

He forms an odd expression, as if I've confused him.

"*Isla*." He stares into my eyes now. "What are you doing?"

"What do you mean, what am I doing?" I'm so confused by his about-face I think I might be losing my mind. "Some things have happened, Ben. Big things. You're not going to believe it. Meet me tomorrow. *Please.*"

"I can't be involved in this mess," he says, looking over my head at a cheering crowd after a strike. "You need to take care of whatever it is you've done before you drag anyone else into your fantasy world."

"What I've *done? Fantasy world?* But you were just with me—"

"It'll be my turn soon." He's focused on his team now.

The place is packed, not just with clammers, but everyone who wants to support them and their families. Local real estate agents, lawyers, shop owners, fishers. Cassandra's a few lanes away playing on a team with a sword boat captain and a few scallopers I recognize, guys who've appeared around town lately to prepare for dredging season in a few weeks.

There's one person I don't see, one who would be the loudest in the room, the most vocal about strikes and gutter balls. Angélica isn't here, and that concerns me, because all her friends are.

I'm choking back panic. After our talk on Wailing Beach, I took solace in the fact that Ben Cassidy, who knows me better than my own mother currently living her life forty miles from here in Boston, was a safe harbor. I knew he couldn't be my rock, but he could be my true north. Somone to remind me there's a destination worth braving the obstacles for.

"I thought of all people you'd have my back, Ben. I don't know if your...your about-face or whatever this is...is about Michele or the Millers or what, but I can't do this alone."

I realize I'm almost yelling now, over the din, my voice shrill and desperate amid the joyous roar of shared purpose filling this room.

Ben shakes his head and sighs as if I've caused him great angst.

"I *have* had your back, Isla. More than you know." He lowers his voice. "But you haven't been honest with me. You should've told me everything if you wanted me to risk my reputation for you. I just…it's too late."

"What haven't I told you?"

"Are you seriously going to stand here and pretend everything's fine? I can't be pulled into whatever this is," he says. "I won't."

He shakes his head again and walks away from me, back to his team, where Michele is turned ninety degrees away from the lane pretending not to be watching us out of one eye.

I stride away, wanting to break into a run, angry and hurt, needing to scream. I stand on the fringes, alone, watching friends and families socialize, wondering where the community was for my father.

Someone is coming, beelining for me.

Shep Clancy approaches, arms out. I allow a quick, light hug. "How you holding up, Isla?"

I have to tilt my head to hear him; he's high as a beanstalk and just as sinewy.

"Same," I reply. "Still looking. Still in limbo."

He nods. "I can only imagine. It's tough. Hey, listen. The teams are already set, but if you want to join in, maybe we can find a group with a no-show, but if you don't…"

"I'm not here to bowl," I reply.

"I figured," he says, dropping the folksy act. "But tonight is about everyone. It's not the time and place for…whatever this is." He cocks his head toward Ben's team. I didn't realize we'd had a rapt audience.

"Nick Banks has been there for all of you for his entire adult life," I say. "Doesn't charity start at home?"

I don't say, *What about me?* It's not my style. But it's implied, and he hears it.

"That's not fair," Shep says. "We invited you to this event months ago. We wanted to raise money for you. You said no. You said any money should go to people who are struggling to feed their families and pay their bills in the low season, and you didn't have time to get involved. You said all you wanted was for us to search for your family. And we did."

"I know how much you all did when it happened," I say. "I've thanked everyone. Then and now. Every time I see them. I appreciate it more than you know. But where have you been lately, Shep? When you all gave up, I was on my own, and everyone went on with their lives."

He holds out two hands as if serving up a silver platter. "Exactly."

I hug myself as if to trap the information about Clive inside me. Shep and his friends—my father's friends, my family's friends—still think he was a victim of the elements, or of something that can never be known. Soon they'll realize I was right all along, that the sea didn't get Nick and Clive. It was people. It's always people.

"We're all just surviving," Shep goes on when I say nothing. "We're here for you, you know that. But there are other crises with people who are left behind. Linda was laid off from her HVAC job and her clamming can't begin to cover her rent. Oyster's wife has medical bills. You know how hard things are around here. If you work with us, you'll find we never stopped caring, looking, talking about him and sharing our memories. People are devastated because they miss him, but also because we *failed*, Isla. I'm not sure you ever got that."

I shake my head. I don't trust myself to speak.

"Look," he says, his tone softening. "Tonight is about taking a moment to be together without all the shit we have to deal with outside that door." He points to the entrance. "If you'd like to stay, we'd welcome you."

"As fun as this looks," I say, nodding toward the hurtling balls and high fives, "I don't have the luxury of ignoring real life. My father is still missing, and I don't intend to stop looking for him."

Shep takes a moment, searches my face. "We'll be there for Nick and his family in a heartbeat," he says. "Give me something solid. Give me something to grip onto and I'll get every last digger, fisherman and even the lobstermen to come out. But don't you ever suggest we don't show up for our own."

He points at me and walks off, back to his bowling team, and I feel eyes on me, and I wonder when I became the enemy in this little town.

15

I'm woken by a text at dawn. I'm not due to meet Oyster until later, as low tide is inching forward every day. Soon, it will reset with the moon's cycles, and we'll once again go clamming in the five a.m. chill.

Oyster's text is in all caps: HURT CAN U COME OVER.

I grab my keys off the wall, hop in the truck, speed around the point to Oyster's place. As I roll up his gravel driveway, I see him laid out on his back next to his truck. Agnes is kneeling over him.

"What happened?" I cry, throwing on the parking brake and flying out of the truck.

"Was loading up some tools. Back went out," Oyster groans. "Honey, you can go inside. It's cold out here."

"I've got this, Agnes," I say, and she treats me to a curt nod. I catch a glimpse of her walking away. She's steady on her feet, but I can't help but notice construction has begun on a wooden ramp next to the front stairs.

"You can't move at all?" I kneel next to Oyster in the gloom.

"Argggghhh," he groans.

"You need an ambulance," I say. "I'm not sure what I can do."

"No! No ambulance." Oyster lifts his right arm and yelps. "Ow! Take my arm and get me to urgent care. I just need the relaxers, and the damn doctor won't give them to me over the phone."

I take him by the forearm and he wraps his hand around my upper arm. I pull as gently as I can. He screams like he's being murdered. I ease off to give him some relief, he yells louder. "KEEP GOING! I CAN TAKE IT." I do, and as this goes on for another minute, I wonder who will hear the caterwauling and if they'll call 911.

As I close his car door and round the truck, I notice a shiny new van parked outside the open garage. It's almost like a bus, and I can see it's been fitted for accessibility. It looks expensive. I can't ask Oyster about it, though, because he does not like prying. To him, any question more personal than "what are you having for lunch" is prying.

I drive slowly toward town. Oyster yelps at every tiny bump.

Urgent care centers near the marinas on the Cape open early. What the captains can't stich up or crack back into place themselves, they'll task to urgent care before submitting to—*gasp*—the hospital twenty minutes down the highway.

I park out front and run inside.

"I need help," I say to the receptionist-slash-nurse. "I have someone outside who says his back is spasming and he needs a muscle relaxer right away."

"He needs to come in and check in at the kiosk." She tilts her chin toward a screen near the door.

"But he can't move. Can we get—"

"Ma'am, that's not possible. You'll need to take him to the

emergency room or call an ambulance if he needs treatment."

"Can I talk to a doctor? If he can just get him that muscle relaxer…"

She doesn't answer. Picks up a phone. Whispers something.

I poke my head outside and hold up a finger to Oyster. *One minute.*

Two minutes later, a petite woman in periwinkle-blue scrubs, her platinum-blonde hair gathered in a bun at the nape of her neck, emerges. She's not smiling.

"Oh…Michele," I clear my throat. "I mean, nurse Battaglia. Hello."

"I'm a Physician's Assistant now."

"Oh. Of course. Um…" What do I call her, PA Battaglia? I never heard anyone do that. Michele it is.

"We couldn't possibly give him anything without examining him."

"I can try to get him in, but he's in agony. Please, Michele. He says he has a prescription in the computer."

"In the computer?"

"That's what he says…'tell them it's in the computer.'"

"If he can't come inside, he needs a hospital."

"This is *Oyster*," I plead. "He won't go to the hospital, and he won't let me call an ambulance."

Michele is used to crew and shellfishers who don't have health insurance. The local medical community can bend, and it often does.

"Handing out meds without proper protocol could get me in trouble," she says.

I point. Oyster is grimacing, bracing in the front seat, staring at us.

Michele brushes past me and walks out to my truck, opens the door, talks to him, and I see him offer slight nods and more grimaces. She returns with a frown on her face. She makes eye contact with me for the briefest second.

"I'll get his prescription. In the meantime, you can pay at reception."

Sometimes it feels like a lot of people despise me around here for things I never did, or don't know I did.

"Hey." I say it sharply. "What's your problem with me?"

She whirls. "Excuse me?"

"I've done nothing to you. I'm not after Ben, I'm no threat to you, and I assure you I have no interest in ever getting back together with him. There's no need to glare at me every time I see you."

She puts her hands on her hips.

"I'm not *with* Ben," she says. "We're co-parenting. And it's insulting to suggest that if I don't like you, it's because of a man."

"What is it, then?" I'm floored. I'm also happier than I should be about their romantic status.

"Your father was in bed with the Kastics," she says. "That makes you dangerous. I'm a mother, Isla. My daughter is everything to me and I'll be damned if I'm going to let any of the scum in this town get near her. I don't like the father of my child wrapped up with you, your father, your friends. You think you're above us townies, but look who your friends and family are associating with."

She's lucky I'm on thin ice with the cops, because the urge to dropkick her halfway to Goodstone is overwhelming.

"That's a lie," I hiss. "Why would you say something like that?"

"I call it like I see it," she shrugs. "I saw your father with Frisco at the marina. I've seen him taking to Luke. You know," she adds, "you've been running around investigating everyone and their mother since it happened. But maybe you should turn that true crime eye of yours on your own family."

She turns and walks into the facility. "Don't forget to pay," she calls as she goes.

I stay a few paces behind her. Michele has gotten to me, which is what she wanted.

Outsiders think Sandburn is cozy. Is drug-running and death by OD cozy? Sometimes it feels like it's less creamy soups and crusty bread and more heroin in the back room of a dive bar. There are people in town, including law enforcement, still whispering that my father was drunk or passed out on drugs, hit his head, and fell overboard. With Nick incapacitated, the story goes, Clive either got lost at sea, panicked and fell overboard, or somehow expired trying to save my father.

Overdoses are as common here as a red tide. No one's immune to the highs and perils of heroin and fentanyl and whatever new concoction is on the streets at a given time. Over in Marlin Bay, they tell tales of entire families shooting up together between extended fishing trips. The tragedies have lessened as captains enacted stricter rules and Narcan became widely available, but the underbelly of the North Cape squirms away. The Kastics are accepted as one of the outposts of the wider drug trade. Problem is, no one's been able to prove it—or they haven't tried hard enough. You'll never catch a Kastic with their hands on an illegal substance. They're too slippery.

I know one thing like I know my own name: Nicholas Banks

was no drug user, no drug dealer, no money launderer. Beyond that, I have to admit Michele was right about one thing: I didn't know either my father or my husband as well as I thought.

Oyster, slurring and loopy, is slumped against the passenger-side door.

"It's all ending," he mumbles as I turn off the main road toward his house.

I shouldn't ask, but Oyster's not a talker, and this is a unique opportunity. "What do you mean?"

"Thissplace." He lifts a finger and waves it around. "Time was you'd meet your quota every day and help the next guy get his, if there was time and your hands weren't torn up." He sniffs and snorts, as if testing out his sinuses. "There's only so many clams out there. Steamers a course. Razors, nah. Cherrystones, chowder clams. Now they're talkin' 'bout farming, and that would be the end. And the erosion. And all that stuff."

He's struggling to keep his train of thought, but this is as good as it gets with him. "And your father's gone. I lost another son, you know that? He's gone and the flats'll never be the same. Town'll never be the same. Wanna know why no one looks for him anymore?"

I swallow hard. "I do."

"Because *no one wants to know* whodunnit. Too many secrets. Clams are the only things they like to dig up around here. Everything else gotta stay buried."

We're passing the driveway to the Millers' house, and Oyster presses his nose against the window.

"That place is bad news. Noises and lights and secrets. All hours at that house."

"What do you mean?" *Tell me, Oyster. Get a few brain cells to team up and tell me what the hell's going on.*

He's snoring. I pull into his driveway and notice the van is out of sight. My father always worried about his mentor and his wife, knowing the degenerative disease Agnes was facing would progress at a rate no one could predict. She could continue her beloved walks for decades, or not.

The accessible transportation Agnes would eventually need, my father told me, would cost tens of thousands of dollars. Shep and Co. would have to bowl a hell of a lot of strikes to raise that much cash. Her medical bills, including an experimental treatment that would cost five figures every year if she were approved, might as well be the moon for a lifelong fisherman, clammer and occasional construction worker like Oyster.

The clammers threw a fundraiser for Agnes's medical bills at the Rusty Lantern one year, and all of the Cape came out. Afterward, Oyster took my father aside. *Never again,* he said. His pride couldn't take it. My father was unamused. *Helping each other is what we do, Oyster! Otherwise, what are any of us doing here?*

Don't need charity.

For fuck's sake, man. People do online fundraisers for a new pair of tits. There's no shame in trying to save your wife's life.

I poke Oyster in the shoulder and his eyes flutter.

Agnes emerges from the house to help him inside. I step out and meet her at the passenger-side door. "He's a little woozy, but otherwise he's OK," I tell her. "The doctor said he needs to rest."

I keep my fingers wrapped around the handle so she can't open it yet. "What did you mean," I whisper to Agnes, "when you said to stay away from the house?"

She looks at the ground, then through the truck window at Oyster, who's too woozy to grasp anything happening around him.

"You remember," she says. "You *know*. Let it be. Everything works out as it should. The universe doesn't need you fixing everything. Stay away from there."

She gestures for me to step aside, and I do. Oyster slides out and wobbles, but we catch him. They link arms and shuffle off together.

I remember *what*? I know *what*? I know my father hated the Millers' place until he didn't. I can't take all the secrets around here, the half-truths, the generational pain, and the outright lying. Oyster was wrong. There is so much more that needs to be brought to the surface in Sandburn.

I wait in the driveway until the couple is safely inside and shut the front door behind them.

16

I drive home and load my gear into the *Sable*. I step off the dock, pull the cord and motor to the small flat at the back of Lost Island, where I won't see anyone who'll want to chitchat with me.

I'm alone in the haze that hasn't burned off yet. I dig and dig, letting the wind, smells, the grating of the rake in sand take me away. A lot of the local clammers have other jobs to get to. The later tides are great for people like me, because I get to sleep in and mosey out to the beds. For the ones with multiple jobs, the later tide means making a living is that much harder.

It's cold, but I quickly become hot and sweaty, and I keep moving until I collect a bushel. I drag my sled to the beached boat and load it up. I motor back toward the marina, passing a few clammers and a lobster boat as I do, waving as we go.

I'm no longer avoiding Angélica, because suddenly it feels like she's my only friend left in the ruinous shit-show that's become my life.

I find a slot at the Sandburn Marina, hoping Angélica's working here today. I walk through the small warehouse and scan the room for her. It's quiet, but there's one guy ahead of me in line for the broker.

I hear a blustering, grating voice coming from one of the offices. Frisco Kastic, I suspect. The guy's a clown, but a powerful one. His hobbies include intimidating people who can't pay their rent without these dockside jobs. His mother was a diehard soap opera fan in the eighties, thus her three kids' names: Luke, Laura and Frisco. In high school, Luke and Laura were mocked mercilessly for being siblings who were named after a hot romantic couple that gripped the nation in the eighties. I always figured that was part of their villain origin story.

I tap my foot waiting for the guy ahead of me to stop chatting with the broker about the biggest clam he ever saw in the state of Massachusetts.

The broker signals me, and the clammer turns and stares at me blankly, then shoots an unimpressed glance to my catch. As the broker, a guy I don't recognize, gathers the paperwork, I ask quietly, "Have you seen Angélica Vega around here today by any chance?"

"Sorry? You'll have to speak up! Angélica who?"

"Nothing. Nobody," I mumble. I take my receipt and turn to get out of there before Frisco lumbers out of his office.

I hear someone hissing my name from the general direction of a stack of boxes.

"Isla!" It's a stage whisper. "*Pssst.*"

I peek behind the boxes and see a friend of Angélica's, hair net on, blue work shirt tucked in neatly.

"Darcy, hi! What's up?" I whisper back.

"She gone."

"Gone…?"

"Left yesterday. She wasn't doing so good. You know. Like

before. Sad, sad eyes. Sometimes crying while she worked. They were starting to notice."

They. The men who make the money off the people who drench their hands in fish blood for fifteen bucks an hour. Frisco and Luke.

My stomach drops. Angélica is a sweet, kind, strong soul. And so, so sensitive. Another person to worry about. Another ally taken out.

"Where did she go? Who was with her?"

"Dunno." Darcy shrugs. "But she ran out of here and we're told to do her work until someone else comes in."

"Temporarily?"

She shrugs again, her eyes wide, concerned, a little scared.

I know not to talk to her boss. The Kastics' primary management approach is keep 'em scared and pay 'em low. They own the most popular restaurant in town, the seafood processing line from docks to factory, a bunch of fishing boats, and they're about to force out one of the last independent marijuana dispensaries on the cape. Those are just their legitimate businesses.

Speak of the devil. Frisco Kastic's snake-oil voice oozes from the walls behind me, and Darcy and I break apart instantly. Frisco storms out of the office and yells at his crew, clapping to accent each word.

"People! We're thirty minutes behind. Chop chop!"

Chop chop? I have to stop myself from turning around and giving him a piece of my mind. I have enough problems right now.

I sit in my father's truck outside the marina. I check my phone, find no correspondence of interest. I'm so bored and distracted I

Google *What are bowling balls made of?*

Turns out it's some sort of mixture of plastic, polyurethane or resin.

It's nearly two o'clock, which means Clive has about nine hours left of his forty-eight.

I should go home and take stock. Breathe. Prepare for Clive's return. I squeeze the steering wheel, an old plastic one with grooves for your fingers, the truck with the standard stick shift I learned to drive at age twelve.

I pull out onto Main Street, traveling at pace, facing straight ahead. *Keep going. Get home. Get some rest.*

I'm a marionette, a puppet, a victim of a possessed vehicle. Instead of proceeding toward home, I veer down the side road where the Sandburn Police Department resides in a modern, steel-and-glass L-shaped building paid for by taxes from summer people buying up properties at ridiculous prices.

I pause, exhale, then reach into the glove box for some lip balm. This impromptu visit isn't going to get me anywhere. *Nothing good will come of this. They're going to glare at you and call you crazy. Drive away.*

I have a legitimate question about the fleece they found. I have a reason to be here. I pull the parking brake, run a brush through my hair, and head inside.

"I'd like to speak to Chief Wen, please."

The desk sergeant hits a few keys on the phone he's playing with and, without looking up, says, "She's unavailable. What can I help you with?"

"Tell her it's Isla Banks."

He looks up.

"Oh…geez."

I don't know this guy. There are about fifteen members of the Sandburn PD including civilians, deputies and reserve officers, and I've dealt with half of them, including Chief Wen, since the disappearance.

"How did you—I mean, we weren't expecting you…"

He picks up the phone while holding eye contact as if I'm about to produce an Uzi and shoot the place up. "Hi. Uh…tell the Chief Isla Banks is here. Yes. *Here.*"

He puts the phone down and smiles in a sort of half-grimace, like he ate some bad shellfish. "She's coming right out."

What the hell is going on?

I decide to pretend like I know. To stay strong. It's like the entire town is fucking with me and I don't know why.

Lilith emerges from behind a door protected with a thumbprint and card reader. She looks tired. Two young kids at home, a political hot potato of a job, and now me. No hat this time. Her neatly combed bob brushes her earlobes.

"I'm glad you decided to come in," she says as if I'm an outlaw she's been desperately searching for. "It's better this way. Follow me. Carter?"

The uniformed deputy I met the night my family disappeared strides out and looks like he wants to take my arm, but he knows better than to touch me. He guides me with an arm arcing over my back, leaving inches of air between my skin and his hand. I get it. It has to be about my recent visits to the house on the point. I can explain everything, tell them I was invited, that it's all a big misunderstanding.

They usher me down the dystopian gray, underlit hallway. I'm sandwiched between them: Lilith leads, Carter has my back. Like I'm going to run.

I pass a room and look to the right and see a man sitting alone, arms crossed, staring at the wall, facing away from me. It's all coming back to me. I remember thinking last time I was here in October: Why does Sandburn, one of the smaller towns on the North Cape, need two interrogation rooms? *They're building everything now for a predicted population explosion*, Ben told me depressingly.

The man turns and faces the window, though all he will see is his own reflection in the mirrored glass. But I can see him. And it's a face I know as well as my own.

17

oly shit. It's Clive. I stop short.

"What the hell, Lilith? What's my husband doing here? Is he OK? What's happening?"

"Keep moving," Carter barks.

I'm watching Clive. He can't see me, but judging by the look on his face, he heard my voice. His expression is somewhere between irritation and hate. He's dropped the tech bro get-up; he's wearing a flannel shirt and jeans today, like he's trying to blend with the fishing community.

The cops take me to the second interrogation room where I face more grey walls, a gunmetal table, uncomfortable chairs. I hated this cold, hard room when I was a victim, and I hate it now as an apparent perp. Lilith sits, and I dutifully take a seat across from her. She nods toward the one-way glass on the back wall and Carter leaves, shutting the door with a gentle click. He'll be watching and listening.

"Must be a pretty big shock to see your husband here," Lilith says, laying her forearms on an unlabeled folder. "I'm surprised you're not more freaked out."

"Oh, I'm freaked out," I assure her. "Forgive me for not

running through the halls screaming. I've had some time to adjust since I saw him less than two days ago."

She squints and leans forward. "You saw your husband? You, the woman who called me fifty times a week with every new thought after they disappeared, didn't break every traffic law speeding here to tell me?"

"He asked me not to tell anyone," I reply. "*Ordered* me not to. Said it wasn't safe. Said he needed forty-eight hours to sort things out and that he'd explain everything. I expected to see him at my house again in approximately…" I check my phone. "Eight hours from now."

She stares at me.

"You don't believe me?"

"It seems convenient that you didn't say anything before now, considering he turned up here yesterday and told us everything. *Everything*, Isla. Won't you feel better if you get it off your chest? Tell me what really happened. I can help you. Clearly there were mitigating circumstances."

I should ask for a lawyer, but it's hard when you don't have a clue what you're being accused of.

"I'm telling you, Lil. I'm completely lost." I meet her eyes, let her see how baffled and stressed I am. "You're talking in riddles."

She opens her folder. "You can get ahead of this. I want to hear your side of the story. I really do."

"I told you everything the day you came to tell me my family had vanished," I say.

Lilith sighs dramatically, like an exasperated TV detective.

"Fine, have it your way. Here's what Clive says. You and he were arguing that night. You wanted to move back to Sandburn but he didn't want to leave New York. His career was taking off, but you wanted to return home to seek the approval of your father. Things got heated, and you hit him."

"What the—I don't *hit* people, Lilith!"

"—Nick heard a kerfuffle, ran in, and slammed Clive against a wall. Your father forced him out of the house at gunpoint, telling him…what was the exact quote…"

She flips through pages. *Pages?* How long was Clive here? Why is my husband doing this to me? Is this really happening?

"Oh, right," the chief nods. "Your husband said Nick told him he'd been, and I quote, 'trouble since you came into my daughter's life. If she wants to come home, she's coming home. You and I are going to take a little ride.'"

I let out a short, staccato laugh and shake my head. "This is a joke, right? Have you ever heard my father speak like that? It sounds like dialogue from a bargain-bin thriller."

The chief examines me as if she can see the truth though my skin.

"No one knows what happens behind closed doors in families," she says. "We see it all the time. Domestic violence, abuse, even murder. It's never the people you think."

"Are we sure that guy in there is even my husband?" I jerk my thumb toward the other room. "We were *not* fighting when he left that night. We were getting along better than ever. The guy doesn't even look like him."

"It's him," the chief replies. "He says you watched your father force him out into the boat late at night. That you were encouraging it."

"Encouraging it, how? Shaking my pom-poms like 'rah, rah, go shoot my husband on the river! Bye, Dad, thanks for everything, hope things don't go south and I never see you again?' This stinks to high heaven, Lil. You must know that. You're a smart woman."

What I'm hearing is my father's dead. That's what this is. A play by Clive to acknowledge what I knew in my heart, to get ahead of it, because Clive knows he's never coming back. Nicholas Banks, my father, my mentor, my one involved parent, will never return. I fight to hold onto hope, but it gets harder by the day. That the man I pledged to spend my life with has betrayed me in the worst way is somehow secondary right now.

"Next," the chief continues, "Nick drove the boat out to the open ocean with a gun on Clive. He stopped at Magenta Shores, where Clive managed grab an oar when Nick's attention was on landing the boat. A scuffle ensued, and both men were injured. Beyond that, Clive has no memory of any of it."

She stares into my eyes again. I don't know what she thinks is going to happen.

"Let me guess," I say. "Clive got a bad case of amnesia and suddenly, four months later, it all came back to him and he's ready to resume his life as normal. I mean, except now he's going to be single."

"Pretty much," she says with a straight face.

"Talk about convenient," I say. "Just out of curiosity, in this scenario, how am I at fault?"

"You lied, for starters, which prevented rescue teams from properly searching for Clive. He says you had every reason to expect this to happen and should've called the police when you watched your father attack him and frog-march him to his possible death." She clears her throat. "Am I to understand you're disputing his version of events?"

"I told you a million times what happened," I say. "You ever know Nick to be that kind of father? As if he's ever tried to keep me in this town. I took off at eighteen for college, got an internship and then a great job in New York City and never looked back. That is, until my new husband decided he wanted the simple life. You've got it backward, Lil. Clive was becoming obsessed with this town. My husband is lying, and it's *your* job to figure out what he's trying to hide."

I lay my palms on the table and lean forward. "I mean, have you even checked out his ridiculous story?"

The chief cocks her head. "You told me you and Clive had a solid relationship. That you were happily hitched newlyweds. And yet you're quick to dismiss your husband's traumatic experience."

"I'm dismissing it because I was there when they went out for a drink like old friends! I *know* he's lying. I was there."

"To answer your question, Isla," Lilith says, her voice softening, "We've begun verifying his story, and so far, it checks out."

"Oh?"

"He said he ended up in Canada—"

"*Canada*? So now he remembered to grab his passport while being taken hostage by a deranged clammer?"

"—he woke up in Canada in a hospital, where they diagnosed him with amnesia. He says they released him when he was able to take care of himself and sign himself out, though he still had short-term memory loss. He traveled down to Maine to try to recover his memories and figure out who he was. He even saw a hypnotist to help him remember."

Now I let out a full laugh. It sounds like Clive ripped his story straight from a soap opera, and a bad one at that.

"How did he survive winter?" I ask. "Let me guess: a kindly old woman took him in and baked him peach fucking cobblers until he was strong enough to find his way home."

"You're not helping yourself with this display…this anger," Lil cautions.

"Did it ever occur to you he came to you to get ahead of his own crime?"

"Wait a minute," she says, and I can see she's trying to slow things down, take back control. "Are you saying you believe your husband's a killer? Why would you marry someone you're so quick to believe could *murder your own father?*"

This is some next level gaslighting, and I'm not taking the bait.

She's watching me carefully. I watch her right back. "People aren't always who they say they are." I say each word deliberately, so there can be no mistake about what I'm talking about. "You of all people know that. You got played by a charmer, and it ruined people's lives."

Lilith is already pale, in part because I'm pretty sure she's never left her house without sunscreen, but now her lips go bloodless, too. She's making a valiant effort to remain stoic but her micro expressions give her away. The eyelid twitch, the tightening of the mouth ever so slightly, the involuntary nostril flare.

"Oh, I'm sorry—did I cross a line?" I lean back in my chair and cross my arms.

I did, but she deserves to be called out. Two years ago, the beloved gym teacher at her son's elementary school was outed as a pedophile. No one listened to the first few kids who reported him for molesting them. It took a rabid parent of a third accuser to spark an investigation. They all said, *Not him, not him, he's a nice guy, he'd never do that!* Oh, but he did, and he's in prison for the foreseeable future.

Lilith is frozen across from me. It's as if she doesn't trust herself to speak. So be it. I have more to say.

"I'm telling you Clive is lying," I go on. "Of *course* I don't want to believe he's capable of any of this, but I don't have fucking time to wring my hands about how a man done me wrong, or to wonder why this guy chose me. Why he wore a mask, what his endgame is. The *why* doesn't matter right now. I don't know what you see that makes you believe him over me, but I'm telling you you're wrong. Amnesia is a classic catch-all to avoid punishment for bad behavior, and you're playing right into his hands."

"He came back of his own volition," the Chief speaks again, as if coming out of a trance. "And I should tell you we did check it out. The hypnotist is here. We called him this morning and he drove down from Maine to back up Clive's story."

18

"A *hypnotist* is your corroborating witness? This just keeps getting better," I say. This is the point at which someone in my position should get a lawyer, but I don't know any.

"He's well-regarded. He's assisted the Portland police and helped bring a missing child back home." Lilith seems utterly convinced.

"He's so successful that he worked for free on a stranger wandering through Maine with no clothes and no money," I point out.

She half-shrugs. "The Canadian government gave Clive social benefits for the first few months. When those payments expired a month ago, he traveled to Maine specifically to seek Dr. Hyndreth's help."

"How convenient." I can throw that word around, too. "So a well-regarded, famous hypnotist who works for the cops never thought to check the missing-person's registry?"

"Canada couldn't determine Clive's identity. Why would he question that?" Lilith replies. "Down here in Massachusetts we were looking for a two-hundred-pound light-haired guy. They were dealing with a dark-haired man weighing, what, one-seventy-five?"

"This man is here right now? Can I talk to him?"

"Not on my watch. And I wouldn't recommend you bother him outside of here."

Nice try. There's no law against approaching people on the street.

"What's he saying that makes this all so believable?"

"I can't divulge what went on between them, but I can say that we find Dr. Hyndreth credible, and he corroborates Clive's story," Lilith says. "The hospital up in Saint John has confirmed certain facts, including that a man with a head wound was there on the dates Clive said he was."

"What date did he allegedly enter the country? When was he first seen for this alleged head wound?"

Lilith regards me as if I'm an entirely new person to her.

"It would be a good idea to get used to the fact there are confidential details you won't be privy to," she replies. "Now. You need to understand we're going to be digging into your life in New York, and here, in the ensuing days and weeks. If there's anything you want to tell me, now's the time. Because if the state police find out there are secrets in this case…"

Of course there are secrets. Doesn't mean I'm going to tell them to the cops willy nilly. "I'm entitled to my privacy," I say.

"Not in a murder investigation," she argues. "You're going to want to be transparent with everyone in law enforcement from this moment on."

I feel a strange sense of calm. Facts, I can deal with. Knowing the truth is what I always wanted. And a terrible truth is staring me in the face. My father isn't coming back.

"I'm curious about something," Lilith says. "If you didn't know about any of this, why did you come here today?"

"I came to ask you about the fleece. To see if it gave you any new leads."

"We've not recovered any usable evidence. I told you not to expect much."

"Oh, I don't."

Lilith sighs and closes her folder. I have to get out of here. I'm going to have to do her job for her. But this time, I don't have months stretching on indefinitely. I have days, if that.

"Give me a sign you understand what I'm telling you," Lilith says. "I'm letting you go while we investigate every angle. The state police might take a look. Maybe even the FBI, if we discover things happened across state lines and the international border. That would complicate matters. What you do now is on you. Keep your nose clean. I mean it, Isla. For your own good."

I rise and bolt out of there as fast as I can, without another word to her.

As I race by the small room behind the mirror, I see Ben in his Harbor Master uniform, frowning, arms crossed over his chest. He's saying something to Carter. He looks angry. His focus is on the chair I was just sitting in.

I don't know if he sees me walk by, and I don't know if he realizes he's broken my heart.

I fast-walk to my truck, distracted and desperate for food and a shower. Which is probably why I don't notice the man creep up behind me until it's too late.

"Miss Banks…" I have one hand unlocking my phone and one balled in a fist as I whirl.

"It's Mrs. Hooghiemster." I size the guy up. He's about my height, pushing sixty, and looks too mushy to be a workout fiend. I figure I can take him.

"Of course," he says. "Under the, uh, circumstances, I thought, um, you'd prefer to be called—"

"Back away," I snap before he can finish the thought.

He does. I somehow know who he is, and I'm not sure why, though maybe it's because he's straight out of Central Casting. He's got a salt-and-pepper beard and round glasses, and he's wearing a wrinkled grey suit with a waistcoat. All he's missing is the dangling pocket watch.

"I'm Dr. Tony Hyndreth. I-I want you to know that I, um…" He's talking fast and stammering.

"Yes?"

"I want you to know I don't disbelieve you," he says. "Very much the opposite. I think I can *help* you. There are things that happen to the traumatized mind, and if we can simply unearth what's hiding beneath, we can reach down, dig around, and pull up a perfect memory, much like the perfect clam you seek in the sands of Sandburn."

Did he just make an awkward *clamming* analogy? *Who is this buffoon?*

I want to ask him cleverly veiled questions to get information on Clive, but this guy confronting me out of nowhere has muddled my thinking.

"Isn't there some kind of conflict of interest with you treating my shitbag of a husband and sucking up to me right now for some reason I cannot fathom?"

"Oh, no, not at all," he says, his voice shaky. "You see, hypnotherapy is not a medical procedure per se. I think you'd benefit from us all working together."

I can see why Clive, my shrewd, calculating husband, chose this man as his alibi.

"You say you don't disbelieve me, but you're talking to police, backing my husband, and putting me in the crosshairs," I say. "All I've done for months is try to find my husband and my father. I've lost everything. My father is still missing, and Clive won't even give me a hint about what happened to him. Why are you trying to frame me and make this so much harder than it already is?"

"Oh, dear. I don't want you to think—well, I'm not backing him, good gracious no," the doc says, clutching his chest as if having a heart attack. He's so good at being the wobbly submissive that if he is putting on a performance, he deserves the proverbial Oscar. "Hypnotherapy reveals the truth within us. Clive revealed his truth to me."

He coughs into the back of his hand. "Let me conduct a session with you. I can help you remember."

"Why would I need to uncover memories if my memory's fully intact?"

He nods wisely. "Indeed," he says. "One could argue that without hypnosis, you'll never know which are the buried memories and which are the ones your mind invented to protect you."

One could roll one's eyes and tell one to go fuck oneself.

"I believe you are sharing your truth," he says. "I mean, I guess I—I think you have some buried memories, and with my help you can enhance them, clarify them, if you will. Think of a session with me as a sort of reverse polygraph. Instead of trying to catch you in a lie, we'd be trying to get to the truth deep inside you."

"Look, doc," I say, trying to stare him right in the eyes but foiled by the sun's reflection off his glasses. "My husband is lying his ass off to destroy me, not to mention my father's memory, and you're supporting him in doing that. I'm not going to help you. You and I are not allies."

"Oh," he says, taken aback, nodding like a bobblehead doll. "I…I'm sorry you feel that way. All I'm trying to do—well, let's just say there are quite possibly other things you're not conscious of, Mrs. Hooghiemster."

I raise my eyebrows.

"Aren't you curious to know why you're so angry at your father?"

His words hit me like a cannonade of darts. His stammering has abated.

My blood pressure spikes and my fist tightens. "Fuck off, *doctor*," I say.

I open the truck door, get in, and peel out with the screech of rubber on road.

19

After a bowl of leftover chowder stretched out with a handful of oyster crackers, I nestle in my father's favorite chair, a vintage wingback that Angélica reupholstered with cozy tufted material in a deep sea green. The forty-eight hours is up soon. I figure there's a fifty percent chance Clive will show.

I flip through photos on my tablet while I wait in the low light of the one lamp I've left on. There's Clive and me in our first selfie together, which turned out surprisingly well. It was that inaugural photo, the one that says you're ready to have someone on your camera roll and *possibly* on your social media in the near future. His eyes are shining, mine are twinkly, and we both have a healthy flush from our fourth date walking the Brooklyn Bridge.

There we are at our intimate rehearsal dinner at Le Mazet with our two best friends. Clive didn't want to wait, so we married in a small civil ceremony in his living room. We made plans for a proper event the following year, a dreamy beach wedding with a clambake for the ages. It would've been this May, but the planning stopped the day my family disappeared.

I scroll through photos of our wedding, where our friends were the photographers, where Clive tried to put the ring on the wrong finger and we laughed. It's the picture of laughter, relaxation, normality. There were no doubts on show. The fears I had were smashed down into the tiniest crevices. I told myself everyone has doubts. Who pledges their life to another person— the most dangerous animal and one you can never truly know— and feels pure, unadulterated certainty? I don't think that's normal. That's what I told myself.

I'm looking for things I missed, red flags I should've noticed, alarm bells telling me this guy is garbage and possibly pure evil. I'm not seeing any clues in these images. Even Lilith, a woman who used to let me stay up late to watch grown-up television with her, believes Clive is misunderstood, so I must allow a stray crumb in the corner of my mind that maybe he was hit over the head with an oar and lost his mind entirely, and his bizarre story is the result.

I shut down the tablet and stare at the wall. The black-and-white photos hung there are a part of this home. There's one of my great-great-great-great-grandfather knee deep in mud and frowning with his hat and his basket, and one of my father when he was young, posing on the mudflats with a handful of other clammers in the background. The most shocking thing about the photographs is how little things have changed. Same mud. Same physical labor, same scowls, same gear. It's not like the telephone and its evolution from clunky, corded landline to flip phone to smartphone. There's still one rake, one bucket, one sled. There is no iPhone for clamming; there is no one to do the work for you. You dig same as everyone else if you want to fill your basket.

I adjust my position and cross my legs in the comfy chair and sip my father's Blanton's over clear ice. I dare him to stop me. *Come back, Dad. Come back and tell me to quit drinking your rare whiskeys.*

But no. He's not going to, and my husband knows why. Clive is faking amnesia. Why did he come back here? Why the convoluted story and breaking in here while I was gone? He's clearly looking for something. *But what?*

I sip slowly, keeping my wits about me. I have to think ten steps ahead of my husband and the cops.

At 10:01, I hear a noise. He's half an hour late. Someone's trying to tiptoe toward the house, but our wraparound deck-slash-porch creaks. Always has, if you're listening. I stare at the window.

There it is. The rattle, the creaking, the lift, the *slam* as the window gives away and the intruder throws one leg over the sill, tapping his toe on the wooden floor as if he's some kind of international cat burglar and not a hapless unemployed prick. He ducks his head inside.

He's got a black scarf around his head, black makeup on his face, and black cargo pants. "You know I can see you, right?"

I act cool, but I'm scared. Scared he'll try to con me. Or kill me.

He twitches with surprise. "Oh! I see." He throws his other leg over. "I guess I don't have to be so quiet, then."

"You thought I'd be out and you'd be safe breaking in here. Why?"

His expression shifts to anger and confusion, but he's looking up, not at me. Like he's pissed at someone else.

"I didn't know either way," he says, reverting to Mr. Innocent. "I had to make sure I wasn't seen coming here. We have to be really careful now. None of this is what it seems."

"Please don't." I roll my eyes, remaining in my comfy chair. "You've overplayed your hand. We are where we are. I want to know why you're breaking into my home looking like the Hamburglar."

"I'm not *breaking in*," he retorts. "I'm visiting the home of my wife and father-in-law, where I can reasonably expect to have a standing invitation. Now. Before you start hammering me with questions like you do at your job, let's check for recording devices."

He steps to me and hovers. "Touch me and see what happens." I show him the gun resting on the seat next to my thigh. It's pointed at his man parts.

"Ooh…OK. Relax." He laughs and holds up two hands, palms facing me. "That's not what you said on our honeymoon."

"I was drunk on our honeymoon. Incidentally, this is the only gun my father ever owned, so your sob story to the cops won't hold up. I promise you that."

"It'll be pretty tough to prove a negative, though, won't it? So he didn't have a registered handgun. With all the underhanded shit going on in this town, Nick Banks could easily get ahold of an unlicensed gun."

This spiteful creature is not the man who was all flustered on our first real date, desperate for me to forgive him for being late, or the man who held my hands on our wedding day and said he'd met his soulmate, or the one who kissed me on Wailing Beach and said he felt like he was home.

"Why are you being so mean?" It bursts out of me involuntarily.

This is a man I thought I loved, who loved me, who was fascinated by my job and adored his, who took me to his company's gala fundraiser at Cipriani and showed me off to his colleagues like I was the catch of the century though I was nowhere near as glamorous as the other wives.

He's standing over me. I put my finger on the trigger.

"*Mean? Me?*" He touches his hand to his heart. "Please don't turn on the waterworks, Isla. It's beneath you. Phone on the table, please."

I pick my phone up from its place next to the gun, make a show of turning it off, and lay it face up on the side table.

"I was hoping you'd make this easier, but deep down, I knew," he says. "Isla darling, I knew you'd fight me on this. It doesn't have to be so hard."

"Where's my father?"

I make deals with God as I wait for an answer: I'll take whatever this man dishes out if I can just speak to my dad one last time. See him. Ask his advice, hear his answer. *Please. I know I never visit you on Sundays, I've never joined a religion, but if you're real…*

But no. My father doesn't show up; I don't hear his voice. Instead, I get this creep.

"I don't know," Clive shrugs. "Things got heated on that boat, but I can't remember a thing after our scuffle."

That's the second mention of a physical fight, which means that part's probably true; there's always a kernel of truth in the lie.

The corner of his mouth turns up. He wants me to know he's lying, that he knows what happened to my father, that he's consciously trying to frame me. OK, I get it. My husband's a psycho. I should've gone to the police before he did. I should've told them Clive was back the second he left this house. Why did I trust him? I knew better. *I fucking knew better.*

He helps himself to a seat on the sofa like he owns the place.

"Where is it, Isla? Come on, now. As fun as this reunion is, I need to get going."

"Where's what?" So that's what these visits are about. Not just to torture me. He's been looking for something, as I suspected.

I don't know if he's after the key around my neck, but I won't lead him there; I'm going to make him say it.

"So you've been breaking in and searching my home to find…what? Why are you here?"

His mouth is set in a hard line. "Where is it?" He leans forward, and his eyes are stone. "Give it to me and I'll be gone."

"Give you *what*? I don't have a clue what you're talking about." My voice cracks. "If I did, I wouldn't be such an easy target for the cops. And for you."

He stands. I remain seated, but I point the shotgun my father taught me to use for this kind of emergency. If someone broke in. No other reason. He wasn't a gun guy, and Clive knows that. So does Chief Wen.

"You can't shoot me," he laughs. "You'll have no chance of proving self-defense. I can choke you out right now and you'd still be the one they arrested."

As much as I'm enjoying his threats, I'm also interested to hear someone moving outside.

"Did you hear that?" I narrow my eyes.

The creaking effect is like having a dog. It sounds off without fail or favor.

"Stop deflecting," Clive snaps. "Your only chance of getting out of this without a prison sentence and your life destroyed is to give me what I want. Then I'll be out of your hair and maybe, just maybe, you can walk away from this."

It's like having a conversation with a computer. No one's giving in and no one's making sense. "Tell me about the fleece," I say. "What was the point of bringing it back? What was your big plan?

"The fleece? I have no idea." He engages in an exaggerated shrug. "But from what I hear, it got everyone talking."

"It was a distraction," I say. "It kept the cops and me busy. But why did you keep it in the first place? *Where is my father?*"

"No more questions," he says. "I'm here for one thing, and then I'm gone. Last chance. I've searched this house from top to bottom. Every nook and cranny over the past few weeks. The only thing I haven't searched is you."

"You keep forgetting I'm the one with the gun," I say. His cheeks puff out and his eyes go wide, and he reminds me of a tomato in a microwave, like his head is about to explode, and the red skin will stick to my walls.

He's menacing, and it's having the intended effect. I shiver, and he notices. I never knew he was here. It's not a big house, and no one's been around this winter to spot him and his moving flashlight. I must've gotten lucky the other night when I caught him.

Clive's eyes home in on my chest. I reflexively reach up to touch the key hanging off the chain, but I stop myself and scratch my nose instead. I keep eye contact, my finger hovering over the trigger.

I jump in my chair when I hear banging on the front door. "Hello? Isla! You there?"

It's a deep, concerned, friendly voice.

"I'm here, Ben!" I yell. "Hang on and I'll come let you in."

"Isla?" More banging.

Clive's turn to narrow his eyes. He's not sure what this visit is about. Neither am I.

"It seems we're at an impasse," he hisses. "But only for now, for this one moment. Because you're about to see how bad things can get, and you should get used to the idea this will be *my* house before long."

He clambers out the window, banging his knee on the sill and stumbling when his second leg hits the porch. I stifle a laugh. If it weren't so tragic, it'd be funny.

20

I run to the front door, shotgun under my arm.

"It's OK. It's me." His voice is muffled.

"*Ben.*" I throw open the door and choke up when I see his concerned face. "What…what are you doing here?"

"I was worried about you." His voice is a husky whisper. "Is someone here?"

I shake my head. "Clive *was* here, but I assume he slithered away through the neighbor's driveway when you made your grand entrance."

My relief at having backup is rapidly replaced by irritation.

"After the chief told me what was going on, I suspected Clive wasn't done with you yet," he says. "I got here as soon as I could."

"But why?" I ask again. "You assumed I was involved in my family's disappearance. You believed Clive's story. Why are you suddenly playing white knight?"

He winces. "No, no, no. It wasn't that. It was—hey, um… can we do this inside?" He nods his head toward the doorway I'm currently blocking.

I step aside, he walks in, and I lock the door three ways.

I head to the kitchen and pour two bourbons. Neat for him

and rocks for me. He's in the doorway watching me, and I dismiss the way I feel when we're in this small space together. It's a passing hit of pheromones. It's meaningless.

I hand him his cut-glass tumbler and push past him, resuming my seat on the wingback. He sits on the guest chair to my right and sets his glass on the end table between us.

"Talk," I say, engaging the safety but keeping hold of the weapon in case Clive decides to return—maybe with reinforcements.

"I never said I believed Clive." Ben gestures with his glass, sloshing the brown liquor. "I overheard the guys talking down the station about how he came back out of nowhere, and how you knew all about it. I was surprised you didn't tell me. Then I heard Chief Wen say she had new evidence, and that she'd checked out Clive's story. But something nagged at me."

"Oh?"

"Two things, actually. One, that husband of yours is a colossal douchebag." He holds up one finger, then another. "And two, Nick Banks never fought a battle for his daughter in his life. You can fight your own. Everyone who ever met you knows that."

I'm blinking back tears, because he's right, and I didn't even think of it. Nick Banks was no helicopter parent. I had to take care of myself earlier than most.

"But," I say. There's always a *but*.

"*But*," he repeats, "just because you can, doesn't mean you should have to. You don't have to do this alone."

You said that before, I want to scream. But I don't have the luxury of doubt. I tell him everything I remember about Clive's visit. I keep my new "friendship" with Charlotte quiet, because it's unclear if she's involved, and whenever she comes up Ben gets weird.

He exhales and shoots a look to my phone on the table between us.

"You attempted to record him?"

"Yep," I smile, taking the other phone out from under my thigh. "But not with that phone. I sat on my burner with the mic sort of poking out. He was so intent on searching this place I knew there was nowhere safe to leave a device."

I find the recording app on the flimsy phone I bought with cash in New York for when I was working on sensitive news stories. I hit play.

My voice is clearest, though most of the conversation is unintelligible.

"I hear him laughing," I say, closing my eyes from disappointment and exhaustion as the recording plays.

Ben holds up a finger. "Is that…'where's the flygum?'"

I pause and rewind. It's barely discernible.

"Item,'" I explain. "He kept going on about an 'item' as if I knew what he was talking about. He seems to believe I'm hiding something. That my father and I had some sort of secret. But we didn't, I swear, Ben. I have no idea what Clive's talking about."

"*Item?*"

"Yeah. Like he didn't want to name it out loud, or he was testing me." I shake my tumbler just to hear the clink of ice on crystal.

Ben shakes his, too, perhaps not realizing he's mirroring me. "Or," he says, "*he* doesn't know what he's looking for."

"Oh." I blink, as if to wipe away my assumptions. *Of course.*

How did I miss it? "You're right. He *doesn't* know. Which would explain everything, why he's back, why he's dipping in and out, visiting me, then sucking up to Lilith and smearing me, then coming in here like I wouldn't be expecting him…"

"You sure it's not the key you're wearing around your neck?"

I shake my head and pull the chain out from under my shirt. "Obviously that came to mind," I say, grasping the key. "But if he was looking for something this small, surely he'd have to turn this place upside-down—I mean, destroy it. I never even knew he was here. I get the sense it's something bigger."

I'm trying to piece it all together while exhausted and slightly buzzed on bourbon and Ben.

"Isla…"

His tone has changed. His expression is tense.

"Don't go there." I shake my head.

"It makes sense to revisit the drugs angle. It doesn't mean your father was voluntarily involved—"

"My father was not running drugs for the Kastic family," I snap. "Of course I thought Luke could be involved early on. Maybe Nick and Clive saw something they shouldn't out on the river that night. But thanks to Clive, we know the answer is simpler than that. Clive Hooghiemster is pure evil and for some reason he wants to punish me through my father. The question is why. And no, I don't think Clive was a secret drug dealer working with the Kastics. You're barking up the wrong buoy."

Ben sighs, leans back in his chair. "Then there's the fleece," he says. "What's that about?"

"I think Clive took it off my father that night and kept it, either because he needed it himself for whatever journey he took that night, or to mess with me. Like he was expecting trouble down the line with whatever he was planning. I can't think of another reason to drop it at the lighthouse other than to cause a ruckus, and maybe give himself space and time to slip back into town.

"Think about it," I go on, playing out the scenario. "That fleece turns up, neon orange and conveniently visible from land and sea, which means Lilith is guaranteed to be out on the point and I'll likely be there for a good while, plus the Harbor Master, maybe forensics, the coasties…it gets people out of his way to do…what?"

Ben chimes in, "Slip back into town? Emerge from whatever house he's been hiding in? Maybe that's when all his searching in earnest began."

"Which means one thing," I nod.

"What?"

I drain my last sip of bourbon and suck the ice as it hits my mouth. Dad hasn't come back to stop me. When the bottle's empty, I'm not sure my remaining reserves of hope won't be, too.

"It tells me Clive didn't know until now that he *was* missing something. But I still have no idea what any of this is about, like why were he and my father really on the river that night? Because I think it's clear they never intended to go for a friendly beer."

It occurs to me that maybe Clive has been in the area all along. Part of me believes he could've been holed up in the Millers' house with Little Miss Perfect.

Ben drains the last drops of bourbon.

"Another?" I ask him.

"Nah. Got an early morning."

The prospect of Ben leaving reminds me how rattled I remain by Clive's visit. He's proved he can come and go as he pleases, and I feel like a sitting duck in this dead neighborhood. I want to ask Ben to stay, but there are so many reasons not to risk it.

"Hey, Isla," he says.

I raise my eyebrows.

"What did you see in that guy, anyway?" The question is as loaded as the baked potato they serve at the Rusty Lantern.

I have to think about it. I can't say, *He wasn't you,* or *He wanted me, so why not?* or *I liked him and went with it because he took care of everything.*

These are not valid reasons for a modern woman who never thought she'd settle to marry a man who was fine, but not amazing. I said I'd marry him if I didn't have to use his dreadful last name. It's not that I'm a xenophobe who won't embrace other cultures and languages. It's that I couldn't go through life as Mrs. Hooghamster like they call me at the bank or, as the nurse at the gynecologist's office called me, Mrs. Hoggmonster.

"He was funny, he had an accent that I used to think was cute, he was trying to help people…or so I thought."

"Not love, then?"

Can I admit it out loud? To him? Ben and I tried. So, so hard, and for a long time. There are things about a soulmate that draw you together for eternity, like an unsnappable rubber band. But the elements that don't work will destroy you. I want *this* Ben, in this moment. Life isn't always cocktails, cozy rooms by the sea and shared obstacles. I don't want the life of a clammer's wife. My mother proved it can't be done. Then again, I don't think Nick Banks was her soulmate. I think he was her bad boy, her object of lust, her excuse for not making it in television the way she thought she deserved.

"I don't know," I say.

He nods. I know he gets that part. What's love, what's obsession, what's infatuation, what's lust, what's a future? Does anyone, except maybe Oyster Farnsworth, find all five things in one person? During one of our drunken breakups where the liquor brought out honesty and the hidden reasons for why not, Ben and I talked about that very question and agreed we'd met very few couples who got it right for life.

He stands, stretches, yawns. Ben-speak for *Time to go.*

I stand in my socks in front of him. "I'm afraid Clive will come back," I blurt.

"I…I think he probably has no more need for these surprise attacks, don't you? If he wanted to hurt you, he would've by now."

It's obvious he doesn't believe what he's saying. There's no telling what this Clive will do.

"Still…can you…"

He clears his throat, looks at the floor. "I don't know…"

"You're right. It's just…"

I swallow, hard. I won't be able to sleep worrying Clive will come back.

"Fine. OK, I'll stay. Lola is with Michele tonight."

"You could have Nick's room…"

Ugh, Isla, you're really offering him a dead man's bed?

"I'll take the couch, no problem," Ben says, throwing a glance to the couch that is very much a problem, because neither of us can forget what we did there in years gone by.

I trot out to grab him sheets, a pillow, and a blanket, and I set them down on the sofa as he checks his phone.

"Goodnight," I say.

He looks up. "Goodnight, Isla."

I didn't even know what to look for in a man after Ben. It's not easy meeting your soulmate so young, because everyone else is pre-ruined, and your ability to allow new intimacy, to make good choices, to discern quality from wish fulfillment, is dulled to near uselessness.

Clive was an hour late for our first date. I only waited because the bartender fed me free tequila shots and told me about the celebrities he'd served that week.

When Clive finally breezed into the restaurant, I was buzzed and hungry and had decided I could do better than a man who spills drinks on me and doesn't value my time. I signaled for the check and slapped my credit card on the bar. Clive's dark-blond hair was mussed, his shirt was half-untucked, but other than that, he didn't appear injured or in distress. Everyone in the bar turned to stare at the man with the presence, a tall, big man in a blue blazer.

I'm so, so sorry, Isla. I—

Don't bother. I'm outta here.

I'm sorry. I'm so sorry! I was saving a kitten from a sewer.

Fuck off.

I couldn't let her die down there.

I slid off my stool, pushed past him, flounced out the door. He followed. *Creep.*

I can show you. We saved her, just barely. I really need a drink. Will you sit with me?

His voice was choked, emotional, drawing looks out on the sidewalk, not an easy feat on a New York City street. I'd gone back inside with him out of wanton curiosity, and I watched the video of Clive sticking his arm through a sewer grate, almost getting it stuck, then lifting the broken drain cover and lowering himself down into the abyss as the sounds of a mewling kitten floated up with the steam.

The next day, the New York *Telegram* ran the video on their website, and Clive went semi-viral, and I was hooked.

21

'm up early, so I brew a pot of coffee and take a mug and my laptop back to bed.

The scent of freshly ground beans apparently curled its way to Ben, who appears in my doorway five minutes later holding a steaming cup.

"What are you researching at six in the morning?" He yawns and leans on the doorway, shirtless and unselfconscious.

"I forgot to tell you," I say as I type. "The hypnotist offered to give me a session."

"No?" He laughs as if he can scarcely believe it.

"Yes," I confirm, and he comes in and sits next to me on the bed.

He leans over my shoulder and reads aloud.

"'Dr. Tony Hyndreth specializes in recovering memories from traumatic events. He's been featured on Oprah, ABC Maine, and the top true-crime podcasts in the country.'"

"A celebrity hypnotist, indeed. When was Oprah's last show? Two-thousand-five?"

"Be that as it may, what's a formerly big famous TV guy like him doing helping a man with no name for free?"

Ben gives me a skeptical squint. "You're suggesting Hyndreth in on it? Risking his reputation for a lost Dutchman who wandered into his office?"

"I don't know," I say. "He seemed earnest enough, but I have a bad feeling. If Lilith is falling for his act, it means things are spiraling behind my back and I have no chance to stop it in its tracks. My only choice is to get ahead of it. Or at least next to it."

I put my hand over my mouth to talk directly at Ben. "I'm going to have to debunk Clive's story myself," I say, "one bunk at a time."

"I'm not sure what that means, but I agree," he nods. "What's with the hand?"

"I haven't brushed my teeth yet," I say into my palm.

"*Please*. And I'm April fresh? Been there, done that," he says, reaching out to gently tug at my wrist, and I let my hand fall. "How do you plan to do it?"

I toggle to another tab. "Check this out."

He reads the page and shakes his head. "I can't believe you found that. You've always been a digger," he says. "You really think that's the doctor who treated Clive?"

"I'm as sure as I can be," I reply. "I'm going up there this morning."

Thanks to a Canadian website where pissed-off patients can rate their doctors, I found a guy with a bad case of gout who was in the Saint John hospital's emergency room at two in the morning, which was the same time of day as Clive was allegedly there, though on a different date. Gout guy railed against a "Dr. P" on the site, which is basically medical Yelp. I figure I have a chance of running into him if I show up in that ER at two a.m.

"Saint John is a six-hour drive," Ben points out. "A round-trip to Nova Scotia will be risky with the old truck."

"Which is why I'll be using the other car," I say. "Nick had that Subaru he called his 'practical ride.' It's in the second garage. I'll take that, if it still runs."

"Couldn't you just…call?"

"I'd get hung up on faster than you can say lying husband," I say. "Much better chance if you meet your sources in person. They'll often confide in you before they'll be rude. People don't like confrontation."

"Some people do," he says. He sips his coffee.

I make a face. "I don't *like* confrontation. I'm just not afraid of it when it's necessary."

"Meantime," he says, "I'll try to snap a picture of those original images of your boat with the intact sand piles. I still think the middle one was from Wailing Beach, and we gave up too soon. But with everything going on, I'm not sure what kind of access I'll have to case files."

"Don't get caught," I agree. "You can learn a lot just by being there. You have access to the comings and goings in that station. Just don't let them know you're working with me."

"No chance," he smiles wryly.

I open the garage door for the first time in years. The lump is still there, smaller than I remember. I throw off the tarp ready to dust off the old Subaru, but I'm greeted with a shock.

This is no Subaru. It is, in fact, an apple-red Porsche 911. *What's a hundred-thousand-dollar vehicle doing in my father's ancient garage?* It looks brand-new.

What am I supposed to drive to Nova Scotia in now? I must choose between a conspicuous Midlifecrisismobile and an old clunker I suspect will struggle to make it to sixty mph. My father never cared about possessions or status, and he has a life partner who holds the same values. I check the glove box and am shocked to find the registration of this vehicle is in the name of one Nicholas Banks of Sandburn, Massachusetts. The keys are in it.

I hit the road that takes me up past New Hampshire and into Maine. I've only flown to Canada, never driven. My dad always used to say, *Got no reason to go to Maine. Why leave Sandburn? Nothing holds a candle to our coastline.*

He's right, but also wrong. The drive is dramatic with rocky coastlines and crashing waves, some of it high above the water. With one flick of my wrist I could go over a cliff. I find myself going ninety without realizing it. The car runs like an extension of me.

I creep through traffic at the Canadian border, showing my passport and congratulating myself for remembering to bring it, and I think about the logistics of how my husband got himself from a skiff in the Atlantic Ocean up to Nova Scotia without a passport, wallet, or his phone. Law enforcement wasn't able to ping his or my father's cellphones after that night. Or so they told me.

I park at the back of the lot at Saint John's Central Hospital. I recline the seat as far as it will go, curl up with the blanket and pillow I brought, and set my alarm.

When my alarm goes off, I'm already half-awake. A Porsche 911 is not the place for a peaceful slumber for anyone bigger than a

Smurf. I freshen up, chew some gum, and head into the ER. The waiting room is packed. Every chair is occupied and most of the wall space is taken up by would-be patients leaning while they wait. No one notices when I walk past reception and through the swinging doors to the inner sanctum.

I find the nurses' station easily, checking the monitor on the wall across from the desk, but only patients and room numbers are listed. I select spot against a wall between a doorway and a man moaning on a gurney and listen to what's going on around me. Two nurses are talking loudly about the Greek lady with the bladder problem in Room 4. Medical staff are hustling up and down hallways.

After fifteen minutes of hanging around like a concerned family member with worried eyes and wringing hands, I haven't heard any mention of a Doctor P. I walk purposefully down the hall. Another ten minutes pass, and I'm starting to attract looks from staff. I find another corner to lurk in, and stare at my phone, making eye contact with no one.

And then, finally, paydirt.

A voice coming from around the corner asks where Dr. Parmenter is.

He's so close I can feel him, like The Force. Someone responds with irritation, "He's gone out." Out? Out where? I'm thinking he's on a smoke break. One of medical Yelp's angry reviewers wrote, *Dr. P stank like a walking cigarette butt.*

I might only have moments to catch him alone; I don't even know if it's a sanctioned break or not. If it's a sneaky race for a nicotine hit, I might be screwed.

The hospital is sprawling, and I have to think fast: Where would a busy doctor go for a quick smoke?

A roof.

That's where I'd go if I were a rogue healthcare provider in need of a fix.

I walk the halls until I find a door marked *Emergency Exit.* Praying no alarm will blare, I push it open, gritting my teeth. I let out a sigh of relief when there's no noise.

Up I go, and I make it to the last flight of stairs and a door marked *No re-entry without pass.* Someone's wedged an empty cigarette pack between the lock and the doorjamb. I'm careful to keep it in place as I step out onto the roof.

There he is. A few paces away, near the edge that looks over the Bay of Fundy, is a man in a white lab coat, smoke swirling above his head.

"Dr. Parmenter," I say, praying I have the right man, and that he won't call security on me.

22

The doctor flinches as I, a tall woman with untamed blonde hair and the fashion sense of a dockworker, says his name and comes at him.

"Hi! Dr. Parmenter?" Big smile. "I'm from Sandburn."

He blows it out his nostrils.

"Sandburn?"

"The Clive Hooghiemster case."

A round of thoughtful inhaling.

"The Lost Dutchman," he says.

"Yes. I understand you spoke to our police chief the other day." I'm crisp, confident, like I belong here.

He nods, and I hide my disappointment. I didn't entirely believe Lilith when she said Clive's story panned out; I figured there was a good chance she was bluffing to get me to talk.

"I did, and I was within my rights. Apparently the guy gave permission to share his diagnosis," the doctor says. "Our chief administrator said it was legal to confirm what your department already knew."

More nostril smoke.

I almost feel bad about how easy this is. My guess is the good doctor is drunk with exhaustion and circadian rhythm abuse.

"And it was more helpful than you know," I say. "The police chief just needs to nail down what kind of amnesia Mr. Hooghiemster had. For example, he couldn't recall how he got his head wound, but he remembers who he is now, and knows his family, his job, his friends…"

"Did the patient consent to this?" He's paying close attention now.

"Didn't the administrator tell you?" I bluff. "As you may nor may not know, a beloved fisherman from Sandburn is still missing, so we're dotting every T and crossing every I. I mean, we're crossing every—"

"I know what you meant," he smiles sympathetically.

Saint John, Nova Scotia is nothing if not supportive of the fishing industry. Its own Bay of Fundy is about to dive headfirst into scallop season, right alongside Marlin Bay, where the port will be overrun with dredgers and visiting fishers gathering up the pale-pink shellfish.

"If Mr. Hooghiemster had amnesia as your diagnosis indicated—"

"My notes indicated the patient 'claimed to have amnesia,'" he interrupts.

"*Claimed?* You didn't believe him?"

"You know how kids are always bumping their heads on something? The playground, doing cartwheels, all those little childhood bumps that aren't concerning."

Nope. "Yep." I nod wisely.

"His was like that. There was a bump he kept pointing to, but we wouldn't have seen it if he hadn't led us directly to the spot. No noticeable wound, no sign of a concussion. But we did our due diligence. When there's blood on a patient who isn't sure if he's been assaulted or in a car crash and he's babbling about being lost and he can't remember his name, we do the necessary scans. We found nothing concerning."

We've veered sharply out of the hypothetical and into the specific, but I'm not going to point that out. "The blood was only on his…?"

"His clothes. Not much." He looks at me oddly. I'm on borrowed time.

"From what we understand, one can get amnesia through a traumatic event alone, even without a gaping head wound," I say.

"Yes, except this guy had the kind of 'amnesia'—" Dr. P makes air quotes best he can with a burning ciggie hanging off his fingers— "where you remember the wrong things and forget the right ones. If you forget your name and where you're from, you might have transient global amnesia. But this guy tells the nurses he can't remember how to brush his teeth. If you're that bad off, you can't remember to walk. Maybe you can't swallow. You know what I mean?"

Another drag. His cigarette is nearing the stub, which means I gotta get out of here before he starts to wonder why an American cop is dressed like a college student at a Phish concert.

"Did you call the police?"

"There's no law against lying about your memory," he shrugs. "But yeah, of course we did. They took a report, but considering he only blood on him was from a small cut on his hand that didn't require stiches, and the was physically fine and not a danger to himself or others, they let him go on his way when he requested to leave."

"What about later? Wouldn't they run missing persons reports across borders?"

"I'm not in law enforcement, ma'am."

"Just one more question," I say. "If he didn't know who he was, wasn't Canadian, and didn't have a wallet, how did he leave here? Did they just watch him walk out the door?"

"No!" he snaps. "Our policy clearly states patients must be picked up by a responsible adult."

"So, like…he called an Uber?"

"I mean, maybe, I guess. But I—wait, no. He couldn't have. He didn't have a phone."

"Did one of your staff possibly call a car for him?"

"*No.* We're not a car service."

"Of course. Sorry. Maybe the Canadian government took care of it."

"The…government?"

"You know. They gave him benefits until he got on his feet and put him up in public housing or something. Maybe he took public transportation. I saw a bus stop out front."

Now I've got him. He's cracking up, coughing on his smoke, shaking his head. "Good god, no. Absolutely not." More coughing. "Canada has some great benefits, but we're not a Four Seasons resort."

I can sense he's about to realize what he's done, that I'm a perfect stranger, not a smoking buddy, and we've colored far outside the lines.

"I appreciate you trusting me. This is extremely helpful," I say.

"Who'd you say you were with, again?"

My brief panic apparently shows on my face.

He gets it now. "Ah. You might want to get out of here before I have to report you."

I nod. I'm already gone, backing away, getting ready to run. "Dr. P? Why'd you talk to me?"

"Frankly," he says, flicking his stub on the ground and rubbing it out with the ball of his foot, "the guy was an asshole. He treated the nursing staff like his servants." He points an index finger at me. "I'll deny I ever said that."

That's OK. I'll report back to Lilith and she or the staties or the FBI can subpoena him.

"Who are you?" he asks.

"I'm his wife," I say, and Parmenter's eyebrows fly upward.

I race away before he's done hiding the evidence of his habit, push through the exit door, and continue down to the ground floor. It's a long drive back to Sandburn. I'm going to need coffee.

23

sleep until late afternoon, something I haven't done since college, then sit on the living room rug with a pile of my father's most recent mail and documents between my splayed-out legs.

Tracking Nick's and Clive's movements with bank records, ATM video and cellphone pings was a matter of urgency when the men went missing. The cops said they dug into it all, including my own activity, but found nothing that would indicate where they'd gone. I surrendered my privacy without a moment's hesitation. Far as I knew, they stopped looking after a week, with Lilith mumbling something about needing a warrant to further breach the privacy of people who might've gone missing voluntarily.

My legs are falling asleep, and the papers I've sifted through are outdated and useless. I'm no closer to understanding how—and why—my father bought a Porsche. Nick Banks doesn't own a computer, and yet it appears he went paperless years ago. He must keep everything on that missing phone, because I can't find anything current in his physical files, whether tax records, bank statements or utility bills.

I use my hand and arms to get to my knees, then stand like a wobbly fawn.

The blood rushes back into my lower extremities, and I lean down and pick up the pages. A scrap of paper falls slowly out, dancing and swaying to the ground. I bend and pick it up. The name *Jane* is scrawled on it in my father's old-fashioned script, and under that, *175 Hawthorne Way, Salem, Massachusetts.*

The note has a jagged border like it was torn off a bigger page. I drop the pile on the sofa and paw through it all again, finding nothing ripped in the same way, no partner for this scrap.

My phone beeps with a text from Ben. I don't know if Michele told him about our little chat or not, but suddenly, our communication channels have opened wide.

Got something to show you. You home?

As I read it, I hear the boat. I head out to meet him on the dock.

He's on duty, at the helm of the Harbormaster's boat. He drops his fenders and tosses me his line. He hops off as I tie the ropes to the cleats. We sway as the dock rises and falls with the wake of a boat passing too fast.

"I got it." He's smiling and unlocking his phone.

"Got what?"

He holds the device in front of me. He's snapped a pic of the inside of my father's boat before it was towed, and I can see the three piles of sand, all built and shaped by my father's hand, little anthills like Ben described.

"Well?" Ben clears his throat.

"You were right about the sand. I'll need to search Wailing Beach again."

"I figured," he says modestly. "So, how'd it go with the good doctor?"

I tell him everything about my trip. The wind is whistling through our ears, sunset is coming, and he steps closer to hear me. His windbreaker is puffing with the breeze and I resist the urge to reach up and flatten it over his chest.

"That was risky," he says when I'm done. "I assume you've already brought this to Lilith?"

I shake my head. "I don't have near enough to impress her. I need a pile of incontrovertible evidence to sway her. Clive's got them all feeling sorry for him. By the way," I say. "You ever heard of a clammer named Jane?"

"Jane? Jane…" He shakes his head. "Doesn't ring a bell. Why?"

"Just something I found in my father's papers. Probably nothing."

"Ah. Better go," he says, taking a step toward his boat. "They want me to swing by the lighthouse. Kids been drinking around there."

"Ben," I say, touching his shoulder to stop him. "What were my father's last months like? What was he doing…did you notice anything out of the ordinary?"

When it first happened, everything was an emergency. I focused on the seconds, the minutes, the hours, the days. Now it's time to paint the grander picture, a portrait of who my father was in the years I was gone from Sandburn save for a week or two a year.

"Your father was digging all the time," Ben says. "Every tide, two a day, no matter the time, he was out for as long as I can remember. Far as I could tell, he was often making his quota. And…he was at the Millers' house a lot. He wasn't digging so much with the other guys in the past couple years."

"What about his friends?" I push. "Was he still on good terms with Oyster? Were he and Angélica OK?"

He gazes off in the distance as if he's thinking of a nice way to say something. "When I saw him, he was often alone. But I never heard of a falling out. You know Angélica …your father got untold abuse for the fact he couldn't get her to marry him. Didn't matter. They were sou—"

He chokes on the word.

"Soulmates," I assist him.

He's too close to me.

"There *is* one other thing," Ben says, changing the subject like cracking a whip. "Did you know he had money?"

"What? No, he didn't." I frown, shake my head some more, this time until I feel a crick in my neck. "Nick has this house. That's it."

"And the Porsche." Oh, right. I keep forgetting about the Porsche.

"I don't know how to explain it," Ben goes on. "Two years ago, Michele and I were struggling to find the right school for Lola because she wasn't thriving in Sandburn's schools, and we were doing *everything* to raise money to go private, but we were stuck. Remortgaging the house or borrowing at a high interest rate would risk Lola's stable home and her future. We don't know if she'll ever be able to live on her own or not. We have to plan decades in advance.

"Nick…your father…he heard about our situation. Next thing we know, we get a call from a private school with a reputation for mainstreaming children with Down syndrome, saying Lola's tuition had been paid for the year and can she start school in the fall."

He tears up. I have never seen Ben Cassidy cry. His eyes grew glassy when we broke up the last time, which was officially five years ago with one quick bout of ex-sex in between, but his pain, his emotional baggage, usually takes the form of retreat and, occasionally, anger.

He clears his throat. "I owe him," he says. "When they found that fleece, when you told me about what you've been doing, I knew I'd fucked up." He holds his head in his hands. "I should've been helping you all along. I really thought he was gone, Isla, just like fishermen for centuries on the North Cape."

I'm still trying to figure out how the hell—and why the hell—my father had that money to give Ben. It occurs to me I never drilled down into who would be paying for my and Clive's big beach wedding, and I glossed over my father saying more than once that he'd "take care of everything."

"I've got to go get ready," I say, watching the sky darken, realizing I'm running late.

"Ready for what?"

"I'll tell you when I know more," I say. "Trust me. I'm not about to do anything stupid. But keep your phone on, OK? In case."

I don't know what Charlotte's endgame is or if we've reached it yet, but with Clive pounding nails into my coffin, I can't be so cavalier anymore. If she drugs me, if I start to feel even a hint of a substance I didn't ask for, I'll press one button on my phone and alert Ben. He gives me a suspicious look and then hops into his boat, riding off into the literal sunset.

24

After a hot shower, I pull on some black pants and fitted white top, blow-dry my hair and put on some makeup. I hardly recognize myself. I've grown used to seeing sweatshirt-clad Clammer Isla in the mirror. Dinner Party Isla, until this week, remained back in New York.

I carry my knife, and I have a mini pepper spray cannister and a rape whistle on my keychain. I work late nights and early mornings in Manhattan, and I'm used to having my wits about me.

I'm tempted to take the Porsche, but it's smarter to take the boat. I have the river to myself as I approach the point. The house is fully lit up and guides me in. I focus on beaching the *Sable* and pounding the stake into the sand so it doesn't float off as the tide rises.

I walk up the beach barefoot and carrying a bottle of Grey Goose.

The side door is most convenient, so I ring the buzzer. Nothing happens. I ring again, but there's no reply. A few knocks, hoping she hears me. "Charlotte… Charlotte? It's Isla."

I swing around the front.

When I set foot on the driveway, I see a car that doesn't belong to the Millers. They're BMW people. This one's a Dodge Charger.

Do I try the front door, or do I run?

Run, Isla.

That voice again.

I mount the narrow stone steps to the grand doorway with its beveled glass accents. I peek through the side panel. The entryway is lit up by a chandelier the size of a rose bush. The front door, unlike the back, has a visible camera doorbell, so Charlotte will be able to hear my voice and see me. I smile, wave, hit the button, cling to my vodka.

One more ring, one more wave, and then I'm out. She said eight o'clock. It's now eight fifteen, so not too early, not too late. I stand for a few more moments and then, finally, I hear footfall.

A man throws open the door. Unlike his car, he is marked. Sandburn police officer Carter Waring is in uniform, hand on his gun belt, radio pinned to his shoulder. Before he can say anything, I hear stomping and yelling behind him. Charlotte steps forward. Strands and flyaways have escaped from her normally slick pony, and she's shaking, her mouth twisted in a half frown, half sneer.

I've walked into a trap, and it's my own fault. I knew. The red flags were there, my gut was screaming and my brain was right there with it. I want to run now, oh so badly, but Carter's gun and thoughts of being tackled to the ground stop me.

"Why aren't you *arresting* her?" Charlotte screeches, looking from me to Carter. "I told you she's been stalking me, and here she is, banging on my door! What more evidence do you need?"

"I wasn't *banging*," I say. "I—what is happening—"

Charlotte yells to Carter, "You saw her on the monitor yelling, trying to get in. And now she's brazenly stalking me at my front door, probably drunk again." She nods to my vodka bottle.

"It's *unopened*," I say weakly.

"Arrest her before she runs away again. This woman is *insane*!" Charlotte is putting on a convincing show.

Carter's eyes are hard. "Ma'am, what brings you here this evening?" He asks. "As things stand, you are currently in violation of a restraining order. I have no record showing it was lifted."

"I'm here because I was invited to a fake dinner party," I say, my voice like butter, my demeanor calm. "This woman told me to arrive at eight."

"No, I did not!" Charlotte exclaims, jabbing a finger at me. "There's a restraining order out on you. Why would I invite you? You're the *opposite* of invited!"

"Carter. Come *on*." I involuntarily laugh, and it comes out as an angry chuckle. "This is ridiculous. She's *lying*—"

"Ma'am—"

"Don't *ma'am* me." And there goes the calm, let out like a racehorse from the gate. I jab my finger in his direction. "You were hugging me the night my husband disappeared, and my father is *your* father's mentor, and suddenly I'm 'ma'am?'"

Charlotte steps forward, her eyes flashing and showing zero recognition for our budding friendship. She fixes on Carter. "I showed you the footage. She's here most nights, as the video shows. She's running up the beach and banging, yelling, scaring me. It's terrifying."

"*Please*," I say, shaking my head. "That makes no sense. If you were so terrified, why didn't you call the cops the first time I allegedly breached the order? You invited me, you lured me here from the beach, and I came in and kept you company against my better judgment."

I turn to Carter.

"Check the video on that. It should show her waving me in from the beach when I was passing by in my boat."

Carter squints. "Ms. James?"

"There is no such footage. She's lying. The videos that I showed you speak for themselves. Get her off my property! Now!" Charlotte is huddled in the doorway, shaking.

"Carter," I say, my voice quiet but shaking. "Can I see the video?"

He pauses.

"Don't you dare let her in!"

For some reason, that seems to annoy Carter, and he says to her, "Ma'am, show me your phone again, please."

Charlotte hands it to him, and he shows me. There I am, in full stalker mode, storming up the beach toward the house with an angry face, annoyed at myself for leaving my housekeys behind. There I am, banging on the door trying to wake her up. Me on the beach, searching her property, lingering, looking for the keys she deliberately dropped.

"You can see this has been edited," I tell Carter. "It's cut like a movie trailer, for goodness' sake."

Charlotte hugs herself and hunches like she's going to be hit.

Carter holds up a hand to stop me, like a traffic cop.

"Don't come any closer," he barks. He's serious. I take a step back. His other hand flutters on his holster.

"You gonna shoot me, Carter?"

"The resident of this property has asked you to leave. You are trespassing. I'm going to ask you one last time."

"Fine." I stay where I am, stare directly at Charlotte, if that's her real name.

"You and I both know the truth," I say. "And everyone else will very soon. Make no mistake about that."

"See? She's threatening me! Why aren't you arresting her? She's committing a felony right in front of you!"

I hold up my hands in surrender. "I'm not threatening anyone. I'm defending myself. And now I'm gone."

Before I can move, Carter's radio crackles and a staticky man's voice comes through. Carter brings the radio to his mouth. "Go again?"

"Found. *Scratch*. Code *scratch*. All hands. It's *mumble mumble*."

Color drains from Carter's ruddy face. "Copy." His expression tells me this is going to be bad. The way he holds my gaze lets me know that whatever this is, it involves me. The sirens are piercing the air now. By the sounds of it, there are at least three vehicles screaming in our general direction.

"Ma'am—" He steps out of the house, toward me, the aggression gone, hand off his gun. Charlotte has faded back into the house.

I don't wait for another word from these two.

I turn and race through the dark woods, knowing them like my own back yard, running toward the flashing red and blue lights.

The melee is in the triangle of woods between Oyster's house and the Millers.' I can see flashlights and, suddenly, a spotlight.

Acres of woods surrounds the glass house. Oyster's family has the last homestead within it, the last residence built before the town enacted an ordinance so no other development could happen on this protected land. It's thick with underbrush, roots, rocks, oaks and maple trees.

I weave my way through trees and underbrush, brambles slapping my face, and I hope the crunch of my feet on foliage doesn't announce my presence. The sirens pierce the night air, and the red lights of an ambulance and the blue flashing ones of cop cars illuminate the dark woods.

Please don't let it be my father.

Please let it be him, so I can bury him. Let it be Nick Banks, who died of a brain aneurism and never felt a thing.

I creep up to the edge of the clearing. I've made a circle through the woods, coming back around so we're at the edge of the Miller's beach, but hidden among the grand oaks, some of them hundreds of years old. Lilith is here, directing things in the small space between the woods and the sand.

Don't let it be Oyster. Or Agnes. I can catastrophize with the best of them, and suddenly I think maybe it's Ben.

Someone moves a few steps, and suddenly I see.

It's a man. A long, tall one. With the spotlight, I can tell he has dark hair. His face is covered in blood. He's on his back, arms by his sides, legs out in front of him, like someone posed him. Like he's at rest.

Problem is, there's nothing peaceful about the clamming fork sticking out of his neck, nor about the blood covering the top half of his body, but even with the spotlights, I can't make out his features.

But I can see what he's wearing, and that's how I know.

25

The blue vest gives it away. It's Clive.

My husband is dead. There will be no closure. No confrontation, no way for me to punish him or to make up with him or to do any of the things you want to do to a man you've been intimate with in every sense of the word. The gruesome loss and the unfinished business weighs heavy as a planet.

I am overwhelmed with regret, love, hate, violation, anger, all at once. The amalgam becomes a poison. It courses through my blood, unnamed, unstoppable, wanting to kill me.

I take a breath to get ahold of myself. Before I can do anything, a hand covers my mouth and I feel a body slam into me from behind. He pulls me back. Second time in a week I've had a man accost me, and I've had it. I try to reach for my shucking knife, but he's pulling, pulling, dragging me back into the woods.

He steadies me, then lets go. I whirl, but I stop myself from yelling out. I don't want to draw attention to us.

"Carter! What the hell?" My adrenaline is off the charts.

"I'm sorry," he whispers. "But you can't let them see you. You need to get out of here."

I double over and take some breaths.

"There's no time," he says. "The staties are on their way. Major crimes will be working with SGPD on this one."

I straighten up as it dawns on me it's not just Clive whose life is prematurely over. I could be a suspect.

"They've got their eyes on you," he whispers. "Your father had a lot of goodwill around here. That's why I'm risking my job. He was good to me. To my father. But they have evidence, Isla."

"Evidence? They found the body two minutes ago!"

His face is in shadow. Part of me is shutting down; part of me believes this is not happening. Whether I'm awake or asleep or dead, this is a nightmare all the same.

"What happened back in New York?" he asks. "Because Lilith smells something she doesn't like. Clive told her everything, and I mean *everything*. I'm not privy to all of it, but I know it's not looking good for you."

"Jesus, Carter. I'm not running around stabbing people in the neck with a clamming rake!"

"There's more," he says, apparently unmoved by my protestations. "There's chatter on the radio that the rake was your father's."

Oh, this is bad. This is really, really bad.

"They'll be checking for fingerprints."

"Of course," I say, forcing myself to recover, to stay sharp. "I'm sure they'll find his, maybe one of the Millers.' And yes, maybe mine. I gave him that clamming fork for his birthday when I was a kid."

A wave of shame collides with the tide of dread inside me. I walked right into this. It's the kind of trap the subjects in my news channel's investigations about scams and murder are always falling into. I thought I was smarter than all those sad sacks I'd interviewed, but it turns out I'm just as susceptible to being taken advantage of as the rest of them. I let Charlotte hand me my father's clamming rake and then complied as she casually, nonsensically, took it from me by the sharp end.

"They're going to come looking for you," Carter says. "Go home. Stay inside. They can't arrest you in your own house without a warrant, and they won't get one tonight."

"A *warrant*? You think they'll try to arrest me? Based on what evidence?"

"I have to go," he whispers. "Get the hell out of here. Get yourself a lawyer. If they visit you tonight, they'll claim it's a notification, but their goal is to see how you react, to question you, to catch you off guard. Don't answer the door tonight, but don't leave your home. Do something that proves you're there—call someone from a landline, use your laptop and home Wi-Fi, order a pizza."

"Why are you doing this?" This is a risk for both of us. We're in a lie together now.

"Something's not right," he whispers. "Your father would want me looking out for you. I think Clive wasn't so innocent. Now go."

He strides toward the crime scene. I race out of the woods in the other direction, toward the edge of the wood, then to the slim beach, and finally to my boat tied up at the house on the point.

I do as I'm told and lock myself in the house. The grief will have to wait. Survival is all there is.

Around eleven p.m., someone raps on the front door, and Lilith's best empathetic voice, muffled, speaking words I can't discern from where I am, vibrate into my safe space. I hide under my blanket like a child. I stay in bed, curled up, hugging my knees, tossing and turning.

I stay awake until two, when I figure they'll leave me alone until a more civilized hour, and I make the mile-and-a-half walk to Ben's. It's an emergency, and there's no other way I can talk to him without leaving a trail. I play a hunch and rap on his window.

He opens it, and I can tell from his face he doesn't know my husband took a clamming fork to the neck and everyone thinks I did it.

"I have something to tell you," I say. "And I need a favor."

<h1 style="text-align:center">26</h1>

I wake up in the morning with the goal of evading the cops for as long as possible. I text Oyster and say I'll meet him at the flats as normal, feeling guilty for lying, but knowing it can't be helped.

Two hours before low tide, I don my father's blue windbreaker, his old yellow waders and gloves, and tuck my hair under his fishermen's beanie. I hop in the *Sable*, a red Lund that looks like everyone else's, and race to the Sandburn Marina. I'm out of time, so I'm going to barge into the belly of the beast and attempt to hoover up any scraps of evidence I can find.

I pull into a slip tucked out of sight between two hefty cabin cruisers and hop onto the dock. The gulls are screaming, the cormorants are shitting on everyone's boats, but humans are blessedly scarce. Marlin Bay is where the bigger fleets operate. The wholesalers aren't here yet, as there's no catch coming in right now. The commercial fishing fleet at Sandburn, though never the most robust on the cape, has thinned out, and all the related jobs are going away year by year, decade by decade.

As I head toward the warehouse I spot Cassandra, her braids tied back, wiping her new boat. Her pleasure cruiser lives here, and her tuna boat, the *Courage*, is docked in Marlin Bay. She glances up but doesn't seem to recognize me. Her eyes look tired, like she's been up all night.

In the glint of sunrise, something in her cruiser's window catches the light and blinds me for a moment. I walk closer, and the boat hides the light, and I can see what look like two little security cameras perched in her slim front windows, like two narrowed, suspicious, all-seeing eyes.

Inside the warehouse, I weave between the mini-forklifts and moving palettes. I would normally be nervous, because Frisco Kastic has more power than Luke and is probably more dangerous, but today the only thing that scares me is getting arrested before I can prove my innocence.

I rap my knuckles on the office door at the back and push it open at the same time.

"—no, our usual guy is—" Frisco looks up with a look of shock on his face. "Gotta go. I'll deal with it. *Yes*. Stop worrying." He slams the receiver down.

"What do *you* want?" I'm standing over him in the messy, ugly office with old stainless steel cabinets and Formica desk. For a family so wealthy, they spend a lot of time in shabby surroundings. His workspace has all the charm of a broom closet.

I put on a smile. "Sorry for barging in," I say. "I knocked and I thought I heard you say to come in. Really sorry."

He sighs. "I'm busy. Make an appointment."

"I'm here about the security footage from October twenty-first. The night my father—"

"No, no, no," Frisco shakes his head. "Like we told the cops, we never had any video of that night. I have no idea what happened to your father, but from what I hear, the cops have a new theory."

"Oh?" He's deftly switched the subject.

He points a meaty finger at me. "I hear you're their prime suspect. Shame. I thought you were a good kid."

"I'm a thirty-four-year-old woman, you sexist throwback," I snap. "I'm no one's suspect. I need that footage. I know you have something. Your family watches this marina like the FBI. Nothing goes on here without you knowing it."

"You're right about the second part," he says. "That said, it was a stroke of bad luck that night. We cooperated fully with law enforcement. Now please leave my office."

"Were you doing business with my father?"

"What? You come in here and—"

"It's a simple question. Why was my father talking to you in the weeks before he disappeared?"

"Who told you that?" He springs off his chair, uses his bulk to try to intimidate me. He can join the club of men who've attempted it. I stand my ground. We're so close I hear the faint rattle of his unhealthy lungs.

"If the police are investigating me as you claim they are, then they'll be doing a deep dive into your relationship with beloved local legend Nick Banks. I'll make sure to steer them that way."

"Get out." I don't doubt he'd physically attack me.

"I'm going," I say calmly. "Just one more thing before I do. You seen Angélica Vega around lately?"

He pushes past me to open his office door, knocking me as he does.

"I'll take that as a no." I follow him out, scanning the

warehouse, but neither Angélica nor Darcy are here. They work most days over at Marlin Bay, so I'm not too alarmed.

I leave Frisco fuming as I race outside, unsure what my next move is.

Cassandra's still on deck, wiping, wiping, wiping. Like she's about to sell it. Or maybe she's a clean freak beyond what she's ever displayed to me. Her tuna boat is suitably grimy when conditions call for it, no more so and no less than any others.

I check my surroundings. No one's paying me any mind. Two clammers I know look right through me, thrown, I'm sure, by my male-flavored attire. I stop at Cassandra's boat and call up to her, "She's looking good. I think she's the shiniest boat on the cape."

Cassandra stops cleaning, adjusts her hat, squints.

"Isla? What you doing out here looking like that?"

She should talk. She looks like she hasn't slept in a week.

"I noticed you had cameras on your boat," I say, pointing to the black eyeballs by the front windows. "And I'm praying you had them running the night my father went missing."

Cassandra looks down at the deck, then back up at me.

"I wasn't docked here that night."

"Would've been between ten and eleven."

"I know what happened. I helped search for weeks, if you remember."

"I remember," I croak, then clear the grief from my throat.

"Sorry…it's just there's more at stake here than you and your family." She wrings the dirty cloth between her hands, and I'm positive she doesn't even know she's doing it. I've thrown her, and I don't know why.

"There is?" She's managed to shock me in a week of many shocks; if I didn't know better, I'd say she has footage of that night, and that my father and husband are in it. She hasn't denied it.

She sighs, then moves to the stern, where she looks down on me.

"Things go on at night. You've been away a long time. Your father stays out of it, mostly, but he's part of the ecosystem here. I'm gone most of the winter. He's a stalwart. A guardian of this place."

"Was."

"Was, or is, a part of this place. But it exists without him, and we, each of us, has to look out for ourselves. Ain't no one else gonna do it. No matter what a person says."

My eyes dart around. I hear no sirens, but things suddenly seem a bit too quiet for me. Coincidence, maybe. Maybe not.

"Cassandra, you might've heard my husband is back in town." I watch her face. She knows. "He's spreading dangerous lies about me. I know *you* know I'm not involved in anything illegal or immoral. But he's going to a lot of trouble to frame me. He's not the man I thought he was. Without witnesses, without security footage, without proof, he very well might win."

Cassandra crosses her arms. "You knew that fool husband of yours for how long before he got lost?"

"I don't know…maybe…a year, I guess."

"One year," she says. "You figured him out already, right? Now you know he's a lying dirtbag. Welcome to life. They're never who they say they are. We gotta be more careful than anyone will ever admit. Imma give you a piece of advice. You knew your father your whole life, but you just might not know him as well as you think."

She gazes over my head, her expression changing, her eyes narrowing.

"Isla."

"What?"

"*Run.*"

27

I don't ask questions. I run. The code of the sea and the sand requires us to look out for one another at almost any cost. From her perch, Cassandra could see far beyond me.

I'm in my boat pulling the cord before I have a handle on what the danger is.

There are no sirens, no lights, but I imagine that's by design, so I won't see them coming.

I hunch over like a generic clammer racing to the next flat. In ten minutes I'm at the public beach, away from my home and my usual flats, up toward Plum Island. Ben parked my father's Porsche in the lot at two-thirty in the morning, stocked the trunk with everything I might need for a few days on the run, then drove me home in his car.

I tie my boat tied to a mooring that belongs to summer people, hoping the *Sable* will go unnoticed at low season. I take the community rowboat back to their small dock, then find the Porche in the lot next door.

I gun it out of Sandburn, heading to the last place anyone will look for me.

I hit morning rush hour in Boston, which is a special kind of hell. Driving in New York City is like reclining on a fluffy cloud with a glass of champagne compared to traversing this city, which was laid out by colonizers who didn't think things through. One-way streets, bends, forks in the road, the T in the middle of it all, ragey people who shouldn't be behind the wheel. There's a reason they have a nickname for drivers in our state. We earned it. We are Massholes.

I cross the Tobin Bridge. Then Charlestown to Charles Street, then Beacon Street, then I find the building. I haven't called ahead. I turned my phone off and removed the battery last night. I have the old burner I use for work, but it only has numbers for sources on past news stories I worked on programmed into it. I never added friends or family; the whole point was for it to be unconnected to me.

I ring the bell, fairly certain she'll be home at this hour. It takes a few rings. She opens the door in a towel.

"Hello, mother."

"Isla? What in the world?" That booming newscaster voice will never leave her. Tanya Banks will be on her deathbed ordering nurses around sounding like she's reporting on a car crash on the Mass Pike.

My mother doesn't move.

"Can I come in?"

"Oh. Yes. Of course."

She moves aside and closes the door behind me as I step into the cozy one-bedroom condo she bought with the divorce settlement. My parents opted for a one-time payout rather than being tied together with alimony for years, and my father remortgaged the saltbox to pay her. One of the smartest things my mother ever did was sink her settlement into Boston real estate.

Her tufted white sofa is less bright than it once was, but the faux-fur polar-bear-fur carpet looks new against her beloved exposed brick. I used to worry about her, but people in my life, mostly my father, worked hard to remind me that wasn't my job. The parents worry about the children, not the other way around.

"How are you?" She asks, unwrapping the turban on her head and towel-drying her dark hair.

The genetics gods divided my parents right down the middle and produced me. My father's blue eyes and my mother's brown conspired to create hazel-green that change depending on time of day and mood. My hair gets bleach-blonde highlights like my father five months out of the year, but underneath it all, I have hints of brown like my mother. I'm the split of them in my soul, in my temperament, in my dreams for what my adult life would look like. I am part New York City career woman and part sandfly. Part stay home in the bubble I grew up in, part fly away and do something extraordinary.

"Not too good," I say. "I'm in a bit of a pickle."

"Too *well*," she corrects me. "What's happened?"

"You're going to see some things in the news. It's bad."

"Good god, Isla. How much worse can things get with your father missing and not a peep from him? Let me throw on some clothes and we can talk this out."

No hug. She pads to the bathroom, shaking her head and tutting as she goes. It sounds weirdly like she thinks this is all *my* fault.

After she blows her hair dry and dresses in a pencil skirt and a flowy red silk top, she settles in on the wingback across from me and leans forward, elbows resting on her knees like she's Diane Sawyer.

"I'm going to be late for my shift," she says, "but I don't care. You're my daughter and you're in trouble."

Let me run out and get you a medal for mother of the year.

"Oh? What are you doing at the station these days?"

Whatever her current role is, I know it's not what she wanted to be, which was a news anchor. Not just any anchor, but Boston's most trusted voice. She was never interested in chasing news; she wanted to read it. When I was young, the Boston stations gave her some reporting assignments, but ultimately decided she didn't have the *it* factor. Television news veterans urged her to cut her teeth in smaller markets, but Tanya Banks was never going to go to an affiliate in central Alabama. She stayed in Boston and, last I heard, her title was "research associate," which means they throw her a random weekend assignment now and then, but she'll never be a name. I'm not sure she knows that.

"I'm a reporter," she snaps. "As I always was. I just did a story about how Boston's whale-watching industry is thriving."

I saw it. It ran in February.

"Now. Talk," she commands.

I tell her most of what I know, leaving some things out but hitting the high points: the fleece we found, the surprise Porsche, my husband making a grand and bizarre return and then getting murdered with a clamming fork.

"Isla…I don't know what to say," my mother says, rising and, finally, offering a stiff hug. "This calls for a drink. Hot tea or white Burgundy?"

In my mother's world, these are the two options. "Tap water."

She calls to me as she putters around the small kitchen.

"I can't believe that guy turned out to be such…such an *asshole*," she says. "You just never know with people."

"I feel like such a fool," I say.

She emerges carrying two glasses of sparkling water with lemon.

"You couldn't have known!" Tanya hands me my drink and takes a seat. "Listen to me. These men are good at what they do. Their methods for manipulating their prey are tried and true. You can't see past what people show you, no matter how hard you try, how hard you might want to. We don't know why he did what he did, but I'm glad he can't hurt you anymore. Sorry, not sorry."

I half smile. It's comforting to have her so vehemently on my side.

"I know you look at your father like a hero. I respect that. I still wonder if this whole thing is about drugs, and I don't want you anywhere near that."

"Nick Banks was not a drug dealer." I grip my glass too hard.

"I'm not saying he was," my mother holds up a hand in surrender. "But what if he was approached by someone? The shady characters running the drugs pipeline up there are no joke. If Nick had anything to do with them, even involuntarily, you'll step right in it if you pursue this. You're out on the flats alone in the dark at dawn and dusk. Who's going to save you? Oyster?"

"I'll save myself."

"Against five men and an assault rifle?"

"You don't see too many shoot-outs on the clam flats," I

reply. "And anyway, we already know who the danger was, and he was a lot closer to home."

Out comes a loud, weary-mom sigh. "I just think this can't lead anywhere good for you. I don't want you disappearing, too."

"I have to know," I say. "And whoever did this needs to be held accountable."

"It's so strange," my mother says, a faraway look in her eyes. "I don't know what to think. Nick wasn't someone who'd hold your husband up at gunpoint and take him out. It's preposterous." She stares out the window. "Last time I saw him he seemed happy. Excited, even."

"Last time you saw him?" I'm about to burst with frustration. "I thought that was years ago. Last I heard, you two were making an Olympic sport of living separate lives."

My mother takes a long look at me. "There are a lot of things you don't know," she says. "About me, about him, and about our family."

28

I've been getting a crash course in secrets lately. Shame I haven't dug any up intact yet. I have fragments, shards, and unfinished narratives of the past.

"Why didn't you tell me this back in October?" I cry. "You know how I was trying to track his movements before he vanished! I was looking for anything out of the ordinary. You two hanging out and comparing ancestry is certainly out of the ordinary."

She listens to me as if I'm a toddler gone wild.

"I'm sorry, Isla, but you may recall you were not speaking to me then."

"I was too!"

"You called to tell me he was gone. I told you I wanted to come sit with you. To help you. You said not to bother."

"Can you blame me?"

She says nothing, and we both sip our water, as if swallowing is a better way to justify our silence than the simmering family trauma that caused it.

"What made you think we *hadn't* been talking?" She says after a few moments.

"Because you're always asking me about each other whenever I spent five seconds with either of you," I reply. "'How's your mother?' 'What's your father up to these days? Still digging at dawn for loose change?'" I'm not holding back. "Forgive me if I didn't know you were pals. He hates driving into the city. You hate driving out of the city."

I keep glugging water as if it will drown out the building tension. Clive's murder will be hitting the news any time, and the head start I had will evaporate.

"So? When did you last see him?" I ask. "And why?"

"Your father called me…oh, maybe last May or so. He was interested in the genealogy work I'd done with my family. He wanted to know how far back I'd gotten, and if I could help him trace his ancestry."

"Right," I nod. "You're still trying to claim you're a Mayflower descendant."

"*We*," she corrects me again primly. "As my daughter, you have the same lineage. You know my grandmother was a White. I'm going to prove it, too, and the Mayflower Society will have to accept us—*and* they'll owe me an apology."

"What specifically was he asking about?"

My father knows his family history well. It's easy: Put your finger on Sweden, run it along the map to Sandburn, and stay there. My father's great-great-grandfather times five, Axel Bankson, and his pregnant wife Isabel came over from Sweden during that country's devastating crop failures and found a whole new kind of fertile ground in our clam beds. For some reason old Axel ended up dropping the "on," so our family name became Banks. The adventurous Swedes came for the fishing and stayed for the clams, though that wasn't a living early on. Before we knew to fry them up into delectable appetizers and before baking clams on hot rocks and calling it a traditional New England clambake was cool, the humble mollusks were pig food. Clams were sustenance left for the poor to grit their teeth and tolerate during times of deprivation on the North Shore.

"I told you," my mother shrugs. "He wanted to trace his side of your family as far back as he could go. He said he couldn't get past the nineteen hundreds. No one ever accused your father of being a member of MENSA. I'm not sure he ever wanted a true partnership."

"He and Angélica are…or were…very happy together," I point out. I don't want to rub it in, but she started it.

My mother leans forward. "Angélica is happy to come second to a pile of clams and a man who thinks he's an antihero in a Hemingway novel," she says. "Women like you and I don't need that kind of toxic masculinity."

"*Mother.*"

"Sorry, sorry." She squeezes her eyes shut for a moment, then blinks at me. "Believe it or not, I'm grieving, too. I know I don't always show it. But sweetie…he was my first true love. The father of my child. Losing him left a hole in both our lives."

"We don't know he's…"

"…I think it's important we come to terms with the fact he very well might be…"

No one will say the word: Dead, died, gone.

Don't cry, don't cry, don't cry. I sit with my remaining parent, the one I always felt distance from, and all I want to do is collapse in her arms and let her stroke my hair and tell me *there, there.*

There's more chance of me ending up in prison than that happening at this point, and I'm aware part of that is because I'm prickly. She can't reach out, lest my spikes wound her. I wait futilely for her to understand my sharp corners grew from her early parenting, or lack of it.

"Right now I need to know more about why he was so interested in his family tree. What was he looking for? And did you give him what he wanted?"

She shakes her head. "He was going through it all and grumbling. When he got to the final name he just said, 'Thanks, old bean.' And then he started asking about something else."

"Something else? What something else?"

She waves her hand as if she has the vapors. "Like, oh, something about how to set up a trust, how much the saltbox might be worth now, how a second mortgage might work. I haven't dabbled in real estate for a few years, but I was able to give him some tips. I swear I never thought that man would sell that house."

"But he hasn't."

"Hasn't he?"

Why would he be asking his ex-wife about any of this? I come up with the answer as I'm formulating the question. Because he knew my mother wouldn't be in contact with anyone back home. The number one safest person in the world to keep a secret from Sandburnians—without even trying—is Tanya Banks. And on this one, Nick clearly didn't want tongues wagging.

"Can I see what you found?"

"Sorry," she shakes her head. "It was all on his phone. I helped him get as far as the sixteen hundreds, but he didn't seem interested in any of the people we came across."

Or he didn't want her to know he'd found what he was looking for.

"Even *though*," she says, throwing her hands up, "you're related to Swedish nobility! Let me know if you ever want do dig into it. I'll help you. We can do it over margaritas at the Cactus Club."

Her shaky, unsure smile makes me want to cry. I've been hard on her. I know I have. My father got more of a pass, I think now, because he stayed in the family home, my anchor; that realization hits me like a flying lobster pot. Another secret I need to dig into if I don't end up in prison. Then again, research would be a way to pass the time behind bars.

What the hell the seventeenth century has to do with my father's disappearance is too much for me to think about right now.

"You want to help me?" I ask my mom.

She nods.

I stand and hold out an open palm. "I need to borrow your car."

She rises. "That Porsche you mentioned. It's brand-new, you say?"

She leads me to her spot in the building's cramped underground garage.

My heart sinks when she stops at her car.

I've jumped from the frying pan into the fire.

"*Mom*," I say. "I can't go on the run with a metallic pink convertible Audi."

She hands me the keys.

"At least the roof's black," I observe. "I'll just put the top up."

She shakes her head. "It doesn't work. If it starts to rain, get into a garage *immediately*." She wipes the air like erasing her words. "In fact, get off the road if it even *looks* like rain. The interior is Italian leather."

It's fifty-nine degrees outside, and I'm going to be cruising the Merritt Parkway in a fucking pink convertible. I might as well call Lilith and tell her where to find me.

"Good luck," my mother says, leaning in for a distant air hug. I wrap my arms around her and squeeze until she gasps.

I get in the car and adjust the seat and mirrors for my height.

"Remember," I say, looking up at her as she wipes a stray tear from her eye. "I was never here. If they come for you, I never told you anything and I took your car keys while you were in the shower."

I set the GPS on my burner phone to avoid tolls and head toward the suburbs. I'm running on borrowed time. They'll contact my mother eventually, but she'll be low on their list. Everyone back in Sandburn will tell the police that we barely speak.

29

Sudbury, Massachusetts is Colonial-era porn writ large. As I pull into the town center on my way to Harold and Millicent Millers' primary residence, I'm sucked into the past. Grand white Town Hall with white columns and sloping roof: *Check*. Ye Olde Tyme Church with stunning steeple and a clock tower: *Check*. Revolutionary War Cemetery: *Check*. I'm half expecting Pilgrims to start jumping out of the bushes.

I did my due diligence after the Millers left Sandburn and were never heard from again. Using the same tricks and databases I use to find sources for a news story, I tracked down contact information for people who were probably related to them: A daughter, his wife, and a woman I'm pretty sure is Millie's sister. I identified their neighbors in this quaint, moneyed suburb. Miller is such a common name that I'm still not sure if I found the right people, but I kept the list.

I couldn't do my full investigation back then because of the restraining order. I wasn't going to be calling the Millers' friends and neighbors and possibly getting brought up on charges. But now, all bets are off.

I motor up their long driveway. I can see no one's living here.

The grass is overgrown as spring takes hold. The bushes are untrimmed, and winter's detritus, the dead leaves and blown-down branches, are strewn about the grassy hill. If I were a burglar, this place would be on my hit list.

Their sprawling mansion is white with black trim and has actual wings off the main house, and I imagine Millie calling out, *Harold, daaahling, tell the maids to clean the west wing for our weekend guests.*

I park and step out to inspect the property. If their summer home is a technological wonder, this one's a luddite's paradise. There's no notice of an alarm, no wires on the windows, no visible cameras. I creep around and peek into windows. It's as dead as a house can be. There's not even a porch light on.

I peek through the letterbox. There's nothing out of the ordinary in the foyer. No piled-up mail, no broken glass or blood or dead bodies. I stand back a few yards and survey the home from bottom to top. No one's home. The Millers have vanished off the face of the earth, and I need to know why.

I'll start with the neighbors. I roll down the driveway, take a right, and swing into the next one. This house is closer to the road. It's a newer build, with the obligatory generic beigey-grey siding and white plastic fencing. I ring the bell and brace myself for a frosty greeting. New Englanders don't tend to like strangers at their door.

Within ten seconds, a woman who looks about my age appears in front of me. Her platinum blonde hair is cut in a perfect pixie. On her hip is a toddler with orange gunk on his face.

"Yes?" She asks. I'm surprised she opened the door. I wouldn't have. Maybe she's bored.

"Hi," I smile. "I'm a friend of the Millers next door? They don't seem to be home, and I haven't heard from them in a long time. I'm wondering if you've seen them lately? I'm a bit worried."

"Shouldn't you be calling the family or the police?" She asks, bouncing the baby as he gurgles.

"I don't want to alarm anyone," I say worriedly. "I thought I'd ask around first to see if neighbors have seen them out and about."

She shakes her head. "We moved in over the summer, when I understand they're usually at their other house somewhere on the shore."

"Right," I confirm. "Normally they're back here from November through April."

"I wouldn't know," she says. She has her hand on the door. She's about to close it. I won't resist. I don't want to cause a kerfuffle, get myself noticed.

"I'm sure they're fine. Thanks for your help," I smile. "Cute baby."

I hop in the pinkmobile and double back to the neighbors on the Millers' other side. It looks like they set down roots in Sudbury pre-housing boom. They've got a nice sprawling raised ranch, nothing fancy, and it's glaringly out of place on this road.

I park in their regular-sized driveway and walk up to the door.

They have an ivory doorbell that appears to be from the eighties. I hold it down, but hear nothing. I wait, then try again. I hear footsteps. Slow, methodical.

The door opens, and a man is standing in front of me,

smiling. It took him a while because he's using a walker, and I feel awful for bothering him.

"Can I help you?" He asks brightly.

"Well, yes," I smile in return, then lie to his face. "I'm a friend of your neighbors. The Millers?"

"Oh yes, Harold and Millie. Lovely folks. Are they OK?" His brow furrows.

"I certainly hope so," I reply. "But, well, we haven't heard from them in a while. I wanted to pop by and visit them, but they don't seem to be home. Have you seen them lately?"

He puts a palm to his cheek. "Come to think of it, I haven't," he says.

"When was the last time you saw them?"

"Oh, gee, let me think… let me think…"

He noodles, but no answers are forthcoming. He says, "Why don't you come on in. I just made some Yorkshire tea."

"You're very kind," I reply. "I'd love to come in for a moment, but I'm afraid I don't have time for tea."

He's already shuffling back inside. "There's always time for tea."

I follow him in, thinking about the restraining order against me by the seventy-something Millers. If this visit goes south, it won't be good for my reputation in the senior citizen community.

In the kitchen, a throwback drenched in chartreuse and avocado, he lets go of his walker and moves about, preparing a tray of tea and scones.

"Last time I saw them was November," he says, flipping on his electric kettle. "Come to think of it, it was odd what was going on up there."

"Odd? Like how?"

This information, if legit, could be a game changer. The Millers left Sandburn in mid-November and weren't seen in those parts again, as far as I've been able to figure. If they weren't killed or abducted in Sandburn, it might mean their disappearing act has nothing to do with my father.

"There was a good amount of packing and unpacking of vehicles," the man says as he sets four scones on a delicate bone-china plate. "A lot of suitcases and noise. I was taking my morning constitutional through the woods and couldn't help but notice, you understand." He glances at me to let me know he's not a peeper.

"Of course." I nod my understanding.

He drops a handful of bags into his matching teapot. The kettle shrieks, and he grabs it and pours hot water into the teapot.

"I assumed they were coming and going from their summer house as they do a few times a year, but now that you mention it, it wasn't the same kind of packing and unpacking they usually do. It's hard to explain…it was as if they weren't coming back, but yet…they didn't officially move. I never saw movers or trucks. Do you think something happened to them?"

I'm still not sure which way to go with this guy. Full disclosure, some disclosure, or double down on the lying? "Did you see anyone else with them? Maybe movers or a taxi driver? Family, or anyone like that?"

He swivels and hands me a steaming cup of tea.

"Head on into the good room just around the corner. I'll be right behind you."

I do as I'm told, and find a floral sofa covered in plastic. As I sit on it, I feel the familiar stiffness my grandma Mixie subjected us to in her old house. She used to keep her furniture wrapped in plastic so there was never a comfortable moment in the good room, not ever.

The man has a system. He moves toward me with a tray balanced on his walker. He stops, then lifts the tray of tea, scones and clotted cream, and sets it on the coffee table. He sits across from me. His brown skin is cracked at the knuckles, the joints bulbous and achy. He picks up tiny silver tongs, drops three die-sized sugar cubes into his cup, and stirs.

I sip mine black.

"You asked me if I saw anyone with them," he says. "And for a minute, I didn't think so, but then I remembered there was a gal. She came by a couple times…"

"Oh? What did she look like?"

He smiles. "Like you," he says. "It was funny. I made a mental note because I couldn't figure out how she fit in. She wasn't familiar enough around them to be friends or family. She was more formal than that. She was dressed in a business suit. Like a real estate agent. She was no taxi driver." He gestures to the platter. "Please. Have something to eat."

I do as I'm told and take a blueberry scone.

"I'm Leroy Talbot, by the way," he says. "Silly me, not even making proper introductions."

I can't help it. He's won me over and if he reports me, so be it. "Isla Banks," I say. "It's a pleasure to meet you. So, Leroy, could you describe the woman any further? You say she looked like me?"

He squints, leans back as if to gain some distance, and nods to himself. "Now that you mention it, not so much like you," he says. "She was shorter. Just a little thing. She had bleach-blonde hair. Looked like she'd been on vacation, like she was overtanned. She was a bit orange, if I'm honest."

My heart sinks. That doesn't sound like Charlotte. Could be a disguise, though. Clive showed he could change his entire look to become unrecognizable. My gut says the pair of them were in this together, but the question is, was their coupling romantic? Were they sleeping together while we were married? The thought infuriates me. Not because of the betrayal—that's in the background now—but the possibility of being subjected to whatever STDs the two of them might've been swapping.

Leroy and I sip our tea and munch on scones. I ask, "Did anything about that scene worry you? Did Harold and Millie appear under duress or stressed at all?"

He shakes his head. "Nope. If they had, I'da stopped and poked my nose in. I'm not opposed to asking unwelcome questions when the occasion calls for it."

"Ha," I chuckle. "Same. Would you mind if I used the bathroom before I head out?"

"Of course. Through the kitchen, on your right."

I remain standing when I return to the living room. "I'd better get going," I say. "I can't thank you enough for your help and hospitality."

"Oh, it's no trouble," Leroy smiles with a melancholic twinge. "It's been a while since I've had a visitor."

He rises and leads me toward the door in his walker. I step outside and face him.

"Come back anytime, won't you?" He smiles.

"I wish I could," I say. "But I live up the coast quite a ways."

He nods. "Wherever you're going now, watch your back."

I'm overcome with chills, as if the air conditioning kicked on full blast. "I'm…uh, I'm sorry? What do you mean?"

"You don't look like a murderer," he says. "Whatever it is you're trying to do, I wish you luck."

He pulls a phone out of his pocket and holds up the screen. "I follow the crime blogs and the law enforcement notices. Hasn't made the mainstream media yet."

I read the short bulletin.

Suspicious death in Sandburn, Massachusetts. Victim is a male between 30 and 45 years of age. State Police responding.

"But how did you know? It doesn't say—"

"I wasn't sure until just now," he says, calm as can be after serving a potential cold-blooded killer tea and crumpets. "But ain't no coincidence you're looking for the Millers from Sandburn same day there's a murder in Sandburn."

"Why—but why…why did you let me in?" I stutter.

The obvious answer comes to me. *To stall until the cops get here. This can't be over yet. I need more time. I need more proof.*

"I've followed your case," he says. "Terrible thing, what happened to your family. There's a whole group of us who thinks the Coast Guard gave up too soon. What's a lifelong clammer who knows those estuaries like the back of his hand doing getting lost at sea on a calm night a mile from his own house? Doesn't add up."

"Exactly!" I want to hug him. This is what I've been telling Lilith and Co. since day one.

"You seem like a nice lady," he adds. "The law can find its own way. Let the system work how it's supposed to. Doesn't need help from the likes of me. Now go on. Find the Millers. Don't get caught."

The timer is set. The news is trickling out. It won't be long before it catches up with me.

30

've never felt as exposed as I do in an open-top pink car on Rte. 9 in Framingham on a cold spring day. Other drivers on the congested two-lane road openly stare at the messy blonde shivering in the wind. I stare ahead and grip the steering wheel, white knuckling it all the way.

When I pull into the industrial park, I see the building I'm looking for. Of course it has to be a top secret biotech compound, all clean lines and glass and cameras everywhere.

I keep driving and find an empty lot outside a deserted building with windows papered over from the inside. I park at the far end, tuck my hair under my father's beanie, and walk back along the road to the building I'm here to visit.

I decide my best strategy is to call the main phone number. I punch in the name of the woman I'm looking for and the automated system sends me to voicemail. *Shit.* I don't have time to wonder if someone's in a meeting or working from home today or out for lunch.

This woman is my last chance. I've tried everyone I can find with a connection to the Millers, including a daughter who appears to live in North Carolina, with no luck. No one answers their landline anymore if they have one, and cellphone numbers go quickly out of date. Considering the speed with which I need to get this done, Millie's sister, a Mrs. Sharon Flunch, is my best bet.

I call back, and again I get voicemail. I wait two minutes and try a third time.

"*Yes*," an irritated woman says.

"Hi, Sharon. I'm calling about your sister and brother-in-law. I'm outside your building if you want to come talk to me."

I hang up.

If I know two things about human beings, it's that they're curious, which means Sharon will have to find out what my bizarre call was about, and they're often inherently more fearful than they'll admit. Either way this woman is coming outside.

Less than three minutes later, she strides out with a frown and a friend. She's wearing sensible shoes and sky-blue pantsuit. I never understood what they mean when they say someone has blue hair, but this woman, who can't be more than sixty years of age, has a blue bouffant. She's trailed by an equally frowny security guard with his hand on his hip.

I'm standing on the sidewalk, staring at them. She comes into my space, nearly a foot from my face.

"You're the woman who called? What's this about?"

My manner is a one-eighty from my crisp phone call. "Thanks for coming out," I say. "I'm so sorry to bother you, but Millicent and Harold spoke so highly of you that I *knew* I could come to you about this. You see, I'm a neighbor of theirs from Sandburn—"

"Your name is?"

"Millie said you two were close, and I was up in Boston visiting friends, so I thought I'd stop by. I'm worried about them. I haven't seen them in months, and I wanted to bring them their favorite clam chowder, but I can't seem to reach them."

This woman is not falling for it. "And you are?"

Before I can think of an answer, she turns to the guard. "You can go. I'll handle this. Great work, Bernie."

Bernie seems unsure, glaring at me and keeping his twitchy fingers on his side piece. She jerks her head in the direction of the building and he slinks away. Her LinkedIn profile says she's an Associate Director, which is apparently a big deal at Re-Gene-A Biotech.

"So you see," I chatter on, "I was alarmed when I realized they hadn't put in their usual order. I mean, Millie and Harold live for Sandburn's famous chowder, right?"

Distract, distract, distract.

"Look," Sharon says, checking her watch. "I don't know you, so I'm not giving out private information, but I can tell you Millie and Harold are quite safe. They're hard to reach because they're on an around-the-world cruise."

"*Around-the-world-cruise?*" I can't hide my incredulity. That's the kind of cover story a dumb murderer comes up with on an episode of *Dateline*. "But they never said anything about a big trip before they left…"

…or were kidnapped and possibly murdered.

"They entered a contest, and they were informed last autumn that they won," Sharon says. "It was a last-minute thing. Please tell everyone back in Sandtown that my sister and her family are just fine." Another check of the wrist.

"Sandburn…" I correct her distractedly. "A last-minute around-the-world cruise," I say again. I'm not ready to walk away, no matter how badly Sharon wants me to. "What's that run, a hundred grand? Did anyone check out the contest—"

"We're not *idiots*," she snaps. "Of course it sounded too good to be true, so we nailed it down before Millie and Harold went anywhere. I personally checked with the cruise company. They confirmed a balcony cabin had been fully prepaid."

This stinks to high heaven. I can't wrap my head around how someone employed at a top-tier biotech firm can be so clueless. "What contest? How did they enter it?"

"You have a lot of questions," Sharon says. "Why are you really here?"

"I'm sorry if it seems like I'm prying," I say deferentially. "I just…well, they're very well liked in Sandburn. And when they didn't call in for their beloved chowder, I volunteered to ask around to make sure they were OK."

I clear my throat, push my luck. "Even if the cruise was legit, are you sure they got on board?"

Big sigh. She's about to leave, and/or call security again.

"Not that it's any of your business, but my wife and I video-called them as they boarded the ship. Not to mention the company rep made sure the process was smooth from packing to boarding."

"That sounds heavenly," I say. "What company did you say the rep was from?" Now we're getting somewhere. Let me guess: The "rep" has bleach-blonde hair and an orange-hued spray-on tan.

"Oh…I don't remember." She purses her lips. "She had a business card, letterhead, and a LinkedIn profile with over five-hundred connections. She was *wonderful* to my sister. She helped them plan for their time away, and she was the only one there for them when the locals started blaming them for—"

She checks me out, and I keep a sympathetic face on, so she continues.

"Well, if you're from there, you know what happened. And you know my sister and her husband were unfairly targeted by locals because one of *them* was their handyman. When they started getting hassled by a local girl, this company rep really stepped up and took care of my sister. Mille was way too nice. She was getting taken advantage of, so the rep helped her and Harold put together their statement and take it to the police. She even helped them put in a security system."

Not clapping back at her fictional little story takes every bit of restraint I possess.

"Didn't you..." I cough to stop myself from setting her straight. "Didn't you think it was odd that a random stranger insinuated herself into your sister's life out of nowhere?"

"Not after she explained everything," Sharon shakes her head, defensive now. "Of course you're not going to get a free vacation for nothing. There was a catch. Millie and Harold had to agree to be part of the company's social media campaign. They're a rival to the AARP, and they said my sister and her husband were perfect for the role, so yes, we questioned it, but the rep quickly put our fears to rest. I was happy for my sister. It was all on the up and up."

"This rep," I say. "She a blonde woman with a killer tan?"

"I don't know," she says. "I never met her."

"Have you been in contact with your sister since they left port?"

Sharon lets out a derisive *pfft* and wags her finger at me. "I'm not giving that kind of information to a *stranger*. I'll ask you to kindly leave."

"What was the rep's name?" I'm running out of time.

"Who *are* you?" She asks again.

"Like I said, I'm just a friend from the North Cape," I say for the last time. "Sorry to have bothered you."

I swivel and walk away, then quickly turn back.

"One last question," I call after her. She whirls, and I know she's about to call someone, but I need to see her reaction. "Is a LinkedIn profile and a business card enough to convince you it's normal to have a stranger squatting in your sister's house while they're on this supposed cruise of a lifetime?"

Her face tells me everything. I've planted a seed of doubt, and I have to let it grow while I keep investigating, even if I only have half a day left. If that.

If anyone's going to drop a dime on me, it's Ms. Pantsuit Executive.

I set a course for Manhattan to avoid tolls as much as possible. I feel the heat of the news of a small-town murder chasing me. The case will attract every reporter, podcaster, and internet sleuth on planet earth once the inevitable clickbait headlines hit.

Some media organizations will play it straight, with headlines like *The Clamming Fork Murder*, while the more tabloidy platforms will get clever. I can see it now: *Clive Cleaved by Clamming Contraption*. It'll be all fun and games to them. I know, because I've worked in newsrooms since college. It's the lure of true crime, the fascination with a human being's grisly demise, the ravaging of a family as we once knew it over hot cocoa and a fortress of pillows. Is there anything cozier than blood, guts and grief?

31

Finance For All's offices are in a drab, warehouse-style building in Hell's Kitchen. I slip past security when they're busy with a delivery and head up to the tenth floor. The receptionist is staring into space. I put on a smile.

"Paul Wright's office, please."

"Name?"

"Isla Hooghiemster."

She doesn't appear to recognize the name; maybe she's new. She hits a button and talks into her headset. "There's an Isla Hugmeister here to see Paul?"

Her eyes go wide. "Oh. Right, sorry, Hooghiemster…OK. Of course." She hits a button.

"I'm afraid Mr. Wright is not available," she says to me.

"Tell me about it."

"What?" The joke flies over her head like a heron.

"Please tell Mr. Wright I'm not leaving until he speaks to me."

She's blinking and whispery as she calls his office again. "She says she's not leaving. Should I call security?"

She nods to no one, then shoots me a suspicious glare.

Seconds later, a woman wearing a pencil skirt and flaming red lipstick bursts into the foyer.

"Follow me." She doesn't make eye contact, but I assume she's talking to me, and I obey.

She ushers me to the boss's office, rolls her eyes, and leaves without a word. The room isn't grand, but it has a small window and enough space for a gray loveseat that's seen better days. Finance For All doesn't have the name recognition of the big boys like breast cancer or children's hospitals, but Clive told me their donors are influential types who like to stay under the radar.

Mr. Wright has a combover and deep-set, porcine eyes. He doesn't get up when I enter.

"Frankly, I find it galling you'd show your face here," he says by way of a greeting. "You have some nerve."

I take the liberty of sitting across from him.

"What choice did I have?" I'll see his belligerence and raise him pure combativeness. "Your company has ignored my calls and emails since my husband went missing. Your star fundraiser disappeared into thin air and you don't seem the least bit concerned."

"*Us?* What about *you?*" Mr. Wright scoffs. "Clive did everything possible to protect you. He bent over backwards to keep everything discreet, and he paid dearly so you could skate away. Frankly, that never sat well with me."

I'm trying to understand, but he's talking gibberish, and I don't speak the language.

He says, "Wait. Our *what?*"

Now we're both confused, apparently. I scoot forward on my seat.

"Your *what*, what? My husband was your Executive Director of Fundraising. I'm looking for information about his employment benefits, about what his last days were like, and anything you know about where he might have gone."

He takes a moment to absorb what I've said.

"Executive Director of fundraising? I'm afraid you're mistaken." He shakes his head.

"Fine. Senior Director. Whatever. Can you just—"

"Clive was a *volunteer*," he says. "In our accounting department."

"What do you mean, a volunteer? He was a top executive! He took me to your gala fundraiser," I argue. "Introduced me to all your top people. I met the VP of marketing, your donors, their spouses…"

"You might've met people, but they weren't Clive's colleagues," Paul replies. "He would've paid for the tickets out of his own pocket. That function was a thousand dollars a plate."

Oh, my god. It's coming back to me. Served up along with decadence and fancy attire that night were awkward introductions, brief hesitations, and the forgetting of names. I chalked it up to workplace tension or miscommunication, then swigged more of my margarita.

"Back up." I hold my hands out like a traffic cop. "You're telling me my husband was not an employee at this organization, nor was he getting paid?"

"I don't know what he told you, but no, he was not. He came to Finance for All on the recommendation of a fellow Wharton grad I know in Amsterdam," Mr. Wright says. "I asked Clive why he'd want to volunteer considering his C-suite experience, and he said he had family money and was looking to learn about philanthropy. I told him there were better ways, but he insisted. We found him a place in accounting."

My husband was a full-on conman, and while I should've accepted it by now, I'm utterly shocked by the depth of it. *How far back, how deep, does this go?*

"And this illegal activity you keep alluding to?" I ask.

"Don't tell me you don't know."

I raise my eyebrows at him.

He ambles to his feet and marches over to a file cabinet. He opens the top drawer, yanks out a thin manila folder, hands it to me, and returns to his seat.

I open it on my lap. It's a contract of some kind. It's written in dry legalese, but what it describes is vividly hideous. I look up at Mr. Wright.

"Am I reading this right?" I ask him. "Clive embezzled a quarter of a million from your charity and blamed me?"

I can't stop reading one passage in particular: *Volunteer will pay back the full amount in ten equal payments over five years. Should the payments lapse, PLAINTIFF will pursue all available legal remedies. VOLUNTEER'S SPOUSE will be added to said action should the need arise.*

Reality seems to be dawning on Mr. Wright. "Clive said—he said you got into the laptop you share at home—"

Mr. Wright stops abruptly. I can see the wheels turning. "He said you'd been pressuring him to get a better job, that he wasn't getting promoted fast enough, that you'd dug a financial hole with your overspending, that you're obsessed with designer clothes and handbags."

I tilt my head and raise one eyebrow, a skill I inherited from my grandfather.

"Exhibit A," I say, sweeping my arms up and down my jeans-and-cotton-top-clad body.

"Yes," he says. "I see."

I pick up my phone and snap a photo of the first page of the contract.

"Excuse me! Delete that *right now*." Mr. Wright is huffing and puffing, red faced and starting to glisten on the forehead. I snap a picture of the next page.

"You're telling me," I say calmly, "that a volunteer stole a ton of money that could've put a bunch of needy kids through business school, and you took his word for it that his greedy wife framed him, you never bother to talk to me, and he goes on his merry way?"

"Of course not. He was let go as soon as we found the errors."

I think back on the one email Finance for All sent to me: *His checks should keep coming until the agreed date.* Clive wasn't *receiving* checks. He was supposed to be *sending* them.

I'm starting to get the big picture. My guess is that embezzling a quarter million dollars from this charity was only the seed money for the real con. Clive was going for the big payday, and while he was setting it up, he was living off his last con. All while pretending to go to work every day.

I, my father, and Sandburn had to be the targets. But what the hell is in Sandburn that could possibly be worth this kind of risk? I'm starting to wonder if I dismissed the Kastic family too quickly. Maybe they're more diabolical than I gave them credit for.

"He agreed to ten payments over two years," Mr. Wright says. "He paid twenty-five thousand before he disappeared."

Enough money to stall, but only ten percent of his takings. That tracks.

"Did it ever occur to you," I say slowly, trying not to let him know how upset I am, "that his disappearing act was *because* he got caught stealing vast sums of cash under your nose?"

"Frankly, no," he says. "We thought you were the bad one."

"You need to destroy this," I say, shaking the folder at him. "I won't have a legal document circulating saying I'm a criminal. I didn't do anything, and I didn't sign anything."

He shrugs. "I'm afraid there's nothing I can do. This document is the reason we let you and Clive 'go on your merry way' as you put it. You pay or we press charges. It's what we call mutually assured destruction."

I smile, and it's genuine, because this man doesn't get it. He's in for a rude surprise, and I'm going to enjoy watching him squirm.

"I'm afraid only one of us will be destroyed by this situation," I say. "Because Clive came back from the dead. I can see by your face you didn't know. Most people don't yet. Check with Sandburn PD if you want. When the news is official, I'm going to shout your name from the rooftops. Finance for All and Clive's hapless boss Paul Wright will be all over the news. You'll have reporters on your doorstep for months. You won't be able to get enough funding to run a lemonade stand."

He looks like he's going to cry. I walk out, taking the folder with me, knowing there are copies, but determined to make a point.

I push through the building's revolving door and step onto the sidewalk, getting my bearings.

A man in a trench coat steps in front of me.

"We need to talk," he says.

32

The stranger and I are jostled and cursed at by New Yorkers rushing along Ninth Avenue. I step back, out of the way, and the guy and I face off. He looks about twenty-five and has a short ponytail and a mustache that needs manicuring.

"I have something to show you," he says. "But we need to go somewhere quiet."

Why men persist in thinking women will follow a stranger into a dark alley or their killing dens or rape rooms is beyond me. Then again, maybe it's because some of us do; we close our eyes and let them lead us, especially when we are very young. I push past him and walk toward my car, still reeling from the extent of my foolishness. Of my willful blindness to Clive's true personality.

"Please, Mrs. Hooghiemster! I just need a minute of your time. It's about Clive. He's not who you think he is."

He said the name right. This kid knew Clive.

We snag a table in a coffee shop on 39th Street.

"Who are you?" I ask as he fiddles with his phone. "And how do you know who I am?"

"No names," the stranger whispers, glancing around like

we're spies in 1930s Berlin. "And, are you kidding? The minute you showed up at the office, word spread like wildfire. You and Clive…well, let's say you're legends."

"You work at Finance for All?" He nods and stares down at his phone. "Now that I'm sure you're not in on it, I can show you this. I'm going to airdrop you a link."

No, you're not. I grab his phone out of his hand and snap a screenshot of the link with my burner, then hand his phone back. "Cue it up. I'll watch it on yours."

I figure this meeting means the news of Clive's premature demise hasn't made it out of Sandburn yet. This walking bag of nerves doesn't act like he thinks I'm on the run for stabbing someone in the jugular with a clamming fork.

"We really should be watching it somewhere quiet…" he mumbles, holding out the device. "Just to warn you, it's pretty bad."

I take the phone. I hit the play button and…

Oh my god.

It's Clive, back from the dead, making my stomach lurch. First the back of his head, then his arrogant grin when he swivels and faces the camera. I see his mouth moving, but I can't hear what he's saying, so I put the phone to my ear, but then I can't see the action.

"I have earbuds," the guy offers.

I don't share earwax. "I'll take it to the bathroom."

I'm gone before he can protest. I can't get into the bathroom without buying something, so I pay cash for a small coffee and take the key. I use my burner to record the video as I watch it, and I'm glad I'm near a toilet because I can't stop myself from retching. Nothing comes out, but I wish I could vomit up the horror.

I watch as Clive lifts a kitten out of a cardboard box, takes it to a sewer grate, and drops the mewling baby animal through a slim gap. He turns back to the camera with a low-lidded smirk. He shakes out his arms and closes his eyes like he's stretching for a performance, and then it begins.

"Oh my goodness!" Clive cries. "Do you hear that? Oh my lord, is that…wait…it's a *kitten*!"

He glances around as if to see who's watching, then kneels and turns on his phone light. The cameraperson, who I assume is Mustache Man, zooms in on the kitten. As the charade unfolds and the camera pans over the crowd, I remember what it felt like to sit at the bar alone that same night. *Why didn't I listen to my gut then? Why didn't I see the red flag and run from it?* I was doing tequila shots while Clive was staging this bizarre act of manufactured heroism. And I fucking fell for it.

I airdrop the video to myself, then take the phone back to the guy.

My hand shakes as I sip my coffee.

"That's the director's cut of the video that went viral," the guy says. "I started recording after he procured the kitten. Don't ask how we got it. You don't want to know."

"What happened to the kitten?" I almost shriek it.

He half-smiles. "She's the one thing I'm proud of in this whole mess. I took her home. Her name is Angel. I thought about Phoenix, but decided that would be derivative."

I don't dash the poor man's delusion that there's nothing new under the sun and everything's derived from something. I'm more relieved about the kitten than I'd like to admit.

"After that day, I started secretly recording certain conversations with Clive," he goes on. "I realized he was bad news, and I wanted to have something to protect myself."

"Why didn't you report him?" I ask. "Why didn't you *do* something?"

I've scared him, judging by his quivering chin. So be it.

"What could I do?" He throws up his hands. "The guy is unhinged, and he works at my company. He's friends with the big boss. I swear I had no idea what he was going to do with the kitten, but no one will care. Everyone would think I was complicit. I had to protect myself. I kept the video and put it up on YouTube with the privacy setting on. I let him know that if he tried to come for me, the evidence would always be there on a public platform and there was nothing he could do about it."

My coffee's getting cold, but I sip it for the caffeine.

"But *why?*" I ask the stranger. "Why would anyone do something like this to me? What was he trying to do?"

This is the part of the puzzle that's blank as a snow-covered beach. The *what* has been written in the sky. I've had to accept my husband was a deranged menace. An asshole. Some version of a narcissist, sociopath and/or psychopath. But the *why* is a fog. What was Clive's endgame? Who would do all this to con a broke news producer who was one round of layoffs away from being an unhoused clammer who lives with her father?

The man nods his understanding. "You don't want to hear it from me—"

"The hell I don't," I snap.

"No, I mean don't hear it from *me*. Hear it from Clive."

He fiddles with his screen, then hands me the phone. "This one's not on YouTube," he says. "Because of privacy and all. It's short, but to the point."

I turn up the volume and put the phone close to my face so I can hear it.

"Fill it up. Don't be shy," Clive says from his perch on a leather sofa. Someone's filling his crystal tumbler with what looks like scotch.

I'm telling you, Hunter, this is the one.

You mean… The One?

Hunter, whose name I am happy to know so it'll be easier to find him later to testify, sounds incredulous.

She's exactly what I need right now. Let's just say there are some things about her family that are very…useful to me. She's uncomplicated. Maybe gay. Maybe asexual.

Clive lifts his scotch like he's the Great Fricking Gatsby in a salon of big thinkers instead of an offensive, judgy prick.

She's interested, I can tell. But she doesn't want the hard sell. No, Hunter, with this one, all I have to do is keep showing up. She'll give in eventually, and she'll never cling. It's perfect.

Nausea spreads, and I sip my lukewarm coffee, but it only roils the acid already eating away at my stomach.

I want to yell at the phone, *I'm not asexual or disinterested or gay. I'm spoken for.* My whole life, there's no one who is home to me the way Ben is. When you know you can't be with your soulmate, you tend to shut down.

But oh, Clive had me pegged. I was ready to marry someone who kept showing up because I knew no one would ever be Ben Cassidy, and we could never be together.

Just like Tanya and Nick Banks. My doomed parents.

History repeats itself.

"Do you have any idea what Clive was talking about?" I ask the guy. "Did he say what exactly was *useful* about my family? It's an odd thing to say."

"I thought so, too," he says. "But I never figured it out. He was too smart to get specific."

His eyes are pleading for me to believe him, and I suspect he truly wants to help, but can't. We were all given different puzzle pieces of Clive's true self. We don't know what the final puzzle should look like, and without everyone he ever met corralled in a room together, you only have your own piece to go on. That's what his type counts on.

"One last question," I say. "Did you ever meet a woman friend of his? Maybe a colleague or a fellow expat he hung out with?"

Ponytail man wrings his hands. "A woman?" He's trying his little heart out. "I…no. I only hung out with him through work. I never met anyone in his personal life."

Again, I believe him. But I can't shake the feeling Clive and Charlotte are in this together, whatever *this* is.

33

I call my mother as I pass through Greenwich, Connecticut on Route 95. "Has anyone contacted you?"

"No," she says. "I haven't heard anything. The cops must've worked overtime to keep it quiet. Won't be long, though."

"I'll park the Audi at the Lynn train station. Do you have someone who can drive you out to pick it up?"

"Of course. Leave the keys on the back passenger-side wheel. Did you learn anything new?"

"Yep," I tell her. "I'll fill you in as soon as I can."

"Isla."

"Yeah, mom."

"I love you."

"I know," I say, and for the first time in years, maybe I believe it. But I'm not ready to say it back.

I call Ben next. He picks up on the second ring. "Hey. You OK?"

I see a cop and put my phone down. With the wind like a jet engine in my ear, I have to keep the device pressed to my head to hear anything. The police car passes and I get back on with

Ben, who's yelling, "Isla. *Isla*? You there?"

"Sorry. The fuzz was on my tail. What's happening there? Anyone looking for me?"

"I don't know," he says. "I haven't heard anything. Been working. I spent some time at Wailing Beach, but I couldn't see a thing. No clues, no overturned earth, nothing with the detector. I'm starting to think we're on the wrong track there."

"Agreed. This isn't the way."

"You still have the key?" he asks.

"Of course." What an odd question. "I'm catching the train out to Marlin Bay. I'll text you when I know my ETA."

"I'll pick you up if I can," Ben says.

"I've got cash. I'll grab a taxi if I don't see you."

"Safe travels," he says, and his tone is intimate, and my insides flutter. He's always done that to me, and it never ends well.

As the train pulls into the Marlin Bay station, I scan the parking the lot for Ben's Jeep. He's had the same red Wrangler since we were seventeen, and it no longer has doors. He doesn't care, and he'll take the Jeep whenever he can, especially on hot summer days on winding roads to the beach.

No sign of it.

I have a bad feeling about this, and I'm wondering how much Ben is truly in my corner. He works part-time for the police. His allegiances are split, but not evenly. The job he needs to raise his young daughter and pay for her future and her health care has to be far ahead of my well-being.

I step off the train and instead of Ben's Jeep, I see slick, generic sedans. Three of them. Two dark blue, one black.

Unmarked cop cars, clearly. Why three of them for little old me? I think about staying on the train, but running is pointless. I went on an investigating trip just now, but if I try to stay on the train, I'll officially be fleeing. They'll catch me at the final stop over in Goodstone. Beyond that is water, and I'm not up for a frigid swim across the North Atlantic.

I look for a way out. Run to the front or the back of the train and try to slip past them?

The train is squeaking to a halt.

It's over.

Goddamn it, Ben. What have you done?

I step off the train with my go-bag hung in the crook of my arm, bracing to be shouted at and thrown to the ground by men in windbreakers. But a few other passengers are disembarking alongside me, so I guess the cops are keeping things chill unless I try to bolt or resist.

I can see Lilith through one of the car windshields. Carter is with her in the passenger seat, struggling with his seatbelt.

They're terrible at this.

I stand still in the lot, presenting myself to them like a gift, and after the last straggler passes me, a bunch of men and Lilith step out from the three cars. They've all got their hands over their hips, ready to draw like I'm a serial killer.

"Is there a problem?" I ask, keeping my hands where they can see them.

"Keep your hands where we can see them," a tall guy with white hair orders me.

"I already am," I point out.

"Well…keep them that way." He sniffs. "Isla Banks?"

I thought it was pretty obvious. "No. I'm Scarlett Johansson. Isla went that way." I nod my head in the direction of Boston.

"I'm Massachusetts State Police Detective Mike Dirgler," White Hair says. "We'd like you to come down to the station with us."

Lilith and Carter are training their eyes on me.

"Am I under arrest?" I ask the group.

The detective sizes me up. I'm not a delicate petal. He can't trick me.

"Not at this time," he says.

I've said this maybe twice in my entire life, and I hate even thinking it, but my mother was right. I should have an attorney. For now, I'll pretend I have one, like most people do in these situations.

"Welp, thanks for the invite, but I'll reserve my right not to say anything. Talk to my lawyer for any further needs. This has been fun."

"You sure you want to play it this way?" White Hair wants to be on *Dateline NBC* so bad.

The tension in the lot is more powerful than I'd initially understood. This is deadly serious. I'm a murder suspect. I'm a victim, a grieving widow and daughter, and yet the pressure is piling up on *me*. It's surreal, and my current method of getting through it is to pretend it's not happening.

I say nothing.

"Fine," the detective says. "Don't leave town again while we complete our investigation." I don't know if he can actually stop me, but I take the warning.

He steps back into his car. No one came out of the third car, but when Dirgler drives away, the third car follows. As a taxpaying citizen, I'd like to protest their spending so many precious resources on one unarmed woman.

Lilith and Carter don't say a word to me. Lilith gets in the car while Carter's focusing on his phone. I walk over to them and open the passenger door.

"What are you *doing*?" Lilith cries as I take the seat next to her.

"I need a ride, and you're going my way," I say. "It's the least you can do, don't you think?"

She pauses, her face ashen, as she ponders the situation.

"I'm not Ted Bundy, Lilith. You and I used to bake cakes by lightbulb in my Kiddie Cooks oven. We played with action figures, and may I remind you that you always wanted to be the bad guy."

My bravado has some real confidence behind it, because it's clear a decision has been handed down not to arrest me on these charges—yet. I've seen it in plenty of cases I've covered: When law enforcement isn't one-hundred percent sure about a suspect, they hold off as long as they can while they gather evidence. If they arrest me and it turns out I'm innocent, then, down the line when they catch the real killer, their case against *that* person is shaky at best. They've handed the defense reasonable doubt on a silver platter: *The police arrested Isla Banks for this crime, but they couldn't make a case, so they're framing my client!*

But this little episode makes it clear they *do* think I'm the killer, which means they're dying for me to pay a visit to the Millers' house so they can arrest me for breaching the restraining order. While I'm rotting in the slammer on an unrelated bogus charge, they can take their sweet time investigating Clive's murder.

I'm not giving them any reason to nab me.

Carter's noticed I'm in his seat and raps on the window. I smile at him.

"Get in the back," Lilith calls out. He pretends he can't hear her through the glass, so she yells louder, pretty much directly into my left ear. "IN THE BACK."

Carter, fuming, does.

Lilith signs, turns the key, backs the car out.

We're on Rt. 128 for only a couple minutes when she can't take the silence anymore. I'm a trained television producer. Silence is one of my greatest weapons. People hate it.

"You shouldn't have run."

"I didn't run. I followed leads. I'm having to do your job for you and investigate the murder of my husband."

Lilith huffs and grips the wheel harder. "You want to play it that way? Fine. Tell me, Isla. What did you find on this investigative trip?"

"How about this," I say. "You show me yours and I'll show you mine."

"Not going to happen."

"I figured you'd say that," I reply. "I guess we're on our own. But you know I didn't do this, and yet you and the staties are focusing on me when the real killer's out there stabbing people with fishing implements."

"What I *know* is that human beings are capable of twisted and impulsive crimes when they think they have no other way out," she says. "The fingerprint analysis came back. Yours were found on the handle of the rake that killed Clive."

"I'm shocked. *Shocked*, I tell you," I deadpan. "I only gave the damn thing to him as a present."

She shakes her head like I just don't get it. Carter is pulling the silent treatment.

We ride in silence until Lilith turns onto the road leading to my father's house.

"On another note…" I say.

She turns to me, raises her eyebrows.

"You get any missing person's reports about Angélica recently?"

"Angélica?"

I wait.

"Oh. Angélica Vega. Your father's… no. Why?"

"No reason."

She brakes at the end of my father's driveway. I grab the doorhandle.

"You sure you don't want to share your side of things with me?" Lilith asks, looking me dead in the eyes. "Because I can tell you the staties are on a mission, and they're coming up with some conclusions I don't think you're going to like. Let me help you. Tell me what you found out."

I step out of the car, slamming the door behind me. As I stalk toward my front door, I hear another door slam. I look back to see Lilith following me, and Carter glaring from the back seat like a child left behind at the ice cream parlor.

"Isla," she calls. I'm at my door. She's on the walkway, keeping her distance. "The state police say they have a motive. Don't you want to know why they think you killed your husband?"

34

Almost without realizing I'm on the move, I meet the chief where she is on the flagstone walkway.

"I told you the staties were liaising with the NYPD," she says, her voice low and quiet. "They sent us the reports, Isla. We know about the trouble in your marriage. Two calls to a Riverside Drive apartment by a woman saying she's been locked inside, crying and screaming in terror. Two police reports, two visits by domestic violence officers."

Her words wallop me. I should've been prepared for this, but I shuttered the windows in my mind, locked the doors, and assumed everyone would forget like I did, as if banishing the thoughts would erase the police files. It worked, too, until now.

"I wasn't *screaming in terror*," I reply. "That's melodramatic."

"The police report literally says the 911 dispatcher described you as 'screaming in terror.'" Lilith is not buying it.

"Well," I say, trying to find the right words. "Then they also would've noted the police were sent away both times. Couples fight. Marriage isn't easy."

"You had a goose egg on your head," she says, her voice raspy, lower now, as if the trees are listening. "The police noted they were concerned for you but couldn't press charges without your help. Clive's landlord says there were complaints from tenants, too."

I moved into Clive's one-bedroom sublet after our engagement. I was all too happy to ditch my room in the Upper West Side apartment I shared with two other news producers from the station, but that decision also meant that when things got heated with Clive, I had no safe space to retreat to without revealing my rushed marriage was already failing. So I stayed.

When we announced our engagement, everyone we knew smiled nervously or flat-out told us we were moving too fast. An editor at work told me there were bets that Clive was using me to get American citizenship.

"Tell the state police I forgave him, and we moved on," I say to Lilith. "We were getting along better than ever on this last trip. We were trying to work it out, like you're supposed to. We talked about counseling, but he thought for our first year we didn't need it. We just needed to never do it again. We promised each other."

Lilith makes a condescending face, which I'm sure she thinks exudes sympathy. "It sounds like it got pretty bad," she says. "If you were defending yourself here in Sandburn, if you felt unsafe and you had no other choice, that's mitigation. It changes everything."

She takes a deep breath, waits. I don't respond, because my mind is like an estuary at low tide: Thick, sludgy, with a squirming underbelly.

"Talk to me. *Please.*"

"You've got it all wrong," I shrug. "It wasn't that bad. They say the first year of marriage is the hardest. And yes, we moved fast. But when you know, you know."

People tried to warn me, but I didn't listen because Clive had me all figured out, and he made it all seem normal. Thanks to Ponytail Man, I now know Clive studied me, gauged me, figured out I was the anti-love bomber. Don't come at me with roses or sickly sweet texts. The man who approaches with the confidence to give me space, the man who doesn't play games and doesn't stick to me like gum on a New York sidewalk, wins.

Even Clive's proposal was low pressure. We were at my co-producer's wedding, the champagne was flowing, a light breeze was spreading the scent of lilac blossoms, and Clive whispered, *Let's get married.*

Should we?

I think we should…do you?

Yes! Let's do it.

In that scenario, you're led to believe you came up with the idea together. You're not accosted by a dude you've known for two months; he doesn't get on one knee and freak you out by asking you to hand him your future on the spot.

There was no ring, no tangible contract of our drunken promise. It simply *was.* We ordered our marriage certificate online and were married in our living room by a justice of the peace, and then we got to work figuring out a date the following year for our beachside gala, the clambake to end all clambakes, otherwise known as the real wedding.

Clive's parents were thrilled to meet me. *We will teach you to speak Dutch. You will come here in the summer.* Lotte and Hans crowded the screen on Clive's phone, melding heads, cheering our engagement. That was my validation that the future would be healthy, new, exciting: A family. Doing life the regular way.

Exotic in-laws, a world of travel. A European passport!

"I don't know why you're defending the guy who abused you," Lilith says, dropping the gentle tone. "But you need to get yourself a lawyer. Stop running around thinking you're solving anything or coming up with anything we don't already know. Find yourself an attorney. I'm telling you this as a friend."

She leaves, and I watch her go, wondering how I'm going to get out of this one.

It's cold today, unseasonably so. I creak along my wraparound porch. There's no one to hear my footsteps. There's no soul here now, no heart. There's dust on the window ledge. I haven't taken care of this home as well as I should have. I didn't have the energy to clean the dust in the cobwebs, and now I can't think of a reason to put effort into it now.

I let myself inside. I plan to live like they're watching me. Part of me believes they're not, but I'm not giving an inch. I won't speak of anything more consequential than new recipes or cat videos, whether I'm in my home or my vehicle. The fact I'm still free when the clamming fork killer is on the loose, when there's so much pressure to catch him, makes me think the cops have something brewing. There is no doubt in my mind I am their primary, and possibly only, suspect.

I have to keep moving, like when your haul is short and the tide is racing in. I can't take a break from clearing my name while a tsunami is bearing down on me.

Everyone knows where I am now, so I pop my battery back in my phone and reactivate it. I have messages from Ben on my burner. *What happened to you? I was only two minutes late and you're not responding to any of my texts. Let me know UR OK.*

I want to block him, but part of me won't allow me to press the buttons, so I ignore him instead. I'm struggling to maintain my trust in Ben. He was the only one who knew what time my train was coming in.

The thing about Ben is this: The reasons I trust him to do the right thing are the same reasons I don't trust him to always do what's right for *me*. He flat-out told me the last time we talked that Lola comes first, Michele is a close second, and I imagine his parents and his brother are near the top of the list, too. Where does that leave me? It's not that I believe Ben might've betrayed me; it's that I believe he'd do what's best for his child, no matter what the cost.

As it should be.

I won't be able to sleep until I find Angélica. My father would want me to be sure she's safe, and in case he's looking down on me—or up at me, as the case may be—I'm going to put some effort into finding her.

When my father asked her to move in with him three years into their relationship, she said no. He offered to rent out the saltbox and move to her inland cape.

No, no, no, she'd stomped her feet to get him to listen to her. *I want my own house. My own space. Comprende?*

This woman adored my father, and he was utterly besotted with her. The sun rose and set in the space between his smile and her twinkling eyes. They made it work.

Angélica's son, Jorge, isn't responding to my texts. He travels frequently, usually to Asia, so it's not unusual. Time difference, meetings, a less-than-stellar opinion of me. All reasons he might not reply. Jorge and I are like chalk and cheese, as Clive, who learned the Queen's English in his Netherlands school, used to say. It's an English saying. Apparently, chalk is the opposite of cheese, and the two inherently clash.

When my father went missing, Angélica went catatonic. A shutter came down over her sparkling eyes. Voicelessness replaced her chatter and her vivid observations. I called Jorge, and he caught the first flight out of San Francisco. My mother of all people picked him up at Logan, because everyone else was searching.

Jorge realized immediately his mother was in trouble, and he signed Angélica into a facility with one of those luxury spa type names like Serenity Now or Lovely Acres. I never visited her there; I was too busy searching.

After she got out, she was alive and alert, but she was not Angélica. She avoided eye contact. She told me to give up. She said that if we didn't start moving on right then, we'd waste our life dreaming about an impossibility. Problem was, I could see she didn't believe a word she was saying. I could see the hope behind her eyes, hear the longing in her voice. I could see the loss and uncertainty over my father's unknown fate was killing her.

I figure she's gone back to the hospital, and I don't want to show up empty handed, so I pop to the Gas 'n' Gulp. Angélica never liked cut flowers. *You take them from the person and they're already dying. You're given a job to keep them alive. And then they die no matter what you do.*

I browse the candy aisle and feel eyes on me. I select a bar of dark chocolate with 70 percent cocoa, a food Angélica and I have sparred over plenty of times, primarily on the chocolate-based holidays like Christmas and Easter.

It tastes like cooking chocolate.

But milk chocolate is nothing more than brown lard. It has to be real cocoa, highly concentrated.

The clerk side-eyes me as I approach the register, one hand on his phone.

"Go ahead, Monkey. Call the cops. I dare you."

35

onkey's eye is twitching nervously. I do believe he's mildly afraid of me. This is the same guy who swore he had no idea there was a woman living in the Millers' house, but something tells me he was lying.

"Go on. Dial 911. See how annoyed they get at you wasting precious police resources."

He rings me up.

Back in the truck with my chocolate, I conduct a quick internet search to find the facility Angélica went to back then. I knew it was somewhere around Marlin Bay and Manchester-by-the-Sea, and there's only one mental health hospital in the area.

Calming Shores is a light-grey one-story building with manicured lawns and a happy, welcoming sign, like you're coming for a massage and a facial instead of sedatives and antidepressants. The logo is a frothy wave. This place will cost a fortune.

As I lay my hand on the door handle, my phone rings. It's the call I've been expecting, and I think about trying to delay the inevitable. I can ignore it. I can make them work for it.

I answer. "Hi, Lane," I say to my executive producer.

"Hey, Isla." She draws out the *Heyyyyy* in a sing-songy tone you use when someone dies. "How are you?"

She doesn't want to know how I am, so I do her a favor and keep it short.

"Hanging in there," I say. I don't tell her my husband came back from the dead and was promptly murdered. "I know I owe you a call about when I'm coming back to work, sorry…"

"About that," Lane says, and I can hear her teeth grinding. "I'm afraid…well, maybe you've read in the news we're having to downsize. I'm afraid they targeted our show. I'm sorry, but we're going to have to let you go. I'm so fucking sorry, Isla. I fought for you. I told them they were utter garbage for doing this to someone while they're on leave for…"

As she's talking, I think about how I could use this to my advantage.

I make a sort of choking, gurgling sound to signify shock and an imminent breakdown.

"I can't believe they're doing this to me now," I cry out, sniffling for good measure. "With everything I'm going through. How could they do this? I think—I think I'm having a panic attack!"

I thought I would be OK when the call came. I didn't expect to be relieved and a little bit thrilled. *I'm free.* Let me get back to solving the mysteries currently destroying my life.

"Oh, Isla. Breathe, OK? Is there someone with you? Is there someone you can call?"

"I'm—I'm—I'll be alright." I take some deep breaths.

"I just feel terrible," she says. "You don't deserve this."

Not to worry. You'll go in the next round, or the next. In today's media landscape, the staffers left behind to run the newsroom on a shoestring have survivors' guilt, plus they live every day waiting for the executioner to beckon them.

"HR will be in touch," she says solemnly. "In the meantime, if there's anything I can do, and I mean anything, Isla, just say the word."

"Now that you mention it," I say. "There is something."

"Anything," she says.

After I bid farewell to Lane, I take my no-frills chocolate bar to the reception desk. "Welcome to Calming Shores," the receptionist breathes. "How may we improve your day?"

"I'm here to visit Angélica Vega."

"Let me check for you," he smiles like he's extremely excited to help me.

He clicks around on his keyboard, keeping his face impressively impassive.

He raises his eyes, now showing disappointment. "I'm afraid there's no one by that name in residence at Calming Shores."

I nod and smile back. "I understand. Perhaps she's been released."

"Due to HIPAA privacy laws, I am unable to tell you if anyone has been released."

"Thanks for your help." I head out, without any idea of where to go next.

I sit in my truck and tear open the chocolate. I break off a square and let it melt in my mouth, but it doesn't, so I chew it. I'm not going to bother Darcy. The woman is vulnerable as an employee of the Kastic family. If she talks to me, she's risking more than I could expect her to.

Where could Angélica be?

I wait until dusk, then head to her house. Angélica lives on a side street on the other side of town, which means I'm forced to travel down Main Street. I decide my father's mountain bike is the best way to go without people immediately realizing who I am. His truck is as old as the rest of them around here, but it stands out because of its cracked side mirror and a faded bumper sticker his mother gave him two decades ago for Christmas that says in all caps, I DIG YOU. I always counted myself lucky he wasn't driving around with HAPPY AS A CLAM on his bumper.

I bring the bicycle around back when I get to Angélica's house. I knock halfheartedly and call out her name, but not loud enough for any neighbors to hear. I look through the window to the kitchen. No lights, no movement, no sound.

Angélica taught me how to get into her house in the first year she was dating my father, when it was clear nothing was going to pry apart Angélica Vega and Nick Banks.

Find the hose spigot.

Measure two palm lengths against the house to the right.

Look down.

Dig.

I crouch, holding my breath as I dig my raggedy nails into the hard dirt, scraping, finding nothing. I move an inch to the right and try again. If the spare key's gone, that means she is, too. I rifle around some more, feel the cold metal, and exhale. I let myself into her home, call her name again as I breach her threshold, get no response.

The house has a smell, like someone's been living here recently, like cooked food and old sneakers. The aura of Angélica's beloved peppermint tea hangs in the air, but maybe that's wishful smelling on my part. I breeze through the kitchen but find no signs she's been here today. I touch the kettle and find it cold.

I tromp to the living room, where her life story is narrated silently by photos and decorations and memorabilia, a bit like my father's home but neater and smaller.

Angélica falls somewhere between a Renaissance woman and a Jane of all trades. She crochets when she's anxious, and she's left an unfinished rainbow beanie on a side table. That gives me some pause; neither unfinished tasks nor clutter are characteristics she's known for.

Magazines are laid out neatly on the glass coffee table: *Angler's Monthly, Vogue, The Economist*. Family pictures of her life in Mexico and her life here; Jorge as a toddler in the surf and at his Boston University graduation; one of my father, Angélica and me at my college graduation brings an instant lump in my throat.

On the back wall, there's a framed photograph of Angélica wrangling a marlin off the back of a fishing boat in turquoise waters in Mexico. On the mantle, her college swimming gold medal hangs on the corner of a framed a picture of her posing with her team, which sits next to an image of her with her chef father and her manager mother in their restaurant back in Mexico.

Angélica's always been open with me, but she'll never talk about why she's in the United States undocumented. It is a story I never pushed her to reveal, and one my father never shared with me; I don't believe he knows. Whenever a conversation veers in that direction, he waits to hear more. I can see it in his face and his eyes: he wants her to trust him with it, but it's hers to hold until she's ready.

I see no sign of a struggle or foul play in the kitchen and front room, which calms me slightly.

I stop in the laundry room.

My blood runs cold.

36

The cream tiles are stained with scarlet. I crouch to get a better look at two smears the size of casino chips. They're dry, and they were surely accidental, a trace left by a person stuffing the front-loaded washing machine with soiled clothes. A bloody finger touches the floor or a droplet falls, and a knee is dipped in it while crouching to load the washer.

I pull open the washer door with a pounding pulse. There are damp clothes clinging to the sides. I peel it off an item. Jeans. A man's. Dark with water. I pick out a long-sleeved tee. Navy blue, probably a man's, impossible to see stains if they exist.

There's no smell. A mildew stench will hit wet laundry within a day, so I know this load was washed recently.

I fight panic. I can't call the police.

But how can I *not* call them?

Something is badly wrong. On top of everything else, it's not like Angélica not to contact me with support during a time like this, let alone ignore my pleading texts.

With the small amount of blood, I opt to leave it be. When your friend is undocumented, when she escaped something she still can't talk about and made a life for herself in a place that's still not safe for her, your options for assistance are always greatly reduced. The "help" you summon is sometimes more likely to destroy them than save them.

I send her a text and pack it with her beloved emojis, more to soothe myself than anything.

Angel, I'm worried. PLEASE let me know you're OK.

I pedal down Main Street toward the marina. Sandburn's fanciest restaurant glows up ahead. I wish I was in there, forgetting everything outside, being served, pampered, sipping their signature Blue Blast martini, a cocktail that looks like windshield wiper fluid and tastes like summer.

The Pearl, they say, is for lovers. It's also for men looking for a quick route to impressing a date, or rich tourists needing a break from the fast-casual fried clams and chowder we're known for. The view out the back of the great marsh, the winding, curvy inlet that leads to the river and then the ocean, is worth the extra cost if you can afford it.

The picture windows are alight with a sexy, moody atmosphere. The Pearl's chef fled New York to cook seafood on the North Cape, and some say his forty-five-dollar striped bass en papillote is to die for. *For that price, it better come with a mountain of mashed potatoes with a gold coin inside*, my father used to say. And then he'd take Angélica there for every birthday when he wasn't spiriting her into Boston's North End for her beloved red-sauce Italian.

With darkness falling and the restaurant lit up, I can see the diners inside clearly. I see someone I know, someone who's more likely to grab a gas station sandwich than visit the Pearl. I brake so my bike skids on the dirt parking area.

Ben's sitting at a prime table by the back of the restaurant against the window facing the water. I can't see who he's dining with, but I can see he's talking to someone. I run through the reasons Ben Cassidy would be at the Pearl.

He and Michele made up again.

He's hanging out with one of his best friends who's a bartender there.

Or…he has a new girlfriend.

I shuffle awkwardly with the bicycle between my legs, and as I draw closer to the restaurant's front door, I'm half hoping he'll look out and see me.

His profile is in view now, but the person he's talking to is hidden by another diner's head. I move a few feet down the sidewalk, and from this new angle, I can see who Ben is with. He's leaning forward, and so is she, in what appears to be an intimate exchange.

It's Charlotte. She's leaning on her elbows and resting her chin on her folded hands as she devours Ben's wisdom. The body language all around is familiar, comfortable, and screams this isn't the first time they've hung out. There are wine glasses on the table.

And then, with one shift of her gaze, she sees me. Like she did from the house the night she caught me spying from the seagrass. Her face lights up, and I'm treated to a lightning-fast smirk and a wink.

I take off, pedaling as fast as I can, trying to burn off the pain.

Part of me still hoped Ben had a plan, one so clever he couldn't let me in on it yet, one he was secretly working on behind the scenes. But this romantic dinner with a woman he said he never met is going to be tough to explain away.

I lock the bicycle to a light post and walk along the harbor, passing stores, a restaurant, and the warehouse that services the marina. I feel eyes on me all the time now, the stares a constant companion reminding me I'm on borrowed time.

The Creaky Schooner is tucked behind the North Cape Lobstermen's Market with its bent aluminum siding, crooked door, makeshift awning and ever-changing price list scrawled on a chalkboard. The market changes by the hour, so there is chalk and an eraser within grabbing distance. The Schooner is a tourist trap May through September, when the Kastics, who own the place, mock the summer people mercilessly behind their backs for paying eighteen bucks for a shitty margarita and thinking they've found a hidden gem.

I push open the door and brace myself for an experience I haven't forced upon myself in years. The aesthetic is a confused mishmash of Applebee's and a dive bar; there are hanging plastic lobsters and a green and white motif, so you're not sure if you're in for an Irish experience or a seafaring theme, or if you should get shepherd's pie or clams casino off the plastic menu.

Doesn't matter to me. The real bar is in the back, where locals retreat when May hits. Those in the know enter through the pub's rear entrance, and if you want to come in through the main bar, the password is *Get out of the way. I'm coming in.*

If you show weakness, you're not getting in.

Luke Kastic is behind the bar in the main restaurant. His

family is made up of shadowy businesspeople, but Luke only ever wanted to be front facing: A bartender, salesman or social media man. He's an evil extrovert, a charming psychopath. In my experience, the people who lack a conscience and possibly a soul are often the most seductive. They study us like professors to learn how a human behaves, and then they do it better.

I wait for Luke to notice me. After a moment, he pokes his head up, bringing with him a plastic container of freshly cut limes. He looks tired, busy, and nowhere near as eager to mess with me as he was when I bumped into him at the Rusty Lantern.

"I need to talk to you. Can we go in the back?" I ask.

"I'm working. You gonna buy something?"

There are a few people drinking frothy beers and eating potato skins and fried clams, but it's not busy.

I lean on the bar, arms crossed. "What's your specialty?"

Luke roots around for something under the bar while a bartender at the other end polishes glasses.

"And don't say sex on the beach," I add.

That gets him. Luke treats me to that cocky lopsided grin. "You think I'm that basic? I'm insulted. How about a screaming orgasm?"

A groan comes from the younger bartender, who I don't know, but it's possible I saw him fishing for striper with Oyster last summer.

I want to tell Luke how gross he is, but I need him to open up to me and as offensive as it is, I'll play his game.

"Nothing I'd love more," I reply, and he chuckles to himself.

He grabs a lowball glass and a cocktail shaker. He adds a scoop of ice, followed by a frightening array of sickly liqueurs:

Kahlua, Amaretto, Baileys. Then vodka and cream.

He shakes, then pours it over fresh ice, stabs a maraschino cherry with a fancy toothpick, pops it into the glass, then sets the drink before me.

I take a sip and, shockingly, it's delicious.

"As advertised," I say in the suggestive way I know he wants me to.

He grabs a dishtowel.

"What are you here for, Isla?"

He keeps busy, and I realize I've made him nervous.

"I'm in a bad place," I blurt. "They think I killed Clive."

"Didn't you?"

He regards me with half-open, dark eyes.

"Of course I didn't kill my husband." I watch his face. He's not sure. "Look," I say, "I'm having to investigate my own case now along with my father's disappearance. I need your company's security footage from the marina, Luke. There must be something we can work out. Something where I get to see it, or you tell me what's on it, or anything that could quite literally save my life."

He shoots a look to his colleague and beckons me to the far end of the bar.

"If I tell you, will you stop talking to everyone about it? You're making trouble for us. You're bringing attention to our family for something we had nothing to do with."

"If you tell me what happened to your security footage from that night, I promise you, Luke, you won't hear another word from me about it."

I cross my heart.

"What was that? Were you trying to genuflect?"

"It's called cross your heart and hope to die. I don't know. I just need to know what's on the footage and then I'll drop it."

"I'll deny I ever said this," he whispers. "But we weren't lying to the police. We *don't* have footage of that night. Or from the entire two months surrounding that night. It's an utter shit show. Frisco blew a gasket when he found out."

"What happened?" I take a drink. It's an odd feeling to believe him.

"Someone hacked us. The footage we'd been checking every day was the same two twenty-four-hour periods on a loop."

"*What?* Are you being straight with me?"

He nods slowly.

"How did someone do that? I mean, and *why*?" I can't imagine who's going to mess with the Kastics.

"Take your pick," he shrugs, showing a shocking level of self-awareness. "Competitors. Law enforcement. Bored hackers. This is why everyone's so touchy. Every time you ask anyone about it, it gets back to us. It's a problem. It's the worst of both worlds. We look suspicious for holding it back, but if we admit we don't have it, we look like bumbling idiots. We'd open ourselves up to people thinking we have vulnerabilities. Frisco can't have that."

"But what do *you* think?" I ask. "You must have a theory."

"Someone's using the marina for something they're not supposed to," he says. "We've suspected it for a while, but we can't nail it down."

"You have your suspicions, though." It's written on his face. I said he was charismatic. I never said he was clever.

"Cassandra's new pleasure cruiser came out of nowhere," he

says. "I mean, we're not accusing Sandburn's only Black tuna boat captain of nothing, but it's…"

"You can't really think she's doing anything illegal?" His eye roll tells me he does. "She's as by-the-book as they come."

"I don't know what to think, but Frisco's losing his shit."

I toss back my drink, letting the ice hit my teeth and filter the sweet liquid, and finish it in one final sip. I set the glass on the bar. Luke is about to talk to another customer.

"Hey," I say. He raises one eyebrow. "You met the English woman who's staying in the Millers' place yet?"

"In passing," he says. "What's the word the Brits use for fancy people? Posh. She's posh, that one."

"Do you know anything about her?"

"I know she's hot and has a sexy accent."

"Do you ever get tired of being a cliché?"

"No." He leans forward and gazes into my eyes like he's about to kiss me. I back up.

"How do you know her?" I push. "Everyone in town says she never comes out and they don't believe anyone's living in the Millers' house."

He makes a face like *What drugs are you on?*

"Of course she comes out," he says like I'm so far out of the loop I can't even see the loop. How dumb I've been. How naïve, how willfully blind. "She gave to the Fisherman's Winter Fund this year. We rang the bell for her." He nods his head toward the bell they use for big tippers. "Hell, I've seen her at the Gas 'n' Gulp. Why are you asking? What's she got to do with anything?"

"I don't know," I say. "But don't you think it's strange this young-ish woman just showed up one day and stays in that house by herself all the time?"

"Do I think it's strange a new person moved to Sandburn, fills up on gas, loves the best restaurant in town, and patronizes the coolest pub?" The eyes, dark-rimmed, sultry, staring right into mine, hoping I'll be another one sucked in by his seductive come-ons. *Not today, Luke.*

The Pearl. The Creaky Schooner. The gas station furthest from my house.

Places I'm *not* known to frequent.

Interesting.

I pedal through the dark back roads toward home, fearing every bright headlight and red taillight, waiting to be arrested. To distract myself, I organize my feelings into tiny drawers like the jewelry box my mother gave me. I'm no worse off without Ben. You're on your own in this world, and as a wise woman once said, you always have been. You enter alone and you leave alone. No one's coming to save you.

37

I drive to Wailing Beach before sunrise. Ben claims he conducted another search and found nothing, so I decide to shift my focus. He is fastidious and he is stubborn, and if there was something to find, he'd have dug it up.

It's not a *thing* I'm looking for.

It's a memory. A white wisp of leftover skywriting, a hint of poetry scrawled in the sand, an imprint of the past. A thought that's been swirling in my mind becomes a vice. It's time to think like a man with no time and few options.

I walk barefoot onto the beach. The wind is ferocious, blowing my hair back so none of it touches my face or neck. My bare feet are cosseted by cool white sand. My eyes are trained on a spot in the distance. I can make out only shapes before the sun comes up. The sunrise's miraculous burst of color, the show that will light up the world, is yet to begin.

I swing my mind back to the time my father and I spent here, forcing myself to swerve away from the present and plow into the murky past. The ground I'm standing on is special. Wailing Beach presents a stunning, picturesque New England scene, but it is the way the sand speaks to you that gives it its name and makes it one of a kind.

When you first set foot on the beach, the sand cries out beneath your arches.

Squeaks and moans. Sings, sometimes.

Dad and I would come here when the tourists didn't, before the summer people and their noise and their coolers and their crowds sullied its majesty.

I think back to that time my father showed me why it's not the best clamming beach. *No one knows why. It's for tourists, not for us.*

I must've been eleven or twelve years old. He raced up the beach, kicking sand as he went, and found a stick in the dirt. He stomped back to me and chose a spot close to the waterline. I watched as he drew long lines and arcs and circles.

When he finished, he said, "Read that."

I stood over the lines and couldn't make sense of them. There was a P and a V, maybe an I, maybe an L.

I can't see the whole word.

Stand back. Move away, into the surf, and try again.

I took ten steps back, and in front of me the letters became a word. PERSPECTIVE.

When you're too close to anything, and you're struggling with it, take a step back. Take time. Create distance. Look at it again.

Perspective is everything, Isla girl.

There was a trick he used to show me.

I wait in the pre-dawn darkness, and then the faintest furnace electrifies the horizon, tinges the dusty earth with an outline of rippling fire. What my eyes can't see, the sun can still reach, weaving through spaces between trees and soaring birds and new spring buds.

The prism hanging in Oyster and Agnes's window a mile from here, nestled in the woods among thick, towering trees, takes in the sun's rays and focuses their light into a laser. As the yellow-orange sun pokes its fire above the horizon, light blasts through the crystal and falls on one spot.

The house on the point.

The light from the prism hits the spot directly in front of the Millers' patio, beyond the hot tub sunken in expensive stonework, on the sand where the footprints of clammers, shellfishers, their children and families and helpers can still be seen when I close my eyes.

The spot that my father showed me years ago from this very beach when he showed me this trick, is now the sign he left for where the answers lie. I know what to do now.

Something is under that sand. Now I must figure out how to get to it, whatever *it* is, without getting caught.

I grab a breakfast sandwich from the main street diner, killing time until a civilized hour so I can pay a visit to an old acquaintance.

Ben hasn't contacted me since I ignored his previous entreaties. He knows me well enough to understand he should live in fear of me from here on out. Forever.

When the clock strikes nine, I motor out along winding back roads to find my sober witness to my father and Clive in the boat on that fateful night. Theodore Rainwater lives in a manufactured home out by the Goodstone River. I wait in my truck for a few minutes, figuring nine-fifteen a.m. for an unannounced visit strains the boundaries of politesse.

When the two witnesses first came forward about seeing my father and Clive floating in the *Sable* that night, I took law enforcement's word that they vacuumed up every crumb of viable information. Now I know better. And, as I learned in the news business, letting a few months pass can settle nerves and yield fresh results from reluctant or anxious witnesses.

I step out of the truck and knock on the door. A man with wild, wiry silver hair dressed in a paint-splattered smock and apparently nothing else opens the door.

"Well, hello," he says in a deep, smooth voice as I work hard not to stare at his bare legs, lest something peeks out from below the smock.

"Come on in."

This is not a usual New England greeting. "Go away" is by far the preferred choice when a stranger knocks.

"Oh…thank you," I say, stepping into the small, clean home that smells of varnish.

"Who's that?" A grouchy voice comes from a back room.

"It's Isla Banks, darling," the painter yells. To me, he says, "Call me Lippy. You know, because of the big mouth. Would you like a cup of tea? Or a shot of tequila? Which kind of visit is this?"

I'm disarmed by his kindness and the fact he knows who I am, and I giggle. "I'll tell you once I've talked to Theodore."

"Tequila it is," the man winks. I notice he's wearing a thick platinum wedding ring. I didn't know Theodore was married.

He steps aside to let me in, then closes the door. Several canvases painted in stunning colors and textures, modern splashes of paint, and a half-finished oil painting that looks like it'll end up as a portrait of Sandburn decorate the room.

"These are beautiful," I say. "Do you ever show them?"

"I do, up in the Marlin Bay galleries," he says. "But you're not here to talk about my career. Come on through. I'll try to cajole him into being helpful."

Theodore is in a leather recliner sipping coffee and reading his tablet.

"Hello, Theo," I say.

"Hey, Isla. Long time."

38

I warm my hands on the coffee mug Lippy gave me. I'm thankful he didn't bring me tequila.

Theodore is thinking hard, twisting up his mouth, his brow, his nose, to show me how hard he's trying. "Buoy?" He finally says, pursing his lips until they nearly disappear inside his mouth.

"Yes…Chief Wen said there was a red buoy between the two men in the boat, but—"

"Oh." He clears his throat with a crackle and a gurgle. "Well, sure, I mighta said something about a buoy when they interviewed me, but that's because I didn't know what it was. They kept pressing me to say what it was, but hell if I knew."

"Could you describe what you saw? You don't have to label it."

"I guess," he says. "It was red, like I told 'em. And it wasn't square or nothin' with any sharp pointy edges. It wasn't no lobster trap. But it wasn't like any buoy I ever seen. The guys were all shifty around it, too."

"Shifty?"

"Like, oh, I don't know…restless, like trying to keep from touching it or something."

I try to picture the scene. Two men and a big lump in the boat. A red lump.

Oh, my god. Why didn't I figure this out sooner? It's so obvious I could cry. It should've been obvious to me from minute one. Then again, I trusted Lilith's version of the witnesses' statements. One of many mistakes through all this.

Lippy returns with a tray.

It's the dreaded tequila. "Oh, I couldn't—"

"Yes, you could." Lippy sets the tray down. "This is medicinal. Trust me."

He picks up a shot glass and I follow suit. It's the least I can do now that his husband has changed everything.

"Lick, shoot, suck. *Go!*"

I do, and the tequila goes down like honey. "That's good," I say, smacking my lips. "What is that?"

"It's from my friend's micro distillery down in Jalisco," he says. "One hundred percent the best blue agave you could imbibe."

"I'd better go before I'm tempted to have a few more of those," I say, rising, having an urgent matter to attend to.

"Thank you so much," I say.

"Come back and visit any time," Lippy says, and I do believe he means it.

I race the truck too fast around hairpin turns. I don't know how I know where to go. I just do. As I fly over the uneven roads of inland Sandburn, my pressing thought, besides how to keep my anger at bay until I have more information, is how much I want to call Ben. This is the break we've been looking for, and to not share it with him is physically painful, a tightening of the throat and the ribcage.

The marina is busy enough so that I don't stand out. I can hear the chop slapping against the dock and the boats. Of the three harbors on the cape, ours is the smallest.

The boat is in its slip and the windows are glowing subtly, just enough to let me know there's someone on board. I storm up to the stern, put my foot on it, and step hard, loud, deliberate on the slick fiberglass.

I walk toward the cabin. There's no one on the bridge, so I'm guessing they're doing their thing below. I don't know what Cassandra's using this boat for, but it's not for luxury trips to Bermuda to sip piña coladas.

I knock on the cabin door. I hear scrambling, then, "Who's there?"

"Why not check your cameras?" I snark.

"Isla?" Cassandra sounds shocked, and a little nervous. Unusual for our steadfast captain.

I hear mumbling that sounds a lot like a woman saying *Let her in.* Either that or *Hit her pin.*

The door opens. There she is, in the flesh.

Angélica, my stepsomething, friend, and big fucking liar.

"Not bleeding anymore, I see."

"Isla…guapa…come in."

I cross the threshold and am hit with the smell of extreme cleaning products, the kind with chemicals that'll kill anything that touches it.

"Isn't this cozy," I seethe.

Cassandra's sitting on the "sofa," which on this mid-range

cabin cruiser is more of a bench constructed with glorified flotation devices. Angélica has moved to the galley, where she's surrounded by sponges and cleaning supplies. There are grocery bags everywhere.

"You provisioning? I didn't know this boat could bring in much of a catch this time of year," I say to Cassandra.

Angélica gestures to a barstool at the galley counter.

"Tell me," she says. "Tell me what is wrong."

"What is *wrong*," I reply, "is that there was never a red buoy in my father's boat that night, was there? There was no weird-looking lobster trap."

Her eyes go wider, if it's possible. "I—"

"All this time, everyone from the police chief to the coast guard assumed there was an *object* in that boat. But the lump Theo Rainwater saw wasn't a buoy. It was *you*, hunched over and trying to stay out of sight, covered with your favorite red jacket."

She closes her eyes. I keep talking. "You survived whatever happened that night because you're a championship swimmer. Those currents would be tough for some, but not for you. You know this river well as I do. You got away, safe and sound. I just want to know *why*, Angélica." My voice cracks. "Why didn't you give me a fighting chance and tell law enforcement this was all Clive's doing? That he forced my father out on the river that night?"

"How did you know?" she asks softly.

"When I went to your house, desperate to find you, worried sick, finding blood on your floor for god's sake, I saw your swimming trophies. It didn't hit me then, but when I talked to Theo just now, it all slotted into place."

I move to the sofa across from Cassandra and pick up Angélica's red windbreaker. "I didn't see it at your house, of course, because you were wearing it, like you do most days in spring and fall. Don't I feel like an idiot not figuring it out until now."

I shake my head. "How stupid I was to think you were on my side. I thought my second mother would have my back. Would look out for me."

I am regressing. I am a child standing in front of the parent who betrayed her. I am holding her to a high standard, I know, but she started it. She made sure to draw me in when she got serious with my father, becoming a friend and a bonus parent I could share anything with. She's the cool aunt who will never judge me, never leave me, never betray me. Yet she has.

Angélica puts up two hands in surrender.

"The first thing I need you to know," she chokes out, "is that I have no idea what happened to either of the men."

Her tone is pleading, her eyes big, shining, and meeting mine without wavering. "I don't know why Clive did it. Neither of them would tell me. Your father said I must know nothing, in order to keep me safe. Clive said I should not know because it was my best chance to live."

I see nothing but honesty on her face, but then again, some people are really good liars.

"Let's say I believe you. What *do* you know?"

"I wanted to tell you so many times, but it would be selfish—"

"*Selfish*?" I guffaw at that.

"Selfish, because it would make *me* feel better, but it would put your life in danger. You understand? Remember the other day at the marina, when you were with Oyster? I was weak when I saw you. I almost told you. I'm glad you left before I could."

"Tell me what happened," I say coldly. "From the beginning."

39

Cassandra is watching Angélica and me like a tennis match. I feel her leaning almost imperceptibly in my direction, as if readying herself to leap up and block me from attacking Angélica. I've no doubt the rage in me is visible on the outside.

"Clive forced your father out of your house, onto the water, at gunpoint," Angélica says.

I nod. "There was never any trip to the pub. I figured that out when Clive came back pretending he had amnesia."

Turns out Lilith was on the right track when she'd asked me on day one, *Why go out for a beer in the cold just before the Rusty Lantern closes when you could sip one on your private dock?*

Angélica's ponytail swings as she shakes her head. "That was a lie for your benefit. Your father wouldn't say why they were heading up toward Plum Island, but when I saw them at the edge of Sandburn Marina, where Cassandra had just dropped me off, I waved and called to them.

"No one was around, but Clive was furious that I was bringing attention to them. Your father steered the boat to me, and Clive told me to get in. Nicholas tried to convince Clive not to pick me up, but Clive said he'd shoot me if he didn't, so your father agreed. As soon as I got on board, Clive told your father to take us to Magenta Shores."

"Magenta Shores is the opposite direction of Plum Island. What were they doing up by the marina in the first place?"

"I don't know. All Clive could talk about was what to do with me. He was close to killing me on the spot. I could feel it. He kept yelling in a whisper, like, 'what do we do with her? Dammit, Nick. She's going to ruin everything. I can't afford to have her out there knowing about this.' Nick promised him I wouldn't talk."

She puts her head in her hands and emerges from behind the galley counter. She stands in front of me. "He made me swear not to tell. I begged. 'Let me go. None of this ever happened. I don't even know what you're doing out here.' Clive told me that if I told anyone, that he'd kill *you* that night. Then he'd kill Jorge. Then he'd have me deported so I'd be alive to know the pain of losing my home, my son, my love. My daughter."

She reaches out, touches my shoulder. I jerk away. She has the nerve to look wounded. "If my father told you to jump out of a boat with a man holding a gun," I say, "he must've believed Clive was ready to kill you in cold blood."

"Yes. That is what I thought, too," she agrees. "Clive was pretending he would let me go so I would stay quiet in the boat. Your father knew of my skills in the water, and he knew how close the nearest shore was, and how long I could survive without getting hypothermia. When we floated closer to Lost Island, he told me to 'jump, jump, Angélica! Get out.'

"It was so dark, he hoped I would be lost among the waves so

Clive could not see me to shoot me. So I jumped, and I swam, and I swam, and I made it to the island and called Cassandra." Clive wouldn't have known that people in the fishing industry often keep their cell phones in water-tight pouches.

I turn and check the captain's reaction. Cassandra remains seated and unruffled. "You were in on this too?" I screech. "Great! Another so-called friend of our family who betrayed us in the worst way possible. I don't get it. I really don't."

My eyes well up, but I manage to beat back the tears. I don't have time for the nervous breakdown I deserve.

Cassandra stands, and three of us face off in close quarters on this mildly rocking vessel. "Don't judge us," she shakes her head, wags her finger at me. "Listen to what Angélica is saying. Really *listen*, Isla."

I say to Angélica, "That's why you checked yourself into Happy Sunsets or whatever? To avoid having to talk to the police and look me in the eye when you lied to me?"

"She didn't check herself in," Cassandra answers for her. "Jorge and I did. I told them she'd been traumatized and was having a breakdown. Angélica could barely speak. Her life was over that night. Do you get that? It wasn't having to live with what happened on that boat that would've destroyed her. It was the decision your husband forced upon her. She had an impossible choice to make, and it was one she had to keep making *every single day* when she woke up. It's torture, and it's not fair. Give her a break, Isla."

Angélica half-smiles at Cassandra, then says to me, "I won't ask you for a break. But please understand that the last thing your father said to me was, 'Don't let him hurt Isla, Angie. Do what he says. Keep yourself and Isla alive. Don't tell anyone. You hear me? Never tell.'"

Cassandra chimes in as I process what's happening.

"She didn't ask for this any more than you did. She had no choice."

"There's always a choice." I step away from this cozy threesome. I need air.

"You weren't there. You don't know," Cassandra says.

"To keep all this from me, from the police and the Coast Guard, when everyone was thinking the men were lost at sea, is unforgiveable," I say, my voice shaking. "You knew all along it wasn't a drug deal gone wrong, a rogue wave, a heart attack. My god."

Angélica's eyes are closed, like she's wishing the past, or maybe me, away.

"This isn't on you, Cassandra," Angélica wakes up. "This is on me. I'm undocumented. If I told, Clive could come out of nowhere, kill you, and destroy me and my family without even trying, and then he could disappear again."

"There's more to this," I say. I turn to Cassandra. "What are you not telling me? You have something to protect, too. What is it?"

"Let it go."

"What are you using this boat for, Cassandra? Because I know you're not out sunbathing or indulging in happy hour cruises."

She snorts at that. Angélica stays silent.

Cassandra regards me, and I hold up under the gaze of the sea captain who's dealt with death on board, sexist crew, racist crew, fighting fish, and killer seas to become one of the most successful fishers in a dying industry.

"If I tell you, you must promise on your mother's life you'll take it to your grave," Cassandra rasps, stepping to me so there's no misunderstanding.

"Those are some heavy asks," I say.

"It's a heavy secret," she hits back.

I nod, and Cassandra nods back, and the contract is signed.

"I have some friends down in North Carolina who educated me about some things," Cassandra says. "Showed me there are some fine folks in terrible circumstances who could use a lift back to shore. Now. The less you know about this, the better it'll be for you, but I feel you deserve to know your father's role in this."

"You've lost me."

"I've been…well, helping people up here along with the network down south. Your father caught me one night. He was out doing his thing, whatever that is—"

"What's that supposed to mean?" I snap. "You trying to connect him to the Kastics and drugs again?"

She gives me a cynical half-smile. "Girl, if you can only come up with drugs as the answer, you're not thinking creatively enough." She pauses. "Don't tell me you don't know your father was out at all hours in strange places. Been doing it for years. It was an open secret."

She's the latest person to allude to my father's mysterious obsession. Not drugs. Nothing to do with bivalves, shellfish, mollusks…or so they say. Was he out passing messages and codes from a spy network he was a secret agent in? Was he digging for pirate's treasure? Or…was his obsession the sand itself? It's worth a lot of money, and sand thieves will pillage and plunder beaches and riverbanks and dunes, like heroin by the ton. There are sand mafias in some parts of the world that use intimidation and bribery to traffic it. It is one of the most mined commodities in the world, and it is finite, and we are using it up quickly. You can't build without it. There are no homes or skyscrapers or hospitals without sand. Cranberry growers spread it by the ton on their bogs to rejuvenate old vines and protect buds from frost and insects, and the politics of it in the towns where they operate have been known to become adversarial, even threatening.

"Anyway," Cassandra continues. "Nick asks me the next day what we're up to. I tell him, because if I don't, I'm afraid he's going to start talking. So he says, 'Cass, just so happens I'm looking for an investment right now. You need a better boat.' Then out of nowhere he comes back the next week and gives me the down payment for this cruiser in cash. You could've shut me up with a crab claw. I tell you." She shakes her head as if she still can't believe it.

"You're picking up refugees…" It took me a moment, but I get it now. That's the action going on in the marina that the Kastics can't nail down.

"We are." Cassandra nods. "You run into them in open water, they need help, you don't know who they are. Maybe someone tells you where they might be, maybe it's a big coincidence. You take them on board and drop them off on land. Maybe someone picks them up. Not my business. So you see, we're operating on technicalities, but if we're caught, it'd be bad."

I sigh, thinking of how to put this next question. "You're bringing people into this place illegally? Isn't that…dangerous?"

Cassandra shakes her head. "These aren't mass immigration runs with coyotes and human trafficking," she says. "These are select rescues of family members and people known to a small network along the Eastern Seaboard. People escaping the gangs and the knowledge they'll die if they don't get out. A captain in Ocracoke took me out, and I saw for myself a family, *little children*, dehydrated in a makeshift life raft hanging on in the swells, and I couldn't look away."

"My father helped with these rescues?"

Cassandra waves the thought away. "No, no. Just the donation. He had nothing to do with this work."

I ask, "What about the blood at your house? Angélica, you involved in this?"

"Ah, guapa," she shrugs. "I couldn't look away either. It was just a little nick when we were cutting the ropes."

I'm in crisis mode, and I'm ready to get out of here. When I think of what could've been saved in time and stress and wrong turns, it's almost unbearable.

"You have to come forward," I tell them. "I'm fighting for my life here. Tell the police everything. They think I killed Clive and set this whole thing up. They won't even look for my father."

"Did you hear a word we said?" Cassandra asks sharply. "That ain't going to happen."

She's fierce and unmoved. My one life is nothing compared to the many she can save. I can read her mind, because I'd be thinking the same thing if it wasn't my head on the chopping block.

"I could go to jail for life. Probably will, the way things're going," I reply. "You're going to stay silent while an innocent person goes to prison?"

Cassandra moves past me as if preparing to escort me off her boat, then faces me at the door. "I don't know why you're worried about that," she says. "I heard someone walked into the police station this morning and confessed to killing your husband."

"*What*? What are you talking about?"

"I assumed you knew," Cassandra says. "Everyone knows everything around here."

She leads me up the stairs to the stern. Before I hop onto the dock, I ask her, "You know anything about hacked security cameras at the marina?"

She slides a pack of cigarettes out of her pocket and taps it on the base of her palm.

"Let it be, Isla," she replies.

40

I fast-walk to my truck parked on a side street a quarter mile away, not wanting to draw attention to myself breaking into a run. I text Ben as I go. *You there?*

Anything I write to him can and will be used against me, so that's as specific as I'm able to get right now.

I can't begin to guess who confessed to killing Clive. It can't be Charlotte. That woman intends to live a deliberate, unfettered life, free to con and seduce whoever catches her fancy. I plan to behave as if the cops are still after me, not least because of the phonied-up security footage Charlotte gave them. That's all they need to arrest me on violating the restraining order, and I'm not going to hand myself to them on a silver platter. I feel an urge to get out of town, even if for a few hours.

I'm out of breath when I make it to the truck. I pull the scrap I found in my father's papers out of the glove compartment.

Jane

175 Hawthorne Way, Salem.

I drive at a reasonable speed down Rte. 128. I imagine who this Jane person could be. She's a brown-haired fifty-something with bangs. *She's my father's accountant. No. She's an old friend from high school who slid into his DMs, and he met her for coffee for old time's sake and they hit it off like old pals.* She's got the answers I need wrapped up and waiting, tied in a pink bow. She'll serve me hot tea. My father will burst out of a back room and say, *Surprise, Isla girl. Sorry for all the cloak and dagger. It'll all be over soon, and life will get back to normal.*

I turn off the highway in Beverly, and the GPS leads me toward the water and over the Essex Bridge. Parking is a nightmare in this town, so I grab a spot on the street well before my destination and travel the rest of the way on foot.

I follow the red dot on the map and come upon 175 Hawthorne Way. It appears to be a small pirate's museum I've never heard of in an old building with wooden slats, possibly the originals, painted black, and a sign written in old tyme cursive: *Museum of North American Pirates.*

The map says this is the place, so this must be the place. Maybe Jane lives above the museum. I push the door, and as I step inside the darkened entryway, instead of a tinkling bell, the call of an overexcited man bellows out of a scratchy speaker, "Ahoy, matey! Shiver me timbers!"

I find the reception area, which contains a desk and a man who seems happy to greet me. He's dressed in full pirate regalia and sports a short black beard.

"*Arghhhh,*" he growls without a hint of self-consciousness. "Does ye fancy some pirate lore? Ye came to the right place!"

I try to keep my smile friendly, though I want to laugh. He's doing his job, and I would never want to hurt his feelings, but this scenario is so surreal it occurs to me I might be dreaming.

"*Garrrrr,*" I growl back gamely. "Could ye possibly tell me if Jane is working today?" I ask the question with the confidence of a person who knows Jane very well and has spoken to Jane often about her employment at the Museum of North American Pirates.

"Jane?" He squints. "Jane…"

"Jane," I confirm.

"I don't know any Jane," he says. "I'm the senior tour guide here. My mother is the director, but she won't be in today. Are you sure your friend's not working over at the Witches Museum?"

I don't say what I'm thinking, which is, I know the difference between a witch and a pirate. "Positive."

"Of course you are," he shakes his head. "You wouldn't be so silly as to confuse witches for pirates." He's earnest. I'd say he's in his mid-twenties.

"It's OK," I say. "What about in the past few years? Anyone with that name here?"

He squints again, and his heavily made-up eyes turn to black holes. "I don't know if I'm supposed to share private employee information…"

Now I've piqued his curiosity, which is not a good thing. "No, no, of course. I just…"

I'm about to spin a tale of an old high school best friend I lost touch with, but he's turned his back to me. This is a dead end. This note could be from any time, and maybe the rest of the message is, *Jane…who was never at this address.*

The pirate is hunched in his chair, and I hear papers shuffling.

"Hey, thank you for your help," I call, and turn to head out. I push open the door and it starts on me again. The animatronic pirates along the back wall are laughing evilly and repeating "Ahoy, matey! You've been sentenced to walk the plank!"

"Ma'am?"

I have my hand on the door handle. I turn to answer him. "Yes?"

"I *do* know a Jane, now that you mention it," he says. "Maybe she's the one you're looking for?"

He holds up a document.

I walk back in as he moves out from behind the desk, and I see he uses a wheelchair. He leads me to a back room with maps papering the walls. It smells musty, as if it's as old as its subject matter. He pulls his chair up to a table strewn with brochures.

"Have a seat," he offers. I sit across from him. "My mother knows much more about this than I do, but I can give you the basics. We don't feature this woman in our literature. She's mentioned only as a footnote on the tour these days, because she's lesser known and, sadly, the folks who come here tend to want the big names. Your Captain Kidds, your Blackbeards. Don't get me started on the wreck of the Whydah Gally. Black Sam Bellamy went down with his ship in 1717. Found off Cape Cod, but you can see some of its treasure down the street at the museum here in Salem. It's the only fully authenticated pirate treasure in the world."

"That's fascinating," I nod. I never studied pirates, never understood the fascination.

"If someone sent you to a pirate museum looking for a Jane," he says, "then I figure there's every chance they're talking about Jane Ree."

He spreads out some pages on the table and points to a passage. I lean in to read it.

Jane Ree was a pirate who stalked the New England coast in the late seventeenth century in the Golden Age of Piracy. Her most famous ship was the Red Ghost, thought to be carrying fine silks, jewelry, gold, and silver coins, and bullion. She was never captured, and no one knows what happened to her, but on his death bed, the pirate Hawthorne Buckley was said to have ordered his crew to find deposits Jane was rumored to have buried along Massachusetts' North Shore.

Some of the booty was alleged to be her own plunder. But it was also thought she stole from a ship she crewed on while disguised as a man named Gene Ree. Historians and experts believe she was a pirate in her own right for a time, but they add that it's unlikely Jane Ree was in the North Cape area long enough to bury treasure during the brief period she was active.

What does any of this have to do with my father? I'm trying to put the pieces together. They don't quite fit yet, though, because as much as I'd like to believe my father found buried treasure left by an obscure yet inspirational woman pirate, I have to believe there would've been signs. A map in the house. Dear old Dad going on a spending spree beyond a single Porsche hidden in his garage. Sharing the news with me. Something.

"I never knew any of this," I say to my pirate-loving friend. "Do you know which towns she was known to frequent?"

"I've heard talk about the Isles of Shoals up in New Hampshire, you know, standard stuff," he says. "But some say she was seen at night walking on the Cape at all hours. Marlin Bay, Manchester-on-Sea, even Sandburn. Most historians don't put much stock in those claims, though."

My face must be betraying my distraction, because he races to lure me back in. "That's not to say there's not treasure along the North Shore! They say there's a trove hidden in the cave at Dungeon Rock in Lynn. John Quelch had a two-million dollar treasure said to be at Star Island, or possibly just down the road in Marblehead."

"I have so much to learn," I say. "Thank you for everything. I'm not sure this is the Jane I'm looking for, but you never know. I'll leave you to your work."

I'd stick around to see what this guy's pirate expert mom knows about Jane Ree, but I have the modern world to deal with. I get in the truck, check my phone, but there's nothing from Ben. As uneasy as I feel about him right now, he's still the only person I can talk to about all this. It has occurred to me he's gone dark because the cops told him not to contact me. It occurs to me I'm going to be arrested as soon as I set foot back in town, but I'm willing to take that risk. I don't have a choice.

As I'm turning off Route 128 onto the road to Sandburn, a text comes through.

It's Ben.

Agnes in hospital. Don't know how bad it is

I'm about to pass the on-ramp. I hit the brakes in time and swerve back onto the highway toward Beverly.

41

I have experience slipping past emergency room staff, and I do it this time even though Beverly Hospital's waiting room is considerably less packed than Saint John's. I walk the halls and, within two minutes, I find Oyster emerging from a room, his hat off and his shoulders hunched.

"Oyster," I call to him, striding quickly, meeting him halfway as he moves down the hall.

My friend is shaking with grief. As I grow closer, I get a shock; it is rage, not sadness making him tremble. He's gritting his teeth and his nostrils are flaring. I haven't seen him like this since a new guy in town tried to sell him heroin as he helped a sword boat load provisions up in Goodstone a month after Oyster's son died of an overdose.

"Hey," I say gently. "You OK? How's Agnes? What happened?"

He comes at me, jamming his finger in my face, coming so close I can feel the vibration of his anger rattling the air.

"I—Oyster! What—"

"*You*," he growls. "You couldn't leave it, could you? I asked you to stop, but you were so stubborn. So fucking stubborn, Isla, just like your father."

"Back off and tell me what the hell's going on." I stand my ground.

"Agnes—" he clears his throat. "Agnes is in a hospital bed right now because her body couldn't take the stress of what she did for you. She went and confessed to the murder *you* committed."

He takes a deep breath and exhales with two words. "*Dammit, Agnes.*"

"Wait a goddamned minute," I snap. "First, I did not commit any murder, and you of all people know that! And second, what exactly did Agnes confess to, and why?"

I'm not going to crumble under this man's rage, as horrifying it is to have Uncle Oyster, Dad's best friend, his mentor, the one he set up a fundraiser for when Agnes needed an experimental medical treatment that costs tens of thousands of dollars, shouting at me with hatred in his eyes.

"She told Lilith she came upon your husband during one of her walks," he says. The darkness of the emotion directed at me clashes violently with the sterile white hallway. "She claims Clive attacked her, and she was forced to defend herself."

"I...I can't..." I can't comprehend what I'm hearing.

"If you're wondering how a seventy-seven-year-old woman with multiple sclerosis overcame a six-foot-tall young man, well, my Agnes says he stumbled and somehow ended up on his back, and she took the rake and stabbed him in the neck before he could get back up and attack her again.

"Thing is," he adds as I stand speechless, "she's got all kinds'a bruises and old scratches from her woodland walks and her falls. So the story's believable to the cops. All too believable."

That's one thing I can hit back at. "Lilith Wen is not going to believe Agnes Farnsworth killed anyone, and neither is the district attorney. Even if Lilith does arrest her, no one would prosecute her, Oyster!"

He's shaking his head. He's simmering down like a teakettle taken off the boil, but he's still furious at me.

"You know what the messed up thing about this whole nightmare is?"

I stand quietly, assuming it's a rhetorical question.

"You're sacrificing everything to find a father who wouldn't do the same for you. He *didn't* do the same for you. He abandoned you, but you won't abandon him. Worse, you've created a fantasy that Nick Banks was some hero. But we both know that's not true. You blindly blaze through everyone and everything to prove some kind of point you don't even understand yourself. You don't know what your father was into, Isla, and going around town saying he didn't do this or that, that he was entirely innocent, doesn't make it so."

I'm still unclear about why there's any crime in searching for a lost father and husband, but Oyster's old school, and he and many of his fellow Boomers in this town like to keep things quiet. Don't rock the boat. Pretend it's not happening. Leave it buried. Whatever *it* is. I'm not sure I'll ever know, at this rate.

"I'm not going to apologize for looking for my family," I say. "And I don't control what your wife does. What if it were you or Agnes out there, lost in the ocean for no fucking reason?" He's not the only one who can point fingers.

Oyster glares at me. His breathing is heavy. I hope he's not having a heart attack. He shakes his head and says, "You ever wonder why you're so obsessed with the beach but you'll never swim? You ever ask yourself why you and your father glamorize this strange obsession you've had since you were little? What kid doesn't play in the surf? What father doesn't take her to the park, to the Swan Boats in Boston, on a bike ride? Why were you always in the sand, Isla? Where was Father of the Year then?"

"Where is this coming from, Oyster?" I plead. "If you have all this anger toward me and my family, why didn't you say anything before now?"

It's always disconcerting when someone you're close to goes from friend to aggressor without any hints in the space between. I usually cut people out of my life for that. But Oyster…it's not so easy. Plus, it seems he might be doing the cutting himself, right here in the hospital.

"I did," he cries. "That's the problem. You didn't listen. You kept obsessing about the house, the woman, the search, when everyone on the Cape gave everything to find them. You didn't care who you hurt."

"I need to talk to Agnes," I say.

"The hell you do." Oyster stands firm, blocking my way, and his delivery carries a *You shall not pass* level of fierceness, so I back away.

One way or another, I will speak to her about this. Oyster has jostled something in my deepest memory, like sliding down a dune that's about to crumble into a landslide. When it will collapse, you don't know. How much force it will take is impossible to tell. But it's going to happen, and it's best not be under it when it does.

I race out of the hospital, laser focused on getting to my truck, and I almost collide with another distraught hospital visitor.

"Sorry," I mumble, and keep going.

"Isla?"

I stop and turn around. The voice from hell has seeped through the earth's crust and offended my ears.

"What are you doing here?" It comes out as a screech.

"I heard about Agnes," Charlotte purrs. Her hair is worn down, curled under, landing below her shoulder, and the change pings me because in all my days spying, she wore it in that slick, low pony. "Naturally, I came to see if they need anything, and to support Oyster."

"You don't even know them."

The slow smile, the one I'll see in my nightmares for years to come, spreads across her face like blood on a white handkerchief.

"I know people in this town. Better than you do in some cases, from what I've been able to gather," she says, her voice smooth as Matty's aioli. "I noticed you noticing me and my date at The Pearl. Sorry you had to find out that way."

I curl my right fist, picturing my knuckles smashing her lip into her teeth.

Stay calm. She wants you to attack her.

I'm not a violent person, but on a scale of one to ten, I'm at an eleven. Double digits demand blood.

"I know you've been watching me for months, Isla banks," Charlotte says, and if I didn't know better, I'd say she's flirting with me. "I know you've seen the men's jacket at the bar in my home, the shadow of a male figure in the background, the kisses I've blown to him in another room. He never let you see him.

He knew you'd be jealous and come for both of us if you found out we were together."

Breathe, Isla girl.

I am, Dad. I'm still alive, aren't I?

"You and Ben?" I try my best to sound calm and neutral, but my voice comes out squeaky. "You're telling me you two have been dating?"

I think back to every time I thought another person was skulking around the glass house with her. I remember the messy foyer when Charlotte invited me inside. The jackets, the fleece, the raincoats. I picture the royal blue windbreaker that looked a lot like the one owned by our trusty Harbormaster, Ben Cassidy. Recognizing someone on the water out here is the color of a jacket, of a fleece or a hat, the barnacles on a boat, the name painted on the side. Not the faces or the names of the people as they race by, heads down, their features indistinguishable, but the mark of their possessions.

"I wouldn't call what we're doing dating," Charlotte says. "It's deeper than that. I'm surprised you didn't pick up on it until now. Denial is a powerful thing…"

I wasn't sure whether to trust Ben's texted apologies after the ambush at the train station, but in this moment, Charlotte has told me everything I need know about him, and about how I'm going to proceed from here to prove my innocence.

More to the point, how I'm going to prove Charlotte's guilt.

I leave her standing alone in the parking lot.

The Sandburn High School varsity lacrosse team won the state championships one time. Ben was the star. He was a junior, and the captain, and the MVP of the tournament. After the school-wide celebration, a smaller crew headed to the dunes at Castle Neck and built a bonfire in the powdery white sand.

Ben was like a celebrity that night. Michele, the pretty freshman cheerleader, was following him everywhere, and next to me by the fire, Shana and her crew of cool girls were plotting, giggling, taking bets on who'd get him, who should try.

He smiled at me across the bonfire. I smiled back. The smores were a fail, because there is no marshmallow hot enough to melt a cold Hershey bar on a cold graham cracker, but I ate mine anyway, and got sticky fluff on my mouth, chin, fingers.

I walked away from the fire to clean myself up and get away, because for an introvert, social events are endured in shifts.

Ben met me at the base of the dune. We were out of the flickering light of the fire, and he was a tall, dark shape in front of me. He took my hand, and I followed like I was caught in a tractor beam. We sat together in the sand, thighs touching, watching the stars and the fire in the distance.

"You're kind of a big deal," I said.

"You're not impressed," he replied. He reached out and I flinched, but he kept coming. "You've got marshmallow on your chin." He wiped it off.

"I never said that," I insisted. "I *am* impressed you've got half the girls at Seagrass High chasing you just because you can throw a ball with a net on a stick."

He threw his head back and laughed, and leaned into me, and I rested my head on his shoulder.

"I can't help it if I'm devastatingly attractive," he said.

"You're seventeen. Give it time." We were quiet for a moment, and I heard people calling for him. The MVP couldn't go missing for long, not when there were beer bongs to do.

"Do you think we'll be friends forever?" I was thinking of college, of our divergent plans and dreams, of our fathers' rift that had proved to be permanent.

"I hope not," he said.

"Stop it." I sat up and jostled his shoulder with mine.

He turned to face me. I looked up at him.

"I mean it. I don't want to be your friend, Isla. Don't pretend you don't know that."

I knew it was coming, and I could've stopped it before we even got to the dune. I leaned in without meaning to, and we met halfway. His lips met mine for the first time since we'd shared a peck on a junior-high party dare. This one was as real as it got, buzzed by an attraction neither of us had control over.

He ran his fingers through my hair, pressed harder, tried to lean me back. I pulled away.

"I—I'm sorry," I said. "I just…shouldn't. I…um…" I babbled while he gazed at me cooly with some amusement and some confusion.

I didn't want to be *the one* that night. I didn't want to be his post-game conquest or the girl he couldn't get, the challenge, the new high he chased after the post-game adrenaline crash.

"That's fine," he said. "I can wait."

He leapt to his feet and offered his hand. I took it, he helped me up, and we walked together down the dune, back to the fire. I saw the rest of the girls try that night, from freshmen to seniors, watched them laugh at everything he said, sit in his lap, feed him smores.

Ben didn't hook up with any of them that night.

Ten minutes after Charlotte's ambush I'm outside his house. I know he's not on marine patrol, and the tide's high and useless for clamming. The odds are on my side. I knock, and I yell, not caring if the neighbors hear, knowing the fear of that very indiscretion will make him come to the door faster.

"Bennnn. Ben Cassidy! Come on out. I'll wait as long as I have to. We need to talk."

I hear footsteps, and I prepare myself for the big talk we need to have, like I practiced on the way over here.

42

I shower for the first time in days, shave, blow my hair dry. I feel human, and with the last gasps of winter sticking around like houseguests you can't get rid of no matter how many hints you give them, I build a fire.

As I poke the kindling to bring the flames to life, the doorbell rings. I rise, brush off my hands, and throw open the door.

"You're early," I smile.

Ben holds up a grocery bag. "This thing's leaking. May I?"

"Please," I smile, unsure what he's got up his sleeve. He brushes past me and rubs my arm as he goes.

I lock the door and follow him to the kitchen, where he's already unpacking. I see two bottles of my favorite wine, a viognier no one sells for twenty miles, a bag of fresh linguine, and a tub of littlenecks.

"The beauty of Clams ala Ben is that it's super-fast," he says. "All I need is for you to direct me to a pasta pot. I can find the rest." He swivels around the small kitchen. "I hope so, anyway. I forgot the Bankses aren't a family of chefs."

"We're more like barbecuers," I admit. "Or taker-outers."

I reach over him and grab a bottle of wine. "I'll pour."

I grab two white wine glasses from the cupboard, which I'm certain was stocked and organized by Angélica, open the wine, and taste it before pouring two full glasses.

"Ah, that's good," I say, and it hits me that I'm having a cozy dinner while I may or may not be about to be arrested for the most heinous crime our constitution recognizes.

That, I think, was Ben's plan. Bless him.

As the pasta water heats up, he roots around for cooking-related items while I sit at the island drinking wine.

"At least we've confirmed Charlotte's not as smart as she thinks," I say. "As if I'd believe you two were an item."

"I appreciate your faith in me," he says. He's found a knife and is chopping garlic. "Then again, you were quick to believe I'd ratted you out to the cops. If I didn't know you better, I'd be profoundly insulted."

He adds olive oil to a sauté pan he miraculously found. He wasn't kidding. This is speed cooking.

"Can you blame me? I bought the train ticket at the last second, and you were the only person I told."

"The staties have all sorts of wacky ways of finding people," he says with a dash of snark. "Like following a murder suspect's credit card charges in real time."

"Well...duh."

As soon as Charlotte tried to tell me she and Ben were romantically involved, I knew she was lying about everything, and that the "date" I saw was a setup. I suspected, but I wasn't sure, and the worry nagged at me until her ambush. Ben and I ironed a few things out two hours ago in his living room, but he was running out to watch Lola's soccer practice, so he promised to come clear the air tonight. I, for one, am happy he's clearing said air with pasta and wine. My self-care has been nonexistent for too long.

"So? Can we address the British elephant in the room?"

"You got a decent cheese grater anywhere?" He's holding a ragged hunk of parmigiano Reggiano. I point to the cabinet next to the oven, and he roots around. "I was in the Pearl helping Frank behind the bar. His trainee called in sick."

"A *fourth* job?" Ben is going to wear himself out before he's forty. If he makes it that long.

"Joe's a friend. I was helping him out. That's all." He emerges from behind the island holding a vintage cheese grater that's probably as dull as a rubber hose. "Charlotte somehow knew I was there, or maybe she goes there all the time. Who knows. Anyway, she laid it on thick about how fascinated she was by clamming, and I agreed to have a drink with her to see what I could find out. I played her game."

"And?"

"I learned she's a little obsessed with you," he says as he grates the cheese into a fine fluff. "She made it seem like she was trying to get to know me, but it was all about you. How long have we known each other, what was the state of our relationship, why you don't like it here. She wanted to make sure we were seen, so word would get back to you. It worked better than she'd planned, I think."

"What did she learn about you?" I ask slyly.

"She learned I have three jobs, am single, have a daughter, and I love pina coladas and walks in the rain. Oh, and that I'll never live anywhere but Sandburn because I can't imagine anywhere better."

He's grated a pyramid of parm while I've grown nice and buzzed on wine.

He's never said anything around me about being unattached, and I'm feeling a level of relief I shouldn't. We both need to move on for real, and even though I've been terrible at it, he still has a chance.

"Why don't you check on the fire?" he suggests. "Ten minutes to dinner."

I toss back my drink and polish off my first glass. "Easy on the wine," he says. "I need it for the recipe."

"Not my problem," I wink, then leave the kitchen as ordered.

Ben twirls linguine around his fork.

"Pirates," he says. He takes a bite, chews, sets down his fork. "Pirates? I never thought to suspect *pirates* in any of this."

I swirl some pasta around the garlicky butter, wine and olive oil sauce on my plate, and take a messy bite. This dish is next level, and I feel myself growing jealous of the woman who gets to eat Clams ala Ben for life. I sip some wine, then reply, "Tell me about it. I tend to think that scrap of paper with 'Jane's' name on it could be literally anything."

"Well, not *anything*," he argues. "The address did send you to the pirate museum. It would explain all your father's extracurricular digging…his secretiveness…his sudden influx of cash."

"Do we know it was sudden, though? For all we know, he's mortgaged this house to the hilt. Or got a Robin Hood complex in his later years."

"And got the bags of gold how? Robbing banks?"

My food is gone, the clam shells left on a side dish, a slick of oil and butter and flecks of parsley all that's left on my plate. My eyes go to the distinctive round bottle of Blanton's on my father's mini bar, where Malibu rum left over from my college years gathers dust next to unopened cheap brandy someone gave him in the nineties. My father is of the "liquor can't go bad" school of expired food and drink. The good stuff, the Blanton's, is running out like a timer. There are a few fingers-worth left, from the same bottle my father served Clive from on what was possibly his last night alive.

"I have a bunch of pieces of the puzzle now," I say, "but no idea how they fit together, or what the picture on the box is."

Ben drains the last of the wine with one long sip, then says, "You have some good evidence. The bizarre videos of Clive's double, life, the doctor up in Canada, the embezzling…"

"Which actually points to me," I wince. "I've got nothing that would tantalize the cops more than a murder weapon with my fingerprints and my father's name on it."

The fire crackles as it begins to die.

"Fair point," he says. "So, let's get off defense. It's not enough to try to show law enforcement you didn't do it. Let's give them a viable suspect. Because if you don't, either you or Agnes are going down for this."

"I know," I say. "Any idea how to achieve this feat?"

He rests his elbows on the table.

"Fuck it," he says after a few moments. "Go meet with Lilith."

"I don't have a lawyer yet." I shake my head.

"Go there and get *her* to talk. You do that for a living, right? Use what you know to manipulate her into giving up the information you need."

I take his suggestion into consideration. The wine is messing with my head, and my thoughts float to the secrets in this town. Clams are the only thing people here like to dig up; secrets are meant to stay buried. I want answers that no one can give me.

Why do I dream of sandcastles? Why is a bed of sand my safe place, not warm, soft blankets like normal people? Vague memories, sensory imprints, the feel of the sand, the whoosh of the waves. The fat seagulls squawking at me.

I ask him, "Do you remember when we used to play while our fathers were digging?"

"Of course. Bits of it, anyway. Images. I was too young to really remember many specifics."

"I remember being alone in the sand a lot," I say. "My father used to take me out all over Sandburn's flats, the big ones, small ones, hidden ones. And he…he wasn't there. My memories are all of me alone, playing, singing, staying away from the water."

"You think your father left a four-year-old alone on the sand while he went to work?"

"I'm sure someone was watching me," I reply.

"But you couldn't see or hear them?" Ben is listening intently, like he's been waiting for this strange, vague conversation to happen, and he has answers ready.

That's all it takes. Ben's question loosens the truth out of my brain like salt out of a grinder.

"What are you getting at?" I ask him.

I know, though.

Finally, I know.

I shake off the melancholy, stand, take my plate and stack it on his. "You cooked, I clean," I say.

He rises. "That wasn't the deal. I'm here to give you a break, even if it's just from a few dishes for one night."

I move into the kitchen and set the plates next to the sink. He is suddenly next to me.

"What did I just say?" His body is touching mine.

"I want to help," I protest. It comes out as a croak.

He looks down at me, and I look up at the brown eyes I've loved for most of my life.

"I meant it when I said we were through last time," I whisper.

"So did I," he says, his lips inching closer, his breath smelling of wine.

"This is a terrible idea." *Shut up, Isla.*

His lips are about to brush mine. I can feel his hand gripping my upper arm, his hips pushing into me. And then he pulls away.

"You're right," he says. "We know where this leads."

He pulls back, and his face is unreadable.

Why must I test him every single time? Why can't I be normal? Why can't I let myself be happy? Why am I so afraid to be home?

I'm emotional from exhaustion and wine, and my face is scrunched up in preparation for an involuntary cry. Ben, seeing this, gives me pass.

"Let's get these dishes done," he says casually, brightly. "And after a good night's sleep, you'll enact our dastardly plan, and then you'll be free and this will all be over."

I laugh, get a grip on myself, and start rinsing.

43

Since the day I worked on my first crime story as a working journalist, I've shaken my head at suspects who are stupid enough to speak to the cops without an attorney. There are no exceptions. No matter what, keep your mouth shut. Or, as the social media attorneys like to say, *Shut the fuck up.*

Even if you think you're smarter than law enforcement, remain silent, because if they want to get you they will. Even the dumb ones can outsmart you. They're allowed to lie, and only *they* know their true agenda during an interview. You might think you know, but if you're wrong, the stakes are catastrophically high.

And yet here I am, back in the dystopian interrogation room voluntarily talking to Chief Lilith Wen. Worse, something's different about her now. After the men's disappearance, she was annoyed at my perseverance, but her irritated sighs were sprinkled with a dash of grudging respect and a pinch of understanding. When Clive came back and threw me under the bus, her anger was served up with a dollop of doubt, hold the sympathy.

Not today. Today, my erstwhile babysitter appears to genuinely believe I murdered my husband.

"If you have evidence germane to this case, by all means, let's see it," Lilith is saying. "And no, I cannot discuss any other persons of interest, including Agnes Farnsworth. The state police are covering every base and chasing every lead. Until we've completed our investigation, we'll consider all the evidence. No one has identified a suspect in this case yet."

"Sure you have," I say. "You decided I was guilty on day one."

"Notice you're still free," Lilith snaps.

I get it; we're both playing our best hand, trying to out-psych the other. May the best woman win.

"Even though you have no alibi to speak of," she adds, folding her hands on the table. "'Home alone sleeping' is a tough sell. Plus, it was your father's clamming rake that killed Mr. Hooghiemster, *and* your fingerprints were all over it."

She leans forward, locks eyes with me. "We can end this right now. Don't you want it to be over? Everyone will understand," she says. "You'll have to face consequences for what you did, but we can mitigate them. Help me help you. I'll make sure the DA knows Clive was an abuser. No one would blame you. If it was self-defense, tell me. That changes everything."

I smile as if I appreciate her phony sympathy.

"That's a hell of a story," I say. "But there are several problems with your assumptions."

"Oh?" Lilith says, still playing good cop. Playing like she's my friend.

"The murder weapon isn't my father's clamming fork."

"Why do you say that?" The chief appears intrigued, but also exasperated that I didn't spill like a gutted bass.

"It can't have been his," I shrug. "He lost it in the marsh two years ago. It was a big deal because I gave it to him when I was young, embossed it with his name, and he thought it was the best gift ever. He used it for years until it rusted, and then he threw it at Old Caleb during an argument about the Red Sox's new short stop. He thought he'd just go back and easily find it in the shallows but he lost in the weeds. It was never seen again."

Lilith shakes her head with a confidence of a woman who is certain of her facts.

"I don't know what your father lost or when, but the rake that killed your husband belonged to Nicholas Banks, and your fingerprints were on it. I'm afraid there's no talking your way out of this one."

I shake my head hard and fast. "You're lying. There's no way you have Nick's engraved rake."

Lilith pushes back from the table with a shriek of chair legs on linoleum flooring, rises, and leaves the room. I remain still. I know I'm being recorded.

A minute later Lilith opens the door, slams it behind her, and sits across from me again. She slaps a file down on the table.

"I'll warn you: These images are graphic. You don't have to look if you're not up to it," she says magnanimously. "But if you want to face the truth and understand that we have the evidence whether you want to believe it or not, it's in your best interest to face it head-on. Now's the time, while things are still quiet. We're waiting for the Dutch embassy to reach Clive's family to make the notification, and once that happens, this case will make national news. Nothing will be the same around here. You know that better than anyone."

She opens the folder and slides it over to me. The images are face-up and visible in all their bloody gore. The color photos depict my husband splayed out on his back in the sand, clamming fork stuck in his neck, the handle resting on his chest like a calling card from Nick Banks. Sadly, there aren't any written reports in the folder; Lilith wasn't going to risk it, I presume, so I'll make do with the photos, which are what I wanted all along anyway.

I had to make up the lost rake story so she'd show me the crime scene. The myopic Sandburn cops aren't going to know what to look for around Clive's sandy deathbed. I stare at the rake, eyes wide as if I'm shocked at the sight. Lilith believes she's proving me wrong with these photographs. Au contraire. She gave me exactly what I wanted.

I look for anything out of place around Clive's body, any clue to who might've done this and framed me for it. I shuffle through the photos until I find one with a closer look at Clive's cold, dead hands. His right one is in a grasping pose, like a claw.

I flip through a few more as quickly as I can and find one shot from a greater distance, and place it next to the photo of his frozen hand. BINGO. With the images side-by-side, I see it. It's shining under the police lights if you look close enough, though most of it is buried in sand on the Millers' beach, about three feet away from the body.

"I can tell you who killed Clive," I tell Lilith as I memorize everything about the photograph before she whips the folder away from me. "And I know how we're going to prove it."

44

I place the tip of my index finger next to the shining piece of jewelry on the glossy photo.

"See that?" I ask her. She pulls the folder in her direction.

"See what?" She's squinting.

"It's a silver chain," I say. "I assume it's in evidence, because if it's not, that means someone didn't do their job."

"That's none of your concern," she snaps.

"You're trying to put me in prison for life. Everything about this is my fucking concern."

The refreshing thing about our new relationship is that I no longer have to appease her. I'm out of fucks to give.

"Say it *is* a piece of women's jewelry. It could be yours," Lilith says.

"It's not," I say. "Everyone knows I don't wear jewelry, including you. This isn't just a chain. It has, or had, a unique pink stone on it."

"There were no gems, stones or other shiny objects around the body," Lilith says.

"Charlotte James wears a rose quartz necklace," I inform her. "She wears it all the time and plays with it when she's nervous. It means something to her. If she lost it, that's going to be a problem for her."

I noticed the necklace during my first encounter with Charlotte, and again when we took a hot tub. Half the women I know in New York have hunks of the pink stone on their nightstands, on their wrists, on their desks at work. Rose quartz, in addition to helping to give Magenta Shores its color, is considered a fertility booster. You're supposed to keep it close to you to get the full benefit of its vibrations.

"I'm telling you it's there. Put the work in and search the Millers' beach."

Lilith doesn't flinch. "You think I don't do my job," she says. "I get it. I'm done defending this department to you. You're caught, Isla. You have no evidence to justify allowing an expensive search for a little stone in a sea of sand."

In the past she would've been intrigued, trusted me, knew there was truth in what I said. Today she's talking to a murderer who will say anything to save herself.

"This isn't about you!" I gesture at her with both hands. "I'm telling you that necklace belongs to Charlotte. This is so obviously a setup. Do you seriously think I'm going to go out and murder my husband at the house where I'm not legally allowed to be, leave my father's beloved clamming rake sticking out of his neck, and make sure my fingerprints are slathered all over it?"

"It sure looks that way," Lilith replies.

"If you and the staties or the FBI or whomever sifts through the sand around the body, you'll find Charlotte's pink stone," I say. "I think she lured Clive out there with a cover story, whether for a romantic beach walk or she claimed she saw a prowler, and when she attacked, he tore her necklace off defending himself."

"You're telling me that petite woman took down your husband?"

"Maybe she had help, or maybe…"

Something occurs to me.

"Maybe he was in on it…at first. Maybe they were setting something up for a photo or a scam, only she killed him for real when he was vulnerable. That would explain how someone her size was able to take him down so neatly. Or maybe she drugged him, then got him out there, he wobbled, reached for her necklace, tore it off, the charm went flying while the chain fell to the sand…"

"But why? What's Charlotte's motive? There's no evidence she ever met your husband, let alone had a reason to kill him."

I watch her body language, her expression, her eyes. If I was a betting woman, and I am, I'd say she genuinely has not connected Clive with Charlotte. Which is *not* a good thing for me, because linking those two grifters is exactly what I need to steer the cops away from me as their only suspect.

"Regardless," Lilith goes on, "Charlotte James has an alibi. A damn good one. She was at home on a property with cameras at every angle. Whereas you, on the other hand, have no witnesses to your whereabouts."

I'm not going to melt the way she thinks I will.

"So what you're saying is, Charlotte's alibi is footage I know for a fact she altered."

"No," Lilith shakes her head. "The smart home doesn't lie. It has her entering at six p.m. the night before and not leaving until after Carter arrived."

I stand up. "I've got to go."

"We're not finished." She stands too, her tone like she's an animal trainer and I'm a bad dog.

"Am I under arrest?"

I wait. We face off. She closes her eyes as if she's being forced to unleash Jeffrey Dahmer, Charles Manson and the BTK Killer on the world all at once.

"Not at this time."

I tear out of the room before she can change her mind.

In my truck, I rifle around in the glove compartment and find some old sticky notes and a pen and get to work. When I've drawn the best likeness I can, I head to the Rusty Lantern.

I figure there's a fifty-fifty chance the guys I'm looking for will be there now.

Chance is on my side today. He's sitting at a table with Joe and Frank finishing off a ketchup-smothered burger.

"Shep," I say, standing over him as he dabs the sides of his mouth with a paper napkin, the messy condiment coating his fingers like blood. "You said you needed something solid to grip onto. Grip onto this."

I slap the paper down, turn on my heel, and walk out of the bar.

I'm not counting on my sketch of Charlotte's rose quartz pendant and a terse note scrawled on a sticky note to inspire Shep and my father's other friends to get involved, so it's quite possible this is over. The entire police department is dying for an excuse to arrest me. I'm not allowed on the Millers' property, but there's no other way to prove my innocence.

A few hours later, at high tide when there's no clamming to be done, I wait in the woods with a view of the Millers' beach, as if divine intervention will strike me like lightning. I'm drawn to that sand as forcefully as magnetite is to iron at the beach. I've seen it myself, when my father would bring a magnet from my toy box and watch some of the crystals move and jump like they were alive.

I stare at the patch of sand where the gem most likely is.

Do it.

Don't do it. Save your life; run.

Do it. It's the only way.

It's an impossible choice. It's roulette, but the stakes are my life, and I'm only thirty-four years old.

"Don't, Isla. We've got this." A man's voice comes from behind me, cutting through the sound of rustling leaves.

I know who it is without turning around.

Shep lays a hand on my shoulder. I feel my father channeled through his chapped hand, big as a starfish and just as rough.

What can Shep and a few of his old clammer friends possibly do to fix this? I turn to him, a sad smile on my face, hoping in the gloom he can't see my eyes glistening. He's not looking, anyway. He's focused on the beach beyond, and now he's heading to the Millers' house.

I break past the tree line and see what Shep is walking toward, and all I can do is stare.

45

There are more than twenty of them lined up, a dozen on each side of the beach like a game of Red Rover with grizzled grownups as the players. Linda, Old Caleb, Ben. Ben's talking to someone next to him, telling him how to tackle the sand; I can tell by his gesturing. Smithy, Frank, Joe. And Cassandra, who only digs for clams when her nieces and nephews visit, but knows these shores and these waters as well as God does. There are some I don't know. I don't see Oyster, but I'm sure he's busy caring for Agnes. And also he hates me. But that's not important right now.

"We're looking for a gemstone the size of an olive," Shep yells out, his voice echoing through the wood, across the sand. "It's rose quartz. If anyone can find it, it's this motley crew. We'll be cutting a swath from where I'm standing, then diagonal up to the house."

He throws two arms toward the house like he's directing traffic. Sandburn's finest shellfishers are holding every tool in their arsenal. Metal strainers, spades, rakes, buckets, shovels.

None of them are wearing gloves. I don't see a pair among them. They will need their raw skin, their senses, their fingers to feel for a lone piece of gravel among trillions of grains. I lean on an oak. I need the mighty trunk to hold me up as I absorb what the townspeople are doing for my father, and for me.

Out of the quiet comes the subtle scream of a panicked woman.

Charlotte runs out of the house barefoot, nervous and high-pitched. Her hair is down, wind blowing it around her face. She's wearing pajama bottoms. *Not so put-together when you're not in control, are you, Char?*

"Um, hello? Hi! Can I help you?" She's smiling, trying to sound friendly and helpful, but her gummy, toothy grin and subtext of *Get the fuck off my property* shines through.

I hide behind the oak, out of her sight, in shadow. Will it end here? If anyone can stand up to Charlotte without being accused of harassing or threatening the delicate English rose, it's Shep Clancy.

"Good afternoon, ma'am," Shep says, meeting her halfway in the middle of the two lineups, like two gladiators.

"I'm sorry for the unannounced visit. I rang your bell, but I guess you didn't hear us."

"I have only just returned home," she says. "I'm sure you understand it's quite upsetting to see an army of strangers on my property. I'd like it if you and your friends would kindly leave."

"The thing is, Miss James," Shep says slowly, calmly, convivially, "Millie and Harold were friends of this community, and they've let me know I'm welcome to use their property at any time. Now, I could call 'em. I could get their permission, or perhaps their daughter's permission. I could do that."

Charlotte is frozen in place. He's got her. She must've been appeasing locals from day one, because they seem to know her, and she didn't go directly to calling the cops upon seeing a crowd of clammers descending on her lawn of sand.

"Or, you could be kind enough to let us proceed for the benefit of the Sandburn community. You see, something's been lost. And with a case as serious as murder, well, we watch out for our own. We gotta do everything we can to see justice is done."

"What's been lost?" Charlotte squeaks. The accent's sliding again as she begins to panic. I *knew* she was putting on the posh.

"We'll know when we find it, ma'am," he says, tipping his hat, a frayed baseball cap, to her. "Now, mind if we get going before we lose the light?"

Shep's height and his presence, a kindly yet stern and authoritative manner, gets him places I'd never get as a woman.

"There are so many of you," Charlotte says desperately. "I'm concerned you'll dig up our beach like a common—"

"You have my word your beach will be left in perfect condition," Shep says. "In fact, aerating the sand is good for the environment and for the appearance of your property."

Oh, he's good. I smile to myself. He's got her.

"Dig all you want." She throws up her arms, then crouches, roots around, apparently searching for something. She throws some sand in the air. "All you'll find are bits of rubbish, soda can tops, bits of old beer cans, things left behind by the construction workers twenty years ago." She tosses them in the air. "The bloody slobs left so much litter. Typical of the townies—"

She stops herself. A tide of crimson washes across her face. I can see it from where I'm hiding. "Anyway. Dig away, gentlemen. And ladies. Best of luck to you."

There is no starting call, no whistle; Shep bends over and begins digging. He's closest to the body, where the forensics team ostensibly already searched, but you never know.

They work silently, some straddling and bending, some sinking to their knees, all of them focused on their own patch of sand. This is what we do. It's what we were meant to do. I wish I could be out there, but it's not my time.

No one looks in my direction nor do they worry about the house. It is only the ground, the job at hand, the digging the sifting as they search. They're used to discarding 99% of what they find in search of the one gem, in this case, a literal jewel.

I grow nervous and start to bite my thumbnail as they march forward, closer and closer to meeting in the center, without finding the quartz. They don't give up, they don't grumble. Sometimes they stretch, sometimes they grunt, sometimes they sneeze.

The two groups are staggered now with the front four on both sides getting closer like opposing teams in a football game. From where I stand, I estimate there's anywhere from two to six feet of unsifted sand between them.

It feels like it's over.

And then I hear the beautiful music of the grouchiest clammer in the land, Old Caleb himself, calling out three life-changing words as he holds up a cupped hand: "I got it!"

Shep walks to him and, appropriate or not, applause, whoops and a few laughs erupt from the group. Perhaps not so much because he found the vital item but because, for maybe the first time in decades, Old Caleb is smiling. Shep gives him a nod of thanks and takes the stone, examines it between his thumb and forefinger, holds it up to the last of the day's sun.

"We're done here," he says.

I run out of the woods to see the gem, to check it and thank the searchers, but Ben races toward me, pushing silently, shaking his head. "Get back! *Don't*, Isla."

He's right; it takes only one step to trespass, and for me to be breaking the law. I fade back into the woods.

"We're gonna get this to the police," Shep says, pulling a plastic baggie from his pocket, dropping the stone in, and sealing it. "It's their job to say why this is so important."

Shep and the gang head back to the front of the home, and another handful push out their skiffs and motor home through the cold bay.

Charlotte screeches from her doorway as the fishers head out, none of them paying attention, not even throwing her a glance back.

"You could've planted that! This is all a big show. That could be *anyone's* pendant. You've got it all wrong. Wait and see!"

She is alone, screeching into the wind, as Ben leads me away through the woods.

46

L ilith won't want to see my face right now, so I head to the hospital to see Agnes and Oyster. I make it to her room before he confronts me in the hallway.

"I told you to stay away." He's less angry now, more agonized. "Agnes needs her rest. She's still under observation. Couldn't take the stress of talking to the cops, and she fainted and hit her head."

"Jeremiah. Let us talk." Agnes's voice floats out of the room, quiet and firm.

Oyster nods to no one, defeated, exhausted. He shuffles away, finding a piece of wall to lean against.

"Hi, Agnes," I say from the doorway.

She beckons me in, makes a patting motion toward the chair next to her bed. The seat is still warm from Oyster's vigil.

"I thought you knew," she says. Her white hair is spread over the pillow. "This whole time, I thought you understood everything."

The words tumble out of her throat like gravel. I offer her some water from the plastic cup on the side table. She takes it and drinks.

"I don't know if my memories are of what happened, or if they're images I created based on what people told me later," I tell her. "If I made up a story to fill in the blanks. So many blanks."

My shoulders relax, my posture settles, my lungs expand. For the first time in weeks, I feel safe. No longer alone.

"I was on my night walk," Agnes says. "I never miss it if I'm well enough. The sound of the woods, of every living thing within them, collides with the sound of the ocean after everyone else is asleep, and it's richer than I imagine it to be anywhere else on earth. How many people get to hear a gull cry in response to an owl's hoot? That night, though, I heard the call of a human. A child's song coming from the edge of the wood. I was certain I was imagining it. I was hearing Jack as a child, playing with his stuffed animals and making up songs about them.

"I walked toward the sound. And there you were," she says, breaking into a smile. "Sweet little Isla. You weren't even five yet. You wouldn't let anyone short-change you: I'm not four, I'm four-and-a-half!"

I laugh through the tears that have begun to settle in my eyes. There's nothing I can do to hold them back, and I don't want to.

"You'd built a tiny city for yourself on the beach, a few paces from the woods. Sandcastles and a fort, roads, a bed, a pillow. You'd dug yourself into the ground to sleep, and the sand was your blanket. You'd been there, alone, from afternoon until one in the morning."

I swallow. "If you hadn't been there…"

"You were sunburned, and *so* dehydrated," she recalls. "But you were alive and unharmed. Nick did something right. He taught you to never go near the water without an adult holding your hand. And you didn't. I found you at high tide, and you hadn't moved from where Nick left you. You kept saying it, over and over. *No water. No water. No water. See?"*

I remember two strong, sure hands hooking under my armpits, pulling me up, holding me to a chest, and carrying me, cooing in my ear, singing me home. Gentle, whispered sweetness, like an angel. *I'm thirsty*, I said.

"You were real," I say. "The angel was you."

"I was there," she replies. "I'm glad I was. But I'm earthbound. I'm no angel."

"I remember a stray dog kept me company," I say, feeling a pang of longing. "I named him Scruffy." My father knew he could never take care of a dog, so we never had pets, but he couldn't take the memory of Scruffy from me. "Was he ever taken in, or rescued? Did anyone ever find him?" *Was he real?*

Agnes swishes her head back and forth on the pillow. "My dear, Scruffy wasn't a dog," she says. "There were nocturnal animals all around. I had to shoo away a mama coyote with a den not far from where your father left you.

"The locals liked to believe you were saved by the motherly instincts of a wild animal, like a children's bedtime story. The experts said you likely survived because the eating was good that year. Prey animals were overpopulating the area, so the coyotes were well-fed. If it'd been a drought or a bad year, if they'd been hungry…"

"You 'shooed' a wild animal that could've eaten you alive?" I take a sharp breath in. "You're tough."

"Other people are afraid of the woods at night," Agnes says, her voice growing stronger by the minute. "Not me. The moon guides me, my flashlight, my knife, my wits. Nature is not the enemy."

I'm listening, and I'm formulating questions so fast they keep getting lost amongst each other. "How could my father have done that? How can he take his little girl out to the beach and leave her after he finished work? That's…"

Agnes sighs. "Human beings are nothing if not flawed," she says.

"There's no excuse for what he did."

"Ah, Isla. Excuses are for the perpetrators to escape responsibility. Reasons are for us to understand why it happened. Your parents had reasons. No one is excusing them. Your parents weren't ready for you. After you were born, they simply didn't know what they were doing. And when you were old enough for nursery school, your mother was living part-time in Boston, trying to get her career going. Nick wasn't used to being your sole caretaker. To go to the beach with you and, then come back to his house without you, was normal to him because your mother would often pick you up from the flats while he kept working."

I'm not buying it.

"No one's ever ready to be parents," I argue. "A lot of people lose their minds when they bring home a screaming baby. There must be something more to it. Who leaves a child in the woods by the ocean alone all day and night?"

"Your parents made a bad mistake, and they were punished dearly for it," Agnes says. "Everyone in town knew about it, and the state made a show of stepping in. Oyster and I offered to foster you. You lived with us for a year until you were almost six. You were like our own. You were my baby for that year, Isla, and I loved you as much as a mother could love her own child."

Loved. One word in the past tense carries a surprisingly heavy pain with it.

"If that's true, Agnes," I say, "why have you…why does it seem like you've disliked me for so long? Did I do something to anger you?"

"It wasn't anger, Isla." Oyster's voice comes from the doorway. He's been listening, and now he enters the room and stands on the other side of the bed next to Agnes. "It was unbearable heartbreak. Losing Jack turned her into a different person. Losing you, well…she grew more attached to you than she expected. It was like tearing her second child away from her. She couldn't take the pain." He coughs. "*We* couldn't."

I reach for a tissue from the box on the side table.

"So why cut me out of her life? I don't understand…"

"You don't have to understand," Oyster replies. "She coped the way that worked for her. It doesn't have to make sense to anyone but her."

He clears his throat and shoots a look to his wife, who nods.

"Agnes knew we'd have to give you back," Oyster goes on. "But after a year, we thought they'd given up, that maybe it was best for you to live with us. We know, we know." He holds his hands up as if he's ashamed to even think it. "It was a silly dream, and one that would never be the best thing for you. Your father knew it, too. Nick picked you up the *second* the law allowed. Eight a.m. on the dot on that last day, he was at our house."

Agnes lays a hand on his. "There's something else you should know," Oyster says to me. "Your mother was living part-time in Boston, crashing with a friend, interning, filling in at the station, doing everything to get a foothold. Nick's neglect didn't just hurt you. It hurt your mother."

"How?" I'm not sure I want the answer.

"Nick let you believe Tanya was given the opportunity to come back and be your mom, but chose her career over you," Oyster says. "That's a lie. Your mother wasn't given a chance. She was deemed a bad parent, too, for being at work when you were abandoned, and because she wasn't living in the family home. She wasn't permitted to be your primary parent, which is why we applied to foster you. Your mother was punished for what your father did, and because she made excuses for him."

My childhood was not terrible, and I won't feel sorry for myself. It is the lies that disturb me. It's always the coverup. You live your life believing you know those closest to you, but how can you? My mother let herself be the villain in story of my childhood, and with my father gone, I don't know if she'll ever come clean about who he really was.

I throw a glance at Oyster before I ask my next question. He's as tired as she is, deflated from worrying all day. I lean in and ask Agnes softly, "Why did you tell the police you killed my husband?"

"Why do you think?" Oyster interjects.

"It could've been me," Agnes replies, and I can tell she's growing tired. I should leave her to rest. "It's a plausible story. I'm out that way every day and night. Your husband was a violent man."

"You didn't see him that day, though, did you? You didn't do it."

There is no good way to ask a person if they murdered your husband.

Agnes's face goes even whiter than it already is. "Well, that depends. I…well, if someone I love had a good reason for putting a person down, and if there's a way to ensure they aren't punished for it…"

We seem to be having a pale-off, because I feel myself draining of all color and life. "I didn't kill Clive, Agnes! I swear."

She closes her eyes. I think I see relief cross her face, but then again, it might be regret for taking the rap for something neither of us did.

"Oh, my darling." She takes my hand and squeezes it. "Of course. I'm sorry for even thinking it. It's just that man was so horrible, and I thought…"

"You confessed to save me, even though you believed I did it?" The answer is obvious, but it's difficult to comprehend nonetheless. I've had a woefully small number of people make big gestures for me in my life.

"Family takes care of family," she says. "Bumps in the road, mistakes, apologies, forgiveness. It's all in the same basket. Your father had a philosophy. He said it about clams, and good fishing spots, and he said it about life. Life is choices. Regretting a choice is like wishing you were someone else. You can only go one way, so you must decide which path to take, and then live with your decision. If you take time to breathe, feel the sand under your feet, you'll see everything was pointing to the right decision all along."

Pointing.

Pointing?

Pointing…

Oh, my god. How did I miss it?

was so busy flitting about the dunes and obsessing about the Millers' house I didn't see what was in front of my face. They were right about me all along. My tunnel vision hurt us all.

I look into her eyes, red-rimmed with white lashes, and I tell her, "I don't know how to thank you for saving my life, Agnes."

"You having a happy, healthy life is thanks enough," she says, reaching out for my hand, and as she lays her warm, dry palm over mine, she gives me another squeeze.

"Stop blubbering, you two," Oyster says, forever uncomfortable with displays of genuine emotion. "Agnes needs her rest."

"I'm going straight to the cops," I say. "I'm telling Lilith you didn't do it."

Agnes smiles. "No need. You can't change anything that's happened. Lilith is going to do what she's going to do, and so are the state police. They're investigating now. It's up to them to unravel it all. I'm glad I gave them something to distract them."

Ah, Agnes. She knew they'd never believe her. She did it to give me time, to force the police to slow down and consider other possibilities.

At the door, I stop and ask her one final question. "Why did you warn me away from the house on the point?"

She doesn't immediately reply. She takes a sip of water, moistening her lips and her throat. She regards me, as I'm ready to run, with so much to do, and she asks, "Was I right?"

I nod.

She nods back, and our conversation is over.

I feel like a shuddering freight train is barreling toward an unknown destination, but for once I'm driving it, not in its path. Thanks to Agnes, I know where to find the "item" Clive was so desperate to get his hands on. My father put it in the one place no one would ever look; he hid it in plain sight. I'm sure of it.

I race home and head to the living room. I instinctively check the reading glasses on the side table. Still there, unmoved, no dust disturbed.

Nick decorated his cave with three ships in bottles. One is a delicate antique passed down from my great-great grandfather, a fascinating example of craftsmanship with tiny sails and intricate woodworking inside a glass bottle from the olden days. One is a collector's item given as a Christmas present. The third is tacky gift-store junk, a plastic ship with the overdramatic pirate, his handlebar mustache like Oil Can Harry off my father's favorite childhood cartoon, *Mighty Mouse*, pointing his sword at a cowering crewmember…or is he? Nick's favorite aunt gave it to him, and he thought it would be bad luck to not display it.

I bend and examine the bottle like I'm watching a fish tank. I follow the tip of the captain's sword. It's pointing *past* the crewmate.

Behind the cowering man is a toy treasure chest, a plastic

piece smaller than my fist. *That's* what the sword is pointing to. I lift the bottle. You can unscrew the bottom, and you can see the seam if you look close. It's not real glass, but a reasonable facsimile.

I'm shaking as I get a grip and struggle to open it. I bang it against the table to loosen it. It's stuck good, but with a few more attempts, like a giant mayonnaise jar, I ease the bottom off. I shove my hand inside and fiddle around on the deck of the S.S. *Skull and Bone.* My fingers find the chest. I pull it out, breaking a sail as I do.

I turn the chest in my hands like a Rubik's cube, looking for a keyhole. This bottle, shoved against a wall away from the good stuff, blended in with the room so it became invisible, unremarkable as wallpaper in a space full of history and lore.

I calm myself and find the keyhole.

I pull the silver chain over my head and, hand trembling, insert the key.

It slides in. I turn it. The lock clicks smoothly, easily.

I hesitate before opening the box. Everything changes when I do, and I'm not sure I'm ready for what I might find.

The chest is more substantial than I expected. I carry it to the sofa, balancing it on my palm and feeling its weight. It's not a baby toy made of light plastic. It's a heavier resin of some kind, which explains the regular-sized key.

I open the chest. Stuffed inside it is a handkerchief I haven't seen in years. It's a cream-colored hanky, delicate lace yellowing at the edges, sewn by my late Grandma Mixie. I remove it, carefully lay it on the coffee table, and unfold it. Inside is a torn scrap of paper resembling the one *Jane* was written on. My father scrawled two words in his uneven, stick-like print: *How many?*

Under the paper is a plastic striped bass the size of a baby carrot. I pick it up and tug at the swishing fishtail. As I suspected, out comes a USB connector. Of *course* my father would have a fish thumb drive, but only because they probably don't make them in clam.

I run to my room and grab my laptop, bringing it back to the sofa, setting it up on the coffee table.

How many.

Think, think, think.

He would've ensured I'd glean the answer quickly, and that it wouldn't make sense to anyone else. There were two numbers we would talk about out at night when he was digging at the evening low tide. *How many stars are in the sky, Dad?*

I don't remember the answer. It's the other question we'd talk about, analyze, parse: *How many grains of sand are there in the whole world?*

I insert the drive, and it demands a password from me. The answer is 7.5 sextillion, or 75 followed by seventeen zeroes. I punch in the numbers, each one a thump of my heart, because if this doesn't work, it's going to be a long day. After seven careful, deliberate zeroes, the drive lets me in.

I click the one file on the list, and my father blasts onto the screen. I smile and gasp at the same time.

"Hey, Isla girl," he says. He waves at the camera. He's sitting on the middle cushion on the sofa where I am now. At least for today, at least in this moment, Nicholas Banks is alive. He's with me in this room.

"I know it's you, because no one else will make it this far."

He's smiling, and I'm on the edge of tears. "First, they'd have to find the hiding place, then they'd have to figure out the password, and I set it up to be three strikes and you're out."

His blond hair is long like it gets when Angélica hasn't cut it for a while, a swoop of bangs falling to his eyebrows. He's wearing his favorite cargo pants and ubiquitous clammer's fashion statement of white T-shirt under red flannel top, so I know this wasn't recorded in summer.

"No one knows what I'm about to tell you," he says. "If you don't find this, no one ever will, and I have to believe there would be a cosmic reason for that. There are no copies of this video. The stakes are high, Isla girl. You ready? Let me show you what I've been working on all these years."

He reaches down and brings his right hand up to the camera.

In it is the front page of the *North Cape Caller*. He jabs at the newspaper, producing a crinkling sound so crisp I jump as if he's next to me.

"Today is March fifteenth." I see the date when he shoves it closer to the camera. One year ago. Six months before my most recent visit with Clive.

He reaches down again, and when his hand is back in view, the paper is gone, in its place a golden disc held between his thumb and forefinger. A gold coin, flattened, misshapen, imprinted with something. A cross? Hashmarks?

"I've been digging my life away," he says. "What did I find, dear girl? Gold. I found *gold*."

48

My father pauses for effect.

"Actually," he goes on, pointing at me, "*you* found it. You were about four years old. You were such a good girl. All the clammers watched out for you, so I never worried when I brought you out while your mother was working in the city. One evening at low tide, I strayed a bit far because the steamers were hiding, and everyone else had given up and gone for a bite at the Lantern.

"I lost track of time, and when I returned, you were exactly where I left you. You'd dug a moat around yourself, and you were holding this coin. 'Daddy, I found a treasure!' You were so smart.

"I knew instantly it really *was* a treasure. We were at the edge of the woods by the house on the point." He frowns. "There was no house then. Just thriving clam flats, a secret little beach, and peaceful woods.

"I took you home, and the next morning, after we were done clamming, we went to the pirate museums. Two in Salem alone. There were no cellphones, no internet, not in Sandburn anyway, so we did it the old-fashioned way. We went to the library. I needed to learn everything I could about who could've buried coins like the one you found by the point."

I pause the video to work out the timing of my supposed find. I don't remember anything about that day; there's no mental image, no specter of time spent alone, abandoned, a virtual toddler striking gold. It seems clear that it wasn't the night I was left behind, because you don't obsess and leave your child behind because of clams. You dig until they're cleared out or your quota's met, and you go for a drink. Treasure, though, is a lure, a siren song in the sand instead of the sea. It's an infinite pursuit, and no matter how much you find, I imagine you convince yourself there's more, and no one can disprove it.

I hit play.

"I learned about a pirate called Jane Ree, who was said to have buried a bunch of small treasures around the North Cape. But," he says excitedly, holding up his index finger, "there's *also* a chest somewhere by Rogue's Rock." Seeing my father animated about something other than fishing, Angélica, or bourbon is eye-opening. "The point isn't far from there, and when you found that coin, I knew there had to be more. The chest was from a Central American ship Jane's crew captured, most likely. Supposed to be a ton of gold and silver. Look her up. Her story's fascinating.

"I started metal detecting and digging right away, starting at the spot where you showed me the coin. I didn't find anything at first. The more I read about Jane, the more I came to believe she worked mostly alone, and had been burying small caches over a greater area, possibly over a few years."

He's not said a word about leaving me, or about Oyster or Agnes stepping in as responsible parents. No wonder I buried any memory of my night alone. I got the denial gene from my father.

"And I found 'em, Isla girl," he grins. "I found small treasures over twenty-five years, about one every two years. You see, I couldn't dig all the time. Agnes was always out walking, and we had you, your school, events, activities. Your mom was working, and I had to rake up my quota to keep my clamming license. It was a busy time. Plus, I couldn't let anyone wonder why I was metal detecting in the same area month after month. No one could know. It'd spark obsessions and battles between brothers around these parts. A race to a treasure would've blown this place up. And this place is precious."

He takes a sip of ginger ale, then clears his throat like he's about to deliver a monologue in a play.

"You have questions. Let me start with the big ones," he says. "Why did I keep it a secret?" He shifts on the cushion and winces. My father wasn't far behind Oyster and Old Caleb in the back problems department. "Because, dear girl, there are loopholes in the finders keepers laws. If you find a treasure, you're supposed to be able to keep it. But if it's on government-owned land, what if they claim imminent domain or historical value, and determine it should be in a museum? If it was on private land, could the homeowner make a claim? I couldn't risk it.

"After a few years, I had enough money from the coins to buy the land on the point. It was going for a fair price, and without a house on it, I could afford it by using proceeds from coins I sold to a guy who doesn't ask questions. But those damn Millers swooped in and outbid me before I knew it. Now it was the Millers' land. So *then,* I had treasure I'd found on private property *and* on the bordering conservation land, and at that point I realized no one could ever know. Just you, in case something happened to me.

"I sucked up to Harold and started working for the Millers so I'd be able to keep digging on their property. I spent years securing the treasure where no one would ever find it, selling it off piecemeal so Uncle Sam doesn't come after me. It ain't easy, I tell you. I wasn't just searching. I was moving, hiding, covering. Like I said—I couldn't have anyone finding out about it. The most precious treasure of all is a place, a history, a community.

"To have tourists swarming this place digging for treasure would've sold more chowder, but if we're already struggling to make our quotas, there won't be enough fish for the tourists anyway. I didn't want to be responsible for destroying Sandburn. Not for Oyster, Frank, Linda, Joe, Shep and their descendants. Uh uh."

He shakes his head. It's obvious he spent a lot of time adjusting his moral compass to fit his position.

"I did take one little risk recently." He smiles again. "I talked peripherally about the situation with your mother. We had a wild time remembering the old days. Seems she's forgiven me, and it was cathartic for both of us. Anyway. That's for another time. I asked her about her genealogy work. You see, the treasure was all around where the Bankses have been clamming for centuries, and I thought old Axel might've bumped into Jane. I found no evidence of that, but it sure was fun trying. Who knows. Could still be true."

More ginger ale, and then, "You want to know what I've done with the money. I gave back quietly, in pieces. Agnes needed help immediately. We got her into the experimental treatment. That's why she's walking so strong," he smiles. "Little Lola needed a better school. Look at her thriving! Cassandra needed a new speedboat to do to her important work."

Here he tilts his head, widens his eyes to tell me there is meaning behind that, something he mustn't speak of. So far, he hasn't mentioned the Porsche, perhaps his only indulgence.

"You ever wonder why you never needed student loans?"

At eighteen, I didn't, not really. My father paid the bills, and I was grateful, but I wasn't going to a sixty-grand-a-year school, so I figured the fishing was good during those years.

"No," I reply out loud, and my heart breaks. For a moment I forgot he's not real, that this conversation is predetermined and finite.

"Isla girl, I plan to keep digging until it's all brought up, until I find that treasure chest or I croak. The big one's still out there. And now, for the finale," he says. "You're gonna want to know how much it's all worth."

I nod at the screen.

"Far as I could tell, the coins were borderline seventeenth, eighteenth century. I could hardly believe it! And there was bullion. A gold bar helped pay off the mortgage on this house and…other things. I've had to sacrifice some numismatic value, of course. I was limited regarding who I could ask things of and where I could go for advice. I couldn't have people wondering why I was asking about buried treasure. I couldn't sell to just anyone."

He yawns, looks around, squints as if he hears something.

"Last answer, until next time," he smiles at me. "You're wondering where the treasure is. I don't keep a map. It's all up here." He taps the side of his head with an index finger. *Not funny, Dad.* He used to say that whenever we ventured outside the North Cape. We always got lost or took the long way. We were late for everything for my entire childhood.

"There will be a part two, when I know more," my father assures the camera. "I'm working on something to secure this thing for us. Something big. The only thing I'll say now is, if you want to find the treasure, look beneath. Dig deeper. You got this, Isla. It's all for you. You found it. I only followed the trail *you* discovered."

He stops for a moment. My father appears at peace, comfortable, excited. He wasn't always those things, and it's comforting to see.

"But you know what?" He breaks out into a full, genuine smile. "You'll never need these clues, because we're both going to live long, happy lives, and I'm going to be here for every big moment. I didn't do such a great job early on. I'm sorry for that. But we've got time to make up for it."

He freezes. He turns his head slightly, so his ear is pointed toward the same window Clive climbed into days ago. I hear what my father hears: The faintest sound of wooden slats squeaking and crackling.

"That old porch," Nick says in a husky whisper, leaning in so I can see up his nostrils. "Who needs a guard dog? Wouldn't change a thing about this place." He winks. "Gotta go. Part two will come as soon as I know what part two is. Love ya, Isla girl."

He smiles, his eyes sparkling, dripping with optimism, full of hope. He reaches out one arm, and the screen goes dark.

When he's gone, I double over and weep.

My father's happy, animated face and voice was a gift. The end was like a horror movie. Not for him, because he hadn't a clue what was to come. He thought his daughter's new boyfriend was returning from a delightful outing and we'd all have a drink and then plan dinner.

But the creak of those boards was a harbinger of doom. I want to reach through the screen to warn him, and to beg his forgiveness for bringing Clive into his life.

Clive and I were in Sandburn the day my father made this recording. We'd only been dating for a short time, nowhere near seriously enough for a visit home to meet the parents, but expats are travel whores. They'll go anywhere with anyone to tick the box that says *I've been there*, because they know they'll eventually return to live in their home country.

I'd taken Clive on a fishing trip in the *Sable*, but we returned home early after he caught a fishhook to the fleshy pad of his thumb. He went into the house to treat his wound while I stayed on the dock to tie off and put away the gear. I suspect my husband lurked on the porch, listening to my father, perhaps even seeing the gold coin, because after that day Clive pursued me carefully but relentlessly, stalking me like a panther, finding my weaknesses and pouncing.

If only my father knew then how little his treasure would mean to me, that he was the precious one, not the gold in his hand.

My burner phone vibrates. It's Ben.

"Everything OK?" I answer, knowing it's not.

My smartphone rings, and it's a number from inside WCN's newsroom.

"I think it's happening," Ben whispers. "I'm at the station finishing up my shift report, and I'm hearing talk of two cars getting ready to meet the state police at a subject's house. I think you should prepare yourself."

The fear is a monster chasing me, but I'm ready, so its impact is lessened.

"Don't worry about me," I tell him. "I've been expecting this. Gotta go. I'll call you later…if I can."

I end the call and pick up the other phone.

"Isla? It's Lane. How are you holding up?"

"I'm hanging in there," I say, letting out a long, sad sigh. "I still can't believe I'll never be in the WCN newsroom again."

"Maybe this will help," Lane says. "After we talked the other day, I did some digging. I got something on your Charlotte James."

49

Michele was right when we had our confrontation days ago. A storm *was* coming, and it's introducing itself with cooling temperatures and a blustery wind turning sand into swirling dust devils. Carbon-grey clouds dance around the moon as if considering whether to blot it out entirely.

At the house on the point, I ring the bell, then bang on the door. "Charlotte! It's Isla. Open up!"

Bang, bang, bang.

Give her what she wants: A reason to get me arrested, a certainty that *she* is in control, some juicy footage to show the cops. *Crazy Isla is here, send help!*

I hear footsteps thumping down the soapstone stairs, and a few seconds later Charlotte throws open the door, hand on her heart, with a shaky smile and wild eyes.

"You scared me to death," she breathes. Jittery as she is, she appears happy to see me, like we're old friends. She's wearing khaki shorts and a grey sweatshirt.

"What are you doing here?" She pokes her head outside, past me, seeing if I have company. She thinks it's a trap. "I thought…"

"You thought I'd be in jail for a murder you committed," I smile back.

Her mouth falls open. I suspect she's shocked not by my accusation, but my bluntness.

"I…OK." Her expression changes, her eyes narrow, her shrewd nature bubbles to the fore. "I'm sorry to ruin your big plan, but I'm not interested in speaking to you. I don't need you. You are, as you say, a murderer, and I'm a victim of your stalking. I'll be moving on soon and you'll be in prison."

"You might reconsider when I tell you I have the item," I say.

I've shocked her again. She regains her composure quickly, and asks calmly, "Is that what Clive told you? That we're looking for an 'item?' Don't insult me. If that's your leverage, you're in worse trouble than you think."

I say nothing, and after a few moments of silence, she falls for my old interview trick. At our core, human beings are all the same.

"Fine, I'll bite. What's this so-called item you think you know about?"

"I can tell you what it's *not*," I reply. "It's not a treasure map. That's what you assumed, isn't it? You two grifters were looking for directions to a big old chest full of gold coins. Pirate's booty in Sandburn. Who woulda thought?"

Her face tells me I'm right.

"Outside," she snaps. "You first." She gestures for me to walk ahead of her, and I do, leaving my back wide open for her to stab it.

I stop a few paces away. The wind is kicking up, bending trees as angry air rushes through the woods.

"Talk," Charlotte says, and the wind carries her words to me.

"I'm the only one who knows where any of the treasure is," I explain. "Its location isn't written down anywhere, nothing's recorded, and there's no map."

"Where is it?" She demands.

I shake my head. "You're going to tell me what I want to know, and then I'll tell you where the gold is—but only when I'm safe. You can take the treasure and run. You'll have a head start."

"Oh, *please*," she groans. "You think I'm going to fall for that? Try again."

"What choice do you have?"

"I'll be honest," she says. "You're not saying anything to make me believe you…or not kill you."

She pulls a handgun from behind her back and points it at me. I assume she tucked it into her waistband when she saw me on the door camera. "Not only will I get a free pass for self-defense without breaking a sweat, but I'll be on every news show and podcast. I'll be a hero. Better yet, I'll be a celebrity. You don't want to play with me, Isla."

She's right, I don't. But I have no choice. I prepared for a fight, but I didn't expect to face the barrel of a gun. Still, my determination to serve her a cold platter of consequences keeps me outwardly calm. Today, *she's* the one who's off kilter. Master planners like Charlotte tend to think ten steps ahead—but when things go awry, they can't bend. I can. I'm like taffy, twisting and stretching to meet every push and pull.

"I'll start," I say. "You tell me if I'm on the right track. Clive was visiting Sandburn with me when we first started dating. He returned to the house early when he cut his hand, which is when he heard my father talking about treasure buried around the Millers' house. We weren't serious at that stage, but when Clive thought there was a chest full of gold coins in the family, everything changed.

"That's why he became fixated on my hometown and wanted to visit every month. He was searching our house for some sort of treasure map.

"But instead, he discovered Nick Banks's famous system of not writing anything down. That's when Clive, and you, realized you were going to have to go nuclear. He insisted we come for that extended visit in October, saying he wanted to look at Sandburn real estate, and I believed him. He got Nick out of the house by threatening to kill me if he didn't go."

Charlotte hasn't corrected me, so I go on.

"Here's where things get hazy," I say. "From what I've been able to figure out, my father took Clive on a wild goose chase. He made Clive believe there was a circuitous route to caches of gold based on a non-existent map. My guess is that Nick made Clive think the treasure, or signs pointing to the treasure, were on different shores and different islands, that Nick himself wasn't even sure where it was, but his best idea was, where…up at Plum? Maybe he convinced Clive that Blackbeard's buried treasure was found up at Star Island."

Charlotte swallows hard, which tells me I'm right. I know Nick Banks, and I came to understand after talking to Angélica that every move he made, every weird turn and change of direction, was about stalling. Looking for his moment. He would've been throwing around Blackbeard and Captain Kidd and all the big pirate names. Never Jane Ree.

"But something happened along the way," I continue. "My father was heading toward Plum Island when Angélica saw them from the shore. She got in the way, made a scene, waving and greeting my father with a big smile, right?" I'll go on until she stops me. "From there, everything went wrong."

Charlotte shakes the gun at me. I flinch.

"Great story, but if you think you're going to get a TV-style confession, you're more naïve than I thought," she says. "You wired, Isla? You think you're going to get me to say something incriminating while you record me? I know you don't have reinforcements, because the cameras see all. No one in the woods, no one on the beach. Just you, me, and this."

She raises the gun, aims it at my face, squints as if to find the spot on my body she wants to shoot.

"Let's take a hot tub," she says out of nowhere, lowering her weapon. "If you want to continue our chat, those are my terms. I'll hear you out. I want that treasure."

"You're not serious."

"Go on. Strip down. Let's have a look at you."

"I'll go in," I concede. "But only if you put the gun down."

"After I check you for devices, I'll put it down," she says.

The scene is all the more bizarre, all the more spooky, as a sliver of the moon is covered by black, scudding clouds, like splotches of evil trying to hide the light. I shimmy out of my jacket, then lift my shirt, leaving me in a white bra. I step out of my cargo pants and stand in matching basic cotton underwear.

"I'm convinced. Maybe you *are* arrogant enough to come here without backup or a wire. Even if you do have something tucked somewhere, the water'll drown it out. In you go," she says, pointing to the water with her gun.

"You first," I argue.

She sighs, then complies. She sinks in, gun in hand, then holds it up to show me, and slowly, gently lays it on the deck, barrel pointing toward the sea, away from us.

I sink in on the opposite side, just as I did days ago when we were engaged in a game of friend or foe.

"You're wearing that necklace," I say, noticing the pink stone against her wet skin. "The cops gave it back to you?" I speak calmly, but my lungs give me away; I can feel my chest heaving like a heroine in a Jane Austen novel.

"Aw, Isla," Charlotte interrupts with what appears to be genuine sympathy. "You didn't think that stunt would change anything? You're a newswoman. You know about crime and victims and innocent people railroaded for things they didn't do. The quartz was *mine*. It was found in the sand, where I could've dropped it any time. I've lived here for months, after all. The police didn't want to face my lawsuit for malicious prosecution, trespassing, pain, and suffering. So, yes. Chief Wen gave me my necklace back when I demanded it. Isn't it pretty?" She fingers it then lets it fall to her chest, where it dangles just above the roiling bubbles.

"So pretty," I say, using a baby voice beloved by so many of today's alternative pop singers.

"You know what they say about sarcasm," she chides. "It's the lowest form of wit."

"They also say it's the highest form of intelligence." Hot bubbles massage my skin. "Your turn."

50

"That stupid Angélica ruined everything," Charlotte shifts her position on the underwater bench. "Clive panicked and let her go. He thought she'd drown or freeze. But we know she's made of tougher stuff, don't we? Our only chance at that point was to come up with something so convoluted that it would have to be believed. He couldn't stroll back into town and live his life with Angélica knowing what happened."

She's skipped over the most important question: *What happened to my father?*

"What I can't figure is what made Clive quit looking for the treasure that night," I say. "Did my father hit him with an oar? Maybe tip the boat, try to capsize it? The plan turned to damage control. Either my father didn't tell you anything, or something happened so he *couldn't* tell you. That left you both screwed. You were going to get rid of Nick once he led you to the treasure, keep it for yourselves, kill me, and then Clive would inherit the house, the gold, everything. That's why the rush marriage, right?"

Charlotte appears impressed and angry at the same time,

which produces a comical combination of evil eyebrows and a smirk.

"When he said he wanted to propose after two months of dating you, I told him you wouldn't be so stupid," she says. "I told him that you're a career woman, you're cynical, didn't need a man to be happy, that you weren't going to marry the first guy that asked you. But he said no, Isla's still hung up on her high school football star boyfriend—"

"Lacrosse."

"Never heard of it. Clive said you were waiting for someone to make the decision for you." She laughs sardonically. "He was right. You folded like the sad cheerleader who gets cut from the squad and pledged your life to a guy you barely knew, whose parents you met once over Zoom. A stroke of luck for us that you had such poor judgment. You caused all of this just to get over some clammer who probably doesn't even have health insurance, let alone any viable future."

There are so many things I want to say to her right now, but I'll wait until she's in handcuffs. "My father was never going to make it out alive," I say. "He never had a chance."

Charlotte tries to grab and hold onto a bubble, like a child.

"We knew that if Clive killed your father first, you'd inherit everything." She looks up again. "Then it would be your turn, at which point Clive would inherit everything from *you*. It was perfect. But too many witnesses were out that night. We needed Nick alive until he showed us where the gold was. We realized we needed a Plan B."

"Which involved Clive freaking out and contacting you somehow, and you having to rescue him."

"Clive was such an idiot he could barely figure out how to drive the boat." She laughs like we're bonding at a girls' retreat. "He finally did it and got past Marlin Bay, but I told him the tide would carry the boat right back into Sandburn. But by then it was too late; we were risking everyone and their brother seeing us, so he left it in the bay and I picked him up on the shore around the lighthouse.

"We got the hell out of there. Took back roads up to Nova Scotia and dropped him at the first big hospital we came upon."

"Brilliant plan," I say, choosing sarcasm again. "Are you telling me the Canadians had Clive's passport on file, not to mention security video of his entry, and no one figured it out?"

"Spoken like a cultureless American," she snorts. "You gave the cops his Dutch passport. But he's a dual citizen of Holland and Great Britain. He used his British passport to get through."

"You keep saying what a dud Clive was. So why were you ever with him? Why would you get romantically involved with someone like that?"

Her face stretches out like silly putty. "Oh my *god*," she says. "No. Ick. Clive was just some bloke I met on a con. Old lady with too much money and no family." She shudders.

"Anyway, when it was all over, we couldn't let you bring the cops to the scene, so I convinced the Millers to rake the beach to keep you away. I told Harold you were stalking them. It wasn't a tough sell. You were there all the time. You were *obsessed*."

There was never any blood found, so I can't see Clive hitting my father with an oar, stabbing him, or shooting him. It would've had to be a blunt object that incapacitated him.

"I'm funny like that when people I love vanish into thin air,"

I say. "You're not going to tell me, but I've figured it out. My father brought Clive here, hoping to wake the Millers in the melee, but they slept through it all. You were waiting for them. There was a fight, and somehow my father got the gun overboard, but Clive got the jump on him and hit him over the head. My father passed out. You two managed to drag him into the woods and left him there while you searched for treasure in the middle of the night, not having a clue what you were doing. Nick woke up and took off, and you never saw him again."

"That is some wishful thinking right there." Charlotte nods in a show of mock respect. "No, I'm not gonna tell you what really happened. We'll keep that part back until I know I'm far away from this backwater. Now. *Where* is the gold? Because Clive searched bloody everywhere. He took apart pillows and floorboards and pawed through every personal effect you own, and you trusting small-town nobodies didn't even notice."

"That's why you invited me in," I say. "You had to be sure I was out so Clive could search the house. Time was running out and you bumbling buffoons still had no treasure. The embezzled cash from Finance for All was almost gone, too, wasn't it? But he got caught. It didn't occur to either one of you that Nick kept this a secret from everyone, including his family and friends."

"Clive was weak. He thought I needed him because he was smart, and a man. Wrong. I needed him because he was weak as a baby giraffe. So, so weak."

She points at me with both hands, like she's playing wild west shootout. "But you know that, don't you? You realized it too late. You were already in it. Already married, said your I dos in front of God and family. Practically begged your father to validate your choice. And when your husband turned out to be an abusive control freak, you couldn't get out. Too proud."

She laughs, then cackles like a witch.

"Sweetie, I've been there. Unlike you, I didn't take it more than once. That man found out the hard way that no one fucks with me. *No one.*"

"Clive found out the hard way, too," I say.

"He was fucking everything up," Charlotte confirms, shaking her head. "He mangled our plan to keep you onside until we were done with you, he never found the treasure, and he was running around town dressed like Dread Pirate Roberts. He had to go. And framing you, well…it was sublime."

She's so talkative that I don't have time to feel the rage I'm entitled to. "That sounds super fun," I say. "But I don't understand how you got a big lump like him with one clean hit like the cops say. There wasn't much of a fight. One hit and bam, he's bleeding out, and you're gone."

"Don't insult me," she cackles. "That man was gagging for me. He'd do anything I said, including pose for a fake death photo I told him we needed. He didn't ask why."

And that's a wrap. I don't want to share space with this evil creature for one more second.

"I'm hot," I say, and lift myself out before she can argue.

I have my eye on the gun. It happens in slow motion. She sees me seeing it, and lifts herself out of the hot tub like a gymnast. We both lunge for the gun, hitting the deck hard.

51

Charlotte scratches at me, and I grab her forearms to keep her from punching me in the jaw, and we're wrestling on the flagstones. We inch closer to the gun and she grabs it, but I catch her wrist, dig my fingernail into the fragile skin, and she loosens her grip enough for me to grab the barrel, so we're both holding it.

This is never a good position to be in, according to television. They're always saying, *We fought over the gun and it just went off.* She's on her back and I'm straddling her now, and I manage to rip the weapon out of her hand, holding it up for a split second like a game of keep away, but she's grabbing for it, so I throw it as far as I can across the sand.

She's on her feet before I am. She's light, nimble, fast.

But I'm smarter. Running on the beach is all about surface area. If you try to run like you do on pavement, your feet slip back with every step and you end up kicking sand and exhausting yourself. My entire childhood was spent running across sand, through the dunes, sprinting over the beach volleyball court. Chasing Ben or running from him. Touch football on the shore. Never run toe-to-heel. Land flat-footed, take shorter strides.

Charlotte is kicking sand and flailing, slipping backwards with every attempt. I make it to the gun before she does, grab it, and whirl.

The wind kicks up, spins dust devils all around us, blows my hair in my face. I take aim at her chest. She stops short. The moon's out again, and she's like a hologram with the light bouncing off the deep blue sea.

"Tell me where my father is."

She holds her hands up.

"You're not going to *shoot* me."

"You sure about that?"

I take a step closer. "Where is he? Where did you two assholes hide him?"

"I don't know," she says. "Clive probably threw him overboard."

If he had, with the tide going out, my father could've floated out and disappeared forever, or been seen by a passing boat, or caught on something. Whether he became fish food or was retrieved by rescuers would have come down to pure luck. No, that wasn't what happened. The drag marks on this beach that morning were going from the shore to the woods.

"Clive landed the boat here," I say, wishing I could read her facial expressions, but the moon's gone again. "You two dragged my father to the woods and tried to force him to show you where the gold was, but it was too late. You realized he was dead. You both loaded his body into a car and drive him somewhere."

This is the scenario that makes the most sense to me based on the scant evidence I have, and it makes my blood run cold. Nicholas Banks could be anywhere between here and Nova Scotia, in any stretch of woods, in a vast ocean of crashing waves.

Was he still alive when they took him? Was he in their trunk, praying and suffocating and bleeding?

"Careful with that gun, Isla." Ben's voice booms out from the edge of the woods. He emerged without my noticing, invisible as a sand mite.

Red, white and blue lights bathe the beach as sirens shriek.

"What the *hell?*" Charlotte spits and coughs from the sand that blew in her face during the last gust and turns toward the house.

"You were right about one thing," I yell over the incoming reinforcements. "I wasn't wired. But *you* are."

Her chest is heaving as her breath comes louder, faster. Her eyes flash, like she wants to attack me. "Wha—what are you talking about? There's no way."

"I'm afraid there is, darling."

"I'm clearly not wired. Desperate isn't a good look for you, *darling.* Even if I was, the water and the wind would've muffled everything." Her cockiness rises to the surface.

"Not if it was right next to your mouth. Outside of the water," I tell her.

She's not stupid. It takes her a moment of rapid-fire thinking, and then she figures it out. She reaches for her pendant and rips the necklace off. The chain doesn't break easily; it looks like it tore at her skin as she pulled. This amuses me.

"You'll find it inside the setting," I tell her helpfully. "The state police have all sorts of gadgets nowadays."

With that, the state police, SWAT, and Sandburn officers swarm the beach, streaming from behind the house. They were stationed along the road and in the woods in the security cameras' blind spots.

I drop the gun and raise my hands. Charlotte eyes the weapon.

"On your knees! Hands in the air!" Multiple voices yell at once.

I comply, hoping Lilith will release me momentarily. Charlotte sinks in slow motion, but I don't think her reticence makes the point she thinks it does. The cops converge on her, and a man puts his knee into her back while a woman cuffs her.

Lilith approaches me as Charlotte is dragged toward the house. She offers me a hand, and I take it. "You did good," she says. "Sorry we're late. The splashing covered up the gunfight."

"I still don't know where my father is," I say, and Lilith keeps hold of my hand, and I let her, and we walk around the house to the front driveway.

"I know," she says, sucking in her breath as if she's overcome by emotion. "I know."

I grasp the scope of this operation when we make it to the circular driveway. They sent two vans, three police cars, one ambulance, and two unmarked cars.

"Isla! Chief!"

I look to the left and see two people shuffling away from a white BMW. One's wearing a flowery shirt and a pleated skirt, the other an even more flowery shirt and pleated trousers.

"Oh, great. The Millers," I say flatly.

Lilith nods to the couple.

"We've dropped the restraining order," Harold says to me, as if I should thank him. His gray hair is poufy *and* slicked back like he's in a doo-wop group.

"Where is she?" Millie asks in a tone she usually uses on servants. I know, because she used to speak to my father that way.

"We never said she could live here," Harold says, pursing his lips. "She promised to keep an eye on the place for us. She *lied* to us."

Lilith points to the right side of the circular driveway, where the cops appear to be working out which car will take Charlotte to jail while she studies everything around her, clearly thinking of ways to get away.

"*Her*? That's not the company rep!" Millie screams, whirling on Lilith. "Where's Ophelia?"

"Told you," I whisper to the chief out of the side of my mouth. Kindly couple my ass. They're overprivileged snots.

"She's right there," I say, pointing at their squatter. "We know her as a fake British brunette. You know her as a bleach-blonde Southern belle with an orange spray tan."

52

"Her real name is Misty Pumphrey," Lilith tells the confused couple.

"She's a long way from Lock Jaw, Arkansas," I say to the woman of many names, and she turns, like a velociraptor with flashing, dead eyes, her face illuminated in a rotation of blue, then red, then blue, then red as police lights flash.

"*Hog* Jaw," she sneers. There is no fear on display, only contempt and rage. If she's not a textbook psychopath, I don't know who is.

Law enforcement has me to thank for this. When they came to my home to arrest me, I invited them in and showed them evidence they couldn't ignore. I knew every agency wanted to catch the Clamming Fork Killer, and I counted on egos and glory-hunting to transcend the Insane Isla narrative.

To get the warrant to plant a wire on Charlotte, they had to know everything, and I told them how Lane, my guilt-ridden producer, called in a favor to find Misty using facial recognition with the social media accounts I gave her. *It's not the FBI's database*, she said when she called me with her findings, *but it's better than an image search on the internet.*

"Ask her about a con on an elderly woman she and Clive stole from, probably in New York," I say. "And you might want to have the NYPD try to track down the leaseholder on our apartment." I have a bad feeling the man Clive was "subletting" from didn't make it.

As Misty is dragged away, Ben says to me, "There's every chance she'll get a plea deal. She'll tell them where your father is. It's not over by a longshot."

"There will never be a plea." Charlotte/Misty smiles, offering that catlike squint of the eyes, and that purr. "I'll take this to a jury, and they won't convict me of anything by the time I'm through with them. There is no plea you could offer that I'd accept, other than a walk free and clear."

The scary part is she might be right. Her petite, pretty, smooth, British ways only have to make one juror swoon, and that juror will have a ready-made excuse to vote not guilty when he sees the photos of big Clive and the clamming fork, and will struggle to picture a scenario where little Misty jabbed it into his jugular.

The officer has a hand on her head ready for her to duck into the back seat. "Hey, Misty," I say, nice and loud so everyone around me gets it. "You did all of this for nothing."

"What?"

"The treasure. It doesn't exist," I say. "My father was making me an April Fool's video. We prank each other every year. Think about it. You and Clive searched *everywhere*, but never found a trace of anything even hinting at a pirate's treasure."

Officer Carter Waring is nodding along furiously. "Everyone knows there's no pirate's treasure on the North Shore," he says.

"All anyone wants to hear about is Captain Kidd, John Quelch, Blackbeard. Isles of Shoals up in New Hampsha, Smuttynose Island in Maine are *not* ideal places to hide anything, and—"

"*Carter.*" Lilith makes a throat-cutting motion with her right hand.

Misty's face goes white, and I think she might cry. She believes me because it's logical. They ripped my father's house up and found no coins, no maps, no clues. They've been digging around the point for months and found nothing but rubbish and old soda can tops.

A state police officer guides Charlotte into the back seat of the car, and Millie shouts after her, "We'll be pressing charges for fraud!"

Harold Miller turns to me.

"We're sorry we've been out of touch," he says to me as if I have any interest in knowing either one of them. "We had no idea how hard it would be to communicate at sea."

"And how annoying the people would be," Millie sniffs. "This Misty person sent us on a *bargain-basement* cruise, and now we're not even going to go viral!"

"Millie's wanted to go viral since she found out it's not a disease." Harold's deadly serious.

I'm glad they didn't get murdered, but I have no interest in speaking to them. Because of their willingness to turn on my father and me at the most crucial time, I never found the evidence we needed, never got to show the cops those drag marks or any hairs or blood or evidence the murdering grifters—or my father—might've left behind. The raking they allowed "Charlotte" to do was deep, thorough, and deliberate. The cops wouldn't spend a moment of their time on that beach once they realized there was nothing to see.

"I'll see you around this summer," I say, hoping I don't.

"No, dear. Didn't you hear?" Millie squints at me like I'm a rogue maid. "We've sold the house. We're moving down to North Carolina to be closer to the grandchildren. We close on the sale day after tomorrow."

"Moving vans come tomorrow," Harold says, gazing up at the house wistfully, as if this place is anything but cursed.

This news piques the interest of every Sandburn local in earshot. "Who'd you sell it to?" Carter asks point-blank. "Summer people?"

"Sold it to a trust. Forget the name. The lawyers are taking care of all that," Harold replies.

I hope the new people have a boatload of sage to burn over three floors.

"One thing I didn't get to ask," I say to Lilith. "What about Hyndreth? Was the hypnotherapist in on it or not?"

She completes a yawn, then says, "He checks out. Far as we can tell, Clive took a shitty apartment in Maine and conned Hyndreth into thinking he was a sad amnesiac while Charlotte—*Misty*—lived down here, setting the stage and doing some treasure hunting. Hyndreth saw an opportunity to get back on TV by helping this lost soul, and took Clive on pro bono. Speaking of which," Lilith says pointedly to me, "your reprieve is over. The Dutch embassy made the family notifications and the media has already started calling the department. They'll be here by morning, if not sooner."

"Thanks for the heads up," I say, though I already have my

plan in place, and it involves shutting everything down and holing up at the precious saltbox.

"I have a question for you," Lilith asks quietly. "Is there a treasure?"

I was dreading this question. I can feel Ben tensing up next to me. He's the only one who deserves to know the answer, but I don't know what to say. Do I take the path to a healthy relationship, whether an intimate one or a friendship, or do I want to protect my father, the money, my privacy, the hell that wealth can bring?

My mind sifts through the possible responses, and I opt for the truth as I know it.

"It doesn't look like it," I say.

"Let's go!" Carter calls. "We're following the staties to conduct the interrogation."

I yawn, long and loud. "Who should Ben and I ride with to the station?" I ask Lilith.

"Go home," she says. "You've done enough. This will keep until tomorrow."

This time, I think she's right. My knees are wobbling.

"Ben? Can you see her home?" Lilith asks.

He nods and reaches out to put a gentle arm on the small of my back. "I'm parked around the bend," he says. "I've got you."

53

At home, I'm too tired and shocked to find my sleeping clothes, and Ben guides me. I submit. My brain function is on hold, my bones mushy and stubborn.

"It's too late to eat," I say.

"I'll make you breakfast, then." With any other man, that would be a red flag and instant stress: *It's a come on, leave me alone, you're making some big assumptions.* With Ben, it's caretaking. He knows I'll be starving in the morning.

"I'm not afraid anymore," I say.

"Good," he smiles.

"I'm sorry it took me so long."

"It's alright," he says, taking my chin in his hand. "I told you I'd wait for you."

I look up at him, make him understand I'm not going to back away this time and I'm not too tired for this, and he leans down, and his soft lips cover mine.

Ben is gone when I wake up. It was comforting having another person in the house again, but it's disconcerting that he disappeared without waking me, and the silence is somehow more powerful now when I don't expect it. I hear nothing, smell nothing. No footfall, no fresh coffee.

I swing my legs out of bed.

A sharp rap of knuckles comes from the front door of the house. Ben never enters that way, and he certainly wouldn't knock. My heart pumps overtime and my breath quickens. I hear yelling now alongside the rapping, so loud now it's close to pounding.

I thought this was over. Yesterday, I was primed for anything, ready to take the hits. Today I thought I could relax until I was utterly deflated, and so I did, and this urgent knocking is out of place and is giving me heart palpitations.

"Mrs. Hugmeister? Mrs. Hugmeister! I *really* need to talk to you…" *Knock, knock, knock.*

"Hang on!" I throw on a bra, T-shirt and flannel bottoms in record time. I make it to the door and remember too late that normal houses don't have peepholes; this isn't New York City.

"Who is it?"

"My name is Rowan Tangier, with the firm of Tangier and Florence. We're running out of time. Please, may I come in?"

I stand on tiptoes and peek out the panes of glass at the top of the door, then look the guy up. Rowan P. Tangier, Esq., is listed as a partner in Tangier and Florence, which sounds like an exotic travel agency but is, indeed, a Boston law firm. The face of the man at my door matches the headshot on their fancy website. I open the door.

"I've been trying to get in touch with you for weeks," a shorter fellow with a round, bald head says, dabbing at his forehead with a tissue. "Time is of the essence. It might already be too late."

I lead him through the house to the table in the dining nook. We sit across from each other, and Rowan and I notice the scrap of paper on at the same time. He slides it over to me.

Went to get eggs and coffee. You're out of everything. B

"I'd offer you a cup of coffee." I tap my finger on the note. "But I'm out of everything."

Rowan hoists his briefcase onto the table and opens it with two crisp clicks.

"Too late for what?" I ask him.

"To complete the purchase of One Bluff Way, Sandburn, Massachusetts."

"Back up," I say. "I'm not purchasing anything. You have the wrong person."

"I assure you I don't," he says, removing a sheaf of papers from the leather case. "Your father signed a contract through his trust, Sable Holdings. A considerable sum of money is in escrow, and you'll lose it all if you're in breach."

"Your father and the Millers had an agreement that they'd be allowed to keep the place for the holidays last winter, and then they'd have until spring to clear out. The sale is meant to go through tomorrow."

"Why is the first I'm hearing of this? And…how exactly have you tried to reach me?"

"With the information we have on file. An email to NBClammerman@nowmail.com, messages on a cellphone, and of course the landline."

"What number is that? I don't have a landline."

"Your father does, and I've been leaving messages on it for the last month."

Who has a landline anymore? Nick set it has it on silent and it goes to the phone company's voicemail.

"As you are surely aware," I say, "my father is missing."

"Yes, and I'm terribly, terribly sorry for your loss." He sounds terribly, terribly annoyed. "Which means that as his power of attorney, you're needed to make sure this sale goes ahead."

This guy needs to slow down. "Wait a minute," I shake my head in disbelief.

"Are you telling me that before my father disappeared, he bought the Miller's house? And that I have power attorney over…what, exactly?" I don't actually know what power of attorney means.

"You have power of attorney, period," he says. "You can sign any legal document on your father's behalf and access his finances at any time. The seller was getting very antsy. As soon as I leave here I'll call them and hope they're still ready to complete this sale tomorrow.

"Your father made smart investments. Small ones, mostly, but they added up and compounded over time. He has a nice portfolio, so with his house paid for, any excess money from his fishing trips was all invested. You control everything, and you're responsible for everything. If—"

"When."

"*If* and *when* he returns, it will all be his. And of course if he's declared…if the worst happens…well, then, it all goes to you. Oh, except…"

He shuffles more papers and pulls out a pink legal-looking paper.

"The Porsche," he says. "I assume it's on the property? Mr.

Banks was adamant that vehicle go to a Tanya M. Banks, of Boston, Massachusetts as soon as possible."

"But it's in his name," I say. "Not hers."

"He wanted it to be a surprise. He bought it for her and said it's all she ever wanted, an apple red Porsche. That it was least he owed her."

My mother is someone who would appreciate that. She would not feel bought off or placated. She'll be over the moon.

"Tomorrow, then." He snaps shut his briefcase and rises. "I'll text you the time and place later today."

We exchange numbers, and as we do, there's a knock on the back door. "It's open!" I call. Ben straggles in with grocery bags in one hand, balancing two coffees in the other.

Rowan nods to Ben. "Good day," he says. "I'll see myself out." If he was wearing a hat, I'm certain he'd have tipped it.

"What was that about?" Ben asks after we hear the door close behind him.

"Long story," I say

Ben nods and gets to unpacking the groceries. "Omelette or waffles?"

"Uh…"

"You don't have a waffle iron, do you?"

I shake my head.

"Omelettes it is," he says, and leans down to kiss me.

54

In the blanketing silence of the dawn, I run my metal detector over the beach outside my new home. I haven't ventured inside yet. The house doesn't feel like mine; it doesn't welcome me. It shouts *Go away, you don't belong here.*

I don't feel a need to possess this alleged treasure, but I'm impelled to search for it. I have a hunch about where my father hid his stashes, thanks to Charlotte's angry performance for the clammers.

I walk to where she tossed the soda can tops, those silvery aluminum discs with the flipped tab and drinking hole, during her tantrum. I noted at the time that it's not uncommon to find buried refuse, especially considering builders were working on this land for years. But you'll more often find intact cans. There is no sand monster stalking the shores of Sandburn ripping off the tops but leaving the cans themselves missing.

I sink to all fours and brush my hands across the sand like windshield wipers. I find what I'm looking for after a minute, almost cutting my finger in the process, and fall back on my haunches. The aluminum top has been sheared off the can deliberately with a clean, even slice.

I clamber to my feet and pad to the spot where the ray of light from the prism I saw from Wailing Beach landed. X marks the spot. I whip around when I hear rustling fifteen feet away in the brush, and it's still dark enough that I could feel tracked, watched, preyed upon. I think of Scruffy, soft fur and comforting presence with me in those same woods so long ago, and I can't be afraid. Not of wildlife. There are deer, bobcats, fisher cats, coyotes, so many predators, all around Sandburn, and a selection of them could be watching me right now.

I don't know who said it first, but the one who burned the sentiment into my mind was Holocaust survivor Irene Weiss, who said in an interview, *The most dangerous animal in the world is man. Other animals will hurt you if they're hungry…but the instinct to kill is so strong in man.*

I keep going with the detector. It takes only a few minutes to trigger a *beep*. I dig down, my fingernails packed with grit, finally understanding this is my home, feeling like the land is where I am meant to be. A full four inches down I find a beer can top. I put it in my pocket.

I stand again, running the metal detector over the same spot. And there it is: another *beep*. I dig another four inches down until my fingers are raw, and I hit something solid, something that doesn't belong.

It's a small PVC bag sealed with a plastic zipper. This was clearly meant to be here temporarily, not to last through centuries of erosion, movement and storms. I unzip it and, inside, is a stack of plastic coin holders. Each piece of gold is nestled in its own home, protected as much as they can be out here. This system my father came up with is brilliant. Anyone with nefarious intentions would hear the metal detector's beep, find the can top, and move on. They wouldn't think to dip into the layers, and to, as my father said in his last recording, *Dig deeper.*

My father never knew he was hiding the treasure from the likes of Misty and Clive, but it worked. Clearly they'd found the can tops and looked no deeper. Impatience. Greed. No understanding of sand and nature and the ecosystem.

All I can think is, if someone came by right now and asked me for this bag of coins in exchange for my father, I would give it to them in a second. None of this matters without him. But he left a legacy. Agnes, Oyster, Lola, Ben. Who else? My mother, me. He wanted nothing more than to protect Sandburn from a race to find treasure. He tried to control everyone, and now I see why, and I immediately know that I will do the same. As the law itself says, finders keepers. I was the finder. I'll follow in my father's footsteps and make the town a better, safer place.

I drop my blade. I drop my spade and I drop my metal detector and I stare at the sky and I think, *I'm done. My part is over. I can't search anymore.* I'm exhausted, and I'm not responsible for the evil wrought by these twisted people.

I'll keep my father's commercial clamming license, if the town will let me. I'll stay in Sandburn and see what it means to be home, and I'll know whether I ever really needed to leave in the first place.

I told Ben to spread the word about my father buying this house, and when he does, it'll catch fire. I've opened it to Sandburn clammers again. If you have a digger's permit, you can clam here, and you can access the beach however you need to.

55

They come from every corner and nook of the North Cape. The town is packed with vehicles snaking along the road as far as the eye can see, and the boats, so many boats, skiffs and cruisers and fishing, have taken over the sea.

High school students, volunteers and budding clammers, the children and grandchildren of Sandburn's commercial diggers, hand out electric candles, the kind that won't blow out with the ocean breeze. They are a thousand little lights on Wailing Beach.

When my grandfather died, my father read the same poem fishers from around here so often request well before their own demise. *The Unknown Shore* by Elizabeth Clark Hardy is as overplayed at memorials as 1 Corinthians is at weddings, because it is exquisite. No poem is more suited to bidding farewell to Sandburn's legendary fishers and diggers. They seek solace; give it to them. In front of everyone, I read it aloud for Nicholas Banks, legendary clammer, sovereign of the sand.

Sometime at eve when the tide is low,
I shall slip my moorings and sail away…

I choke up and take a moment to catch my breath. I finish the poem with tears streaming down my face. I see the others are crying, too. They're all here.

Shep, Old Caleb, Linda, Cassandra. Lilith, Carter, and some from the Coast Guard in their dress blues. Angélica is in front of me. She didn't want to speak today. I see Leroy, the Millers' neighbor from Sudbury; I greeted him with a hug and with thanks when he arrived with a woman friend.

Lola leaves her spot between Michele and Ben, runs to me and hands me a tissue. She squeezes me at the waist, and I squeeze her just as hard.

"Thank you," I whisper in her ear.

She stands next to me and holds my hand. "I've got you," she says loud enough for everyone to hear. A chuckle ripples through the crowd.

I make eye contact with Michele, who shrugs and mouths, "I don't know where she learned that."

It has to be fun, too. Not so serious, not entirely dark. Nick wouldn't have liked that.

Oyster is next to me, and it's his turn to speak. "Nicholas Banks was a son to Agnes and me. Not *like* a son. A son. To all of us he was something: a friend, a competitor, a helper, a bank, a brother, a father." He looks to me and I smile through silent tears.

Oyster crumples the paper and puts it back into his pocket.

"Fair winds and following seas, my friend."

I lean in and hug him. The Reverend steps forward and leads us in a final prayer.

Heads down, we listen to her words, short, bolstering,

healing. And then a moment of silence.

I hang my head. The quiet is so complete you can hear the flap of a cormorant's wing and the nip of a striper's mouth on the surface of the water.

"Thank you," the Reverend says after a time, and at that moment, the distant horn of a vessel coming home to Goodstone sounds.

"Can we go to the party now?" Old Caleb grumbles loudly. "It's an early tide in the morning."

A laugh ripples through the tearful crowd. I take Lola's hand, and we walk along the beach toward the far end around the bend, where the Clam Shanty has put on the grandest clambake the cape has ever seen, or at least that's what they tell me.

Michele and Ben fall back, and Ben takes Lola's hand and brings her with them while I stay behind for a moment, alone, staring out at the sea, the place where I loved him, and the place where I lost him.

Fair winds and following seas, Dad.

Love you forever, Isla girl.

I throw him a wave and a kiss, and then I run, barefoot, to catch up with the rest of my family.

***

Other Titles by Courtney Hargrove

Mysteries & Suspense

The Duchess Scarlett Mysteries

The Expatriate Mysteries

History of the British Royals

The Harry & Meghan Biography Series,
Volumes 1–4

www.ingramcontent.com/pod-product-compliance
Lightning Source LLC
Chambersburg PA
CBHW020228010826
48973CB00006B/1417